PRIESTESS
OF AVALON

Marion Zimmer Bradley
and
Diana L. Paxson

HarperCollins*Publishers*

Voyager
An Imprint of HarperCollins*Publishers*
77–85 Fulham Palace Road,
Hammersmith, London W6 8JB

www.voyager-books.com

Published by *Voyager* 2000
1 3 5 7 9 8 6 4 2

A catalogue record for this book
is available from the British Library

ISBN 0 00 224709 7

Typeset in Melior by Palimpsest Book Production Limited,
Polmont, Stirlingshire

Printed and bound in Great Britain by
Omnia Books Limited, Glasgow

To our grandchildren

ACKNOWLEDGEMENTS

This is the story of a legend.

The provable facts about Helena are few in comparison with the wealth of stories that have attached themselves to her name. We know that she was the consort of Constantius and the honoured mother of Constantine the Great, and that she had some association with the town of Drepanum. We know that she owned property in Rome and that she made a visit to Palestine, and that is all.

But wherever she went, myths sprang up behind her. She is honoured in Germany and Israel and Rome, where she is hailed as a saint in the churches that bear her name. Medieval hagiography makes her the great discoverer of relics, who brought the heads of the three Wise Men to Cologne, the Robe Jesus wore to Trier, and the True Cross to Rome.

But she holds a special place in the legends of Britian, where it is said that she was a British princess who married an emperor. She is believed to have lived in York and in London, and to have established roads in Wales. Some even identify her with the goddess Nehalennia. Did these stories arise because Constantius and Constantine both had such strong connections with Britain, or could she have originally come from that isle?

If so, perhaps it is not so great a stretch to link her with the mythology of Avalon, and add one more legend to the rest.

Marion Zimmer Bradley and I began this work together, as we have

vi

worked together before, but it was left to me to complete it. At the end of her life Marion attended a Christian church, and yet she was my first high priestess in the ancient mysteries. In telling the story of Helena, who also walked between the Christian and the pagan worlds, I have tried to remain faithful to Marion's teachings.

In the creation of this book, Marion's was the inspiration and origin. The historical legwork was mine.

Among the many sources which were useful I should list: Fry's *Roman Britain*; Gibbon's classic *Decline and Fall of the Roman Empire*, which includes all the gossip; *The Later Roman Empire*, by A.H.M. Jones; Robin Lane Fox's fascinating *Pagans and Christians*; and *The Aquarian Guide to Legendary London*, edited by John Matthews and Chesca Potter, particularly the chapter on the Goddesses of London by Caroline Wise of the Atlantis Bookstore. More specifically, I relied on *Constantine the Great*, by Michael Grant, and Jan Willem Drijvers' classic, *Helena Augusta*; and for Helena's journey and the reinvention of the Holy Land, *Holy City, Holy Places?*, by P.W.L. Walker. The hymn in chapter thirteen was written by St Ambrose in the fourth century.

I would like to express my gratitude to Karen Anderson for working out the astronomical configurations in the third century skies, and to Charline Palmtag for helping me with their astrological interpretation. My thanks also to Jennifer Tifft, for enabling me to make an extra trip to England and find the chapel of St Helena in York, to Bernhard Hennen, for taking me to Trier, and to Jack and Kira Gillespie for showing me Cumae and Pozzuoli.

Diana L. Paxson
Feast of Brigid, 2000

PEOPLE IN THE STORY

* = historical figure

( ) = dead before story begins

* Aurelian – Emperor, 270–275

Aelia – a young priestess, trained with Helena

* Allectus – Finance Minister to Carausius, later Emperor of Britannia, 293–6

Arganax – Arch-Druid during Helena's youth

* Asclepiodotus – Constantius's Praetorian Prefect

Atticus – Constantine's Greek tutor

* Carausius – Emperor of Britannia, 287–293

* Carus – Emperor, 282–3

* Carinus – older son of Carus, emperor, 283–284

Ceridachos – Arch Druid when Dierna becomes High Priestess

Cigfolla – a priestess of Avalon

* Claudius II – Emperor, 268–270, Constantius's great-uncle

Corinthius the Elder – Helena's tutor

Corinthius the Younger – master of a school in Londinium

Julius Coelius – [King Coel] Prince of Camulodunum, father of Helena

* Constantia (I) – daughter of Constantius and Theodora, married to Licinius

* Constantia (II) – daughter of Constantine and Fausta

* Constans – third son of Constantine and Fausta
* Constantine [Flavius Valerius Constantinus] – son of Helena, Emperor, 306–337
* Constantine (II) – eldest son of Constantine and Fausta
* Constantius Chlorus [Flavius Constantius] – consort of Helena, Caesar and later Augustus, 293–306
* Julius Constantius – second son of Constantius and Theodora
* Constantius (II) – second son of Constantine and Fausta
* Crispus – Constantine's illegitimate son by Minervina
  Cunoarda – Helena's Alban slave
* Dalmatius – son of Constantius and Theodora
  Dierna – Helena's second cousin, later Lady of Avalon
* Diocletian – Senior Augustus, Emperor, 284–305
  Drusilla – cook in Helena and Constantius's household
* Bishop Eusebius of Caesaria – Metropolitan Bishop of Palestine, a major writer of church history and later the biographer of Constantine.
* Fausta – daughter of Maximian, wife of Constantine and mother of his legitimate children
  Flavius Pollio – a kinsman of Constantius
* Galerius – Caesar, 293–305, Augustus, 305–311
* Gallienus – Emperor, 253–268
  Ganeda – Helena's aunt, Lady of Avalon
  Gwenna – a maiden being trained on Avalon
  Haggaia – Arch Druid when Helena returns to Avalon
ᴬ Julia Coelia Helena, later, Flavia Helena Augusta – (Eilan) daughter of Prince Coelius, consort of Constantius, mother of Constantine and priestess of Avalon
* Helena the Younger ('Lena') – a noblewoman of Treveri, wife of Crispus
  Heron – a maiden being trained on Avalon
  Hrodlind – Helena's German maid
(* Joseph of Arimathea – founder of the Christian community on the Tor)
  Katiya – a priestess of Bast in Rome

* Lactantius – a rhetorician and Christian apologist, tutor to Crispus
* Licinius – Caesar appointed by Galerius to replace Severus, later Augustus in the East, 313–324
* Lucius Viducius – a pottery merchant trading between Gallia and Eburacum
* Macarius – Bishop of Jerusalem
  Marcia – midwife who delivers Constantine
  Martha – a Syrian slave, healed by Helena
* Maximian – Augustus of the West, 285–305
* Maximus Daia – Caesar appointed by Galerius
* Maxentius – son of Maximian, Augustus in Italy and North Africa, 306–312
* Minervina – Constantine's Syrian concubine, mother of Crispus
* Numerian – younger son of Carus, Emperor, 283–84
  Philip – Constantius's servant
* Postumus – rebel Emperor of the West, 259–68
* Probus – Emperor, 276–282
* Quintillus – brother of the Emperor Claudius II, Constantius's great-uncle
  (Rian – High Priestess of Avalon, Helena's mother)
  Roud – a maiden being trained on Avalon
* Severus – Caesar appointed by Galerius, executed by Maximian
  Sian – daughter of Ganeda, mother of Dierna and Becca
  Suona – a young priestess of Avalon
  Teleri – wife of Carausius and then of Allectus, later, High Priestess of Avalon
* Tetricus & Marius – rebel co-emperors of the West, 271
  Tulia – a maiden being trained on Avalon
* Victorina Augusta – mother of Victorinus and virtual ruler
* Victorinus – rebel Emperor in the West, 268–270
  Vitellia – a Christian matron living in Londinium
  Wren – a maiden being trained on Avalon

Helena's dogs: Eldri, Hylas, Favonius and Boreas, Leviyah

PLACES

BRITANNIA
Aquae Sulis – Bath
Avalon – Glastonbury
Calleva – Silchester
Camulodunum – Colchester
Cantium – Kent
Corinium – Cirencester
Eburacum – York
Inis Witrin – Glastonbury
Isurium Brigantum – Aldborough, Yorkshire
Lindinis – Ilchester
Lindum – Lincoln
Londinium – London
Sabrina estuary – the Severn
the Summer Country – Somerset
Trinovante lands – Essex
Tamesis – the Thames
Tanatus Insula – Isle of Thanet, Kent

THE WESTERN EMPIRE
Alpes – the Alps
Aquitanica – southern France, Aquitaine
Arelate – Arles, France
Argentoratum – Strasburg, Germany

Augusta Treverorum (Treveri) – Trier, Germany
Baiae – Baia, Italy
Belgica Prima – eastern France
Belgica Secunda – the Low Countries
Borbetomagus – Wurms, Germany
Colonia Agrippinensis – Cologne, Germany
Cumaea – Cumae, Italy
Gallia – France
Ganuenta – formerly an island where the River Schelde joins the
  Rhine in the Netherlands
Germania Prima – lands just west of the Rhine, Koblenz to
  Basle
Germania Secunda – lands just west of the Rhine, North Sea to
  Koblenz
Gesoriacum – Boulogne, France
Lugdunum – Lyons
Mediolanum – Milan, Italy
Moenus fluvius – the River Main, Germany
Mosella fluvius – the River Moselle, France, Germany
Nicer fluvius – the River Neckar, Germany
Noricum – Austria south of the Danube
Rhaetia – Southern Germany and Switzerland
Rhenus fluvius – the Rhine
Rhodanus fluvius – the Rhone
Rothomagus – Rouen, France
Treveri (Augusta Treverorum) – Trier, Germany
Ulpia Traiana – Xanten, Germany
Vindobona – Vienna, Austria

THE EASTERN EMPIRE
Aegeum – the Aegean
Aelia Capitolina – Jerusalem
Aquincum – Pest (Budapest), Hungary
Asia – Western Turkey
Bithynia et Pontus – northern Turkey

Byzantium (later, Constantinople) – Istanbul
Caesarea – a port city south of Haifa, Israel
Carpatus Mountains – the Carpathians
Chalcedon – Kadikoy, Turkey
Dacia – Romania
Dalmatia – Albania
Danu, Danuvius – the Danube
Drepanum (Helenopolis) – Hersek in northern Turkey
Galatia and Cappadocia – Eastern Turkey
the Haemus – Balkans
Heracleia Pontica – Eregli, Turkey
Hierosolyma – Jerusalem
Illyria – Yugoslavia
Moesia – Bulgaria
Naissus – Nis in Romania
Nicaea – Iznik, Turkey
Nicomedia – Izmit, Turkoy
Pannonia – Hungary
Rhipaean Mountains – the Caucausus
Scythia – lands above the Black Sea
Singidunum – Belgrade, Yugoslavia
Sirmium – Mitrovica or Sabac on the Save, Serbia
Thracia – southern Bulgaria

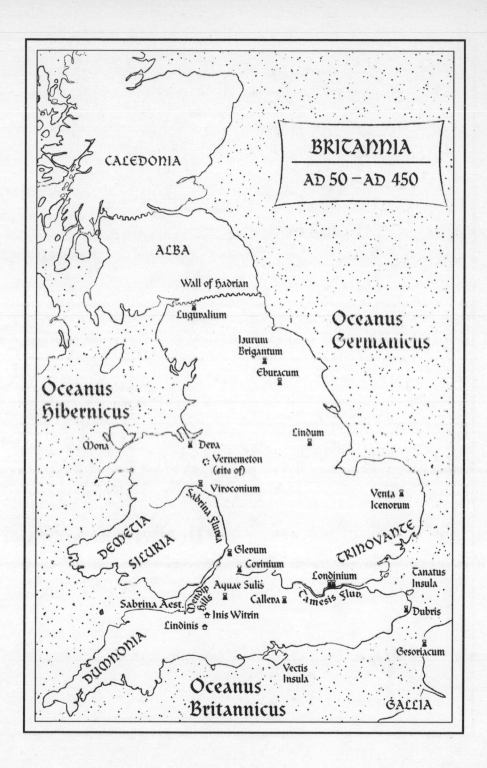

BRITANNIA

AD 50 – AD 450

CALEDONIA

ALBA

Wall of Hadrian

Luguvalium

Oceanus Germanicus

Isurium
Brigantum

Eburacum

Oceanus
Hibernicus

Lindum

Mona

Deva

Vernemeton
(site of)

Viroconium

Venta
Icenorum

DEMETIA

Sabrina Fluma

SILURIA

TRINOVANTE

Glevum

Corinium

Sabrina Aest.

Mendip Hills

Aquae Sulis

Calleva

Londinium

Tanatus
Insula

Lindinis

Inis Witrin

Camesis Fluv.

Dubris

DUMNONIA

Vectis
Insula

Gesoriacum

Oceanus
Britannicus

GALLIA

THE ROMAN EMPIRE
264 BC – AD 565

PROLOGUE

249 AD

With sunset, a brisk wind had blown in from the sea. It was the season when farmers burn the stubble from their fields, but wind had swept away the haze that had veiled the heavens, and the Milky Way blazed a white road across the sky. The Merlin of Britannia sat on the Watcher's Stone at the top of the Tor, his eyes fixed on the stars. But though the glory of the heavens commanded his vision, it did not hold his entire attention. His ears strained to catch any sound that might come from the dwelling of the High Priestess on the slopes below.

Since dawn she had been in labour. This would be Rian's fifth child, and her earlier babes had come easily. The birthing should not be taking so long. The midwives guarded their mysteries, but at sunset, when he had prepared for this vigil, he had seen the worry in their eyes. King Coelius of Camulodunum, who had called Rian to the Great Rite for the sake of his flooded fields, was a big man, fair-haired and massively built in the way of the Belgic tribes who had settled in the eastern lands of Britannia, and Rian was a little dark woman with the look of the faerie people who had been the first to dwell in these hills.

It should be no surprise that the child Coelius had begotten was too large to come easily from the womb. When Rian found that he had got her with child, some of the older priestesses had urged her to cast it from her. But to do so would have negated the magic, and Rian told them she had served the Goddess too long not to trust in Her purposes.

1

What purpose was there in this child's birth? The Merlin's old eyes scanned the heavens, seeking to comprehend the secrets written in the stars. The sun stood now in the sign of the Virgin, and the old moon, passing him, had been visible in the sky that morning. Now she hid her face, leaving the night to the glory of the stars.

The old man huddled into the thick folds of his grey cloak, feeling the chill of the autumn night in his bones. As he watched the great wain wheel ever further across the sky and no word came, he knew that he was shivering not with cold, but with fear.

Slow as grazing sheep, the stars moved across the heavens. Saturn gleamed in the south-west, in the Sign of Balance. As the hours drew on, the resolution of the labouring woman was wearing away. Now, at intervals, there would come a moan of pain from the hut. But it was not until the still hour just as the stars were fading that a new sound brought the Merlin upright, heart pounding – the thin, protesting wail of a newborn child.

In the east the sky was already growing pale with the approach of day, but overhead the stars still shone. Long habit brought the old man's gaze upward. Mars, Jupiter and Venus stood in brilliant conjunction. Trained in the disciplines of the Druids since boyhood, he committed the positions of the stars to memory. Then, grimacing as stiffened joints complained, he got to his feet, and leaning heavily on his carven staff, made his way down the hill.

The infant had ceased its crying, but as the Merlin neared the birthing hut, his gut tensed, for he could hear weeping from within. Women stood aside as he pushed back the heavy curtain that hung across the doorway, for he was the only male who by right could enter there.

One of the younger priestesses, Cigfolla, sat in the corner, crooning over the swaddled bundle in her arms. The Merlin's gaze moved past her to the woman who lay on the bed, and stopped, for Rian, whose beauty had always come from her grace in motion, was utterly still. Her dark hair lay lank upon the pillow; her angular features were

2

already acquiring the unmistakable emptiness that distinguishes death from sleep.

'How—' he made a little helpless gesture, striving to hold back his tears. He did not know whether or not Rian had been his own child by blood, but she had been a daughter to him.

'It was her heart,' said Ganeda, her features in that moment painfully like those of the woman who lay on the bed, although at most times the sweetness of Rian's expression had always made it easy to distinguish between the sisters. 'She had laboured for too long. Her heart broke in the final effort to push the child from the womb.'

The Merlin stepped to the bedside and gazed down at Rian's body, and after a moment, he bent to trace a sigil of blessing on the cool brow.

I have lived too long, he thought numbly. *Rian should have been the one to say the rites for me.*

He heard Ganeda draw breath behind him. 'Say then, Druid, what fate the stars foretell for the maid-child born in this hour?'

The old man turned. Ganeda faced him, her eyes bright with anger and unshed tears. *She has the right to ask this,* he thought grimly. Ganeda had been passed over in favour of her younger sister when the previous High Priestess died. He supposed the election would fall on her now.

Then the spirit within him rose in answer to her challenge. He cleared his throat.

'Thus speak the stars—' His voice trembled only a little. 'The child that was born at the Turning of Autumn, just as the night gave way to dawn, shall stand at the Turning of the Age, the gateway between two worlds. The time of the Ram has passed, and now the Fish shall rule. The moon hides her face – this maid shall hide the moon she bears upon her brow, and only in old age will she come into her true power. Behind her lies the road that leads to the darkness and its mysteries, before her shines the harsh light of day.

'Mars is in the Sign of the Lion, but war shall not overcome her, for it is ruled by the star of kingship. For this child, love shall walk with sovereignty, for Jupiter yearns towards Venus. Together, their radiance shall light the world. On this night, all of them move towards the Virgin who shall be their true queen. Many will bow before her, but her true sovereignty will be hidden. All shall praise her, yet few will know her true name. Saturnus lies now in Libra – her hardest lessons will be in maintaining a balance between the old wisdom and the new. But Mercurius is hidden. For this child I foresee many wanderings, and many misunderstandings, and yet in the end all roads lead to joy and to her true home.'

All around him the priestesses were murmuring: 'He prophesies greatness – she will be Lady of the Lake like her mother before her!'

The Merlin frowned. The stars had shown him a life of magic and power, but he had read the stars for priestesses many times before, and the patterns that foretold their lives were not those he saw now. It seemed to him that this child was destined to walk a road unlike that which had been trodden by any priestess of Avalon before.

'The babe is healthy and well-formed?'

'She is perfect, my lord.' Cigfolla rose, cradling the swaddled infant close to her breast.

'Where will you find a nurse for her?' He knew that none of the women of Avalon were currently feeding a child.

'She can go to the Lake-dwellers' village,' answered Ganeda. 'There is always some woman with a newborn there. But I will send her to her father once she is weaned.'

Cigfolla clutched at her burden protectively, but the aura of power that surrounded the High Priestess was already descending upon Ganeda, and if the younger woman had objections, she did not voice them aloud.

'Are you sure that is wise?' By virtue of his office, the Merlin *could* question her. 'Will the child not need to be trained in Avalon to prepare for her destiny?'

'What the gods have ordained they will bring to pass, whatever we do,' answered Ganeda. 'But it will be long before I can look upon her face and not see my sister lying dead before me.'

4

The Merlin frowned, for it had always seemed to him that there was little love lost between Ganeda and Rian. But perhaps it made sense – if Ganeda felt guilt for having envied her sister, the babe would be a painful reminder.

'If the girl shows talent, when she is older, perhaps she can return,' Ganeda continued.

If he had been a younger man, the Merlin might have sought to sway her, but he had seen the hour of his own death in the stars, and he knew that he would not be here to protect the little girl if Ganeda resented her. Perhaps it was better that she should live with her father while she was small.

'Show me the child.'

Cigfolla rose, flipping back the corner of the blanket. The Merlin stared down at the face of the infant, still closed in upon itself like the bud of a rose. The child was large for a newborn, big-boned like her father. No wonder her mother had fought such a grim battle to bear her.

'Who are you, little one?' he murmured. 'Are you worth so great a sacrifice?'

'Before she died . . . the Lady . . . said she should be called Eilan,' Cigfolla answered him.

'Eilan—' the Merlin echoed her, and as if the infant had understood, she opened her eyes. They were still the opaque grey of infancy, but their expression, wide and grave, was far older. 'Ah . . . this is not the first time for you,' he said then, saluting her like a traveller who meets an old friend upon the road and pauses for a moment's greeting before they continue on their separate ways. He was aware of a pang of regret that he would not live to see this child grown.

'Welcome back, my dear one. Welcome to the world.'

For a moment the baby's brows met. Then the tiny lips curved upward in a smile.

Part I

THE WAY TO LOVE

CHAPTER ONE

AD 259

'Oh! I can see water gleaming in the sun! Is it the sea?' I dug my heels into the pony's round side to bring it alongside Corinthius's big horse. The beast broke into a rough trot and I clutched at its mane.

'Ah, Helena, your young eyes are better than mine,' answered the old man who had been tutor to my half-brothers before being given the task of teaching the daughter Prince Coelius had inadvertently got upon a priestess of Avalon. 'A blaze of light is all I can see. But I think that what lies before us must be the levels of the Summer Country, flooded by the spring rains.'

I brushed back a wisp of hair and peered out at the landscape. The waters were broken up by hummocks of higher ground like islands and divided by winding rows of trees. Beyond them I could make out a line of hills where Corinthius said there were lead mines, ending in a bright haze that must be the estuary of the Sabrina.

'Then we are almost there?' The pony tossed its head as I squeezed its sides and then pulled back on the rein.

'We are if the rains have not washed out the causeway, and we can locate the village of the Lake folk that my master told me to find.'

I looked up at him with swift pity, for he sounded very tired. I could see lines in the thin face beneath the broad straw hat, and he sat slumped in the saddle. My father should not have made the old man come all this way. But when the journey was over, Corinthius, a Greek who had sold himself into slavery as a youth

9

in order to dower his sisters, would have his freedom. He had saved a nice little nest egg over the years, and meant to set up a school in Londinium.

'We will come to the Lake village in the afternoon,' said the guide who had joined my escort in Lindinis.

'When we get there, we will rest,' I said briskly.

'I thought you were eager to come to the Tor,' Corinthius said kindly. Perhaps he would be sorry to lose me, I thought, smiling up at him. After my two brothers, who cared for nothing but hunting, he had said he enjoyed teaching someone who actually wanted to learn.

'I will have the rest of my life to enjoy Avalon,' I answered him. 'I can wait a day longer to arrive.'

'And start your studies once more!' Corinthius laughed. 'They say that the priestesses of Avalon have preserved the old Druid wisdom. It consoles me a little for losing you to know that you will not spend your life running some fat magistrate's household and bearing his children.'

I smiled. My father's wife had tried to convince me that such a life was a woman's highest hope, but I had always known that sooner or later I would be going to Avalon. That it was sooner was due to the rebellion of a general called Postumus, whose war had cut Britannia off from the Empire. Unprotected, the south-eastern coasts were vulnerable to raiders, and Prince Coelius had thought it best to send his little daughter to the safety of Avalon while he and his sons prepared to defend Camulodunum.

For a moment then my smile faltered, for I had been the apple of my father's eye, and I hated the thought that he might be in danger. But I knew well enough that while he was away from home my life there would not have been a happy one. To the Romans I was my father's love-child, without maternal relatives, for it was forbidden to speak of Avalon. In truth it was Corinthius and old Huctia, who had been my nurse, who had been my family, and Huctia had died the winter before. It was time for me to return to my mother's world.

The road led downwards now, winding gently back and forth across the slope of the hill. As we emerged from the shelter of the trees, I shaded my eyes with my hand. Below, the waters lay upon the land like a sheet of gold.

'If you were a faerie horse,' I murmured to my pony, 'we could gallop along that shining path all the way to Avalon.'

But the pony only shook its head and reached for a mouthful of grass, and we continued to clop down the road one step at a time until we came to the slippery logs of the causeway. Now I could see the grey stalks of last summer's grass waving in the water and beyond them the reedbeds that edged the permanent channels and pools. The deeper water was dark, charged with mystery. What spirits ruled these marshes, where the elements were so confused and mingled that one could not tell where earth ended and the water began? I shivered a little and turned my gaze to the bright day.

As the afternoon drew on towards evening, a mist began to rise from the water. We moved more slowly now, letting our mounts choose their own footing on the slippery logs. I had ridden horses since I could walk, but until now, each day's journey had been a short one, appropriate to the strength of a child. Today's ride, the last stage in our journey, had been longer. I could feel the dull ache in my legs and back and knew that I would be glad to get out of the saddle when the day was over.

We came out from beneath the trees and the guide reined in, pointing. Beyond the tangle of marsh and woodland rose a single pointed hill. I had been taken from this place when I was barely a year old, and yet, with a certainty beyond memory, I knew that I was looking at the holy Tor. Touched by the last of the sunlight, it seemed to glow from within.

'The Isle of Glass . . .' murmured Corinthius, eyes widening in appreciation.

But not Avalon . . . I thought, remembering the stories I had heard. The cluster of beehive huts at the foot of the Tor belonged to the little community of Christians who lived there. Avalon of the Druids lay in the mists between this world and Faerie.

'And there is the village of the Lake people—' said our guide, indicating the trails of smoke that rose beyond the willows. He slapped the reins against his pony's neck and all of the horses, sensing the end of their journey, moved forwards eagerly.

'We have barge, but crossing to Avalon needs priestess. She says if you are welcome. Is important to go now? You want that I call?' The headman's words were respectful, but in his posture there was little deference. For nearly three hundred years his people had been the gatekeepers for Avalon.

'Not tonight,' answered Corinthius. 'The maiden has endured a long journey. Let her have a good night's sleep before she must meet all those new people in her new home.'

I squeezed his hand gratefully. I was eager to get to Avalon, but now that our journey was over, I was painfully aware that I would not see Corinthius again, and only now did I realize how fond of the old man I really was. I had wept when my nurse died, and I knew that I would weep to lose Corinthius as well.

The Lake people made us welcome in one of the round thatched houses set on poles above the marsh. A long, low boat was tied up beside it, and a creaking bridge connected it to the higher ground. The villagers were a small, lightly-built folk, with dark hair and eyes. At ten, I was already as tall as a grown woman among them, though I had the same dusky brown hair. I watched them curiously, for I had heard that my mother had been like them in feature, or perhaps she and they were both like the people of Faerie.

The villagers brought us thin ale and a stew of fish and millet flavoured with wild garlic, and flat oaten cakes baked on the stone hearth. When we had eaten this simple fare, we sat by the fire with bodies too tired to move and minds not yet ready for sleep, watching the flame fade into coals that shone like the vanished sun.

'Corinthius, when you have your school in Londinium, will you remember me?'

'How could I forget my little maiden, bright as one of Apollo's sunbeams, when I am striving to beat Latin hexameters into the thick skulls of a dozen boys?' His worn features creased into a smile.

'You must call the sun Belenos,' said I, 'in this northern land.'

'It was Apollo of the Hyboreans that I meant, my child, but it is all the same—'

'Do you truly believe that?'

Corinthius lifted one eyebrow. 'A single sun shines here and in the land where I was born, though we call it by different names. In the realm of Idea, the great principles behind the forms that we see are the same.'

I frowned, trying to make sense of his words. He had attempted to explain the teachings of the philosopher Plato, but I found them hard to understand. Each place I came to had its own spirit, as distinct as human souls. This land they called the Summer Country, all hill and wood and hidden pools, seemed a world away from the broad flat fields and coppiced woodlands around Camulodunum. Avalon, if the tales I had heard of it were true, would be stranger still. How could their gods be the same?

'I think rather that it is you, little one, with all your life ahead of you, who will be forgetting me,' the old man said then. 'What is it, child?' he added, bending to lift the lock of hair that hid my eyes. 'Are you afraid?'

'What— what if they don't like me?'

For a moment Corinthius stroked my hair, then he sat back with a sigh. 'I ought to tell you that to the true philosopher, it should not matter, that the virtuous person needs no one's approval. But what comfort is that to a child? Nonetheless it is true. There will be some people who do not like you no matter what you do, and when that happens, you can only try to serve the Truth as you see it. And yet, if you have won my heart, then surely there will be others to love you as well. Look for those who need your love, and they will return the blessing.'

His tone was bracing, and I swallowed and managed a smile. I was a princess, and one day would be a priestess as well. I must not let people see me cry.

13

There was a stirring at the door. The cowhide flap was pushed aside and I glimpsed a child holding a squirming puppy in his arms. The chieftain's wife saw him and said something reproving in the dialect of the Lake. I caught the word for hound and realized he was being told to take the dog away.

'Oh no – I like puppies!' I exclaimed. 'Please let me see!'

The woman looked dubious, but Corinthius nodded, and the boy came up to me, grinning, and released the animal into my outstretched hands. As I clutched at the wriggling bundle of fur I began to smile as well. I could see already that this was not one of the graceful sight-hounds who used to lounge in noble dignity about my father's hall. The puppy was too tiny, its creamy fur too thick already, and its tail too curled. But the brown eyes were bright with interest, and the tongue that flicked out below the moist black button of a nose to lick my hand was pink and warm.

'There, there now, and aren't you a darling?' I gathered the little dog to my chest and laughed again as it tried to lick my face as well.

'A creature with neither breeding nor manners,' said Corinthius, who was not fond of animals. 'And likely carrying fleas—'

'No, lord,' answered the boy, 'is faerie dog.'

Corinthius lifted an eloquent eyebrow, and the boy frowned.

'I speak true!' he exclaimed. 'It happens before. Mama gets lost, two, three days. Has only one puppy, white like this. Faerie dog lives long, and if not killed, when old it disappears. Dog sees spirits, and knows way to Otherworld!'

Feeling the living warmth of the creature in my arms, I hid my face in the soft fur to hide my smile, for the rest of the Lake people were nodding solemnly and I did not wish to insult them.

'She is gift, will guard you—' the boy said then.

I suppressed a a spurt of laughter at the idea that this ball of fluff could protect anything, then straightened to smile at the boy.

'Does she have a name?'

The boy shrugged. 'Faerie folk know. Maybe she tells you one day.'

'I will call her Eldri, until they do, for she is as white and delicate as the flower of the elder tree.' I considered her as I said this, then looked back up at the boy. 'And you – do you have a name?'

A blush warmed his sallow skin. 'Is "Otter", in your tongue,' he said as the others laughed.

A use-name, thought I. At his initiation he would receive another that would only be used within the tribe. And how should I answer him? In my father's world I had been Julia Helena, but that seemed irrelevant here.

'I thank you,' I said then. 'You may call me Eilan.'

I woke from a dream of many waters, blinking in the morning light. I had been in a long flat boat that slid silently through swirling mists until they parted to reveal a fair green island. But then the scene had shifted, and I was on a galley approaching endless flat marshlands and a great river that split into myriad channels as it entered the sea. And yet again the vision had changed to a land of golden stone and sand washed by a brilliant blue sea. But the green island had been the fairest. A few times in my life I had dreamed things that came true. I wondered if this was one of them. But already the memory was slipping away. I sighed, pushed back the sleeping furs in which I had nested with Eldri curled against me and rubbed the grit from my eyes. Squatting beside the headman's fire and drinking tea from a cup of rough clay was someone I had not seen before. I noticed first the long brown braid and the blue cloak, and then, as she turned, the mark of a priestess tattooed between her brows. The blue crescent was still bright, and the smooth face that of a girl. She had not been initiated for long. Then, as if she had felt my gaze upon her, the priestess turned, and my eyes fell before that detached and ageless stare.

'Her name is Suona,' said Corinthius, patting my shoulder. 'She arrived just at dawn.'

I wondered how the headman had called her. Did the faerie folk carry the message, or was there some secret spell?

'This is the maiden?' asked Suona.

15

'The daughter of Prince Coelius of Camulodunum,' answered Corinthius. 'But her mother was of Avalon.'

'She seems old to begin her training here.'

Corinthius shook his head. 'She is well-grown for her age, but she has only ten winters. And Helena is not without education. She has been taught to use her mind as well as to do the work of a woman. She can read and write in Latin and knows a little Greek, and has learned her numbers as well.'

Suona did not seem very impressed. I lifted my chin and met the dark gaze steadily. For a moment I felt an odd tickling sensation in my head, as if something had touched my mind. Then the priestess nodded a little, and it ceased. For the first time she spoke directly to me.

'Is it your wish, or that of your father, that you come to Avalon?'

I felt my heart thump, but I was relieved when my words came out steadily.

'I want to go to Avalon.'

'Let the child break her fast, and then we will be ready,' said Corinthius, but the priestess shook her head.

'Not you, only the maiden. It is forbidden for an outlander to look on Avalon except when the gods call.'

For a moment the old man looked stricken, then he bowed his head.

'Corinthius!' I felt tears prick my own eyes.

'Never mind,' he patted my arm. 'To the philosopher, all affections are transitory. I must strive for more detachment, that is all.'

'But won't you miss me?' I clung to his hand.

For a moment he sat with closed eyes. Then his breath came out in a long sigh.

'I will miss you, heart's daughter,' he answered softly. 'Even if it is against my philosophy. But you will find new friends and learn new things, never fear.'

I felt Eldri stirring in my lap and the moment of anguish began to fade.

'I will not forget you—' I said stoutly, and was rewarded by his smile.

My fingers tightened on the rail as the boatmen shoved down with their poles and the barge slid away from the shore. Overnight, another mist had risen from the water, and the world beyond the village was more sensed than seen. Only once, when we crossed the Tamesis at Londinium, had I ever been on a boat before. I had felt nearly overwhelmed by the river's tremendous, driving purpose, driven close to tears when we reached the other shore because I had not been allowed to follow it down to the sea.

On the Lake, what I felt most strongly was depth, which seemed odd, since the bottom was still within reach of the boatmen's poles, and I could see the wavering lines of the reed-stems below the waterline.

But the evidence of my eyes seemed to me an illusion. I could feel waters that ran below the lake bottom, and realized that I had begun to sense them as soon as we started to cross the Levels, even when we were on what passed here for dry land. Here, there was little distinction between earth and water, as there was very little separation between the world of men and the Otherworld.

I gazed curiously at the woman who sat at the prow, cloaked and hooded in blue. To be a priestess was it necessary to become so detached from human feeling? Corinthius preached detachment as well, but I knew he had a heart beneath his philosopher's robes. *When I become a priestess, I will not forget what love is*! I promised myself then.

I wished very much that they had allowed my old tutor to come with me this last bit of the way. He was still waving to me from the shore, and though he had bade me farewell with the restraint of a true Stoic, it seemed to me that there was a brightness in his eyes that might be tears. I wiped my own eyes and waved back harder, and then, as the first veil of mist blew between us, settled back onto my bench.

At least I still had Eldri, tucked securely in the fold where my

17

tunica bloused over my belt. I could feel the puppy's warmth against my chest and patted her reassuringly through the cloth. So far, the little dog had neither barked nor stirred, as if she understood the need to keep silence. So long as the puppy stayed hidden, no one could forbid me to take her to Avalon.

I pulled open the loose neck of my tunica and grinned at the two bright eyes that gleamed up at me, then draped my cloak loosely around me once more.

The mist was growing thicker, lying in dense skeins across the water as if not only earth but air were dissolving back into the primal watery womb. Of the Pythagorean elements of which Corinthius had told me, that left only fire. I took a deep breath, at once unsettled and oddly reassured, as if something within me recognized this protean admixture and welcomed it.

We were well out upon the Lake by now, and the boatmen were paddling. As the barge moved forwards the stilt village faded into the mist behind us. The Tor was disappearing too. For the first time I felt a quiver of fear.

But Eldri warmed my heart, and in the prow, the young priestess sat quietly, her face serene. Suona was a plain-looking girl, but for the first time, I understood what my nurse had meant when she told me to sit like a queen.

Though I saw no signal, abruptly the boatmen lifted their paddles and rested them on their laps. The barge floated quietly, the last ripples of its passage widening away to either side. I felt a pressure in my ears and shook my head to relieve it.

Then, at last, the priestess stirred, casting back her hood as she rose. Feet braced, she stood, seeming to grow taller as she lifted her arms in invocation. She drew in her breath, and her ordinary features grew radiant with beauty. *The gods look like this* . . . I thought as Suona gave voice to a string of musical syllables in a language I had never heard before.

Then that too was forgotten, for the mists began to move. The boatmen had covered their eyes, but I kept mine open, staring as the grey clouds began to sparkle with a rainbow of colour. The light spun sunwise around them, colours blending, wrenching reality out of Time. For an impossible eternity we hung between the worlds. Then, with a final burst of radiance, the mists became a haze of light.

The priestess sank back to her seat, perspiration beading her brow. The boatmen picked up their paddles and began to stroke forwards as if this had been no more than a pause to rest their arms. I let out a breath I had not known I was holding. *They must be accustomed to this . . . phenomenon . . .* I thought numbly, and then, *How could anyone get used to this wonder!*

For a few moments, though the paddles dipped, we did not seem to move. Then the bright mist suddenly wisped away, and the Tor was rushing towards us, and I clapped my hands, recognizing the fair green island.

But there was more to it than I had seen in my dream. I had half-expected to see the huddle of wooden huts I had glimpsed from the Lake people's village, but that was Inis Witrin, the isle of the monks. Where the huts had stood, on the other isle on Avalon there were edifices of stone. I had seen Roman buildings that were larger, but none that were at once so massive and so graceful, columned with smooth shafts of tapered stone. Blessed by the spring sunlight, they seemed to glow from within.

If I had been capable of speech, I would have begged the men to stop the boat, to tell me what each house was, now when I could comprehend their harmony. But the land was coming at us too swiftly. In another moment the bottom of the barge grated on sand and it slid up onto the shore.

For the first time, the young priestess smiled. She got to her feet and offered me her hand.

'Be welcome to Avalon.'

'Look, it is Rian's daughter—' the whispers ran. I could hear them clearly as I came into the hall.

'It cannot be. She is too tall, and Rian died only ten years ago.'

'She must take after her father's people—'

19

'That will not endear her to the Lady,' came the reply, with a little laugh.

I swallowed. It was hard to pretend I did not hear, harder still to walk with the proud carriage of a daughter of a noble house as my nurse had taught me, when I wanted to gawk at the hall of the priestesses like a peasant passing for the first time beneath the great gate of Camulodunum.

I could not help gaining some impressions of my surroundings. The hall was circular, like the houses the British used to build before the Romans came, but this one was built of stone. The outer wall was only the height of a tall man, but a circle of stone pillars supported the sloping roof, carved with spirals and triple knots, chevrons and wound about with twisted bands of colour. The beams of the roof did not quite meet, and through the open circle in the centre came a flood of light.

The round gallery was in shadow, but the priestesses who stood there were radiant. When Suona piloted the barge through the mists, she had worn a tunic of deerskin. Here, I was surrounded by a sea of priestess-blue. Some of the women wore their hair braided down their back like Suona, but others had it pinned up or loose upon their shoulders. The sunlight glistened on their bare heads, fair and dark and silver and bronze.

They seemed to be of every age and all sizes, alike only in the blue crescent painted between their brows – that, and something indefinable in their eyes. Upon reflection, I decided it was serenity, and wished I had it, for my tummy was doing flip-flops with anxiety.

Ignore them, I told myself sternly. *You will be living with these people for the rest of your life. You will look at this hall so many times you will no longer see it. There is no need to stare now, or to be afraid.*

Especially now, my thought continued as the women before me moved aside and I saw the High Priestess awaiting me. But the uncertain feeling returned as I felt the faerie dog stir in the bosom of my gown. I knew now that I should have left the puppy in the

20

House of Maidens, but Eldri had been asleep, and it had seemed to me then that if she woke in strange surroundings she might be frightened and run off. I had not thought about what might happen if the dog woke during my formal welcome to Avalon.

I crossed my arms, pressing the warm furry body against my chest in an attempt at reassurance. Eldri was a magic dog – perhaps she could hear my silent plea to be still.

The murmur of women's voices faded to silence as the High Priestess lifted her hand. The women were arranging themselves in a circle, with the senior priestesses closest to their Lady, and the maidens, stifling their giggles, at the end. I thought there were five of them, but dared not look at them long enough to be sure.

All eyes were upon me. I forced myself to continue moving forwards.

Now I could see the Lady clearly. Ganeda was at this time just past her middle years, her body thickened by childbearing. Her hair, which had once been red, was dusted with grey like a dying coal. I came to a halt before her, wondering what kind of bow would be appropriate for the Lady of Avalon. My nurse had taught me the proper obeisance for ranks all the way up to Empress, unlikely though it seemed that any Caesar would ever come so far as Britannia again.

I cannot go wrong if I give her the salute due an Imperial lady, I thought then. *For truly, she is Empress in her own sphere.*

As I straightened, I caught the old woman's eye, and it seemed to me that for a moment Ganeda's scowl was lightened by a gleam of amusement, but perhaps I had imagined it, for in the next moment the High Priestess stood stone-faced once more.

'So—' Ganeda spoke at last. 'You have come to Avalon. Why?' The question was spat suddenly, like a spear in the dark.

I stared back at her, suddenly bereft of words.

'You have frightened the poor child,' said one of the other priestesses, a motherly-looking woman with fair hair just beginning to fade to grey.

21

'It was a simple question, Cigfolla,' said the High Priestess tartly, 'that I am required to put to all who seek the sisterhood of Avalon.'

'She means,' said Cigfolla, 'to ask if you have come here of your own will, and not by any man's coercion. Do you seek the training of a priestess, or only a time of teaching before you return to the world?' She smiled encouragingly.

I frowned, recognizing this as a legitimate question.

'It was by my father's will that I came here at this time, because of the Saxon raids,' I said slowly, and saw something like satisfaction flicker in Ganeda's eyes. 'But it has always been my destiny to return to Avalon,' I continued.

If there had been any doubt, that journey through the mists would have dispelled it. This was the magic at the heart of things that I had always known must be there. At that moment, I had recognized my heritage.

'To walk the path of a priestess is my truest desire . . .'

Ganeda sighed. 'Beware what you wish for, lest you find it has indeed come to pass . . . Still, you have said the words, and in the end it is the Goddess who will decide whether to accept you, not I. So I bid you welcome here.'

There was a murmur of comment from the other priestesses at this grudging acceptance. I blinked back tears, understanding that my aunt did not want me here, and no doubt hoped that I would fail.

'*But I will not fail*! I promised myself. *I will study harder than any and become a great priestess – so famous they will remember my name for a thousand years*!

Ganeda sighed. 'Come.'

With my heart thumping so hard I feared it would wake Eldri, I started towards her. Ganeda opened her arms. *She is scarcely bigger than me*! I thought in surprise as I moved into the older woman's reluctant embrace. The High Priestess had seemed so tall and stately before.

Then Ganeda gripped my shoulders and drew me hard against her breast. Eldri, crushed between us, woke with a sudden squirm and a yip of surprise. The priestess released me as if I had been a hot coal, and I felt the betraying colour flood into my face as the little dog poked her head up through the loose neck of my gown.

Someone stifled a giggle, but my own impulse to laugh died at Ganeda's frown.

'What is this? Do you think to mock us here?' There was an undertone in the voice of the priestess like distant thunder.

'She is a faerie dog!' I exclaimed, my eyes filling with tears. 'The Lake people gave her to me!'

'A rare and wonderful creature,' Cigfolla put in before Ganeda could speak again. 'Such gifts are not bestowed lightly.'

From the other priestesses came a murmur of agreement. For a moment longer that mental thunder echoed in the air, then, as it became clear that most of the priestesses were viewing me with sympathy, Ganeda clamped down on her anger and managed a tight smile.

'A fine gift indeed,' she said thinly, 'but the Hall of the Priestesses is not the place for her.'

'I am sorry, my lady,' I stammered, 'I did not know where—'

'It makes no difference,' Ganeda cut me off. 'The community is waiting. Go, greet the rest of your sisters now.'

With the puppy still peering out of my tunica, I went gratefully into Cigfolla's arms, breathing in the lavender that scented her gown. The woman who stood next to her had the look of a paler copy of Ganeda. In her arms she held a little daughter whose hair blazed like a fire.

'I have *seen* your face in vision, little one, and I am glad to make you welcome! I am your cousin Sian, and this is Dierna,' she said softly. The little girl grinned toothily, as fair and fat a child as one might hope to find. Next to that flaming hair, her mother seemed even more pallid, as if she had given all her strength to her offspring. Or perhaps, I thought, it was growing up in the shadow of Ganeda that had sapped the strength from her.

'Hello, Dierna.' I squeezed the plump hand.

'I'm two!' proclaimed the little girl.

23

'You certainly are!' I answered after a moment's confusion. Apparently that was the right answer, for Sian also smiled.

'You are very welcome to Avalon,' she said then, bending to kiss me on the brow.

At least one member of my mother's family was glad to see me, I thought as I turned to the next woman in the line.

As I moved around the circle, some of the women had a pat for the puppy as well, and others a word of praise for my dead mother. The girls who were currently being trained on the holy isle received me with delighted awe, as if I had intended to play a trick on the High Priestess all along. Roud and Gwenna had the ruddy-fair colouring of the royal Celts, and Heron, the dark, narrow build of the people of the Lake. Aelia was almost as tall as I, though her hair was a lighter brown. Tuli, who surveyed them from the eminence of her approaching initiation, and her younger sister Wren, had fair hair, cut short like that of the others, and grey eyes. This was not the way that I had intended to impress them, but for good or ill, the little dog seemed to be a powerful talisman.

And then the formality of greeting was over, and the solemn row became a crowd of chattering women. But as the girls swept me away to the safety of the House of Maidens, I saw Ganeda watching me and realized that if my aunt had disliked me before, she would hate me now. I had grown up in a prince's court, and I knew that no ruler can afford to be mocked in her own hall.

CHAPTER TWO

AD 262–263

'But where do people go when they visit Faerie? Does the spirit journey only, as in a dream, or does the body really move between the worlds?'

I was lying on my belly with the sunlight soaking into my back, and Wren's words seemed indeed to come from another world. A part of my mind was aware that I lay on the earth of the holy isle with the other maidens, listening to Suona's teaching, but my essence was floating in some strange in-between state from which it would be very easy to travel entirely away.

'You are here, are you not?' asked Suona tartly.

'Not all here—' whispered Aelia, giggling. As usual, she had claimed a place next to me.

'You passed through the mists to come to this place, otherwise you would have ended on Inis Witrin,' the priestess continued. 'It is easier to journey in the spirit only, but indeed, the body may also be translated, by those who are trained in the ancient wisdom . . .'

I rolled over and sat up. It was an unusually warm day in the springtime, and Suona had brought her charges to sit in the apple orchard. Light fell in a shifting shimmer through the young leaves, dappling the undyed linen gowns of the girls with gold. Wren was thinking over the answer, head cocked to one side like the bird from whom she took her name.

She could always be depended on to state the obvious, and as the youngest of the girls being trained on Avalon, she came in for a good deal of teasing. I had seen how it was when a new member was introduced to a pack of hounds, and had expected that they would gang up on me.

But even though Ganeda showed me no favour, I *was* a relation of the Lady of Avalon. Or perhaps it was my size, for at thirteen, Aelia and I were as tall as many of the grown priestesses, or because Wren was such an easy target, but it was the younger girl who got picked on and I who did my best to protect her.

'The Christians have a tale of a prophet called Elijah who went up to heaven in a chariot of fire,' I said brightly. As part of our education we had been taken to a service on the other isle. 'Was he an adept as well?'

Suona looked a little sour, and the other girls laughed. They had become accustomed to thinking of the Christians of Inis Witrin as foolish, if generally kindly, old men who mumbled prayers and had forgotten the ancient wisdom. And yet, if what I had heard of the holy Joseph who was their founder was true, they also had known something of the Mysteries at one time.

'Perhaps—' Suona said unwillingly. 'I suppose that the laws of the Spirit World are like the laws of the world of Nature, and do not operate much differently in other lands than they do here. But it is in Avalon that the old ways are practised and the truth remembered. To most men, this place is a dream and a rumour of magic. You are very fortunate to be dwelling here!'

The giggles subsided and the girls, recognizing that their teacher's patience was thinning, arranged their skirts decorously around them and sat up straight once more.

'I remember how it felt to go through the mists the first time,' said I, 'for I came here only three years ago. It was as if my mind was being turned inside out, and then the world changed.'

Only three years – and yet now it was the world outside that seemed a dream. Even my grief for my father, who had been slain fighting the Saxon raiders, had eased. My hostile great-aunt was now my closest relation, but the other priestesses were kind to me, and among the maidens, Aelia was my fast friend.

Suona smiled a little. 'I suppose that is as good a description as any. But that is not the only way to move from world to world. To travel from the life of the tribes to Londinium is to the spirit as great a journey, and some of those who make it fall ill and pine like trees transplanted to unfriendly soil because their minds cannot bear the change.'

I nodded. I had been to Londinium several times during my childhood, and though Prince Julius Coelius might have been Roman in name and taught his children to speak Latin as well as their mother tongue, I could still remember the shock as we passed through the gate of the city and the noise of the capital rose around us, like jumping into the sea.

'But do our bodies go to Faerie?' said Wren, who could stick to a topic like a terrier when her interest was aroused.

Seeing Suona's frown, I stepped in once more. 'We know that our solid bodies are sitting here in the orchard below the Tor, but except that the weather is sometimes a little different, Avalon is not so unlike the outside world.'

'There are other differences,' said the priestess, 'which you will learn about when you are more advanced in your training. Certain kinds of magic work more easily here, because we are at a crossing of the lines of power, and because of the structure of the Tor . . . But for the most part what you say is true.'

'But Faerie is not the same,' put in Tuli. 'Time there runs slower, and its folk are magic.'

'That is so, and yet even there, a mortal who is willing to pay the price may dwell.'

'What is the price?' asked I.

'To lose the gradual sweet changes of the seasons, and all the gathered wisdom of mortality.'

'Is that so bad a thing?' asked Roud, her red hair glinting as her braid swung forwards. 'If you go when you are young?'

'Would you like to have stayed forever nine years old?' Suona asked.

'When I was nine, I was a baby!' Roud said from the eminence of her fourteen years.

27

'Each age has its own delights and contentments,' the priestess went on, 'that you will miss if you go where time has no meaning, beyond the circles of the world.'

'Of course I want to grow up,' muttered Roud. 'But who would want to be *old?*'

Everyone, thought I, if Suona was to be believed. It was hard, though, to credit it, when young eyes could gaze through the trees to the dazzle of sun on water, and young ears listen to the song of the lark as she lifted skyward, and a young body twitched with impatience to run with Eldri through the long grass, to dance, to be free.

'And that is why, for the most part, we make our journeys in the spirit only,' Suona added. 'And at the moment, yours are bouncing about like lambs in a meadow. If you will be so kind as to focus your minds for a few moments, we have work to do.'

Alas, thought I, it was nothing so exciting as a journey to Faerie. The folk of Avalon, both priestesses and priests, did not spend all their time in ritual. Wool and flax must be spun, the gardens tended, buildings repaired. But at least some of the work involved the heart as well as the hands. Now, when the fruit was setting, was the time for working with the spirits of the trees.

'Sit still, then, and rest upon the earth—' As the priestess spoke, the girls settled obediently into the position for meditation, legs crossed like the Horned One when he blesses the animals.

I closed my eyes, my breathing slipping automatically into the slow, regular, rhythm of trance.

'See with your mind this orchard – the rough and smooth of the bark on the apple trees, the glitter of leaves as the wind moves them. And now, begin to see with other senses. Reach out and touch the spirit of the tree before you. Sense power radiating around it in a golden glow.'

As the gentle voice continued, I found myself shifting into that passive state in which images formed almost as soon as I heard the words. Whether I was feeling or imagining I could not tell, but I knew I was touching the spirit of the tree.

'Let your own power flow outwards – thank the tree for the fruit it has given, and offer some of your energy to help it make more . . .'

I let out my breath with a sigh, feeling myself sinking deeper and deeper, even as the tree became a brighter glow. And soon I realized that what I was seeing was not a bright tree-shape, but the shining form of a woman, who held out her arms and smiled. For a moment I seemed to see another country beyond me, shimmering with a beauty beyond even that of Avalon. A responding joy pulsed through me in a wave that carried all awareness away.

When I came to myself, I was lying on my back in the grass. Suona was bending over me. Beyond the priestess I could see Aelia, watching with a pale face and worried eyes.

'You were to use *some* of your energy—' said Suona tartly, straightening. Beads of perspiration glistened on her brow, and I wondered just how hard it had been to bring my spirit back again. 'A priestess must learn not only to give, but to control, her power!'

'I am sorry.' I whispered. I felt not so much weak as transparent, or perhaps it was the substance of the world that had grown thinner, for I could still see a glow through the trunk of the apple tree.

Spring turned to summer, but Sian, the Lady's daughter, continued to ail. Often, during those long days, the care of her two daughters fell to me. I had become quite a story-teller in my quest to amuse them. Sometimes, one of the boys the Druids were training, like little Haggaia, would join us.

'In the old and olden days, before the Romans came, there was a king in the westlands whose people complained because his queen had given him no son,' said I.

'Did she have a daughter?' asked Dierna, her bright head flaming in the afternoon light that slanted through the trees around the holy well. It was cool here at the end of summer, listening to the endless sweet song of the cold waters that welled from the sacred spring.

Her little sister Becca was asleep on a pile of blankets nearby with

Eldri curled up beside her. The little dog had grown too big for me to carry in the front of my gown, but she was still no larger than a cat. Except for her black nose, she looked like a bundle of white fleece, sleeping there. Haggaia lay on his belly, half-supported on his elbows, his brown hair glinting in the sun.

'Not that I ever heard,' I replied.

'That is why they complained, then,' said Dierna decidedly. 'It would have been all right if she had had a girl.'

This afternoon, Sian was resting. She had never really recovered her strength after Becca's birth last winter, and none of Cigfolla's herbal remedies seemed to help her. I knew that the elder priestesses were worried, though they did not speak of it, from the gratitude with which they accepted my offers to take care of the two girls. But in truth I did not mind, for Becca was as bright and bouncy as a puppy, and Dierna like the little sister that I had always longed for.

'Do you want to hear what happened or not?' I asked her, amused in spite of myself.

Haggaia pulled a face, but it was no wonder that Dierna thought a daughter more important, living on the holy isle where the Druids were subject to the will of the Lady of Avalon. If there had been a Merlin, the authority might have divided more evenly, but the last had died shortly after I was born, and no one had inherited his powers.

'So what happened?' demanded the boy.

'The king loved his lady, and he told his counsellors to give them another year to have a child. And sure enough, before the year was over they had a little daughter—'

This was not the way the singer in my father's hall had told the story, but he was no Druid to memorize the old lore exactly, and had often said that a bard must adapt his material to the taste of his audience. Encouraged by Dierna's grin, I forged ahead.

'The queen had women to watch by her, but they fell asleep, and while they were all sleeping, the little princess disappeared! When the women woke up, they were terrified that the king would be angry. Now that same night the queen's hound-bitch had given birth to puppies, so the women took two of the puppies and killed them and smeared blood on the queen's mouth and set the bones beside her, and when the king came, they swore that the lady had eaten her own child!'

Now, not only were the children frowning, but Eldri had roused from her sleep and was staring at me with reproachful brown eyes, as if she understood every word.

'Do I have to please you, too?' I muttered, trying to think how I could save the story. 'Don't cry, Dierna – it will come out all right, I promise you!'

'Did the queen die?' whispered Haggaia.

'Indeed she did not, for the king loved her and did not believe the accusations, though he could not prove them wrong. But they did punish her.'

'They would have known the bones belonged to puppies, if she had been on Avalon,' Dierna declared. 'But I am sorry for the mother dog who lost her children,' she added in apology to Eldri.

'She was not the only one!' said I, forging ahead quickly without worrying about the traditional form of the tale. 'In the same country there was a farmer whose hound-bitch gave birth to one puppy every year that disappeared, just like the queen's child. So the farmer stayed up one night to see what was happening—' I paused dramatically.

'Was there a monster?' asked Dierna, her eyes round.

'There was indeed, and the farmer swung his axe and cut off the claw with which it had the puppy clutched tight, and then he started to chase the beast he could hear rushing away. He could not catch it, but when he came back to the barn what do you suppose he found?'

'The rest of the puppies?' Haggaia exclaimed.

Eldri yipped approval, and I made yet another change to the story. 'Not only were the puppies there, but beside them was a lovely little girl wrapped in an embroidered cloth, and she looked just like the queen!'

31

'And they took her back to her mother then, didn't they, and they were all happy—' Dierna was bouncing with pleasure as she provided her own ending to the tale. 'And the puppies too, and they all grew up together, just like you and Eldri!'

I nodded, laughing, as the little dog bounded to Dierna and leapt up against her, licking her face enthusiastically. The little girl fell backwards and child and dog rolled over and over across the grass. At the noise, Becca began to stir, and I went to pick her up.

'Is this how you fulfil your trust?'

I looked up in alarm, blinking at the dark shape that stood between me and the sun. I scrambled to my feet, holding the baby tightly, and realized it was Ganeda, her worn features set in a frown. But that was nothing new. The High Priestess usually frowned when she looked at her sister's child.

'Look at them – it is disgraceful! Dierna! Let go of that dirty beast now!'

I blinked at that, for Blossom's curly coat shone like washed fleece in the sun. The dog stopped first, and then the little girl, the laughter fading from her face as she looked up at her grandmother.

'Get up! You are the heir of Avalon! And you, boy – go back to the Men's Side. You have no business here!'

I lifted one eyebrow. Dierna came of the priestly line, to be sure, but so did I. And high priestesses, like Roman emperors, were chosen by their followers on the basis of merit, not bloodlines. *She wants to rule Avalon even after she herself passes on,* I thought then, *and if her daughter dies she will lay the burden on this child . . .*

'Yes, grandmama,' said Dierna, getting to her feet and brushing the leaves from her gown. Haggaia was already edging away, hoping to make his escape before worse befell.

For a moment Eldri glared at the High Priestess, then she trotted across the grass and very deliberately urinated below a tree. I bit my lip to keep from laughing as Ganeda turned back to her.

'It is time for Sian to nurse the baby. I will take the children now.'

With difficulty, I detached Becca's tiny fingers from the neck of my gown and handed her to the old woman. Ganeda strode up the hill, and Dierna, after casting one regretful look over her shoulder, followed her. As I watched them go, a cold nose poked my leg. I picked up the little dog and cuddled her.

'I am sorry you lost your playmate,' I said softly, but in truth, it was Dierna that I pitied most, and for the child there was nothing that I could do.

From time to time some pilgrim to Avalon would bring news of the world beyond the mists. The imperium Galliarum established by Postumus in the year I had come to Avalon now included Hispania as well as Gallia and Britannia, and there did not seem to be much that the Emperor Gallienus, plagued by a series of pretenders in the other sectors of his empire, could do to reassert his authority. It was Postumus, not Rome, who had appointed Octavius Sabinus to govern Lower Britannia. Rumour had it that he was rebuilding some of the fortresses that had fallen into disarray when the troops that manned them had been sent to bolster waning Roman strength on the continent, but there was not much urgency in the matter, for the North had been quiet for some while.

Indeed, though each year it seemed that Gallia suffered the incursion of some new breed of barbarian, Britannia lay lapped in a charmed peace, as if the mists had rolled outwards to separate it from the world. The harvests were good, and the northern tribes remained peacefully on their own side of the Wall. If the western regions of the Roman Empire were to be forever sundered from the remainder, in Britannia, at least, no one seemed disposed to mourn.

Of these events, only rumours came to Avalon. Here, the passing of time was marked by the great festivals that honoured the turning of the seasons, celebrated year after year in an eternal and unvarying symmetry. But each winter Ganeda seemed to grow more grey and bent, and the girls who slept in the House of Maidens blossomed more brightly with the approach of womanhood every spring.

33

One morning just after the equinox, I was awakened by a dull ache in my belly. When I got up and pulled off my sleeping robe, I discovered the bright stain of my first moonblood on the skirt of the nightgown.

My first response was a great relief and satisfaction, for Heron and Roud had already made their passage, though they were even younger than I. But they were small and sleek and rounded, while my growth had all gone into my long limbs. Cigfolla had told me not to fret, that the plump girls always matured first, and put on even more flesh in their middle years.

'When you pass thirty and still have a waistline you will be grateful for your lean build,' the older woman had told me. 'You will see.'

But I was now the tallest girl in the House of Maidens, and if my breasts had not begun to grow, I would have wondered if I ought to have been living with the boys the Druids were training on the other side of the hill instead of with the priestesses. Even Aelia, who was very like me in build, had begun her courses a year ago.

I understood what must be done – Heron and the others had been only too eager to explain. I knew that I was blushing, but I managed to keep my voice matter-of-fact when I went to ask old Ciela for the absorbent moss and the lengths of linen that had been washed to downy softness that I would need to wrap it in.

I bore the congratulations of the other women as well as I could, wondering all the while how long Ganeda would make me wait for my ritual. The body's maturing was only an outwards marker. The inner transformation from child to maiden would be confirmed by my rite of passage.

They came for me at the still hour just past midnight, when only those who kept vigil for the Goddess should have been waking. I had been dreaming of running water. As the hood came down over my head it became a nightmare of drowning. For a few panicked moments I struggled against the hand that had clamped over my mouth, then returning awareness identified the scent of the lavender that the priestesses stored with their robes, and I understood what was happening.

Last year, it had been Aelia who had been missing from her bed when the horn call awakened us to salute the rising sun, and then, Heron. They had been returned, pale with fatigue and smug with secrets, for the celebration that evening, and neither by threats nor by urging could they be compelled to tell the uninitiated girls what had occurred.

But beyond reinforcing a sense of superiority that had seemed to me to be excessive already, whatever had happened to them seemed to have done them no harm. I forced my limbs to relax. I sensed the beginning of a growl from Eldri, who always slept in the curve of my arm, and pressed the little dog back into the bedclothes, stroking the silky fur until the tension left her small frame.

I wish you could go with me too, I thought, *but I must do this alone* . . . Then I sat up and allowed my invisible abductors to help me out of the bed, wrap a warm cloak around me, and lead me away.

Gravel crunched beneath my feet, and I knew they were taking the path beside the Lake. I smelled the dank scent of marsh and heard the wind whisper in the reedbeds, and wondered, for a moment, whether they meant to take me across the water to one of the other isles.

Several times my escort reversed direction, spinning me about until my head whirled and only a firm grip on my elbow kept me from falling. Instinctively I lifted a hand to the hood, and someone else prevented me from lifting it.

'Do not attempt to see,' came a harsh whisper in my ear. 'You have set your feet upon the path to a future you cannot know. You must walk this way without looking back to your childhood, trusting the wisdom of those who have gone before to show you the way. Do you understand?'

I nodded, accepting the ritual necessity, but I had always had an excellent sense of direction, and as my dizziness passed I could feel the power of the Tor to my right, like a pillar of fire.

Then we were climbing, and my skin pebbled as it was touched

35

by chill, moist air. I heard the musical gurgling of water, and the little procession came to a halt as someone opened a gate. I was hearing the stream that overflowed from the Blood Spring at the foot of the Tor, I thought then. To know where I was made me feel a little less vulnerable. I tried to convince myself that I was trembling because of the cold.

Suddenly, through the coarse weave of the hood I glimpsed the red gleam of torches. The hood was plucked off, and I realized that I had been right, for we were standing before the gate to the enclosure around the well. But everything looked strange. Veiled women surrounded me, anonymous in the flickering light. The smallest of them held my arm. They took my cloak then, and the thin sleeping robe, leaving me naked before them, shivering in the chill air.

'Naked you came into the world,' said the same harsh voice that had spoken before. 'Naked you must make your passage into your new life.'

The one who held me pulled me back. I guessed it was Heron, from her size. It must be the responsibility of the most recent initiate to guide the next one. The other women were forming into a line between me and the gate, legs spread wide.

'Through this passage you came into the world. Pass through the birthing tunnel and be reborn—'

'You must crawl between their legs to the gate,' hissed Heron, pushing me down.

'Through this tunnel you are born into the circle of women. Through this passage you will enter a new world.'

Biting my lip as the gravel dug into my kneecaps, I crawled forward. I felt the rough weave of woollen cloaks and the softness of linen gowns brush my back. As I passed between the priestesses' thighs, smooth skin slid past my own and I smelled the musk of their womanhood, dizzying as incense. It was a shock to emerge from the warmth of that tunnel of flesh into the cool air of the garden beyond.

The gate was open. My guide led me through it and the other

women followed, spreading out to either side. The last one to enter closed the gate behind me. Torchlight glittered red on the still waters of the pool.

A tall form stepped forward, blocking my view of the others. The shape was that of Cigfolla, but she seemed taller, and her voice had the unearthly resonance of ritual.

'You have come into the temple of the Great Goddess. Know that She wears as many forms as womankind, and yet She is singular and supreme. She is eternal and unchanging, and yet she shows Herself to us in a different guise with each season. She is Maiden, forever untouched and pure. She is Mother, the Source of All. And She is ancient Wisdom that endures beyond the grave. Eilan, daughter of Rian, are you willing to accept Her in all Her guises?'

I licked lips that were suddenly dry, but I was pleased to hear my answer coming steadily and clear.

'I am . . .'

The priestess raised her arms in invocation.

'Lady, we come here to welcome Eilan daughter of Rian into our circle, and to instruct her in the mysteries of womanhood. Holy One, hear us now! May our words express Thy will as our bodies show the form of Thy divinity, for we eat and drink and breathe and love in Thee . . .'

'Be it so—' came a murmur of assent from around the circle, and I felt myself begin to relax.

Heron draped the cloak around my shoulders again and pushed me forwards. Three chairs had been set on the other side of the well. The other priestesses had unveiled, but the three who were enthroned were still swathed in folds of gossamer linen, white, and black, and in the middle, red. Aelia was sitting across the circle; as she caught my eye she smiled.

'Daughter of the Goddess, you have left childhood behind,' said Heron, with the careful intonation of one repeating newly-learned lines. 'Learn now what the seasons of your life shall be.'

I knelt before the priestess who wore the white veil. For a moment there was silence. Then the sheer fabric trembled as its

37

wearer laughed. The sound came sweet and silvery as a trill of bells, and I shivered, understanding that something more than a human priestess was here.

'*I am the flower that blooms on the bough,*' said the Maiden.

The voice was light, sweet with promise, as familiar to me as my own, even though I was certain I had never heard it before. To hear it was like listening to the song of my soul, and I knew that this was the Goddess indeed.

> '*I am the crescent that crowns the sky.*
> *I am the sunlight that glitters on the wave*
> *and the breeze that bends the new grass.*
> *No man has ever possessed Me,*
> *and yet I am the end of all desire.*
> *Huntress and Holy Wisdom am I,*
> *Spirit of Inspiration, and Lady of Flowers.*
> *Look into the water and you will see*
> *My face mirrored there, for you belong to Me . . .*'

I closed my eyes, overwhelmed by the image of the Lake, half-veiled by a silver mist of rain. Then the clouds parted. Standing on the shore was a young man whose hair shone like the beams of the sun, and nearby, I saw myself, my hair grown long, so I knew that this was some years in the future. I was moving towards him, but as I reached out to touch his hand the scene changed. Now I was seeing the light of a bonfire upon a Beltane tree crowned with flowers. Men and maidens danced wildly around it, and among them I saw the same young man, his eyes alight with exaltation as a veiled figure I knew to be myself was led forwards by priestesses crowned with flowers. Then he was sweeping me into his arms.

Now we were within the sacred bower. He pulled off the maiden's veil and I saw my own face, alight with joy. I glimpsed the crescent moon through the new leaves, and then the scene dissolved in a shower of stars, and I was myself again, looking up at the Mystery hidden by the white veil.

'I hear you,' I whispered in a shaking voice. 'I will serve you.'

'Will you swear now to give up your maidenhead only to the man whom I shall choose for you, in the holy rites of Avalon?'

I stared, wondering if this was a test, for surely the Lady had just shown me the man I was destined to love. But the voice had lost that unearthly sweetness, and I thought that perhaps the Goddess had departed again. Still, I had known that this oath was required of all who served as priestesses on Avalon.

'I swear,' I said gladly, for even in that glimpse of vision my soul had begun to yearn for the young man I had seen.

'It is well,' said the Maiden, 'but there is yet Another whom you must hear—' I sat back, turning a little towards the second figure, whose crimson veil glowed with the torches' fire.

'*I am the fruit that swells on the branches. I am the full moon that rules the sky . . .*' This voice was all golden, powerful as the purr of some great cat, honey-sweet, and comforting as newly-baked bread.

> '*I am the sun in her splendour,*
> *and the warm wind that ripens the grain.*
> *I give myself in my own times and seasons,*
> *and bring forth abundance.*
> *I am Mistress and Mother, I give birth and I devour.*
> *I am the lover and the beloved,*
> *and you will one day belong to Me . . .*'

As I listened to this voice, I understood that this too was the Goddess, and bowed my head respectfully. And in that gesture of acceptance, vision came once more upon me.

I was on a Roman trading boat, wallowing along under full sail. Behind me lay the silver glitter of the sea, but the boat was moving into the mouth of a mighty river that had carved many branching channels through a flat coastal plain. Beside me stood the man who had courted me, his eyes fixed on the horizon. The scene changed: I was heavy with child, and then I was holding the babe at my breast, a large and healthy boy with a shock of fair hair. The shock of sensation as the infant bit down on my nipple sent me back into my body again.

'I hear you,' I whispered, 'and when my season comes, I will serve you.'

'You will indeed,' the Lady replied, 'but there is yet Another whom you must hear—'

I shivered as the dark draperies that swathed the third figure stirred.

'*I am the nut that clings to the leafless bough,*' came a whisper like the rubbing of bare branches in the winter wind.

> '*I am the waning moon whose sickle harvests the stars.*
> *I am the setting sun*
> *and the cool wind that heralds the darkness.*
> *I am ripe with years and with wisdom;*
> *I see all the secrets beyond the Veil.*
> *I am Hag and Harvest Queen, Witch and Wisewoman,*
> *and you will one day belong to Me . . .*'

That whisper was a wind that whirled my awareness outwards once more. I saw myself older, my garments rent and my cheeks wet with tears, watching a funeral fire. For a moment the flames parted and I glimpsed the fair-haired man. At the pain of that recognition, the scene changed to a hall faced with marble and gold in which I stood, wearing a diadem and a purple robe.

But before I could wonder what I was doing there, it shifted once more, and I saw myself draped in black, walking the sandy shore beside the sea. I turned from the merciless glitter of sun on water to a landscape of bare rock with the severe, stripped beauty of a skull. It filled me with fear, and yet I knew it was there that I must go.

And at that, a longing awakened within me for the cool mists and green hills of my own country, and I came to myself once more, sitting upon the grass beside the sacred well.

'You are the Goddess—' I breathed, 'and I will serve You. Only let me end my life here, in Avalon . . .'

'Do you ask for compassion?' asked the black-veiled figure. 'I have none – only necessity. You cannot escape me, for I am your destiny.'

I sat back, shivering, but mercifully, the Wisewoman did not speak again.

I had not been aware of the passage of time, but overhead the sky was growing pale, and I could feel in the air the moist chill that heralds the dawn.

'You have faced the Goddess,' said Cigfolla, 'and She has accepted your vows. Purified, you shall sit your vigil, and when the day is done, return to the community to be honoured in a celebration. Your new life begins with the rising of the sun.'

Heron helped me to get up, and all the women moved towards the pool below the sacred spring. As the sky lightened, they surrounded it in a protective circle. Heron pulled off my cloak, and as I stood shivering, began to pull off her own robe as well. The other maidens and the younger priestesses were doing the same, and I felt a moment's satisfaction to see that I was not the only one whose skin was pebbling in bumps like a plucked fowl.

I realized that for some time now birds had been singing, their triumphant chorus calling up the sun from the apple trees. Mist still lay along the ground and hung in the branches, but overhead it was thinning, and the failing torches burned pale in the brightening air. Moment by moment the world was becoming more visible, as if it were only now coming into manifestation. Slowly, the smooth slope of the Tor emerged from mists suffused with rosy light.

It grew brighter. Heron took my arm and drew me down into the pool. The other young women followed, sea-shells in their hands. I gasped as the cold water touched my skin, and again as the fiery orb of the sun lifted suddenly above the horizon, refracting from each drop of mist and every ripple in the water in a blaze of rosy light. I lifted my arms in adoration, and saw my own pale flesh grow radiant.

41

Heron dipped up water and poured it over me, but the fire within me welcomed its icy flame.

'By the water that is the Lady's blood may you be cleansed,' came the murmur of voices as the other maidens did the same. 'Now let the water bear away all soil and stains. Let all that hid your true self be dissolved away. Be still, and let the water caress your body, as from the water that is the Womb of the Goddess you are reborn.'

I sank down into the water, and the locks of my unbound hair floated upon the surface, shining like the rays of the sun. A part of my mind knew that the water was cold, but my entire body was tingling as if I bathed in light; I could feel each particle of my flesh being transformed.

For a timeless moment I floated in the water. Then soft hands were drawing me upwards, and I emerged into the full light of day.

'Now arise, Eilan, clean and shining, revealed in all your beauty. Arise and take your place among us, Maiden of Avalon!'

CHAPTER THREE

AD 265

It was the end of summer and I was trimming the hazel hedge when something stung my calf. I jumped and turned, striking out instinctively with the branch I had just cut.

'Ah ha!' Dierna danced backwards, waving the twigs she had snatched from the pile on the path. 'Got you!'

At eight, Dierna's red head blazed like a torch. Two-year-old Becca toddled behind her. I reached out to steady the little one as Dierna dashed away once more, then ran after her, swishing my own branch menacingly, though I suppose I rather spoiled the effect by laughing.

'Are you watching Becca today?' I asked when all three of us had collapsed, breathless, on the grass.

'I suppose so,' answered the little girl. 'She follows me everywhere—'

I nodded. I had heard the older priestesses talking, and knew that Sian still tired easily. It was inevitable that Dierna should end up with much of the responsibility for her little sister.

Sian did not seem to be in pain, but her strength waned with each month, and even when the moon grew full once more, it did not return. Ganeda said nothing, but there were new lines in her face. I found myself pitying the older woman, but I knew I was the last person from whom my aunt would accept sympathy.

Long before I felt ready to get up again, Dierna was bouncing to her feet to run after Becca, whose sturdy legs were already carrying her down the path.

'There are ducklings in the reed-beds!' exclaimed Dierna. 'Come with us and see!'

'I wish I could,' I told her, 'but I have promised to finish this hedge before dinner.'

'You have to work all the time!' complained Dierna. She turned, saw Becca disappearing around a corner, and dashed after her.

For a moment I stood watching as the red head caught up with the brown and the two continued down the path towards the Lake, sparkling in the afternoon sun. Then I sighed and turned back to my work once more.

When I was a little child, I had envied my older half-brothers their training as warriors. In those days, to whack away with a broken branch at some laughing guardsman had been my favourite game. They had told me tales of Boudicca, whose armies once made the Romans fear, and called me their warrior princess. But my brothers had smiled with male superiority and assured me that the disciplines they were undergoing were far too difficult for a mere girl.

Sometimes, when I remembered those days, I would wonder whether my brothers could have endured the education I was receiving now. In the three years since the ceremony that welcomed me to womanhood the training of a priestess had ruled my days. True, I still shared some work and classes with the younger girls and the maidens who had been sent to Avalon to learn something of the old ways before going home to be married. But now I also had other training, and additional duties.

The girls who were meant to be priestesses sat with the youths being trained by the Druids to memorize endless lists of names and master the elaborate symbols and correspondences by which meaning could be enriched, or disguised. We ran races around the holy isle, for it was held that a vigorous body was necessary to support a strong mind. We were trained in correct use of the voice, and practised as a choir for the ceremonies. And with the initiated priestesses, we maidens took our turns to tend the flame on the altar that was the hearth of Avalon.

44

To keep watch in the temple and feed the little fire was not physically demanding. But although meditation was encouraged during the vigil, sleep was forbidden. I loved to sit alone in the round thatched hut on the Maidens' Isle, watching the leaping flame, but now, in the lazy warmth of afternoon, my need for sleep was beginning to catch up with me. I found myself swaying, and stared stupidly at the hazel twig in my hand.

Better stop before I cut off one of my fingers! I thought, blinking, and bent to set the pruning knife on the ground. The hedge was an old one, and before me, twisted branches formed a natural backrest. It felt natural to curl into it, and in another moment my eyes had closed.

My lips moved soundlessly. *Shelter me for a little while, hazel sister, and I will finish trimming your hair . . .*

I never knew whether it was some sound from below or a whisper from the hazel hedge itself that woke me. For a moment, still dazed with sleep, I could not think why my heart was thudding with alarm.

The shadows had lengthened just a little, and the afternoon was warm and still. I glimpsed Dierna's red head near the reedbeds farther along the shore – the girls must be watching the ducklings. Then a closer movement caught my eye. Becca was crawling along the trunk of the old oak tree that had fallen half into the water during the last storm.

I leapt to my feet. 'Becca! Stop!'

For a moment I thought the little girl had heard me, but Becca's pause was only to grab at something in the Lake. Then she was on her way again.

'Becca, stop! Hold on!' I cried as I galloped down the hill. Dierna was standing up now, but the shoreline curved inward here and she was too far away. I saved the rest of my breath for running as I saw the toddler stand up, reach towards the water with a glad cry, and fall in.

I felt a flicker of wonder that time, which a few moments before had seemed to drag so endlessly, should now be passing in such a swift whirl. Becca had disappeared beneath the surface. Grass and shrubs flashed past, and then I was thrashing through the shallows, reaching out as the little girl came up, flailing, and snatching her into my arms.

Becca gave one hiccup, coughed up water, and then began to scream.

In moments, it seemed, we were surrounded by priestesses. I relinquished the child to the little dark Lake-woman who had been brought to Avalon to be her nurse and sighed with relief as the sound of Becca's cries faded away. But in the next moment I realized that someone was still yelling.

Dierna was crouched on the ground, whimpering as Ganeda berated her with a violence all the more shocking because her body was as rigid as stone. Only her hair, escaping from its coiled braids, jerked and trembled. I stared, half-expecting it to burst into flame.

'Do you understand me? Your sister could have drowned! And with your poor mother lying ill – do you want to kill her too, by destroying her child?'

She is worried about Sian, I told myself, but even the other priestesses looked shocked at the venom in Ganeda's tone.

Dierna shook her head, grinding her cheek into the earth in an agony of negation. Beneath the freckles her face was as white as bone.

Just as fear had moved me to save Becca, compassion compelled me into action now. A swift step brought me to Dierna's side. I bent, cradling the girl in my arms as if the assault from which I strove to protect her was physical.

'She meant no harm! She was playing – it was too much respon- sibility for so young a child!' I looked up at the High Priestess, beginning to tremble myself as that furious gaze fixed on me instead. I used to wonder if my dead mother had resembled her sister – I hoped that Rian had never looked the way Ganeda did now.

'She must learn discipline! She is of the sacred line of Avalon!' Ganeda exclaimed.

So am I, Aunt – so am I! I thought, but my own mouth was going dry with fear. *Once I hoped that you would love me, but I don't think you even know how*!

'Get away from her, before I forget to be grateful to you for saving the little one. You cannot stand between Dierna and her punishment!'

Dierna gasped and clutched at my waist. I tightened my own grip, staring up at the older woman defiantly.

'She is only eight years old! If you frighten her to death how can she understand?'

'And you are sixteen!' hissed Ganeda. 'Do you think that gives you the wisdom of the Lady of Avalon? You should have stayed with your father in the Roman lands!'

I shook my head. I belonged *here*! But Ganeda chose to take it as submission.

'Gwenlis, take the child away!'

One of the younger priestesses stepped forwards, eyeing the High Priestess uncertainly. For a moment I resisted, then it occurred to me that the sooner Dierna was out of earshot of her grandmother's wrath, the better it would be. I gave the girl a quick hug, and thrust her into Gwenlis's arms.

'And lock her into the storage shed!' Ganeda went on.

'No!' I exclaimed, getting to my feet again. 'She will be afraid!'

'It is you who should be afraid! Do not flout my will lest I lock you up as well!'

I smiled, for I had already been through more taxing ordeals in my training.

Ganeda took a furious step towards me. 'Don't think I haven't noticed how you have been spoiling the child, interfering with my discipline, plotting to steal her affection away from me!'

'I hardly need to do that! You will earn her hatred yourself if you treat her this way!'

'You will have nothing to do with Dierna in the future, do you understand me? Or with Becca either!' Ganeda's anger had turned suddenly cold, and for the first time I felt fear. 'Hear me all of you, and bear witness—' the High Priestess turned to fix the others with that icy gaze. 'This is the will of the Lady of Avalon!'

Even before Ganeda finished speaking, I had decided to defy her. But a stern order sent me back up the hill to finish trimming the hedge, and it was not until the still hour just after dusk had fallen, when the folk of Avalon gathered for their evening meal, that I was able to open the door to the storage shed unobserved.

Swiftly I slipped inside and took the shivering child in my arms.

'Eilan?' The little girl clutched at me, sniffling. 'It's cold here, and dark, and I think there are rats . . .'

'Well, then, you must talk to the Rat Spirit and ask her to keep them away,' I said bracingly.

Dierna shuddered and shook her head.

'Don't you know how? We will do it together, then, and promise her some food for her clan—'

'Nobody has brought me any food,' whispered the girl. 'I'm hungry.'

I was glad that the darkness hid my frown. 'Are you? Well, perhaps I can bring you some of my dinner, and an offering for the Rat Spirit too. We will put it outside, and ask her to take her people out there . . .'

With a sigh of relief I felt the child begin to relax in my arms, and started the familiar litany of counted breathing and relaxation that would put us in touch with the Otherworld.

I had forgotten that after dinner came the story-telling. The bread and cheese made an awkward lump in the corner of my shawl, but even when I went out to the privies there had been too many people around for me to get away. Certainly I would be missed if I tried to leave now, and my absence would attract just the sort of notice I wished to avoid.

The long hall was lit by torches, and a fire blazed on the hearth, for even in early autumn the nights were chill. But I could not help imagining how Dierna must be feeling, all alone in the cold dark.

On the first day of the week the stories told in the hall of Avalon were about the gods. By now, I had heard most of them, but as I forced my attention back to the Druid who was speaking, I realized that I had not encountered this one before.

'Our most ancient wisdom teaches that "All the gods are one God, and all the goddesses one Goddess, and there is one Initiator." But what does that mean? The Romans say that all the gods are the same, and it is only that different peoples call them by different names. Thus they say that Cocidius and Belatucadros are the same as their Mars, and call Brigantia and Sulis by the name of their goddess Minerva.

'It is true that these deities care for many of the same things. But we teach that they are like pieces of Roman glass set one behind the other. In that place where all gods are One, all colours are contained in the pure light of heaven. But when that white light passes through one piece of glass it shows one colour, and a second where it strikes another, and only where the glass overlaps do we see a third tone that partakes of both of them.

'It is the same in this world, where the gods show a multitude of faces to humankind. To the untutored eye those colours may all seem much the same, but vision is often a matter of what one has learned how to see . . .'

I blinked, wondering what else might be explained by this philosophy. I had had to learn how to recognize the aura that surrounded each living thing, and to read the signs of coming weather in the clouds. I was not as good yet at reading faces, although my aunt's scowl needed little interpretation. Surreptitiously I made sure the food in my shawl had not slipped out, wishing I could teach Dierna how to see through the darkness. Still, tonight the moon was almost full, and the woven wicker walls of the storeshed should let in some light.

'And there are some gods for whom the Romans have no analogue at all. They say that it is Mercurius of the crossroads who guides the

49

traveller. But we have a goddess who watches over the roads of the world, and it is our belief that she was here even before the Britons came into this land. We call her Elen of the Ways.'

I sat up, for that was very close to the name they called me here – Eilan . . .

'In body, she is tall and strong,' the bard-priest continued, 'and it is said that she loves good hounds, and the elder tree. All roads that men travel are under her protection, both the paths that cross the land and the ways of the sea. Traders pray to her for protection, and where she passes the crops grow tall.

'Perhaps it was she who first showed our ancestors the way across the sea to this island, and certainly she is the one who teaches us how to safely cross the marshes that surround Avalon, for above all she loves those places where the waters mingle with the land. We call upon her as well when we seek to go between the worlds, for she is also Mistress of the Hidden Ways . . .'

I remembered how reality had shifted around me when we passed through the mists to Avalon. Surely that was one of the roads that Elen ruled. Dizzied by memory, I could almost understand how it had been done. Then the moment passed, and I realized that the Druid had finished tuning his little lap harp and was about to sing.

> *'Oh Lady of the moonpath bright,*
> *and sea-lanes laid by sun's fair rays,*
> *the dragon-paths from height to height,*
> *and all the holy hidden ways,*
> *Oh Lady Elen of the Ways . . .'*

I blinked as the flame of the torch before me separated suddenly and rayed out in spokes of light. For a moment I was simultaneously aware of their infinite potentiality and the eternal balance of their radiant centre, and understood that there was a place where all the roads were One. But the bard was still singing—

'From heath and hill to marsh and fen
Thy dogs shall guide us all our days;
Through crooked paths laid down by men
Sweet Lady show us all the ways,
    Oh Lady Elen of the Ways . . .'

I thought of Eldri, and smiled at the image of the fluffy white
dog trying to tug some poor confused soul up a mountain. But I
knew how many times the little dog's unquestioning devotion had
steadied me when Lady Ganeda swore I would never be worthy of
becoming a priestess of Avalon. Could this new goddess show me
the way to my destiny?

'When vision fades and courage fails
May thy light lead us from the maze;
When neither strength nor sense avails,
Let thy love teach the heart new ways,
    Oh Lady Elen of the Ways . . .'

The harp-notes died away in a sweet ripple of sound. People began
to stir from the trance into which the music, or the good dinner, had
sent them. Now, in the confusion as the group broke up to prepare
for bed, was the time to take Dierna her food.

Carefully I circled around behind the privies, pulling the other
end of my shawl up to hide my pale face from the moonlight. The
moon was not yet high, and the storage shed stood in shadow. I let
the shawl drop with a sigh of relief, but as I touched the door my
belly tensed once more, for it swung freely beneath my hand.

Surely, I thought desperately, I had secured the latch when I crept
away before! I slipped inside, calling softly, but beyond a faint
scratching from behind the baskets of nuts, there was no sound,
and no sign of Dierna apart from my sash. *Dierna was right*, one
part of my mind informed me. *There are rats in here . . .*

The other part was speculating frantically. Perhaps Ganeda had

51

taken pity on the child and released her, or one of the other priestesses might have stepped in. But I knew that the High Priestess never modified her judgments, and none of the others had the courage to gainsay her. *When I am grown*, I thought grimly, *I will . . .*

This time I took care to latch the door behind me. Then, forcing myself not to run, I sought the snug little house where the smaller children slept, asking, as an excuse, whether they were playing with Eldri there. But neither the dog nor Dierna were to be seen, and the children were unusually quiet, as if the thought of her punishment oppressed them all.

I bade them a hasty good night and returned to the House of Maidens. I should give the alarm now, but I trembled at the thought of the beating Dierna would receive for running away. Eldri jumped up, whining, as she sensed my anxiety, and I hushed her. Then I stilled. Eldri was no scent-hound, but she had proven her intelligence. Perhaps there was another way.

To wait, while the other girls put on their nightrobes and brushed out their hair, made a final visit to the privies and blew out the lamps and turned and coughed until sleep took them, was an agony. But after an eternity had passed, all was still. And still I waited, until I felt my own eyelids growing heavy. Then I slid out of bed, and hiding my shoes beneath my shawl, tip-toed towards the door.

'What is it?'

I stifled a gasp at Aelia's sleepy question.

'Eldri has to go out again,' I whispered, pointing to the little dog, who unless told to stay put, was always half a step behind me. 'Go back to sleep.'

But instead, Aelia sat up, rubbing her eyes and staring. 'Why are you carrying your shoes?' she whispered. 'And your heavy shawl? Are you doing something that will get you into trouble?'

For a moment I could say nothing. Then it came to me that perhaps I had better let *someone* know where I had gone, and I could trust Aelia not to betray me.

'It's Dierna who's in trouble—' Swiftly I gave her a whispered account of what had occurred. 'I think Eldri can find her,' I finished. 'At least I have to try!'

'Oh Eilan, be careful!' Aelia breathed when I had finished. 'I will worry every moment until you return!' She reached out to me and I bent to give her a quick hug. Then she sighed and subsided back into her pillow, and with my heart thumping so hard I thought it should wake them all, I let myself out of the door.

By now the moon was fully risen, limning the hall and outbuildings in harsh black and white. I would have to be swift, for there was little cover. I darted from shadow to shadow, Eldri trotting behind me, until I reached the storeshed once more.

Breathing hard, I took up the sash and held it under Eldri's nose.

'This is Dierna's — Dierna — you know her! Find Dierna, Eldri, find her now!'

For a moment the dog sniffed at the cloth. Then she whined and turned towards the door. I held it open, then slipped out myself, easing it shut behind me as Eldri began to move purposefully across the yard.

The dog's certainty lifted my spirits. As we passed the last of the buildings, I let out a breath I had not known I was holding, and as I breathed in again, felt a hint of the same tingling tickle across my skin that I had noticed sometimes when the priestesses were working with power. I hesitated, peering around me. It was not yet time for the full-moon ritual, nor was it one of the great festivals. Perhaps the Druids were engaged in some working; I did not know their ceremonies. But surely something was going on, for the night was full of magic. With luck, no one would have time to realize I had gone.

Nose to the ground, Eldri moved around the base of the Tor. Dierna must be heading towards the higher ground to the east — at this season it was dry enough to cross into the pasturelands beyond. But though the sky above the Tor was clear, beyond it mist lay heavy on land and water alike, so that Avalon seemed to rise from a sea of cloud.

In a ground-fog it was easy to lose one's bearings, and even if Dierna avoided the Lake, there were bogs and hollows aplenty that could be more treacherous still. Had I not had the dog to guide me, I would never have dared this path in darkness, and even so, I watched my footing, for the dog could dance easily over ground that beneath my weight would give way.

Now the first wisps of mist were curling across the path. Was it even possible to pass beyond them, I wondered, without the spell? And if I did so, would I find myself forever banished to the outside world?

'Elen of the Ways,' I whispered, 'show me my path!' I took another step and a shift in the wind brought the mist billowing around me, catching the light so that I was surrounded by moonglow.

I called to the dog, for I could see nothing but nebulous light, and waited, shivering, until Eldri's pale shape appeared as if it had precipitated from the mist. I tied one end of Dierna's sash to the dog's collar, but in this strange state, in which air and water, light and dark were intermingled, as the druids said all elements had been joined at the beginning of the world, there was no sense of progress. There was only the tingling touch of power, that grew stronger as we went on.

The mist continued to brighten, and then suddenly thinned. I stopped short, staring. Ahead, a pale light that came neither from sun nor moon showed me trees whose leaves were edged with brightness, and meadows starred with flowers. Just where I stood the path branched into three. The left-hand path curved around and disappeared back into the darkness. The narrow path on the right twisted its way over a small hill, and it seemed to me that when I turned my head in that direction, I could hear the sweet ringing of a bell.

But the middle way was broad and bright and fair, and it was towards that path that Eldri was pulling me.

Fear was replaced by a great wonder. Before me rose a venerable oak tree. Gazing up at its mighty branches, I knew that I had passed beyond the borders of Avalon, or any land inhabited by men, for surely the Druids would have made an enclosure around such a tree as this and hung offerings upon its branches. I touched the trunk, so wide that three people together would scarcely be able to embrace it, and felt a thrumming in the wood, as if the life of the tree pulsed beneath my hand.

'My greetings to you, Father Oak. Will you extend your protection to me while I walk in this realm?' I whispered, bowing, and shivered as the leaves whispered in answer.

I took a careful breath, focusing my senses as I had been trained to do. In my first days on Avalon everything had seemed much more *alive* than it did in the outside world. Now that sense was intensified a hundredfold, and I understood that as the moon was to the sun, so was the magic of Avalon to this realm which was its source and its original.

The sash had come loose from Eldri's collar, but it no longer mattered. The little dog was a glimmering shape that danced ahead of me, and white flowerets starred the track where she had passed. Did I see the dog this way because we were in Faerie, I wondered, or was it only in Faerie that her true nature was revealed?

The path led to a copse of hazel, like those that I had been trimming only this morning – when Becca almost drowned. With a pang I realized that I had nearly forgotten why I had come here. Time ran differently in Faerie, I had heard, and it was easy to lose one's memory as well as one's way.

But these hazels had never known the touch of iron. And yet, though untrimmed they might be, surely some mind had guided their luxuriance into this interlace of supple branches in which there was only one opening, through which Eldri had disappeared. For a moment I hesitated, but if I could not find Dierna, I might just as well lose myself in Faerie, for I would surely never dare to return to Avalon. Only the thought of Aelia, anxiously waiting, kept me going forwards.

As I passed through the opening, there came a sudden singing, as if the branches hid a chorus of birds, and yet I knew, and I had been trained to notice such things, that these were no birds I had ever heard on Avalon. I looked up in delight, hoping to see the secret singers. When I lowered my gaze, a strange woman was standing there.

I blinked, finding it curiously hard to focus, for in the lady's mantle were all the shifting pale golds of the leaves of the willow when autumn comes. Red berries were strung like a diadem upon her dark hair and across her brow.

She looks like Heron, I thought in wonder, *or like one of the little dark folk of the Lake village*! But no woman of the Lake people had ever stood as if her surroundings had only been created to be her setting, stately as a priestess, noble as a queen. Eldri had run to her, and was leaping up against her skirts as she did to me when I had been away.

Stifling a pang of jealousy, for Eldri had never shown such affection to anyone else before, I sank down in the obeisance due to an empress.

'You bow to me, and that is well, but others will bow to you one day.'

'When I become High Priestess?'

'When you fulfil your destiny,' came the answer. The Lady's voice held the sweetness of bee-song on a summer's day, but I remembered how swiftly that music could turn to fury if one threatened the hive, and I did not know what might anger this queen.

'What is my destiny?' heart pounding, at last I dared to ask.

'That will depend on what you choose . . .'

'What do you mean?'

'You saw three roads when you came here, did you not?'

The Lady's voice remained sweet and low, but there was a compulsion in it that turned my memory to the scene, and at once it was before me – the path that led back through the mists, the rocky road, but the middle way was broad and fair, bordered with pale lilies.

'The choice that you must make lies in the future – to seek the world of the Romans, or the Hidden Country, or Avalon,' the Faerie Queen continued as if I had answered her.

'But I have already chosen,' I answered in surprise. 'I will be a priestess of Avalon.'

'So says your head, but what does your heart say?' the Lady laughed softly, and I felt a prickle of heat flush my skin.

'I suppose that when I am old enough to think about such things I will know,' I said defiantly. 'But I am sworn to give myself to no man save as the Goddess wills, and I will not break my vow!'

'Ah, daughter—' the Lady laughed once more, 'be not so certain that you understand what your vows mean, and where they will lead you! This much I will tell you: only when you understand who you truly are will you know your way—'

From somewhere, words came to me. 'Eilan I am, and Elen shall guide me . . .'

The Faerie Queen looked at me and suddenly, unexpectedly, smiled.

'Just so. And if you know that much, then you have set your foot already upon the path. But enough of such serious matters – for now, you are here, and that is a thing not given to many mortals. Come, my little one, and feast with us in my hall!' Gazing at me with a sweetness that touched the heart like pain, she held out her hand.

'If I go with you . . . will I be able to return to Avalon?' I asked hesitantly.

'If you wish it,' came the reply.

'And will I find Dierna?'

'Is that what you truly wish?' the Lady asked.

'With all my heart!' I exclaimed.

The Faerie Queen sighed. 'The heart, again! I tell you now that if you find her, you will lose her, but I suppose you cannot understand. Come and be happy for a little while, if that is the only gift that you will accept from me . . .'

Then the Lady took me by the hand, and led me by ways winding and unknown, and we came presently to a hall all built from wood, not cut and pegged, as I had seen in the lands of men, but woven and grown all together, so that the beams were of living wood, roofed with branch and leaf of living green. Jutting branches held torches along the walls, their pale flickering light dancing in the bright eyes of the folk who sat at the high table there.

They gave me a sweet, yeasty drink in a cup that was neither silver nor gold, and as I drank, I found my weariness dissolving away. There were baskets of strange fruits, and pies with roots and mushrooms in a rich sauce, and bread with honey.

The food refreshed my body, although, as I remembered tales I had heard about the Faerie country, I wondered if it were illusion. But the harping fed something in my spirit that I did not even know had been hungering. A young man with merry eyes and a wreath of golden wheat upon his dark curls took my hand and swept me into the dance. At first I stumbled, for this was nothing like the stately measures that were thought suitable for the maidens being trained on Avalon. The rhythm was like the drumbeat that came from the Tor when the initiated priestesses danced with the Druids at the Beltane fires and the girls in the House of Maidens lay in the darkness listening, their blood pulsing to a beat they did not yet understand.

I laughed and let the music lift me, but when my partner would have drawn me away from the dancing into a leafy bower, I knew it for another temptation and slipped from his embrace and back to the feasting table once more.

'Was not the young man to your liking?' asked the queen.

'I liked him well enough,' said I, and felt my cheeks grow hot with a betraying flush, for though his beauty struck no answering chord in my heart, his touch had stirred my senses in a way I did not entirely understand. 'But I have stayed here too long. I hold you to your promise, Lady, to lead me to Dierna and thence back to my home.'

'There is time and enough for that. Wait just a little: the greatest of our bards is about to sing . . .'

But I shook my head. 'I must go. I *will* go— Eldri! Eldri, come to me!' I looked around in sudden terror lest the little dog, who had after all brought me to this place, should have abandoned me. But in the next moment I felt the drag on my skirts as the dog pawed at them. I bent to scoop her into my arms and hugged her fiercely.

'Yes . . . your will is very strong,' said the Lady thoughtfully. 'What if I were to tell you that by returning to Avalon you will take the first steps on the path that leads away from it, and in doing so, you will set events in motion that will end by forever separating it from the world of men?'

'I will never do so!' I cried angrily.

'The wind that is stirred by a butterfly's wing may cause a tempest half the world away . . . in the Hidden Country we do not think on the passing of time, and so for us it runs slowly, or not at all. But when I look into the world of men, I can observe the results of actions that you swift-living mortals will never see. Learn from my wisdom, daughter, and stay!'

I shook my head. 'I belong to Avalon!'

'Be it so,' the Faerie Queen said then. 'This much comfort I will grant you: that however far you may wander, so long as you have your hounds you will find your way home . . . Go then, with the blessing of the Elder Folk, and perhaps, from time to time, you will remember me—'

'I will remember you . . .' said I, tears pricking my eyes. I set Eldri on the ground once more, and the dog, after looking back to make sure that I was following, trotted towards the door.

We passed into the leaf-filtered light of the faerie wood, and then, between one step and another, into a darkness in which the glimmering white shape of the dog ahead of me was the only thing I could see. And then I felt the cold touch of mist upon my skin and slowed, shivering, testing each step before I trusted my weight to it to be sure of keeping to the path.

I could not be certain how long I continued in this way, but gradually I became aware that the mist was brightening, and then it thinned, and I passed through the last of it and onto the grass of the Tor. The moon still rode high – as high, nearly, as it had been when I set forth. I stared at it in amazement, for surely in Faerie the feasting, and the dancing had gone on for hours. But here I was

59

back again, and it was the same time of night as when I had gone. But was it the same night, I wondered in sudden fear? Or the same month, or year? Did Aelia wait for me still?

I started forwards, looking anxiously about me to see if anything had changed, and sighed in relief to see before me the hazel hedge, still half-pruned as I had left it. Something pale stirred in its shadow – Eldri, sitting beside a curled heap of clothing that on closer inspection proved to be the sleeping child.

I fell to my knees beside her, heart pounding in my breast. 'Blessed Goddess!' I breathed, 'never again will I doubt you!' And then, when my pulse had slowed nearly to its customary beat, I gathered the child into my arms.

'Dierna, wake up, little one! You are such a great girl now, I cannot carry you!'

The child stirred, burrowing sleepily against my breast. 'I can't go back there – I'm afraid . . .'

'I will stay with you,' said I, 'and so will Eldri.'

'But she's so little,' Dierna giggled, reaching out to ruffle the dog's curly hair.

'Do not underestimate her. She is a magic dog,' I answered her. In the shadow, it seemed to me that a little of the glamour of Faerie clung to that pale fur still. 'Come now—' I got to my feet, and after a moment's hesitation, Dierna followed me.

I told myself that I could sneak back to the House of Maidens before I was missed in the morning, but even if Ganeda learned how I had disobeyed, I found it hard to care. There was enough straw in the shed to make a bed, and when I had persuaded Dierna to lie down, I told the child tales of my adventures in Faerie until she slept once more.

And at that, the fatigue of my own night's adventuring came fully upon me, and so it was that that when Suona came to release the child in the dawning, she found us curled up together, with Eldri beside us guarding the door.

CHAPTER FOUR

AD 268–70

In the year that I turned eighteen I left the House of Maidens to dwell in a separate enclosure with Heron and Aelia and Roud, for the time of initiation was approaching, and the disciplines which prepared us to receive the Mysteries required solitude. But though we three novice priestesses were to be kept apart from the rest of the community, we could not be isolated completely from the rumours that swept the isle.

It was a time of death and omens, on Avalon as well as elsewhere. A network of connections kept the High Priestess informed of what was going on in the Empire, and from time to time one of the boatmen of the Lake village would bring a leather tube containing a message, or the messenger himself, who was led blindfolded to the house of the Lady to give his news. I always suspected that the High Priestess heard much that was never passed on to the rest of our community.

However, the news that the self-made emperor Postumus had been assassinated by his own troops when he refused to hand over the spoils of a captured town was deemed essential knowledge, for it was he who had divided the West, including Britannia, from the remainder of the Empire. A man called Victorinus had assumed his title, but rumour held that he was a warrior of the bed-chamber whose adulteries were already eroding his support. It was his mother Victorina, said the reports, who really ruled the Imperium Galliarum now.

61

But to those of us who dwelt on the holy isle these tales meant little, for at the end of the winter Sian, Ganeda's daughter and likely heir, lost her own battle with the illness that had come upon her after the birth of her second child, and the community of Avalon was plunged into mourning.

The year that followed seemed to promise little improvement. We heard that the people of the Mediterranean, swept by plague and famine, were blaming their troubles on the Emperor, and Gallienus, like his western rival, fell to an assassin's blade. Of his successor, Claudius, little was known save that he came from somewhere on the Danu, and was said to be a good general. We worried more about the Saxon sea-raiders who were attacking the southern coasts of Britannia in ever greater numbers.

Still, the Saxon shore was far away. As the year turned towards harvest, my own time of testing was approaching quickly, and that gave me a more immediate reason to fear. Our final lessons were the responsibility of the High Priestess, and now that Ganeda was once more forced to acknowledge my existence, it was clear that she had not learned to love me any better than before.

Sometimes it seemed to me that she blamed me for being alive and healthy when her own child lay cold in the ground. I knew that she hoped I would fail the tests that determined who was worthy to be called a priestess of Avalon. But would she so far betray her own vows as to use her powers to make sure?

I woke each morning with a knot in my belly, and approached the garden beside the house of the High Priestess where we had our lessons as if it were a battlefield.

'Soon you will be sent out beyond the mists to the outer world, to bend time and space, if you can, to return to Avalon.'

It was a fair day just after midsummer, and through the leaves of the hawthorn hedge I could glimpse the blue glitter of the Lake. Today the mists were only a thin haze on the horizon. It was hard to believe that beyond them lay a different world.

It seemed to me that the gaze of the High Priestess rested on me a little longer than on the others. I glared back at her, but I retained a vivid memory of how it had felt to come through the mists the first time, when Suona opened the gateway between the isle of the priestesses and the world of men. At that moment, with no training whatsoever, it had seemed to me that I almost understood what was happening. If the test was a fair one, with all the training I had received I did not think that I would fail.

'But you must understand,' Ganeda continued, 'that you are not only being given a challenge, but a choice. You will go forth in the dress of a woman of that world, with gold enough to take you wherever you might wish to go, and provide you with a dowry when you have got there. No vows will bind you, save only a *geas* against revealing the secrets of Avalon. You are young yet, for all our learning, and have barely begun to taste life's joys. To discipline the mind and the body, to go without food or sleep, to lie with a man only for the Lady's purposes, never your own, is to give up what the Goddess offers every woman born. You must consider whether you truly wish to return.'

There was a long silence. Then Aelia cleared her throat.

'This is my home, and I want no other, but why must it be so hard? If those folk out there know nothing of Avalon, what is it that we are doing for them, and why?'

'The princely families know,' I ventured to reply. 'When the crops in their lands are failing, they send for one of us to perform the Great Rite – that is how I came to be born. And they send their daughters to us for training in the old ways of our people.'

'But the Romans have temples, and tax the people to support them. Let them win favour from the gods with their offerings. Why must we give up so much, when we receive so little in return?'

The High Priestess was watching with a sour smile, but she did not seem angry, so I dared to answer once more.

'Because the Romans have forgotten what the rituals mean, if indeed they ever knew! My father used to say that they think that if every word and action of a ceremony is performed correctly, the

63

deity *must* do their bidding, and that no amount of sincere belief will matter if one syllable is wrong.'

My tutor Corinthius, that kind and gentle man, had believed that rituals were only a means of holding society together, and the gods were some kind of philosophic ideal.

'The people of my village knew better than that!' exclaimed Heron. 'Our festivals put us in harmony with the cycles and seasons of the world.'

'And the rituals of Avalon can change them,' Ganeda put in at last. 'We are halfway to the Otherworld already, and what we do here resonates on all the planes of existence. There have been times when we worked more openly within the world, and times when we have stayed behind our mists, invisible, but we work with the energies of the cosmos, according to the teachings that have come down to us from the land of Atlantis that lies now beneath the waves. It is real power, that would destroy the mind and body of any who tried to channel it unprepared or untrained . . .'

Aelia's eyes dropped before the fervour in her gaze, and then Heron and Aelia looked away. Her gaze moved to me, and I realized I was looking not at my aunt, who hated me, but at the Lady of Avalon. I bowed my head in homage.

'And that is why we offer ourselves to the Goddess, to do Her work within the world, not in pride, but because She has called us in a voice that compels an answer,' she said softly. 'Our lives are the sacrifice.'

After that day, the tension between Ganeda and myself seemed to ease a little, or perhaps it was only that I was beginning to understand her now. Indeed, each day seemed to bring new understanding, as we refined skills we thought we had mastered before.

The vision was fading. Reluctantly I released the image of the Tor, ablaze with light, and willed myself to retrace my steps around and around and back again to the garden. The Voice of my Guide continued in its steady direction, keeping me from straying until the brilliant memory of my inner journey became the familiar scene I saw every day.

I opened my eyes, blinking at the sunlight, and set my hands upon the earth to root myself once more in her power. The hawthorn hedge and the carefully-tended herbs were still beautiful, even though they had lost the glowing edges I saw in the Otherworld. Roud and Heron were beside me. I took a deep breath of the scented air and blessed the Goddess for bringing me safely back again.

'Does the Sight come only to those who have been trained in the old ways, as you are training us here?' asked Roud.

The High Priestess shook her head. Since the death of her daughter, age had come fully upon her, and the morning light that filtered between the leaves of the apple tree showed each line and furrow in her face with merciless clarity. If Ganeda had not made it so obvious that she was teaching me with the others only because it was her duty, I could almost have pitied her.

'There are many among our people in whom the Gift runs strongly,' she answered, 'but it does them little good, for it comes unbidden, without direction or control. Untrained, they know neither how to keep such vision from coming when they do not want it, nor how to focus and control its power when they do, and so for them the Sight is more a curse than a blessing.'

Heron frowned thoughtfully. 'And that is why you are so careful about when and where you allow it?'

Ganeda nodded. I wondered whether she feared for the safety of the visionary, or that the vision might be beyond her control? It seemed to me presumptuous to think that one could set such limits upon the speech of the gods.

For a week now she had been speaking of the many ways in which one might divine the future. The Druids knew the craft of reading omens, and the bard-trance, and the dream-vision that comes when the priest sleeps wrapped in the hide of the sacrificed bull. Such skills were also practised by the Druids of Hibernia. The folk of the Lake village used the little mushrooms that can bring visions even to the ungifted, and would trade them to us in exchange for our medicines.

But there were other means, practised only by the priestesses. One of them was the art of scrying in the sacred pool, and another the rite in which a priestess was set on high to seek visions at the time of the great festivals. I had heard talk of this last, but if the rite had been performed since I came to Avalon only the priestesses of the higher grades knew.

'Go now and rest,' Ganeda said then. 'You think you are seers already because you can journey in the spirit, but that is only the first step. Roud has her moonblood, and must wait for another opportunity, but tonight the other three will attempt to scry by fire and water. We shall see if any of you has the Gift to be an oracle.'

Her voice had grown harsh, and none of us dared to meet her eyes. Her daughter Sian had been highly gifted in that way, and since her death Avalon had no seeress. It must hurt my aunt to be reminded of her loss, even as her duty pushed her to seek a replacement. The inner work had always come easily to me, and I wondered whether I would have an aptitude for scrying as well. Such gifts were said to run in families, so it was quite possible. But somehow I did not think Ganeda would be pleased to see me step into her daughter's shoes.

That afternoon was spent in scrubbing the stones of the Processional Way, for Ganeda was a great believer in physical labour as a way to tire the body and occupy the surface of the mind. Also, I suppose, the drudgery was intended to keep us from putting on airs, now that we were training to be seeresses.

But even with the distraction, I could feel tension knotting my belly as the shadows lengthened. When the bell summoned the rest of the community to dinner, we four went instead to the Lake to bathe, for this work was best done purified and fasting.

By the time we were brought to the sanctuary above the holy well darkness had fallen. We were dressed alike in plain white garments that hung uncinctured from an shoulders to our bare feet, and cloaks of undyed wool. Our hair lay loose upon our shoulders. Torches had been set along the path; their wavering light gleamed from Heron's dark locks, and touched Aelia's hair with fire. My own fine hair, undisciplined since its recent washing, blew across my face, edged with light.

Seen through that golden veiling the familiar way appeared mysterious and strange. Or perhaps it was only that the day's fast and the expectation of trance was beginning to affect me. It seemed to me that it would be very easy to let go of ordinary awareness, and travel between the worlds. I wondered whether the rule that one must seek visions while fasting was always wise. It was keeping control of the vision that was likely to be a problem now.

A stool had been set upon the stone terrace. Before it, coals glowed in a brazier. A small carven table stood nearby bearing a silver pitcher and a piece of folded cloth. Silently we took our seats on the bench beyond it and waited, hands resting on our knees, breathing deeply of the cool night air.

It was some sense other than hearing that made me turn. Two priestesses were approaching with the silent gliding step it had taken me so long to learn. I recognized the rigid set of Ganeda's shoulders even before she came into the light. Suona followed, bearing something wrapped in white linen in her hands.

'Is it the Grail?' Aelia whispered beside me.

'It cannot be – the only novice who is allowed to see it is the Maiden who is its guardian,' I murmured in reply as Suona set her burden on the table. 'This must be something else, but clearly it is very old.' Old, and holy, I thought then, for it seemed to me that I could already feel its power.

Suona drew the linen cloth away from the thing she held and lifted it so that it caught the torchlight. It was a silver bowl, a little dented, but lovingly polished, chased around the rim with some design.

'It is said that this bowl was used for scrying at Vernemeton, the Forest House whence came the first priestesses to dwell on this holy isle. Perhaps the Lady Caillean herself once gazed into it. Pray to the Goddess that some of her spirit may touch you now . . .' She set the bowl beside the pitcher on the little table.

I blinked, my sight of the bowl overlaid for a moment with another image, of the same vessel, bright and new. Was this imagination, or *recognition*?

But I did not have much time to wonder, for the High Priestess stood before us, and between one moment and the next she drew the glamour of her calling around her, so that from a little bent woman, always frowning, she became tall and stately and beautiful. I had seen that transformation many times now, but it never ceased to amaze me, or to remind me that I must never discount this woman's powers, no matter how she treated me.

'Do not think,' said the High Priestess, 'that what you are about to do is any the less real because you are still being trained as priestesses. The face of Fate is always both wonderful and terrible – beware how you lift Her veil. Certain knowledge of what is to come is given to few. For most, even a holy seer, foreknowledge comes in glimpses only, distorted by the understanding of the one who sees and the ones who hear the prophecy.' She paused, fixing each one of us in turn with a gaze that pierced to the soul.

When she spoke again her voice had the resonance of trance. 'Be still, therefore, and make clean your hearts. Let go the busy mind. You must become an empty vessel waiting to be filled, an open passageway through which illumination can flow.'

Smoke swirled up from the brazier as Suona sprinkled the holy herbs upon the coals. I closed my eyes, awareness of the outside world already beginning to slip away.

'Heron daughter of Ouzel,' said the priestess, 'will you look into the sacred waters and seek wisdom there?'

'I will,' came the answer. I heard the rustle of clothing as she was assisted into the chair.

I did not need my eyes to know when she looked into the bowl, nor did I need to hear the murmur of instruction by which the Lady drew her deeper into trance. As Heron spoke, I also glimpsed the images, broken and chaotic – storms and armies, and dancers at the sacred stones.

Presently they ceased. I was vaguely aware that Heron had been brought back and it was now Aelia's turn to look into the bowl. Once more I shared the visions. The Lady's voice had sharpened, commanding her look for a time closer to the present, and events of import to Avalon. For a time there was only swirling shadow, and then, dimly, I saw the marshes that edged the Lake. Figures with torches moved along the shore, calling. Then the image disappeared. There was a splash as the bowl was emptied, and Aelia sat down beside me once more. I could feel her shaking, and wondered what it was that her mind had refused to see.

But now I could feel the High Priestess standing like a flame before me. 'Eilan daughter of Rian, are you willing to seek visions?' the voice came out of the darkness.

I murmured agreement, and was assisted to the chair. Awareness shifted once more and I opened my eyes. Suona poured more water into the bowl and set it before me.

'Lean forwards and look within,' said the quiet voice beside me. 'Breathe in . . . and out . . . wait for the waters to still. Let your vision sink beneath the surface, and say what you see.'

Suona had put more herbs on the coals. As I breathed in the heavy sweet smoke my head swam and I blinked, trying to focus on the bowl. Now I could see it – a silver rim surrounding a shifting darkness shot with gleaming flickers of torchlight.

'If you see nothing it is no matter,' the priestess continued. 'Be at ease—'

It does matter, I thought with a twitch of annoyance. *Does she want me to fail?*

Perhaps it would be easier without the distraction of external vision. I did not quite dare to close my eyes again, but I let them unfocus, so that I saw only a dim blur surrounded by a circle of light. Look for the marshes, I told myself; what had Aelia been trying to see?

And at the thought, the vision began to emerge before me, first in scattered flickers, and then complete and whole. Dusk was fading into evening. The Lake gleamed faintly in the last of the light. But the mixture of marsh and islet that stretched around to the south and east were all in shadow. Torches moved along the higher ground, but my vision was drawn to a dark pool in the shadow of a twisted willow tree.

Something moved there. With a gasp, I recognized Dierna's bright head. With one arm she clutched a fallen log. The other reached down as if she were holding onto something beneath the surface. I strove to see more clearly, and the scene shifted.

The searchers had found her. In the torchlight I could see Dierna sobbing, though I heard no sound. Two of the Druids were in the water beside her. One lifted her into Cigfolla's waiting arms. The other was fixing a rope around something beneath the water. The men pulled, a pale shape surged upwards—

'Becca! Drowned!' The words tore from my throat. 'Please, don't let me see it – don't let it be true!' I convulsed away from the table, and bowl and pitcher went flying. I fell to the ground, curled in anguish, grinding my palms against my eyes as if to erase what I had seen.

In another moment Suona had my wrists and was holding me close, her voice a soothing murmur beneath my sobs.

'Of course she will be all right,' Ganeda's voice came from behind me. 'These hysterics are only to gain attention.'

I jerked upright, though the movement made my head spin. 'But I saw it! I saw it! You must guard Becca or she will drown!'

'You would like that, wouldn't you?' snarled Ganeda. 'One less of my blood to compete with for my place when I am gone!'

The manifest unfairness of this deprived me of speech, but I could feel Suona stiffen with shock at her words.

To move into the trance state had been easy. Recovering, especially when I had been so suddenly recalled from it, was harder. For several weeks thereafter I was disoriented and subject to fits of weeping. In the days immediately after the scrying session even my sense of balance was upset so that I could hardly walk, and at every step a headache stabbed my skull. When it became clear that a single night's sleep would not restore me I was sent to the House of Healing. The reason given was that the other maidens would tire me, but I think now that it was really because Ganeda did not wish me to speak to the others, and especially to Dierna, about what I had seen.

And so it was that I was still there, being cosseted by Cigfolla whenever I emerged from my uneasy dreams, when I heard shouting from outside the house, and sitting up, saw the flicker of torches in the darkness through the open door.

'What is it?' I cried. 'What is going on?' But a familiar fear had begun to uncoil in my belly. I tried to get out of bed, but the pain in my head struck me back down, moaning.

I was still sitting there, trying to control the agony by careful breathing, when the door flew open and Heron darted in.

'Eilan – we cannot find Dierna or Becca!' she whispered, looking over her shoulder to make sure she had not been seen, and from that I knew that no one had come to see me because Ganeda had forbidden them to come. 'In your vision, where did you see her? Tell me quickly!'

I clutched at her arm, describing as well as I could where the willow pool that I had seen lay in relation to the path. Then she was gone and I lay back, tears leaking from my closed eyes.

An eternity of misery later I heard the searchers returning, voices deadened by sorrow or hoarse with weeping. I turned my face to the wall. It did not help that without my vision Dierna might have died with her sister. I had wanted so desperately to prove to Ganeda that my Seeing was true, but now I would have given anything to have her accusations proven right, and little Becca safely home again.

Gradually my own health improved and I was allowed to return to the House of Maidens. Heron told me that Dierna had gone hunting herbs in the marshes, leaving her sister behind. But Becca, who since their mother's death had been her sister's shadow, had

71

followed, and fallen in, and by the time Dierna reached her, had already been sucked under by the bog. Even if no one else blamed her, Dierna must be tormenting herself with guilt by now.

I was not surprised to hear that the chill she had taken from the water had turned to lung fever. Now it was her turn to be nursed in the House of Healing. I asked to visit her, but Ganeda forbade it. I remembered a story that my tutor Corinthius had once told me about an oriental king who responded to bad news by executing the messenger. It made no sense for her to blame me for what had happened, particularly since she had not believed me, but I had learned long since that where I was concerned the actions of the High Priestess rarely made sense at all.

Our training went on, but we were given no more lessons in scrying, and I for one was content to have it so. I had learned the first paradox of prophecy, which is that glimpsing the future does not necessarily mean one can understand it, much less alter what one sees.

In time, Dierna also recovered, to creep about with eyes like holes in a blanket and a face pale as whey against the fire of her hair, as if she had died with Becca, and it was only her ghost who remained with us on Avalon.

And so that dreadful summer drew to a close at last. The cat-tails in the marshes grew full and brown, nodding in the wind that fluttered the turning willow leaves, and the mists that surrounded Avalon seemed suffused with gold. One evening as the new moon was rising I was returning from the privies when I glimpsed a pale shape moving down the path towards the Lake and recognized Dierna. My pulse leaped in instant alarm, but I stifled the cry that rose in my throat and whistled instead to Eldri to go after her.

When I caught up with them, Dierna was sitting beneath an elder bush with her arms around Eldri, weeping into the little dog's silky fur. At the sound of my footstep she looked up, frowning.

'I was all right. You didn't need to send Eldri after me!' she said sullenly, but I noticed that she did not let the dog go. 'But maybe you think I ought to walk into the Lake and just keep going, in punishment for letting my sister drown!'

I swallowed. This was worse than I had thought. I sat down, knowing better than to try to touch the girl now.

'They all say it wasn't my fault, but I know what they're thinking . . .' she sniffed, and wiped her nose on her sleeve.

'I *saw* what happened, you know, in the scrying bowl,' I said finally. 'But nobody believed me. I keep thinking that if I had only tried harder to convince them . . .'

'That's stupid! You couldn't know when—' Dierna exclaimed, then paused, eyeing me suspiciously.

'We both feel guilty,' I said then. 'Perhaps we always will. But I will try to live with it if you will. Perhaps we can forgive each other, even if we cannot forgive ourselves . . .'

For a moment longer she stared at me, her blue eyes filling with tears. Then, with a sob, she threw herself into my arms.

We stayed that way, weeping, while the white sickle of the moon swung across the sky. It was only when Eldri growled and pushed her way out from between us that I realized how much time had passed, and that we were not alone. For a little while I had felt peace, holding the child, but now my belly tensed once more. The cloaked shape confronting us was that of the Lady of Avalon.

'Dierna—' I said softly. 'It is late, and you should be in your bed.' She stiffened as she saw her grandmother, but I was already pushing her to her feet. 'Run along now, and may the Goddess bless your dreams.'

For a moment I thought she would insist on staying to defend me. But perhaps Dierna realized that to do so would only increase Ganeda's wrath, for although she glanced backwards several times, she left us without arguing. I confess that as I sensed the menace in the Lady's silence I almost called her back again, but this confrontation had been a long time coming, and I knew I must face it alone.

I got to my feet. 'If you have something to say to me, let us walk out along the shore, where our voices will disturb no one.' I was surprised to hear my own voice sounding so steady, for beneath the shawl I was trembling. I led the way down to the path that edged the Lake, Eldri trotting at my heels.

'Why are you angry?' I asked when the silence had grown unbearable, like the stillness before a storm. 'Do you begrudge your grand-daughter a little comfort just because it comes from me?'

'You killed my sister when you were born . . .' hissed Ganeda, 'you ill-wished Becca, and now you are trying to steal the last child of my blood away.'

I stared at her, anger replacing my fear. 'Old woman, you are mad! I loved that little girl, and surely my mother's death was a greater loss to me than to you. But have our choices no part to play in all this, or has all the teaching of Avalon been a lie? My mother chose to act as priestess in the Great Rite, and when she knew she had conceived, to keep the child, understanding the risk she ran. And Becca had been told not to follow her sister and chose to do otherwise.'

'She was too young to know—'

'And you *chose* to keep me away from both girls!' I raged on. 'Don't you know I would have watched them like a mother bear with two cubs to stop what I had seen from coming to pass? From the moment I first set foot on Avalon you have hated me! What have I ever done to deserve that? Can you tell me why?'

Ganeda gripped my arm, and as she jerked me around to face her, I sensed her energy expanding, and before the wrath of the Lady of Avalon, my anger seemed suddenly the petulance of a child.

'You dare to speak so, to *me*? With a single Word, I could obliterate you where you stand!' Her arm swung up in a sweep of dark draperies like the wing of the Lady of Ravens, and I cowered. For a moment the lapping of wavelets against the shoreline was the only sound.

And then, from the rich scent of wet earth and the whisper of water another kind of power began to flow into me, a steady, enduring strength that could absorb whatever lightnings Ganeda's majestic fury might call down. For a moment then I touched something fundamental within, although whether it was the Goddess or my own eternal soul I could not tell. Slowly I straightened, and as she met my gaze, the power ebbed from Ganeda's body until she was no more than an old, bent woman, shorter than me.

'You are Lady of Avalon,' I said with a sigh, 'but we are both daughters of the Lady who rules over all. In everything that concerns the good of Avalon I will obey you, but it is because I choose to do so.'

She looked up at me, her seamed features carved in lines of light and shadow by the moon.

'You are young,' she said in a low voice, 'young and proud. Refuse to fear me if you will – life itself will teach you to be afraid, aye, and the meaning of compromise!' She began to make her way back along the shore.

'Dierna is my kinswoman too,' I called after her, 'and I will not let you keep me from being with her!'

At that Ganeda turned once more. 'Have it your own way,' she said tiredly, 'but when I was younger, I too had visions. I have looked into the Sacred Well, and seen that it is Dierna who will be my heir. You do well to make a friend of her, for I tell you now that it is *she*, not you, who will be the next Lady of Avalon!'

Slowly, the terrible summer of Becca's death faded into memory. I knew what that tragedy had done to her sister, but as time passed it became clear that Ganeda had also been affected, more deeply than we, or perhaps she herself, knew. In body she was still vigorous – indeed, I do not believe that anyone without superior stamina could do the work required of the Lady of Avalon. But the edge that could cut friend and foe alike, was gone.

I found it hard to be sorry, and being young, I did not understand how life's buffets can wear down the spirit. Nor did I care enough to try. Strong in body and delighting in my own rapidly maturing powers, I went eagerly to my testing, and, certain of my decision, bestowed the bag of gold aureii with which I had been provided upon the family of the boy who had given me Eldri ten years before.

And so I entered the mists, and drew up from the depths of my being the Word of Power that would open the way, laughing because in the end it was so easy, as if I were simply remembering something I had learned long before. Heron and Aelia did likewise when their turn came, and like me were received back with rejoicing. But Roud never returned to us.

In the year of silence that followed, I was forced to look inward in a way that the myriad demands of my training had never before allowed. It was this, I think now, that was the true initiation, for it is not the adversaries outside oneself, that can be confronted and defied, that are most dangerous, but the more subtle antagonists that dwell within.

Regarding the oath with which that year ended, I must also keep silence, save that it was, as Ganeda had promised, an act of making sacred, of *sacrifice*. But though I offered myself to the Lady to be used as She willed, I did not then understand the warning that we cannot predict or control what the Goddess will do with us once that commitment has been made. Nonetheless, when my oath had been given, I passed through the Mystery of the Cauldron, and the blue crescent of a priestess was placed upon my brow.

With my attention fixed upon my own struggles, I did not at first realize that things were not going so well in Avalon. During our year of silence, Aelia and I grew ever closer. I was surprised to find that wordless, I understood more of what was in her heart than ever I had when we concealed our thoughts in conversation, and knew she felt the same for me. Using our voices only to sing the offices of the Goddess, words themselves took on a new and sacred meaning.

Thus, the deliberations at the first full meeting of the consecrated priests and priestesses to which I was admitted after my year of silence seemed charged with unusual significance. In truth, matters were serious enough. It had been several years since any new youths

76

or maidens had come to be trained at Avalon, and Roud was not the only one who had gone out for her testing and never returned. In addition, the princes whose contributions helped to maintain the community on the isle had become increasingly unwilling to pay what was due.

'It is not that we have no money,' said Arganax, who had become chief among the Druids the previous year. 'Britannia has never been more prosperous. But the Emperor Claudius in Rome seems to have forgotten us, and with the death of Victorinus, the Imperium Galliarum has concerns more pressing than collecting taxes here.'

Cigfolla laughed. 'It is his mother, Victorina, who rules there now, despite those young cousins she has set up to warm the throne, and she is twice the man he was, from all I hear. Perhaps *she* would welcome the assistance of Avalon!'

'The princes supported us gladly when the foot of Rome was on their necks,' said Suona. 'It is almost as if they feel they no longer need us — as if they can abandon the old ways of Britannia now that they are free of direct control by Rome.'

For a moment we stared at her in bemused silence. Then Ganeda cleared her throat.

'Are you proposing that we work magic to bring the emperors back again?'

Suona flushed and fell silent, but the others were babbling with speculation.

'We can decide nothing without knowing what we face,' Ganeda said finally, 'and we have exausted the knowledge available by any ordinary means . . .'

'What are you proposing?' asked Arganax.

Ganeda looked around the circle with the exasperated frown I remembered so well from my days as her student.

'Are we Greeks, to waste our lives debating the limits of our philosophy? If our skills are worth preserving, let us use them! The Turning of Spring is almost upon us — let us make use of this balance point between the two halves of the year to invoke the Oracle!'

CHAPTER FIVE

AD 270

'Seekers on the ancient ways,
Seekers on the Path of Light,
Now the Night gives way to Day,
Now the Day has equalled Night . . .'

Singing, the line of dark-robed priestesses moved with gliding steps around the circle, matched by the Druids in their white garments marching in the opposite direction. Dark and light in perfect balance completed the circle and came to rest. Arganax stepped forwards, lifting his hands in blessing. Behind him another priest stood waiting with the gong.

The Arch-Druid was a vigorous man in his middle years, but Ganeda, who had moved out to face him, seemed ageless, empowered by the ritual. Her robe, of so dark a blue it was almost black in the lamplight, fell in straight folds to the polished stone of the floor and the moonstones in the silver ornaments of the High Priestess glowed unwinking from her breast and brow.

'Behold, the Sun rules in the House of the Ram, and the Moon rests in the arms of the Twins,' the Druid proclaimed. 'The winter is past, and herbs are pushing their way towards the sunlight, birds return, proclaiming their readiness to mate, beasts emerge from their long sleep. Everywhere life arises, and ourselves with it, moved by the same tides, kindled to action by the same great energies . . . Keep silence, and behold the rebirth of the world, and as we are all One, behold the same great transformation within . . .'

I closed my eyes with the others, trembling to the vibrations of the gong that echoed from the pillars of the Great Hall of the Druids. It seemed to resonate in every atom of my being. Lost in the beauty of the moment, I forgot to feel envy that it would be Heron and not I who would be sitting on the three-legged stool and descending to the Well of Prophecy.

'Awake! Awake! Awake!' came another voice, high and clear.

> '*Companions of the Cosmic Light,*
> *The hidden splendour will appear*!
> *Greet it on high and in your hearts,*
> *Return to life, cast off your fear*!'

I opened my eyes. Four youths stood now in the corners of the hall, bearing torches. Someone had cast the first handful of herbs onto the brazier, and in their light the sweet smoke glowed as if it had ignited the air. Now I could see the images painted on the plaster of the walls – an island surrounding a harbour, great temples, a pyramidal mountain spouting flame, and other scenes from the fabled land that in one day of doom had sunk beneath the wave. Like this ritual, those tales belonged to a wisdom of which the Druids were only the inheritors.

With question and response, the ritual rolled onwards, defining the sacred moment when, Night and Day being equal, a doorway opened between Past and Future and one who was properly prepared and guided might see between the worlds.

The circle opened to reveal a veiled figure, half-supported by Wren and Aelia. Carefully they guided her to the three-legged stool, steadying her until she found her balance there. *The sacred drink has taken her swiftly*, I thought, watching. *Goddess grant it does not take her too far* . . .

In the old days, I knew, they had called on the Goddess Herself to speak through the lips of Her priestess. Now, though the gods might come down sometimes to dance with us at their festivals, it was considered more useful for the Seeress to become open and empty

79

of any personality, even her own, with no will save to describe the images she saw.

The High Priestess moved forwards to stand at her side. The little table with the silver bowl had already been set before her. Berries of mistletoe floated on the water along with other herbs. From where I stood I could see the glitter of torchlight on the dark water. I felt myself sway and blinked quickly to break the spell, then turned my gaze away, hoping no one had noticed my momentary disorientation. I was a trained priestess now, and should have had better control.

'Sink down, sink down . . . sink deeper and sink deep . . .'

Ganeda's voice was a murmur, leading the Seeress on her journey inwards, downwards, until the bowl of gleaming water became one with the sacred well beside the white cypress tree. Then she straightened and stepped away.

'What passes now among the Romans? What is the Emperor Claudius doing now?' Arganax asked.

For a long moment there was silence.

'Tell us, Seeress, what you see?' Ganeda prompted her.

A shudder vibrated through the sheer folds of the veil. 'I see . . . cypresses against a sunset sky . . . no, it is firelight. They are burning bodies . . . one of the watchers staggers and falls . . .' Heron spoke softly, her voice calm as if she watched from some vantage point outside of the world. 'The scene changes . . . an old man lies in a rich room. His bed is hung with purple, but he is alone . . . he is dead . . . Would you know more?'

'Plague—' whispered someone. 'May the gods grant it does not come here . . .'

'Is the Roman power ended, then? Will they return to Britannia?' the Druid asked, and this time Heron's answer came without prompting.

'I see armies and ships – Briton fighting Briton . . . blood, blood and fire—' she shook her head in confusion, as if the images were overwhelming her.

'Sink back down to that place where there is only the shining water,' said Ganeda in a low voice. 'Tell me, who will come to our aid?'

Heron stiffened. 'The Sun! The sun blazes in splendour! It blinds my eyes!' For a moment she remained transfixed, then let out her breath in a long sigh. 'Ah— He comes . . . his armour is Roman, but his eyes are those of one who knows the Mysteries. There is a city . . . I think it is Londinium. In the streets people are cheering— *"Redditor lucis . . . redditor!"*'

She stumbled on the unfamiliar Latin, but I could translate it: *Restorer of the Light!*

So could Arganax. He traded glances with Ganeda. 'If this man is an initiate, he could help us greatly,' he said in a low voice. Then he bent forwards again.

'Who is he – no, *where* is he now?'

Once more Heron swayed above the scrying bowl. 'I see him . . . but he is younger. Hair like dandelion—' she added in response to further questions. 'He is riding a chestnut mule along a Roman road . . . but it is in Britannia . . . the road to the lead mines in the hills . . .'

'Here!' exclaimed Arganax. 'Surely the gods have destined that he shall come to us!'

The seeress was still mumbling to herself, but at the Druid's words she straightened, quivering like a drawn bow. 'Destiny!' she echoed, and then cried out suddenly in a great voice quite unlike her own. 'The son of the sun, greater than his father! A cross of light burns in the sky! All things changing! Fate hangs in the balance, the son will blaze across the world!' With a last ringing cry the Seeress threw out her arms, sending the scrying bowl spinning across the floor. I saw her begin to crumple, and Aelia and I were just in time to catch her as she fell.

After the noble stonework of Avalon, the round daub-and-wattle huts of the monks on Inis Witrin seemed clumsy and mean. I drew down my veil to hide the crescent on my brow as we climbed the slope, and Con, the young Druid who had been assigned to escort me, moved forwards to take my arm. Nearly six weeks had passed since the Oracle rite, and Beltane was hard upon us. After the usual debate regarding the meaning of the oracle's pronouncements, Arganax had sent out some of his young men to the Mendip Hills to see if any Roman fitting Heron's description could be found, and we had had to wait for their reply.

'You will have to let me talk to them. These holy men are forbidden to speak with a female,' he said softly. The monks allowed us to keep the few horses belonging to Avalon in their pasture, in exchange for herbs and medicines. I wondered where they thought we came from.

'What, do they think I will tempt them to impurity?' I snorted derisively. 'I will need to put on the guise of an ugly old woman when we meet the Roman. I might as well begin practising now.' My father had made sure his children learned good Latin – it was one of the reasons I had been chosen for the task of bringing the Roman to Avalon.

As the path curved around, I could see the round church, the lower ambulatory supporting a central tower, whose thatch shone golden in the sun. Con showed me a bench near the sanctuary where I could wait while he went off to see about the horses. It was a surprisingly peaceful place in which to sit, listening to the soft drone of chanting that came from within as I watched the meandering progress of a butterfly above the grass.

The singing in the church soared suddenly and I turned to listen. When I looked back, the butterfly had alighted on the outstretched hand of an old man. I blinked, wondering how he had come there without my seeing him, for the area all around the church was clear. The other brothers I had seen wore rough tunics woven from the undyed fleece, but the old man's garment shone snowy white and the beard that covered his chest was as white as the wool.

'The blessing of the Most High be upon you, my sister,' he said softly. 'And my thanks to Him for allowing me to speak with you once more.'

'What do you mean?' I stammered. 'I have never seen you before!'

'Ah—' he sighed. 'You do not remember . . .'

'Remember what?' Defiantly, I pushed back my veil. 'You are a follower of the Christos, and I am a priestess of Avalon!'

He nodded. 'That is true — today. But in ages past we were both of the same order, in the land that now is sunk beneath the waves. Lives and lands pass away, but the Light of the Spirit shines still.'

My lips parted in shock. How could this monk know about the Mysteries? 'What—' I stammered, struggling for focus. 'Who are you?'

'My name in this place is Joseph. But it is not my name you should be asking, but your own.'

'I am called Eilan,' I answered swiftly, 'and Helena . . .'

'Or Tiriki . . .' he answered, and I blinked, finding a strange familiarity in that name. 'If you do not know who you are, how can you find your way?'

'I know where I am going—' With an effort I stopped myself from blurting out my mission, but it struck me that the old man already knew.

He shook his head and sighed. 'Your spirit knows, but I fear that the flesh you wear now must walk a weary way before you understand. Remember: the symbol is nothing. It is the reality behind all symbols that is all.'

I was still no closer to comprehending who or what this old man might be, but I had training enough to know that what he said was true.

'Good father, what must I do?'

'Seek ever for the Light . . .' he answered, and with his words, the sunlight on his white robe grew blinding.

I blinked, and when I looked up, Con was standing before me, saying something about the horses, and the old man was gone.

'The horses are waiting down by the gate,' the young Druid repeated, 'and the day is wearing on.'

Still wondering, I allowed him to help me to my feet. I knew better than to speak of what I had seen, but I knew that I would be thinking about it for a long time to come.

*   *   *

Dusk was drawing its cloak across the Vale of Avalon, covering marsh and meadow alike with the same dim purple-grey. From my post by the Mendip road I could see from the higher ground in the east almost all the way to the Sabrina estuary, where the sun was setting into the sea. Now all but the Tor lay in shadow, with a gleam of water below. For ten years I had said farewell to the sun from within that scene; it was fascinating to observe it from outside. Indeed, it was in all ways strange and fearful and oddly exciting to be back in the world of humankind, even if only for a little while.

Con touched my elbow. 'It is almost dark. The Roman should be coming soon.'

'Thank you,' I nodded, glancing up at the clouds that loomed to the north. Even the folk of Avalon could not call rain from an empty sky, and we had had to wait for a weather pattern that would serve my purpose. I had held the clouds at bay throughout the afternoon. Now I released some of the energies that bound them, and felt on my cheek the chill damp breath of the storm.

To learn that Heron's vision of the death of the Emperor had been a true Seeing was encouraging. The men who drank at the taverna near the lead mines were full of gossip. It was said that Claudius had willed the Empire to another general called Aurelian, by-passing his own brother, Quintillus, who, after an abortive attempt at a coup, had died by his own hand.

'He will come, never fear,' said the Druid who had been waiting for us. 'These Romans are creatures of habit, and every evening for the past week he has come this way.'

'He is fair-haired?' I asked once again.

'As fair as bleached flax, with the mark of Mithras between his brows.'

I reached up beneath my veil to touch the blue crescent tattoed on my own forehead. *He is an initiate*, I reminded myself, *and may see more than an ordinary man. I will have to be careful.*

From beyond the curve of the road came a curlew's piping call, an unlikely sound for the high moors, but the Roman whose coming it

84

signalled would not know that. I took a deep breath, lifted my arms to the heavens, and released the clouds.

In moments I felt the first spatterings. By the time the figure on the red mule came into view the rain was driving down in sheets, as several storm fronts that would have passed over one at a time simultaneously released all their stored rain.

Our quarry had pulled up in the tenuous shelter of an elder bush, holding his sagum cloak half over his head in a vain attempt to protect it. For a little longer I watched him.

'Stay out of sight,' I told the two Druids, wrapping my mantle more securely, 'but when I move, follow me.' I gave my mount a kick and reined it across the slope below the road.

'Help— oh, please, help me!' I called in the Roman tongue, pitching my voice to carry above the storm and hauling on the reins of the pony, who had started to plunge as if to make my plight a reality. For a moment nothing happened, and I let the pony move forwards, clutching its mane. 'Can anyone hear me?' I cried again, and saw the red mule at the rim of the hill.

I was wearing a white mantle so that the Roman should be able to see it even through the storm. I screamed and gave the pony a good kick, hanging on desperately as it galloped down the hill. I heard a Roman oath and the crashing of brush as the mule scrambled after me, but we were all the way down the hill and well into the tangle of oak and alder beyond before the Roman caught up with me.

'Lady, are you hurt?' His voice was deep, and so far as I could see beneath his sagum, his body seemed sturdy, though he was tall. He grabbed for the reins that I had artistically allowed to fall as he arrived.

My pony ceased to struggle, recognizing a master's hand, and freed of the need to divide my strength between my mount and the storm, I drew the next squall shrieking down upon us.

'Thank you! Thank you! The pony ran and I feared I would fall!'

He edged the mule closer and put his arm around my shoulders. I leaned against him gratefully, aware now just how long it had

85

been since I had done much riding. His warmth spread through me faster than I would have expected. Perhaps Heron was right, I thought dimly, and he really was the sun.

'I must get you to shelter,' he muttered against my hair, and a shiver ran through me at the touch of his warm breath. The storm had expended its first fury, but the rain was still driving down.

'That way—' I said, pointing south. 'There is an old tile shed.' The tile-makers had not yet started work for the summer: we had slept there on our journey here.

By the time we reached the shed, I did not have to feign exhaustion. My knees gave way as I slid down from the pony, and only the Roman's quick reactions saved me from falling. For a moment he held me, and I realized that we were matched in height. In what else would we be a match? I wondered then, feeling the strength in his arms.

Not that I was likely to find out. The Council, in its wisdom, had decided to bind the Roman to our cause by giving him one of our number in the Great Rite at the Beltane fires; but the priestess whom the lots had selected to be his consort was not me, but Aelia.

I watched, shivering, as the Roman proceeded with swift efficiency to build a fire. At least the tile-makers had left plenty of fuel for it. The little flame leapt and kindled, revealing a sinewy arm, strong cheekbones, short hair plastered close to his head and darkened to old gold by the rain. As the fire began to catch in the larger branches, he stood to unfasten his sagum and drape it, dripping, over one of the low beams. He wore a tunic of good, grey wool edged with red. A short sword in a well-worn leather sheath hung at his side.

'Let me take your mantle, Lady,' he said, turning. 'The fire will warm the air in here soon, and perhaps it will dry—'

The fire flared suddenly, for the first time revealing him fully, and my world stood still. I saw intelligent grey eyes that enlivened a rather ordinary face, permanently reddened by exposure to sun and wind and pinker than ever from the cold. Tired and wet, he was hardly at his best, but he would never be famous for beauty. His

86

colouring proclaimed him Roman by culture rather than ancestry; he hardly seemed the stuff of prophecy.

Yet I knew him.

In the ceremony that made me a woman, the Goddess had shown him to me. He was the lover who would claim me at the Beltane fires, and I was the woman who would bear his child . . .

The Druids found the wrong man, I thought desperately. *This is not the hero of Heron's vision, but of my own . . .*

And if they were the same?

I do not know what my face showed at that moment, but the Roman took a step backwards, lifting his hands in self-deprecation.

'Please, domina, do not be afraid. I am Flavius Constantius Chlorus, at your service.'

I felt myself flushing as I realized that I hardly looked my best either. But that was as it should be. He must see me as ugly, old even, until I knew . . . until I knew whether he was *my* destiny . . .

'Julia Helena thanks you,' I murmured, giving my own Roman name. It felt as strange on my tongue as the Latin. The girl who bore that name had lived another lifetime, ten years ago. But suddenly I wondered if she was destined to live again.

A leather flask hung at his side. He pulled the strap over his head and held it out to me. 'It is only wine, but it may warm you—'

I managed a smile, and turned to rummage in my saddlebags. 'And I have here a little bread and cheese and dried fruit that my sisters packed for me.'

'Then we will feast.' Constantius seated himself on the other side of the fire and smiled.

It transformed his face, and I felt a rush of heat that seared my flesh like fire. Wordless, I held out the loaf of bread, and he took it from my hand. I had heard once that in the hill country, to share a meal, a fire and a bed made a marriage. We had the first two already, and for the first time in my life I felt the temptation to deny my vows.

When my fingers brushed his, he had trembled. My extended

senses knew that at a level below thought, he was responding to my nearness. My Druid escorts were outside somewhere. They would not disturb us unless I screamed. It would take very little, a step in the Roman's direction, a shiver as if I was cold and needed his arms to warm me. A man and a woman, alone together – our bodies would do the rest without direction.

But what of our souls?

To come to him without honour would destroy that other thing, sweeter even than the desire that heated my body: the potential that I sensed between us. And so, although I felt like a starving woman pushing food away, I edged back, drawing ugliness around me like a tattered cloak, the reverse of the glamour a priestess knows how to wear.

Constantius shook his head a little, cast a frowning glance at me and looked away. 'Do you live nearby?' he asked politely.

'I dwell with my sisters on the edge of the marshes,' I answered truthfully, 'near the isle where the Christian monks have their sanctuary.'

'The isle of Inis Witrin? I have heard of it—'

'We can come to my home tomorrow before the sun is high,' I said. 'I would be grateful for your escort—'

'Of course. The men who oversee my family's holdings would rather I had never come here – they will not care if I miss a day or more,' he added bitterly.

'How did you come to riding the back roads of Britannia? You seem a man of authority,' I asked with real curiosity.

'Not to mention family connections.' There was an edge to the bitterness now. 'My grandmother was sister to the Emperor Claudius. I wanted to make my own way by ability, not patronage. But since my great-uncle tried to seize the Imperium, and failed, I will settle for simply staying alive. The new Emperor has good reason to distrust men of my family.'

He shrugged and took a pull from the wineskin. 'My mother's family has investments here in Britannia – an import company in Eburacum, and an interest in the lead mines, and it seemed a good time to send an agent to check on them. At the moment, the Gallic Empire is safer for me than Rome.'

'But will not Tetricus and . . . what is his name, Marius, consider you a danger?'

Constantius shook his head and laughed. 'It is Victorina Augusta who really rules. They call her the Mother of the Camps, you know, but she has little attention to spare for Britannia. So long as she gets a share of the profits, they will leave me alone. Emperors may come and go, but business makes the world go round!'

'You do not sound very happy about it,' I observed. 'I would not have guessed you for a merchant.'

For a moment that grey gaze held my own. 'And what did you think I was?'

'An army man,' I answered, for thus, in vision I had seen him.

'Until a few months ago that was so.' His face darkened. 'I was born at an army post in Dacia. It is all I know, all I ever wanted to be.'

'Are you so eager for battle?' I asked curiously. He did not *seem* bloodthirsty, but how could I know?

'Say rather, that I want what battle can win,' he corrected. 'Justice. Order. Safety for the folk beyond the frontier so that peace can grow . . .' He fell silent, his ruddy skin reddening further, and I judged he was not a man who often let his feelings show.

'Your fortunes will turn,' I assured him. For a moment he eyed me uncertainly, and I reinforced the illusion that disguised me. 'But now we should sleep,' I went on. 'Tomorrow's journey will be difficult after such a storm.' But in truth, it was not the riding that had exhausted me, but the effort to conceal my essence when what I really wanted was to offer him my body and my soul.

The rain had stopped by morning, but as I had anticipated, as the day grew warmer, the saturated ground gave up its excess moisture in wisps of fog. As we rode it grew thicker, until tree and meadow disappeared and the only thing visible was the path.

'Domina,' said Constantius, 'we must halt, before we wander from the road and end up sinking in some bog.'

'Do not be afraid. I know the way,' I answered him, and indeed, I could feel the power of Avalon drawing me forwards. We had come around by the higher ground to the north and east, where a narrow neck of land ran out to the isle.

'I am not afraid, but I am not a fool, either!' he snapped back at me. 'We will go back to the shelter and wait for the weather to clear.' He reached out to take my bridle rein.

I kicked the pony forwards and reined it sharply around. 'Flavius Constantius Chlorus, look at me!' I let the illusion of ugliness fade and called up the power of the priestess to take its place. I could tell I was succeeding when his face changed.

'Lady—' he breathed, 'now I see you as I did before . . .'

I wondered what he meant, as this was the first time I had used the glamour, but the power was continuing to build around me.

'I have been sent to bring you to the holy isle of Avalon. Will you come with me freely and of your own will?'

'What will I find there?' He was still staring at me.

'Your destiny . . .' And Aelia, I thought then. For a moment I wanted to cry out to him to turn, to flee.

'And will I return to the human world?'

'It is there that your fate will be fulfiled.' Ten years of discipline spoke through me now.

'And will you go with me? Swear!'

'I will. I swear it by my eternal soul.' Later, I told myself that I had believed he was asking if I would go with him to Avalon, but I think now that a deeper wisdom made that vow.

'Then I will come with you now.'

I turned, lifting my arms to draw down the power, and as I spoke the spell, the world changed around us, and with the next step the mist was rolling away to either side and we entered Avalon.

Since dawn the drums had throbbed through the earth of the holy isle, the heartbeat of Avalon, filled with the excitement of the festival. White hawthorn weighted the hedges, and creamy primroses and bluebells flourished beneath the trees. It was Beltane eve, and all the world trembled with expectation. All but Aelia, who was trembling with fear.

'Why has the Goddess laid this upon me?' she whispered, curled upon the bed that had been hers while we awaited initiation. There were currently no priestesses in training, and they had given the house to us to prepare the Beltane Bride for the festival.

'I do not know,' I answered her. 'But we have been taught that often Her reasons for setting our feet upon a path are not apparent until we reach its ending . . .' I spoke for my own sake as much as for hers. In the three days since I had brought Constantius to the isle I had not seen him, but he haunted my dreams.

Aelia shook her head. 'I never intended to go to the Beltane fires. I would happily have lived a virgin until my life's end!'

I put my arms around her and rocked her gently. Our unbound hair mingled on the pillow, dark gold and light. 'Constantius will not hurt you, darling. I rode with him for two days – he is a gentleman . . .'

'He is a *man*!'

'Why did you not tell them of your fear when they chose you?' I stroked her hair. And why, I asked myself, had the lot not fallen on *me*?

'We swore obedience to the Council at our initiation. I thought they must know best . . .'

I sighed, understanding how it must have been. Of us all, Aelia had always been the most biddable. For the first time I wondered if the lot had fallen upon her entirely by chance.

'They said the Goddess would give me the strength to do it, but I am afraid . . . Help me, Eilan! Help me to escape this, or I will drown myself in the sacred pool!'

I stilled, understanding in a single instant how I might fulfil both her desire and my own. Or perhaps I had already planned it in some secret part of my soul, and only now, like some moulting insect hidden in the soil, had the idea emerged into the light of day. Justifications came easily – Aelia was the choice not of the Goddess, but of Ganeda. All that was required was a virgin priestess.

It did not matter who she was, so long as she came willingly to the fire. And the substitution would be so *easy*. Though she was paler in colouring than I, and thinner as well, Aelia and I were enough alike for newcomers to mistake us. The younger girls nicknamed us the sun and the moon.

The one reason I did not give myself was the true one – that Constantius Chlorus was *mine*, and it would be like death to see him lead another woman to the bridal bower.

'Ssh . . . be easy . . .' I kissed Aelia's soft hair. 'Both the Bride and her attendants go veiled to the ceremony. We will exchange clothing and I will take your place in the ritual.'

Aelia sat up, gazing at me wide-eyed. 'But if you disobey, Ganeda will punish you!'

'It doesn't matter . . .' I answered. *Not once I have spent the night in Constantius' arms*!

The firelight, seen through the sheer linen of my veil and the screen of branches, filled the circle with a golden haze. Or perhaps it was the aura of power that the dancers were raising, for with each circuit around the bonfire it grew stronger. All the folk of Avalon were here in the meadow at the foot of the Tor, and most of the people from the Lake village as well. My whole body vibrated as the earth shook to their footfalls, or perhaps it was the beating of my heart. I could feel the dancing building to its crescendo. Soon . . . I thought, licking dry lips. It would be soon . . .

The other maidens shifted restlessly on the bench beside me, Heron and Aelia and Wren, all of us clad alike in green gowns and veils and garlands of spring flowers. But only I bore the hawthorn crown. My skin still tingled from the water of the sacred pool, for we had all helped to bathe Aelia, and in the process been cleansed ourselves. I had shared her fast and her vigil; all the ritual requirements had been completed. This substitution might be disobedience, but at least it would not be sacrilege.

'The Roman has been bathed and prepared as well,' said Ganeda, who waited with us. 'When he arrives, you will be brought out to

92

him. Together, you will partake of the sacred food, and together you will enter the bower on the far side of the dancing floor. You are a virgin field, in which he will sow the seed that will engender the Child of the Prophecy.'

'And what will I give to him?' I whispered.

'In the outer world, the female is passive while the male initiates action. But on the inner planes, it is otherwise. I have spoken with this young man, and at present fortune does not smile upon him. It is for you to awaken his spirit, to arouse and activate the higher soul within him, that he may fulfil his own destiny and become the Restorer of the Light for Britannia.'

I dared not ask more, lest my voice be recognized, and then I heard a change in the drumming and my throat began to ache so with tension that I could not have spoken if I had tried.

The Druids were coming in, their white robes washed with gold by the firelight, wreaths of oak leaves upon their hair. But as I watched I caught a glimpse of brighter gold among them. The people were cheering; the air throbbed with wave upon wave of sound. Dizzied, I shut my eyes, and when I opened them again I blinked, dazzled by the golden figure who stood before the fire.

As my sight adjusted I saw that it was only a saffron tunic to which the light had added a deeper gold, but the wreath that crowned Constantius was fashioned of the true metal, like that of an emperor. I realized that when I had last seen him, splashed with mud and worn out by our battle with the storm, Constantius had not been at his best either. Now, his skin glowed against the tunic, and his fair hair was as bright as the wreath of gold.

'He is Lugos come among us,' breathed Heron.

'And Apollo,' whispered Aelia.

'And Mithras of the Soldiers,' added Wren.

He stood like the sun god in the midst of the Druid oaks. If I had not loved him already, in that moment I would have adored him, for the body of the man had become a clear vessel through which shone the light of the god within.

If I had watched for much longer, I think I might have passed into an ecstasy that precluded movement, but now the drumming was giving way to the music of bells and harpstrings. The maidens beside me assisted me to my feet as the screen of branches was lifted away. The noise of the crowd became a hush of awe, and there was only the music.

Constantius turned as we came forward, and his exalted expression focused suddenly, as if he could see past the veil to the woman, or the goddess within. Wren scattered flowers before me, Aelia and Heron walked to either side, and then they too fell back and I went on alone. Constantius and I faced one another, priest to priestess, across a little table that bore a loaf of bread, a dish of salt, and a cup and flagon filled with water from the sacred spring.

'My lord, the gifts of the earth I offer you. Eat, and be strengthened.' I broke off a piece of bread, dipped it in the salt and offered it to him.

'You are the fertile earth. I accept your bounty,' Constantius replied. He ate the piece of bread, tore off another and held it out to me. 'And I shall spend my strength to care for the sacred soil.'

When I had eaten, he picked up the flagon, poured some of the water into the cup and held it out to me. 'I am poured out for you like water. Drink, and be renewed.'

'You are the rain that falls from heaven. I receive your blessing.' I sipped from the cup, then offered it back to him. 'But all waters are at last reborn from the sea.'

He took the cup from my hand and drank.

The drum began to beat once more. I took a step backwards, beckoning, and he followed me. The music moved faster, and I began to dance.

My feet no longer seemed to belong to me; my body had become an instrument to express the music as I bent and swayed in the sinuous spirals of the sacred dance. My garment, of a linen almost as fine as the veils that hid my face, clung and flared as I whirled. But always as I circled, Constantius was my centre, to whom I turned as a flower to the sun.

First he swayed, and then, as the music broke through the last

94

of his Roman conditioning, he began to move, a stamping, vigorous kind of dance, as if he marched to music. Closer and closer we came, mirroring each other's movements, until he caught me in his arms. For a moment we stood breast to breast. I could feel his heart beating as if it were my own.

Then he lifted me, as easily as if I had weighed no more than Heron, and bore me away to the bower.

It was a round hut in the ancient fashion, made from branches loosely woven together. Flowers had been twined among them, and firelight gleamed through the gaps, dappling the rich cloth that covered the bed, and the walls, and our bodies, with golden light. Constantius set me on my feet again and we faced each other, silent, until the golden leaves of his wreath no longer quivered with the swiftness of his breathing.

'I am all that is, has been, and will be,' I said softly, 'and no man has ever lifted my veil. Make pure your heart, oh you who would look upon the Mystery.'

'I have been purified according to the Law,' he answered me. Then he added, 'I have eaten from the drum; I have drunk from the cymbal. I have seen the light that shines in the darkness. I will lift your veil.'

These words were not the ones the priests had taught him. Clearly, he was not only an initiate of the Soldiers' God, but of the Mother and the Daughter as they are known in the southern lands. He reached out, and with steady hands lifted the hawthron wreath from my brow, and then drew off my veil. For a moment he simply stared at my face. Then he knelt before me.

'It *is* you! Even in the storm I knew you. You are the Goddess indeed! Did you show yourself to me first in the guise of a hag to test me, and is this my reward?'

I swallowed, gazing down at his bent head, and then, bending, took off his golden crown and laid it beside my wreath of flowers.

'With this crown or without it, you are the God to me . . .' I managed to say. 'It was I indeed, and even then, I loved you.'

He looked up at me, his eyes still wide and unfocused, set his

95

hands upon my hips and drew me forwards until his bent head rested at the joining of my thighs. I felt a sweet fire began to build between them, and suddenly, my knees would no longer bear me, and I slid down, down, between his hands until we knelt together, breast to breast and brow to brow.

Constantius gave a little sigh then, and his lips found mine. And as if that had completed a circuit of power, suddenly the fire was everywhere. I clutched at his shoulders, and his arms came tight around me, and together we fell to the bed that had been prepared for us.

Our clothing had been made so that at the removal of a few pins it would fall away, and soon there was no impediment between us. His body was hard with muscle, but his skin was smooth, sliding across mine, and his strong hands tender as he taught me ecstasies that had never been mentioned in my training. And then we came together. I set my arms about him as the power of the God came down, shaking him until he cried out in his extremity. And as he gave his soul into my keeping, the power of the Goddess bore my own away to meet him and there was only light.

When time had come back from eternity once more and we lay quiet, clasped in each other's arms, I realized that outside the hut, people were cheering. Constantius stilled, listening.

'Are they cheering for us?'

'They have lit the bonfire atop the Tor,' I said softly. 'On this night, there is no separation between your world and Avalon. The priests will huddle in their cells for fear of the powers of darkness, but the fire that is lit here will be visible all over the Vale. On other hills, folk are waiting to see it. They will kindle their own fires then, and so, from hill to hill, the light will spread across Britannia.'

'And what about *this* fire?' he touched me once more and I gasped as flame rippled upwards.

'Ah, my beloved, I think the fire we have kindled between us will light the whole world!'

96

CHAPTER SIX

AD 270

When I woke, the pale light of early morning was filtering through the leaves of the bower. The air was moist and cool on my bare skin. I burrowed back under the covers, and the man beside me grunted, turned, and flung out a possessive arm to draw me close against his side. For a moment I stiffened in confusion, then my awakening senses flooded me with memory. I turned, fitting myself more closely against him, astonished, despite the unaccustomed soreness in my body, by how *right* it felt to lie this way.

I could hear no human sounds, but the birds were singing a triumphant welcome to the new day. I raised myself on one elbow, gazing down at the sleeping face of my – lover? That seemed too light a word for our union, and yet what had passed between us had surely been more personal than the transcendent joining of priest and priestess as they manifest the power of the Divine into the world.

Though that, certainly, had been part of it. A reminiscent tremor of energy quivered in the area of my solar plexus as I remembered. When we came together, the awakening earth had been filled by the radiant power of the sun. If I extended my senses groundward I could feel the aftermath of that conjunction, like ripples spreading through the stillness of a pool.

And what else had the ritual accomplished? I focused on my own body, lips swollen with kissing, breasts awakened to an exquisite sensitivity, the muscles of my inner thighs sore with unaccustomed stretching, and the secret place between them beginning to throb once more as memory stimulated new desire. I forced awareness deeper, into the womb that had received Constantius's seed. Was I pregnant? Even my priestess-trained senses could not tell. I realized that I was smiling. If last night's love-making had not planted a child in my belly, we would have to try again . . .

Relaxed in sleep, Constantius had a serenity I would not have suspected. His body, where the sun did not touch it, was like ivory. I gazed upon his face with growing delight, memorizing the strong lines of cheek and jaw, the high-bridged nose, the noble sweep of his brow. In the pale light the brand of Mithras was barely visible to the eye, but to my inner senses it glowed, focusing the radiance of the soul within.

As if that awareness had been a physical touch, he began to waken, first with a sigh, and then with a flutter of the eyelids, and then the muscles of the face tightening into their accustomed lines as he opened his eyes. He was, it would seem, one of those fortunate people who pass in one instant from unconsciousness to full awareness. The grey eyes that gazed up at me were wide, not with sleep, but wonder.

'*Sanctissima Dea . . .*' he whispered.

I smiled and shook my head, unsure whether that had been a title or an exclamation. 'Not now,' I answered. 'Morning has come, and I am only Helena.'

'Yes – now,' he corrected. 'And when you came to me last night, and when you sat as a hag beside my fire, and when you summoned me to Avalon. The Greeks say that Anchises trembled in fear because he lay with a goddess all unknowing. But I knew—' He reached up, and very gently brushed the hanging lock of hair back from my brow. 'And if the gods had blasted me for my presumption, I would have counted the price well paid.'

The gods had not blasted us, though there had been moments when we might well have been overcome by ecstasy. It was Ganeda, I thought suddenly, who was going to blast me when she realized I had taken Aelia's place in the ritual.

'What is it?' he asked. 'What is the matter?'

'Nothing – nothing you have done,' I said quickly, and bent to kiss him. Clearly reverence did not unman him, for his response was instant. He pulled me down beside him, and in the flood of sensation as he made love to me all thought was for a time submerged.

When I became capable of coherent thought once more, the light that was filtering through the leaves of the bower was bright and golden, and I could hear the murmur of voices from outside.

'We should dress,' I murmured against his cheek. 'The priestesses will be coming soon.'

His grip tightened suddenly. 'Will I see you again?'

'I . . . do not know . . .' Yesterday, I had not really thought beyond the ritual. I had known I wanted Constantius, but I had not considered how difficult it would be, once I had lain with him, to let him go.

'Come with me—'

I shook my head, not in denial, but confusion. I believed that I had been justified in taking the place of the Beltane Bride because Constantius was the lover promised to me by my vision. But if that was so, then what of the images of foreign lands that I had seen? Much as I loved him, I did not want to leave Avalon.

'What does this mean to you?' Gently I brushed the sign of Mithras on his brow.

For a moment he looked taken aback. I waited as he struggled to frame an answer, understanding how deep was the inhibition against speaking of the Mysteries.

'It is a sign . . . of my devotion to the God of Light . . .' he said finally.

'As this sign signifies my own dedication to the Goddess—' I indicated the blue crescent between my own brows. 'I am a priestess of Avalon, and bound by my vows.'

'Was it only obedience to your vows that brought you to me last night?' he asked, frowning.

'Can you truly think that, after this morning?' I tried to smile.

'Helena — I beg of you, let there always be truth between us!' His face had gone grim.

For a long moment I met his gaze, wondering how much I dared say. But surely he was going to hear about it as soon as I emerged from the bower and they saw it was not Aelia.

'I took the place of the priestess they meant for your bride. I have the Sight, and it showed me your face long ago. And then I was sent to bring you here, and . . . I began to love you . . .'

'You disobeyed?' In his face anxiety warred with satisfaction. 'Will they punish you?'

'Even the Lady of Avalon cannot change what has happened between us,' I managed a smile. But we both knew that I had not really answered him.

There was a sound outside and I stiffened. Someone was knocking softly against the upright of the door.

'Eilan, can you hear me? Is the Roman asleep?'

It was Aelia's voice, and I remembered suddenly that she had been told that after she lay with him she must make sure Constantius drank the contents of the silver flask in the corner so that he would sleep while she slipped away.

'Eilan, come quickly, and no one will—' She broke off with a gasp. I heard the sound of several people approaching, and the pit of my stomach went suddenly cold. With a leaden certainty I knew it would be Ganeda even before I heard the next words.

'Is she still sleeping? It would seem she did not fear a man's touch so greatly after all. You will have to go in and wake her . . .' The laughter stilled. 'Aelia!'

There was a short, charged, silence. As I started to drape the coverlet around me Constantius gripped my arm.

'You shall not face them alone—'

After a moment I nodded, and waited while he twisted my veil about his loins, reminding me of the statues I had seen in Londinium. One arm went protectively around me. With the other, he pushed aside the woven curtain that covered the doorway, and

100

together we emerged into the uncompromising illumination of the new day.

It was worse than I had expected. Not only Ganeda and the priestesses, but Arganax and his Druids, were standing there. Aelia still crouched by the doorway, weeping silently. I reached down to touch her shoulder and she clung to me.

'I . . . see . . .' said the High Priestess in a voice like grating stones. She looked around her at the dancing floor, and I saw that the people who had dropped down to sleep there, in couples or alone, were beginning to awaken and cast curious glances at the scene by the bower. With an obvious effort she controlled the words that trembled on her lips.

'Aelia . . . and Eilan—' she ground out the names, '—will come with me.' Her gaze turned to Constantius. 'My lord, the Druids wait to attend you.'

His grip on me tightened. 'You will not harm her!'

Ganeda's face darkened further as she realized just how much I must have told him.

'Do you think we are barbarians?' she snapped, and he responded to the note of command and let me go, though in truth that was no answer at all.

'It will be all right,' I said in a low voice, though my gut was still knotting in apprehension.

'I will not lose you!' Constantius replied, and it occurred to me that not only had I not anticipated how this night would bind me to him, I had not even imagined how it might affect his feelings for *me*.

I helped Aelia to rise, and putting my arm around her, started towards my reckoning.

'Why does it matter?' I exclaimed. 'Both of your purposes have been accomplished. You wanted a man of destiny for the Great Rite, and you wanted to win his friendship for Avalon.'

The sun was nearing noon, and we were still arguing. By now, my belly was cramping not from fear but from hunger.

101

'You forget the third reason, and that was the most important of all,' Ganeda said grimly. 'Constantius was to engender the Child of Prophecy!'

'And so he shall, with me! In my womanhood vision I saw myself with his child!'

'But not the child of the Great Rite—' the High Priestess said grimly. 'Why do you think Aelia was intended as his consort in the ritual?'

'Because you could bend her to your will!'

'You little fool – she was chosen, indeed, but not for that reason. In your arrogance you thought you knew better than the Council of Avalon, but you were an untried maiden, ignorant of the Mother's Mysteries. Last night Aelia was at the height of her fertile time. If the Roman had lain with her she would have come away pregnant, and the child would have been born here in Avalon.'

'How do you know I am not?'

'Your moontime is barely three days past,' she answered me, 'and I have examined you. There is no spark of new life in your womb.'

'There will be. Destiny cannot be denied—' I answered, but the first breath of doubt stole the force from my words. 'Constantius has pledged his faith to me – a priestess will bear his son!'

'But when? Even now do you not understand? A child begotten last night would have preserved the Mysteries for a thousand years. Even if your fantasies were true, what stars will rule the fate of the babe you finally bear?'

'He will be my son,' I muttered. 'I will raise him to serve the gods.'

Ganeda shook her head in disgust. 'I should have sent you back to your father long since. You have been a trouble-maker since the first day you arrived!'

'You missed your chance!' I hissed, touching the crescent on my brow. 'He is dead, and I am a priestess now.'

'And *I* am the Lady of Avalon!' she snapped in return, 'and your life is in my hand!'

'All your anger, Ganeda, cannot change what has been done,' I said wearily. 'At least I have won Constantius's friendship for Avalon.'

'And what about that which was undone? Do you think the man will come back every Beltane like a stallion to stud until he gets you with child?'

Some tension eased within me. I had feared she would forbid me ever to see him again. Surely he would come back, I told myself, and somehow I would endure until that day.

'So, what is my punishment?'

'Punishment?' There was venom in her smile. 'Did I not promise the Roman I would do you no harm? You have chosen your own condemnation, *Helena*. When Constantius leaves, you shall go with him . . .'

'Leave . . . Avalon?' I whispered.

'That is what he is demanding — be grateful you are not being turned out like a beggar to wander the world!'

'But what about my vows?'

'You should have thought about your vows last night, before they were broken! In the old days you would have burned for that crime.' In her lined face, a sour satisfaction was replacing the fury.

I stared at her. I had disobeyed her order, certainly, but surely I had given myself to Constantius as the Goddess willed.

'You have until the sun goes down to make ready,' Ganeda said then. 'When the sun goes down and the festival is over, you will be banished from Avalon.'

The Christians, I had heard, had a legend that told how the first parents of humankind were exiled from Paradise. When the mists of Avalon closed behind me I understood how they must have felt. Had it comforted Eve to know that Adam was still beside her? Knowing that my own choices had forced this destiny upon me was little comfort.

I told myself that if Constantius had gone alone, leaving me behind, I would have been weeping bitterly, but the grief that kept me numb and silent as the barge bore us through the mists was of a deeper order entirely.

As we slid up onto the shore below the Lake people's village I felt a sudden disorientation, as if one of my senses had disappeared. I staggered, and Constantius lifted me in his arms and bore me up the bank. When he set me on my feet again I clung to him, trying to understand what had happened to me.

'It is all right,' he whispered, holding me against him. 'It is all behind us now.'

I looked back across the Lake, and realized that the psychic sense that had always told me where to find Avalon was no longer there. Physical sight showed me marshland and blue water, and the beehive huts on the Christian isle. But when I had left before, I had only to close my eyes in order to sense, at an odd angle to the mortal world, the way to Avalon. I had taken the link for granted. Through it, the High Priestess could check on the well-being of her absent daughters, for even when priestesses were sent on errands away from the holy isle a thread of connection remained.

But now, Ganeda had severed it, and I was like a sapling that the flood uproots and whirls away. By the time I ceased my weeping, a cold grey dawn was breaking once more.

I do not know whether the fact that Constantius tolerated me for the next few weeks was a measure of his honour or his love. He told the keeper of the posting-inn where we spent the next night that I was ill, and it was true, though my sickness was not of the body, but of the soul. By day, my only comfort was Eldri's devotion, and by night, the strength of Constantius's arms. And when it became clear to him that it was a constant torture for me to live where every clear day showed me the Vale of Avalon, he concluded his business at the mines and we set out for Eburacum, where the workshops his family owned turned some of the lead into pewterware.

Constantius hired a trader to guide us cross-country through lanes and by-ways to the great Roman road that runs northeast from

Lindinis to Lindum. For the first few days I rode in dismal silence, too wrapped up in my own grief to notice my surroundings. Still, if any time of the year could reconcile one to the loss of Avalon, I suppose it must be the smiling season that follows Beltane.

Cold though the wind might sometimes blow, the bone-deep chill of winter was gone. The triumphant sun laid a golden blessing across the land, and the land with joyous abandon made it welcome. The brilliant green of new leaves resounded with the songs of returning birds, and every hedgerow and woodland ride was adorned with flowers. As day followed glorious day, my body, like the earth, responded to that radiant light.

For so long – too long – I had searched out herbs only for their utility. Now I picked the creamy primroses and the nodding bluebells, bright celandine and hidden violets and forget-me-nots like pieces of fallen sky, for no other reason than that they were beautiful. The training of Avalon was intended to develop the spirit, and all the resources of mind and body were put at its service, under the direction of a disciplined will. The needs of the flesh were given grudging recognition only at the festivals, and those of the heart, no honour at all. But Constantius had conquered my awakening senses, and my heart was carried along in their triumph, a willing prisoner. I made no attempt at resistance: banished from the realm of the spirit, the world and its pleasures were all that remained to me.

We travelled slowly, staying sometimes at villas and farmsteads, and sometimes sleeping under the stars in some woodland thicket or in a field by the side of the road. The first significant town along our route was Aquae Sulis, tucked into the hills where the Abona curved round on its way to the Sabrina estuary. I know now that it was a small place, but at the time I was impressed by its elegance. Since ancient times the healing springs had been considered holy, but the Romans, for whom bathing was a social necessity, had made of the place a spa that could compete with any in the Empire.

As we rode in I marvelled at the buildings, constructed from warm golden stone. The people who thronged the streets were well-dressed, and I became abruptly conscious of what a week of journeying had done to my only gown. And my hair—I drew my veil up hastily, and nudged my pony closer to Constantius's mule.

'My lord—'

He turned with a smile, and I was surprised by how naturally he fitted into this civilized scene.

'Constantius, we cannot stay here. I have nothing to *wear*.'

'That is precisely why I wanted to stop here, my love,' he grinned back at me. 'It's little enough I have to offer in return for all you have given up for me, but Aquae Sulis contains, in miniature, the best of the Empire. I have enough funds for us to stay for a few days in a decent inn, and enjoy the baths, and buy clothing that will do justice to your beauty.'

I began to protest, but he shook his head. 'When we arrive at Eburacum, I will be introducing you to my associates in business, and you must do me credit. Think of the shopping as something you can do for *me*.'

I sat back in the saddle, my face flaming. It was still a wonder to be reminded that he thought me beautiful. I did not know if it was true – there were no mirrors on Avalon – but it mattered little so long as I found favour in his eyes.

Shopping in Aquae Sulis was rather overwhelming to one who had grown up with one gown for everyday and one for ritual, though even Constantius widened his eyes at the prices. I came away with a tunica the colour of terra cotta, banded at the hem with green and gold, and a palla of green wool to wear with it, and another ensemble in the rosy shades of dawn. I acceded willingly to whatever Constantius wanted me to wear, so long as it was not priestess-blue.

Leaving Eldri to guard our gear in the inn, we dined in the garden of a taverna on the main street, and then proceeded to the temple complex that included the baths. It was becoming clear that Aquae Sulis was not an ordinary Roman town. Dominated by the religious buildings that had grown up around the sacred spring, it was as dedicated, in its own way, as Avalon. I was accustomed to fine stonework, though the carvings that adorned the buildings seemed

106

ornate after the stark simplicity of the isle. And though it was true that my people had carved images of their deities, the Druids of Avalon taught that the gods were most truly worshipped beneath the open sky.

Thus, I could tell myself that the image of Sulis Minerva that stood in the round *tholos* in the square before the bath precincts was only a statue, though I avoided meeting the calm gaze of the bronze head beneath the gilded helmet as I hurried by. I hung back as Constantius purchased a bag of incense to cast on the fire that burned on the altar in the courtyard, resenting his unselfconscious piety even as I admired it. But what had such observances to do with me, who had known the Mysteries of Avalon? *Known, and lost them* . . . a deeper self reminded me. Very well, I told myself, I would learn to survive with no gods at all.

A Gorgon-face glared fiercely from the portico of the temple, its hair and beard writhing in contorted rays. Another solar deity reigned from the arch that led into the baths. For Constantius's sake, I thought then, I might make an exception of that one.

He paid our fees and we passed beneath the arch, and I coughed at the sudden gust of moist, heated air. It had a faint odour of old eggs, not strong enough to be unpleasant, but distinctly medicinal. Before us, glimmering faintly in the light that came through the high arched window, lay the sacred pool.

'The water rises here and is piped to the other pools,' said Constantius. 'This place has been sacred since long before the Divine Julius brought his legions to this isle. It is customary to make an offering . . .'

He opened his pouch and took out two silver denarii. Other coins gleamed from the bottom of the pool along with lead votive tablets and other offerings. He drew the hood of his cloak up over his head, his lips moving silently, and tossed his denarius in. I followed his example, though I had no prayer to offer, only a voiceless need.

'You are in luck: the attendant told me that the hot pools are reserved for women at this hour. I will go to the steam room at the

other end of the baths and meet you at sunset by the altar outside.'
Constantius squeezed my hand and turned away.

For a moment I wanted to call him back again. But after a week on
the road all other considerations were overwhelmed by the desire
to get truly clean. I turned in the other direction and passed from
the first chamber into the colonnade adjoining the large pool. Talk
in the taverna had suggested that it was early in the season for the
numbers of visitors the baths were built to receive. The warm pool was
almost empty, its water green where sunlight slanted in from above, its
sides mysteriously shadowed by the colonnade. I continued around it,
looking for the smaller pools I had been told lay beyond it.

The pool I chose was heated by water that rushed from beneath
a stone slab, its stones blurred by an accretion of minerals from the
spring. It reminded me of the Holy Well at Avalon, but this water
was as warm as blood. Sinking into its embrace was like a return
to the womb.

I lay back with my head on the smooth curve of the coping, letting
the water support my body, and muscles I had not known were tense
began to unkink at last. The two women who had been soaking
when I arrived climbed out of the pool and went off, chattering
about a new cook. A slave girl came in with an armload of towels,
saw I needed no assistance, and departed. The water grew still. I
was alone.

For a timeless interval I floated, without need or desire. In that
moment, undisturbed by demands from either mind or body, I did
not realize that the defences I had thrown up around my spirit were
dissolving away. The gentle lapping of wavelets against stone faded,
until the murmur of the water flowing into the pool was the only
sound.

And after a while that subtle murmur became a song –

> 'Ever flowing, ever growing,
> from the earth to the sea,
> ever falling, ever calling
> ever coming to be . . .'

I relaxed into the music, and without intention, my soul stirred and reached out to the spirit of the waters. The singing continued. I found myself smiling, uncertain whether my own imagination was supplying words to the music or I was indeed hearing the voice of the spring. Now new words were whispering through the hushed trickle—

> 'Ever living, ever giving,
> all my children are free;
> ever turning, ever yearning,
> they return unto me . . .'

But I was cut off from that eternal source, and forbidden to return. At that, a great grief rose up in me, and the tears rolled down my cheeks and mingled with the waters of the Goddess in the pool.

It seemed an eternity before the slave girl came back into the chamber, but I suppose that in truth not so much time had passed. I felt empty, and when I left the water and saw the blood running down my inner thighs, I realized that I was empty in truth. Ganeda had been right in her calculations, and despite the ecstasy of our loving, Constantius had not got me with child.

When the girl had provided me with clouts and padding, I sat for a long time in the moist shadow, gazing at the swirling waters and waiting for more tears to come. But for the moment I had no more emotion. My life stretched before me, devoid of magic. But not, I reminded myself, of love. By now, Constantius would be waiting. It was not he who had broken my heart – I had done that all by myself.

Deceived, lured from his ordinary world into Avalon and then burdened with a disgraced and weeping priestess when he left it, Constantius had not complained. He at least deserved a cheerful companion. By this time my hair was drying, the shorter strands

109

curling in moist tendrils around my brow. I called to the slave girl once more to dress it high with pins and help me to disguise my puffy eyes with kohl and my pale cheeks with rouge. When I looked into the bronze mirror I saw a fashionable stranger.

When I came out of the baths the sun was about to sink behind the hills that sheltered the town. I turned from the dazzle of light and stopped short, facing a pediment that was the twin to the one that led to the sacred spring. But here, the dominant figure was a goddess, her hair twisted up on each side and caught in the middle by a ring. She was haloed by a crescent moon.

For a moment I simply stood, staring, as a traveller will stop who suddenly glimpses someone from home. Then I remembered how I had come here.

'It will do you little good, Lady, to lie in wait for me,' I said softly. 'It is you who cast me out – I owe you no loyalty!'

From Aquae Sulis, the military road angled northeast across Britannia. After we left Corinium it rose gradually, passing through wild hill country as it approached Ratae. Nonetheless, we continued to find mansios and posting inns spaced a day's travel apart along the road, and from time to time I would glimpse through the trees the red-tiled roof of a villa. This, Constantius assured me, was a gentle land compared to the mountains near Eburacum, but I, accustomed to the marshlands of the Summer Country, gazed at the blue distances and wondered.

As we neared Lindum, we came to flat green countryside like the Trinovante lands where I had lived as a child. I took refuge in those memories, and began to talk to Constantius about my father and my brothers, fitting together my memories like some Roman mosaic of the life of a British prince who had adopted, for the most part, the ways of Rome.

'My own family is not so different,' said Constantius. 'My people come from Dacia, the land away to the north of Greece, where the Carpatus mountains curve around the great plain. I was born in a villa on the Danuvius, where the river cuts through the grasslands.

Dacia is still a frontier province – we became Roman even later than you Britons – and the Goths keep trying to make us barbarian once again . . .'

'We heard that the Emperor Claudius had beaten them at Nissa,' I said when the silence had continued for too long. It had been some time since we had passed a villa, and though the road was elevated, a tangle of trees pressed close on either side. The clip-clop of our mounts' hooves seemed loud in that empty land.

'Yes . . . I was there . . .' answered Constantius, rubbing at the spot on his thigh where I remembered seeing a scar. 'But it was a near thing. They came from the east, across the Euxine Sea. Our garrison at Marcianopolis fought them off, but they sailed south and managed to break through into the Aegeum, where they split into three armies. Gallienus wiped out the Herulians in Thracia, but the Goths were still rampaging around Macedonia.

'We finally caught up with them at Nissa. It's hard to defend against wandering bands that hit a village and run, but barbarian troops can't stand against our heavy cavalry . . .' His eyes were bleak with memory. 'It was a slaughter. After that, it was mostly a matter of mopping up. Hunger and bad weather killed as many of the stragglers as we did. That, and the plague.' He fell silent, and I remembered that the plague had killed Romans as well, including his great-uncle the Emperor.

'Was your home safe?' I asked in an attempt to turn his mind from thoughts of battle.

He blinked, and managed a smile. 'Yes, it was – the Goths were after older and richer towns. It was one time when living on the frontier worked to our advantage. My people have been there since Trajan conquered the land.'

'My father's family ruled the country north of the Tamesis even before the Romans came,' I observed a trifle smugly. The sun was breaking through the clouds, and I unhooked my broad hat from the saddle and put it on. 'But my ancestor made alliance with the Divine Julius, and took his family name.'

111

'Ah—' answered Constantius, 'my own ancestry is less illustrious. One of my ancestors was a client to Flavius Vespasianus, the great Emperor, hence the family name. But the first of my line to settle in Dacia was a centurion who married a local girl. But that's nothing to be ashamed of. Some say that Vespasianus himself was descended from one of the founders of Rome, but I am told that the Emperor laughed at that idea, and admitted that his grandfather had been a ranker in the legions. It does not matter. We are all Romans now . . .'

'I suppose so,' I replied. 'I know Coelius kept the Roman festivals. I remember going with him to the great temple of Claudius in Camulodunum to burn incense to the Emperor. In matters pertaining to government he was a Roman, but he kept to the old ways when it was a question of the health of the land. That is how I came to be conceived,' I added unwillingly. 'In the year of the great floods he appealed to Avalon, and my mother, who was the High Priestess then, travelled to Camulodunum to perform the Great Rite with him.'

'So you are royal on both sides.' Constantius smiled at me, then grew thoughtful. 'Did your father ever formally adopt you?'

I shook my head. 'What need?' I said bitterly. 'I was always intended for Avalon . . . Does it matter to you?' I added, seeing his frown.

'Not to me—' he said quickly. 'It may have some legal implications . . . for our marriage.'

'You want to marry me?' In truth, I had not thought much about it, having grown to womanhood in Avalon, where the priestesses did not bind themselves to any man.

'Of course! Or at least,' he added, 'make some legal arrangement that will protect you – was not that ceremony we performed at your festival a wedding?'

I stared at him. 'It was the union of the earth and the sun, meant to bring life to the land – the god and the goddess were wedded, as was the case with my parents, not the priest and priestess who performed the rite.'

112

He reined in abruptly, blocking my pony, and faced me. A pair of warblers lifted from the hawthorn hedge, calling. 'If you do not consider yourself my wife, why did you come with me?'

My eyes filled with tears. 'Because I love you . . .'

'I am an initiate, but not an adept of the Mysteries,' Constantius said after a long moment had passed. 'The only way I knew how to make those vows was as a man. And you were my lady – the first time I saw you I knew you were the woman whose soul was bound to my own.'

It occurred to me suddenly that Ganeda's plan could never have worked even if I had not interfered. If Aelia had been the priestess, Constantius would have refused to go through with the ritual. He reached out and seized my hand.

'You are mine, Helena, and I will never abandon you. This I swear to you by Juno and all the gods. You will be my wife in fact, whether or not you bear the name. Do you understand?'

'*Volo*—' *I am willing*,' I whispered past the lump in my throat. At least I had had a vision. Only honour, and his noble heart, kept this man at my side.

I think it was at that moment, standing in the road somewhere in the middle of Britannia, that my marriage to Constantius truly began.

CHAPTER SEVEN

AD 271

The wicker back of my round chair creaked as I leaned into it. The pose was deceptively casual: from here I could see past the frescoing of fruits and flowers around the doorway to the kitchen, where Drusilla should be readying the next course of the meal. Our guests, two of the more successful merchants based at Eburacum, had just about finished the pickled eggs and the oysters served raw in the shell with a sharp sauce. This was one of several little dinners Constantius had held in the year we had been here, building a network of goodwill among the merchants in the town.

It seemed to be working. The pewter business was prospering. I knew that Constantius would rather have been with the men of the Sixth Victrix in the great fortress across the river, though in truth, since the wild tribes beyond the Wall had for some time been peaceful the legion was rather under-strength, and there was not much activity there. The busy town, which since the time of Severus had been the capital of Britannia Inferior, was where the real power lay now, and Constantius seemed to be one of those men who could do well at anything to which he put his mind.

I glimpsed Philip, a Greek boy whom we had recently added to the household, hovering in the passage, and beckoned to him to clear away the platters. Constantius, who was still listening attentively to the older of the merchants, one of the large Sylvanus clan who traded in linen from Eburacum and pottery from Treveri, gave me an encouraging smile.

114

I smiled back, though acting the part of a Roman lady still felt a bit unreal. Avalon had trained me for many things, but they did not include planning a formal banquet and making small talk over the wine. For this, I would have been better prepared if I had grown up with the other simpering girl-children in my father's hall. Still, Constantius needed a hostess, and I did my best to pretend I was at ease.

I had learned to paint my face, and dress my hair in a complex knot with a Greek bandeau to hide the crescent moon upon my brow. Constantius's business was prospering, and he delighted to give me things. I now had a chest full of linen shifts and tunicas in finely-woven coloured wool, and earrings and a pendant of the locally worked jet, the roundel carved with Constantius's face and my own.

Spinning was a traditional woman's occupation among the Romans, and that was a craft that I knew well. But when we arrived in Eburacum I had no more known how to manage a house than fight a battle. I had no time to pine for Avalon — there was too much to learn. Fortunately, we had an excellent cook in Drusilla. Constantius had grown visibly more solid this past year. She would have resented any attempt on my part to direct her, even if I had had any notion of cookery. She did, however, require me to memorize the ingredients, so that if any of the guests inquired, I could do justice to her artistry.

Philip brought in the next course, a dish of tiny cabbages called coliculis cooked with sweet green peppers and mustard greens. It was seasoned with thyme and served over a purée of jellied hare. With the gravity of one engaged in some holy rite he served out portions onto the plates, good red Samian ware, probably purchased from Lucius Viducius, whose couch was next to my chair. His family had been leaders in the pottery trade between Eburacum and Rothomagus in Gallia for as long as Constantius's relations had been manufacturing pewter.

I took a bite, then set the spoon down again. It tasted well enough, but my stomach was rebelling. I had not even attempted the oysters.

115

'You do not eat, domina – are you unwell?' asked Viducius. He was a big man with blond hair going now to grey who looked more like a German than a Gaul.

'A momentary upset,' I answered. 'No need for concern . . . Please eat, or my cook will never forgive me. Constantius tells me that you travel to Gallia twice a year. Will you be going oversea again soon?'

'Very soon,' he nodded. 'Your man is hoping to persuade us to carry his wares to Germania on the ship that will bring back our own. May Nehalennia keep us safe from storms!'

'Nehalennia?' I echoed politely. This was a goddess of whom I had not heard.

'She is a goddess much favoured by traders. They have made a shrine for her on an island where the Rhenus flows into the ocean. My father Placidus set up an altar for her there when I was a child.'

'Is she then a German goddess?'

I cast a swift glance around. Constantius had drawn the second man, a ship-owner, into his conversation. There were more dishes on the table now: broiled mullets braised in olive oil with pepper and wine, and lentils with parsnips cooked with herb sauce. I took a little of each, though I did not try to eat them, and turned back to Viducius with a smile.

'Perhaps,' he was answering, 'my father came originally from Treveri. But I think she likes best the lowlands that face the north sea. It is there that the sea lanes and the land roads meet; from there, she can guard all the ways . . .'

My face must have shown something then, for he stopped, asking what was wrong.

'Not wrong: I was only reminded of a British goddess, whom we call Elen of the Ways. I wonder if they could be the same?'

'Our Nehalennia is shown sitting, with a dog at her feet and a basket of apples in the crook of her arm,' the trader replied.

I smiled and leaned down to pat Eldri, who lay, as usual, at my feet hoping that some morsel would fall. She sat up, nostrils quivering, and I realized that Philip was bringing in the roasted boar. I saw it come with mixed feelings – the rich scent further upset my stomach, but its appearance meant that the meal was almost over. I took a careful sip of watered wine.

'Elen is said to love dogs as well, for they show the way,' I said politely. 'Did your father make a dedication to the goddess here in Eburacum as well?'

Viducius shook his head, 'Only to Jupiter Dolichenus, sovereign of the sun, and to the genius of this place – wherever one may go, it is always wise to propitiate the spirits of the land.'

I nodded, aware by now of the Romans' compulsion to honour, not only the *genius loci*, but any concept or philosophical abstraction that brought itself to their attention. Every crossroads and public well had its little shrine, with the name of the donor prominently displayed, as if without such a label the gods would not know his identity. Even Constantius, who had studied the philosophies of the Greeks that were so close to the theology of Avalon, insisted that his ancestral *lares* and the *penates* that guarded the storeroom of this house must receive their offerings.

'Your man has a good head for business, but he was never meant to spend his life as a trader,' Viducius went on. 'One day the Emperor will call him back to his service. Perhaps then you will cross the sea yourself, and pay your respects to Nehalennia.'

I tried to say something polite, but the odour of the roasted meat was too much for my rebellious stomach. Excusing myself, I made a dash for the atrium and vomited into the terra cotta pot that held the rose tree.

By the time I had finished, I could hear the louder murmur of conversation that meant our dinner guests were leaving. I sat down on one of the stone benches, taking deep breaths of the cool, herb-scented air. It was close to the ending of the month of Maia, and the evening was still pleasant. There was yet enough light for me to appreciate the graceful lines of the two-storeyed wings that formed the long atrium, bordered, on the inside, by a colonnade. The house had been built by the same architect who had designed the nearby palace of the Emperor Severus, and though, like most homes in this part of town, it stretched back from a narrow frontage, it had a classic elegance.

I felt much better, now that my stomach was empty. I hoped, for our guests' sake, it was not anything I had eaten. I washed out my mouth with water from the fountain and leaned back against a column, gazing up at the open sky above the atrium where the young moon was already high.

And as I contemplated the moon, I realized that by now I should have had my courses. My breasts, too, had been unusually tender. I touched them, acutely aware of their new weight and sensitivity, and began to smile, understanding at last what was wrong with me.

A shadow moved among the potted shrubs. I recognized Constantius and stood up to meet him.

'Helena – are you all right?'

'Oh yes . . .' My smile grew broader. 'Were your negotiations successful, my love?' I put my arms about his neck, and he murmured something into my hair as his own tightened around me. For a moment we stood locked together. He smelled of good food and wine and the spicy oil his slave rubbed into his skin at the baths.

'You may congratulate me as well . . .' I whispered into his ear. 'I am about to bring you a greater profit than any trader. Oh, Constantius, I am going to bear your child!'

As spring ripened into summer, and my own body began to ripen with pregnancy, for the first time in my life I tasted true happiness. I even knew it, a gift not always allotted mortal men. I had defied, if not the gods, at least the priestesses of Avalon, and now I carried the child the oracle had foretold! It was not until many years later that I questioned that prophecy, or reflected that in order to obtain the right answer it is necessary first to have asked the correct question.

It was a smiling season, and Eburacum was the queen of the north, where traders from all over the Empire brought their wares.

Merchants prospered here, and shared their good fortune with their gods, from Hercules to Serapis. The square before the basilica was studded with dedicatory altars, set up in payment of vows. I paused sometimes to pay my respects to the *matronae*, the triple mothers who guarded fertility, but otherwise I had little to say to the gods.

With Eldri trotting at my heels, every day I would go out of the gate by the bridge and walk down the path by the Abus River to its confluence with the Fossa, where the boats that came up from the coast to the wharves disputed the right of way with the swans. In the evening, the white walls of the fortress were reflected in the water, and the setting sun overlaid the shining surface with opal and pearl. In the past year the little dog had slowed down, as if age had suddenly come upon her, but these expeditions, when she had a chance to nose through all the fascinating detritus left at the water's edge, were the high point of her day. I hoped that it consoled her a little for losing the freedom of Avalon.

But more than trade goods came in with those ships, and though the western and eastern parts of the Empire might be politically divided, news travelled freely between them. Just after midsummer there came two arrivals which were to alter our lives: a messenger with a letter from the Emperor, and the first case of plague.

We were sitting in the atrium, where I had asked Drusilla to serve the evening meal. I was just beginning to enjoy food again, and our cook delighted in finding ways to tempt my appetite. I was not certain whether it had been diffidence on my part or the lofty scorn of an old family retainer for a native-born concubine on hers that had initially created the distance between us. But my incipient motherhood had clearly elevated my status in her eyes.

I had made my way through several of the appetizers when I noticed that Constantius was not eating. After a year in his company, I could see the man in him as well as the hero. I now knew, for instance, that he was at his best in the mornings and increasingly irritable after sundown; could be honest to the point of tactlessness; and except when he was in bed with me, lived more

119

in his head than his body. What some people perceived as coldness I would have called focus. He could not abide shellfish, and when his interest was engaged in some project, he had to be reminded to eat at all.

'You haven't touched the food,' I said. 'It is very good, and Drusilla will be upset if you do not appreciate her effort.'

He smiled and speared a piece of leek and sausage, but sat with it uneaten in his hand. 'This morning I received a letter.'

Suddenly I felt chilled. 'From Rome?' With an effort I kept my voice calm.

'Not exactly. When he wrote it he was in Nicomedia, though he has undoubtedly moved elsewhere by now.'

I looked at him, thinking. No need to ask who *he* might be. But if the Emperor wanted Constantius's head, surely he would have sent an officer along with his message to take him into custody.

'It was not, I take it, a warrant for your arrest?'

He shook his head. 'Helena, he has offered me a place on his staff! Now I can make a real life for you and our child!'

I stared at him, suppressing my first panicked assumption that he meant to leave me. Constantius had done his best to seem happy, but I knew how much he had missed his military career.

'Can you trust him?'

'I think so,' he said seriously. 'Aurelian has always had the reputation of being honest – a little *too* forthright, in fact. It was because he did not hide his anger that it seemed best for me to go into exile. He is already rid of me – to lure me back just so that he could have me murdered would require uneccessary subtlety.'

Too forthright? I suppressed a smile, understanding why Constantius had been exiled, and why the Emperor might want him back again.

His gaze went inward, calculating, planning, and I realized with a pang that if he was to fulfil the destiny I had foreseen for him, his attention would be inevitably drawn away from me. In that moment I wished passionately that he and I could have been ordinary people, and lived out an ordinary contented life together, here at the edge of the Empire. But even in the fading light there was something luminous about him that drew the eye. If Constantius had been an ordinary man, he would never have come to Avalon.

'With Tetricus still in power in the West, I wouldn't be able to use the posting relays anyway,' he said at last. 'It is just as well, with an entire household to transport. We can do part of the journey by water – make the crossing over the British Sea, and then take a barge up the Rhenus. That will be easier on you . . .' He looked up at me suddenly. 'You *will* come with me, won't you?'

One advantage to not being properly married, I reflected wryly, was that Constantius had no legal right to compel me. But the child in my belly bound me to him – the child, and the memory of a prophecy.

Constantius might have been able to leave at a moment's notice when he was a bachelor, but now there was an entire household to shift, and control of a business to transfer into competent hands. The pewterworks had grown in the year he had been in charge of it. The slaves who did the actual labour were all very skilled, but the volume of production was beyond the capacity of the agent who had handled things before, and it took time to find a suitable manager and break him in.

And in that time, the first case of plague became many. It occurred to me that if the disease had decimated the Emperor's staff the way it was going through Eburacum, Aurelian's invitation might be less a mark of magnanimity than of desperation.

The slave boy Philip fell ill, and despite Drusilla's protests, I nursed him. This disease was characterized by a racking cough and a prolonged high fever. But by wrapping him in cool wet cloths and giving him the infusions of white willow and birch that I had learned to use in Avalon I managed to keep Philip alive until the fever broke at last.

No one else in our household took the illlness, but the long hours of strain had drained my strength. I began to bleed, and after a few hours of wrenching cramps, I miscarried my child.

*　　*　　*

121

The summer, and our preparations to leave Britannia, were drawing to an end when Philip came into my chamber to announce a visitor. I was lying wrapped in a shawl on one of the couches with Eldri at my feet. It was summer, but clouds had moved in from the sea the night before and a damp chill weighted the air. Constantius had gone off to a meeting at the Mithraeum – not a ritual, as those were always conducted by night, but some business connected with the temple. I did not know what rank he had attained in the Mysteries, but his administrative responsibilities suggested it was a high one.

I had been pretending to look at the romance by Longus that Constantius had brought home so that I could brush up on my Greek. It was called *Daphnis and Chloe* and its exotic adventures should have been a potent distraction. But in truth I had been asleep. I slept a great deal – it made it easier to forget that the bright spirit that for a little while had made its home in my womb was gone. As Philip spoke I let the parchment roll up again.

'I will tell her to go away—' said Philip protectively. Since his recovery and my own illness, he had been my shadow, as if we were bound together by our pain.

'No – who is it?' I asked, with a quick glance around the room to make sure it was fit to be seen.

The walls had been painted in tones of warm gold, with festoons of acanthus leaves, and some of the striped rugs the local people wove took the chill off the tiled floor. A basket with wool and a spindle had been left on one of the tables, and several book rolls lay on another, but the room was clean. If the wife of one of Constantius's associates had come to see me, I should make the effort to be polite to her.

'I think she is a seller of herbs. She has a covered basket . . . She said she had a medicine for what ailed you,' he added unhappily. 'I didn't tell her, mistress, I promise you—'

'It is all right, Philip. These people all talk to each other – no doubt she has learned of my trouble from someone in the town.

Perhaps she will have something useful.' I sighed. 'You may as well bring her in.'

In truth, I had little hope of it, but it was bad enough that Constantius must drag a wife halfway across the Empire; he should not have to deal with an invalid. But deep down I understood that for any of the nostrums with which well-meaning people were plying me to work, I had to truly *want* to get well.

In a few moments Philip was back, standing aside as an old woman came into the room. Even before I saw her face, senses long unused were sending a prickle of shock across my skin. As the woman began to unwrap her basket, I realized it had been *recognition*.

One moment she was an old, bent woman in a tattered shawl, like a hundred others who came to sell their wares in the town. In the next, she had gathered the glamour around her, and stood in all her majesty before me, seeming almost too tall for the room. Philip's eyes widened.

'Lady—' Without thinking, I had risen to my feet, head bowed in salutation. Then anger flared through me and I straightened. '*What are you doing here?*'

Philip, bless him, took a protective step forwards. I bit back my next words.

'I could ask the same question of you,' said Ganeda, 'shut away within these walls! We must talk. Come out into the light and the air.'

'I have been ill—' I began, automatically on the defensive.

'Nonsense – you will never be better if you curl up like a lapdog! Come!' Assuming obedience, she started through the door.

Eldri jumped down from the couch, growling faintly, and my lips twitched in the beginnings of a smile. At least in the atrium we would be less likely to be overheard. Motioning to Philip to stay inside, I picked up my shawl and followed her.

'So, what have I done to deserve this honour?' I asked dryly, seating myself on a stone bench and indicating that Ganeda should do the same.

'Stayed alive . . .' the High Priestess answered starkly. 'The plague has come to Avalon.'

I stared at her in horror. How could that be possible? The holy isle was separated from the world.

'A girl from Londinium was sent to us for training. She was ill by the time she arrived. We did not recognize the sickness, and by the time word of the plague had reached us it was too late to stop the contagion. Four of the maidens and six of the senior priestesses have died.'

I licked dry lips. 'Not Dierna?'

Fractionally, Ganeda's grim expression lightened. 'No. My granddaughter is well.' I listened as she gave the names of those who had succumbed, women with whom I had shared the unique intimacy of ritual, some who had cared for and taught me, and others whom I had taught in turn . . . and Aelia.

I shut my eyes against the tears I could feel leaking out beneath my eyelids, drawing hot tracks across my cheeks. If I had not left Avalon I could have nursed her, I thought numbly. I had saved Philip, for whom I felt no more than kindness, surely my love would have kept Aelia in the world. Or perhaps the plague would have taken me too. In that moment both fates seemed equally desirable.

'I thank you for coming to tell me . . .' I said at last.

'Yes, I know you loved her,' the priestess answered tersely, 'but that is not why I have come. You are needed by Avalon.'

At that, my eyes flew open. 'How . . . generous . . .' Through stiff lips I got out the words. 'You are desperate, so now you will welcome me back again!' I rose to my feet, the shawl slipping from my shoulders, and began to pace back and forth along the path. 'No.' I turned to face her. 'You severed my link to Avalon. During that first moon, when the wound was yet bleeding, you might have called me back again. Now there is only a scar.'

Ganeda shrugged impatiently. 'The link can be restored. It is your duty to return.'

'Duty!' I exclaimed. 'What about my duty to Constantius?'

'He has no legal authority over you, nor are you linked in the flesh since you have lost the child—'

'Is that all you can understand?' I cried, hands crossed protectively before my empty womb. 'What of the bonds that link the heart and the soul? *What of the prophecy?*'

'Do you think that justifies your rebellion?' Ganeda sniffed scornfully. 'A simple attack of lust would have been more forgivable, my dear—'

'I don't need your forgiveness! I don't *want* it!' I could hear my voice rising, and fought for control. 'You had the right to banish me, but not to jerk me back and forth like a child's pull-toy on a string. It was you, not I, who cancelled my oaths to Avalon. Nor shall I break the vows I have sworn to Constantius. I lost this child, yes, but there will be another. I have *seen* the babe in my arms!'

Ganeda contemplated me sourly. 'When we planned that ritual, Arganax calculated the movements of the stars. We know what they would have destined for a child conceived in that Beltane ritual. Who knows what the child you bear to Constantius will do? I tell you now that there may come a day when you wish he had never been born!'

I lifted one eyebrow and looked down at her. 'Oh – I see. It is wrong for me to set my will above yours, but you are perfectly justified in setting yours above that of the gods! Did you not teach us yourself that the Fates weave our lives as they will, not as you or I would have it? My son will not be the tool of Avalon!'

'Then you had better pray that he will at least know how to serve the gods!'

'Can you doubt it?' I exclaimed in my pride. 'He will be the son of the Restorer of the Light and a Priestess of Avalon!'

'I do not doubt the gods,' Ganeda answered very quietly, 'but a long life has taught me not to put my trust in men. I wish you well, daughter of my sister.' Leaning heavily on her staff she got to her feet, and now she looked truly old.

'Wait,' I said despite myself. 'You have had a long journey and I have offered you no refreshment—'

But Ganeda only shook her head. 'You shall be troubled no longer, either by me or by Avalon . . .'

I understood her words, but as I watched her go it seemed to me that the memory of this conversation would haunt me for a long time to come.

Whether it was because my healing was complete or Ganeda's challenge had stimulated me, I do not know, but from that time onward my energy began to return. I took a more active part in preparing to move the household, and when, a few days before we were scheduled to take ship for the continent, Constantius mentioned that he had to ride out into the countryside to bid farewell to one of his father's cousins, I asked if I could come along.

As our sailing date approached, I found myself viewing Eburacum with new eyes. I had not been there long enough to think of it as home, but it was nonetheless part of Britannia, which I was so soon to lose. Still, the town itself was Roman, not British, and only along the river could I feel the spirits of the land. In the countryside, I would surely sense them more easily, and be able to make my farewells.

Constantius had rented a two-wheeled cart for the journey, drawn by the faithful red mule. The land here was low and rolling, rising gradually to the west, where mountains lay on the horizon, more sensed through the misty air than seen. On the second day we came to Isurium, the old tribal capital of the Brigantes, which was now a thriving market town. Isurium lay in the bend of the Abus, just before the road crossed the river once more.

Flavius Pollio had retired here after a successful career in Eburacum and was now a magistrate. He was clearly delighted to show off his newly-built townhouse, particularly the mosaic of Romulus and Remus with the wolf which adorned his dining room floor.

'I see that your little dog appreciates fine artwork,' said Pollio, flipping a bit of roast mutton to Eldri, who had flopped down next to the mosaic of the bitch-wolf as if to join the twins in nursing from her dugs. I blushed.

'I am sorry – she always sits at my feet when we dine at home. She must have got out of our bedchamber—'

'No, no – let her stay. We are not formal here.' Pollio smiled at me. 'This is a country of goddesses and queens, and ladies have their privileges . . . Cartimandua, you know—' he added when I looked inquiring. 'She held the Brigante lands for Rome, even when her husband rebelled.' He shook an admonishing finger at Constantius. 'Let that be a warning to you, my boy. A man is only strong when his wife is behind him!'

Now it was Constantius's turn to colour, always a notable sight with his fair skin. 'Then I must be Hercules,' he answered, but I shook my head.

'No, my dear, you are Apollo.'

He blushed even more brightly then, and I laughed.

When the meal was over, the two men retired to Pollio's study to go over the papers Constantius had come to see, and I took Eldri out for a walk through the town. After a day and a half of jolting in the cart and a heavy meal, I needed exercise, and soon found myself striding through the gate towards the open country beyond the town.

Here in the north country the day lingered longer than I was used to. A ground fog was rising from the fields, catching the sunset light so that it looked as if skeins of golden flax had been laid across the land. Soon after I crossed the bridge I saw a cowpath leading away to the west and turned off the road. With Eldri to guide me I had no real fear of being lost, even if the mist should thicken as darkness fell.

My steps slowed as I went on, for at last I had found the solitude I was seeking. The air had the peculiar hush one finds at dawn and at sunset, broken only by the cawing of three crows flying towards their roost, and the distant lowing of a line of cattle moving towards the milking shed and home.

I came to a halt, hands lifting in instinctive adoration. 'Brigantia,

Exalted One, holiness upwelling! Lady of this land, I am soon to fare across the sea. Grant me your blessing, goddess, wherever my wanderings may lead . . .'

The stillness deepened, as if the land itself were listening. Although the air was cooling rapidly, I felt on my cheek a breath of warmth, as if the earth were giving back the last heat of the day. Eldri scampered up the road, more energetic than I had seen her for some time. The white tuft of her tail wagged as it did when she was on an interesting scent, and I hurried to follow her.

I reached the top of the rise just in time to see her white form disappearing into the alder thicket that edged the right side of the road.

'Eldri! Come back here!'

The dog did not turn, and I began to run, calling again. I could see now that a path led through the thicket, barely wide enough for me to force my way through.

The meadow beyond it was hazed with gold. Through the glimmer of ground mist I glimpsed Eldri, trotting towards a pillar of dark stone. I stopped short, staring. There were three of them, spaced across the meadow in an uneven row, about the width of a forum apart. I had seen megaliths before, but never any as tall as these, nearly the height of the columns in the Temple of Serapis's portico.

'Eldri, be careful,' I whispered, but I should have remembered that she was a faerie dog, accustomed to marvels, for she sat down before the nearest, panting, and waited for me to catch up with her.

'Well, my dear one, what have you found?'

The dog cocked her head and then turned back to the pillar, watching it expectantly. Slowly I circled it, out of habit moving sunwise. The stone was very dark, more smoothly finished than was usual for one of the works of the ancients, narrowing slightly towards the top, which was marked by several grooves. Orange and white lichens spread lacy swathes across the dark surface. I understood the purpose of circles like the one upon the Tor, but I could not imagine why these three pillars had been erected here.

Very softly I approached and set my two palms against the stone. The surface was cold, but I let my awareness move out through my hands and into the rock, seeking the flow of energy that rooted it to the earth below.

It was not there. Instead, I felt as if I were holding onto some firm object while floating, except that the thing I held was floating too, as if I had taken a boat to the centre of the Lake to go swimming there. The sensation was rather pleasant, like the dislocation of trance, and for me, starved for over a year of such sensations, far too seductive. I let out my breath in a long sigh, allowing my awareness to sink ever more deeply into the stone.

For a timeless moment I knew nothing but sensation. Then I realized that the sense of vertigo was passing. The pillar was once more solid beneath my hands, but as I straightened and looked around me, I realized that the world had changed.

The pillars stood now on an open plain. The golden light of sunset had transmuted to a silvery radiance that had neither source nor direction, but was quite sufficient to illuminate the radiant figures that danced in a double helix around the stones. Eldri was running with them, darting in and out among the dancers like a puppy, barking with joy.

I stepped away from the pillar to go after her, and found myself being swept into the dance. Strong hands swung me around, fair faces invited me to join in their laughter. Suddenly my feet were light, the last, dragging exhaustion from my miscarriage vanishing. I felt joyous and free as I had not been since . . . I had wandered into Faerie.

In that moment I understood how, coming to the stones at sunset, I had opened a doorway between the worlds. Or perhaps it was Eldri who had led me here. Certainly she was gambolling about as if she had shed the years, ecstatic as one who, having been long exiled, returns at last to her home.

I saw her coming to rest at last at the feet of one of the fair folk who stood before the central pillar, and at last the dance cast me up in the same place. With the blood still racing in my veins from the swift motion, I halted, realizing that the person who waited there was the Faerie Queen.

This time she wore the colours of summer's harvest, a crown of woven wheat and a gown of pale gold. Eldri was nestled in her arms.

'Lady, how come you here?' I stammered, straightening from my bow.

'Where else should I be?' Her low voice was honeyed with amusement.

'But we are far from Avalon—'

'And when you dreamed of it the other night, how far away were you then?' she asked.

'I was there . . . but it was only a dream.'

'Some dreams are more real than what men call reality,' the Lady said tartly. 'The gateways to Faerie are fewer than the Doors of Dream, and yet there are more than most men believe. One has only to know the times and seasons to find the way.'

'Will I be able to find the way from the lands across the sea?' I asked then.

'Even from there, if you have need, though you may see us in another guise in those lands where men know us by other names. Indeed, unless you learn to honour the spirits that dwell in the other lands, you will not prosper there.'

And she began to tell me of the beings I should encounter, names and descriptions that dissolved into my awareness, not to be recalled until many months, or even years, had passed. In the timeless present of Faerie I had no sense of hunger or fatigue, but at last the Lady ceased her instructions, and it occurred to me that I ought to be returning to the human world.

'My thanks to you, Lady. I will endeavour to do as you say. Now let me take the dog, that she may show me the way home.'

The queen shook her head. 'Eldri must stay. She is old, and her spirit is bound to this land. She would not survive your journey. Let her remain – she will be happy with me here.'

In that land where there is no weeping, nonetheless tears came to my eyes. But the gaze of the Faerie Queen was implacable, and it was true that Eldri looked very happy, nestled in her arms. For the last time, I scratched behind those silky ears. Then I let my hand fall.

'How shall I go back, then?' I asked.

'You have only to walk widdershins around the stone.'

I began to move, and with each step the light faded until I found myself standing in the meadow in the gathering darkness, alone.

When I reached the bridge I saw torches bobbing along the main road and found that Constantius had come out to look for me. I told him only that Eldri had run away, and I had been searching for her. He knew how I had loved the dog, and so my sorrow needed no explanation. And that night I found comfort in the shelter of his arms.

A week later, we were on one of Viducius's ships, bound for the mouth of the Rhenus and Germania.

Part II

THE WAY TO POWER

CHAPTER EIGHT

AD 271–2

To travel on the sea is to move outside time. One sits, with neither tasks nor duties, contemplating the dim grey ribbon of shoreline on the horizon, and the ever-changing, undulant landscape of the sea. The scene in the boat's wake alters as swiftly as the view from the prow, so there is no way to recognize where one has been, and after a time the succession of ridges and valleys begins to repeat itself, so that one wonders if any progress has been made at all.

Still, after a week of travel I could sense a new warmth in the air, and the land wind brought me a scent that I recognized from childhood. Since we had left Eburacum the weather had been fair, with a following wind. The big trading ship wallowed doggedly southward, not even needing to anchor when night fell. But now we were angling towards the shore. I put my arms around the curving prow, leaning out over the water.

'You look like the figureheads I have seen on some Greek vessels,' said Constantius behind me. He seemed younger and more sturdy somehow than I remembered, and I realized for the first time just how much it meant to him to be returning to his real life once more. Thoughtfully, I let him assist me back to the deck.

'What is that?' I gestured towards the headland, where the grey-green waters of a great river flowed steadily down to mingle with the blue sea.

'It is the Tamesis,' said Constantius, beside me. I turned to gaze

135

with new interest at the low, rolling country above the line of sandspits.

'I played on that beach when I was a little child, while my father inspected the watchtower on the point,' I replied. 'I remember wondering where the passing ships were going.'

'And now you are going with them,' Constantius smiled.

I nodded, leaning against his solid strength. There was no need to burden him with my sudden longing to go home. It was, in any case, impossible. My father was dead, and one of my brothers as well. The other was serving with the false emperor Tetricus in Gallia. In the palace at Camulodunum a distant cousin ruled now. The home of my childhood was gone as surely as the little girl who had once gathered shells on that sandy shore.

I clutched at the rail as the ship leaned into the wind that blew down the river, tacking across its mouth towards the narrow channel between the isle of Tanatus and Cantium. We spent two nights at an inn, while Viducius supervised the loading of additional cargo, but before I had quite got my land-legs back we were afloat once more.

Now, we had not even a glimpse of shoreline to show us our direction, only the sun and the stars, when the clouds parted and we could see them. But I began to wonder if the senses that Ganeda had stripped from me were returning, for I found that even when the mists surrounded us I could feel Britannia behind us, and as the hours passed, I began to sense a new energy ahead. On the third day, as the sea-mist dissipated in the morning sun, I saw ahead a horizon smudged with islets, the many-branched channels of the delta of the Rhenus that guarded the way to Germania Inferior.

Our destination was Ganuenta, where the River Scaldis flowed into the delta of the Rhenus, a major transfer point for shipping from the continent to Britannia. While Constantius made arrangements for our transport up the Rhenus, I was free to explore the marketplace that adjoined the port, the faithful Philip at my side. Like all frontiers, it was an amalgam of cultures, where the gutturals of the Germanic tongues mingled with the sonority of Latin. Since the days when Arminius destroyed Varus and his legion, the Rhenus had been the border between Free Germania and the Empire. But for over a century it had been a peaceful boundary, and the folk who brought their furs and their cattle and their cheeses across the river to market seemed little different from the tribes on the Roman side.

I was looking at wood carvings at one of the market stalls when someone called my name. Turning, I recognized Viducius, got up in a toga with a basket of apples under his arm.

'Are you going to a party?' I asked, indicating the fruit.

'No, although I will see a noble lady – I am on my way to the temple of Nehalennia to give thanks for the safe voyage. You would be welcome to accompany me.'

'I would like that. Philip, you must find Constantius and tell him where I have gone. Viducius will escort me home.'

Philip eyed the trader a little suspiciously, but after all, we had just spent an entire sea voyage in his company. As the boy trotted off, Viducius offered me his arm.

The temple was located on the rising ground at the northern end of the island, a square cloister surrounding the central shrine, whose tower was just visible above it. In between the votive altars that lined the path, vendors had set up stalls offering copper medals with images of dogs or the figure of the goddess, more apples for offerings, and wine and fried breads and sausages for hungry worshippers. The fruit Viducius was carrying was much better than anything for sale here, and we swept past disdainfully and passed through the entryway into the cobbled courtyard.

I had seen finer temples, but there was a comfortable informality about this one, with its red-tiled roof and cream-coloured walls. There were more altars here – Viducius paused to show me the one his father Placidus had dedicated long ago. Then he handed an aureus to the priestess, and pulled the end of his toga up to cover his head as we entered the sanctuary, lit by arched windows high in the tower. On a plinth in the centre of the chamber stood

137

the image of the goddess, carved from some warm reddish stone. She held a ship in her hands, but a basket of apples was carved at her feet and beside it a dog that looked so much like Eldri that tears came to my eyes.

When I could see again, the trader was setting his apples down before the plinth. The image of the Goddess gazed serenely past him, her hair drawn back into a simple knot, her draperies falling in graceful folds. Meeting that carven gaze, I felt a shiver of recognition, and put back my veil to bare the crescent moon upon my brow.

Nehalennia . . . Elen . . . Elen of the Ways . . . Lady, in a strange land I find you! Guard and guide me on the road I must travel now . . .

For a moment then, my inner silence overwhelmed all outside sound. In that hush, I heard, not a voice, but the sound of water flowing from a pool. It sounded like the Blood Spring at Avalon, and it came to me then that all the waters of the world were connected, and where there was water, the power of the Goddess flowed.

Someone touched my arm. I blinked and saw Viducius, his prayers completed. The priestess of the shrine was waiting to escort us out. Without intention, words came to me: 'Where is the spring?'

She looked at me in surprise, then her gaze moved to the crescent on my brow and she nodded with the respect due a colleague.

Motioning to Viducius to stay where he was, she led me around the image to an opening in the floor. Carefully I followed the woman down the wooden steps into the crypt beneath the sanctuary, walled with raw stone and smelling of damp. The flickering light of oil lamps glinted from plaques and images fixed to the walls and gleamed in slow-moving whorls from the dark surface of the pool.

'The water of the Rhenus is brackish where it mingles with the sea,' she said softly, 'but this spring is always pure and good. Which goddess do you serve?'

'Elen of the Ways,' I answered her, 'who may be the face your Lady wears in Britannia. She has guided me here. I have no gold, but I will offer this bracelet of British jet if I may.' I worked the round bangle over my hand and let it fall into the hidden depths of the spring. The reflections scattered in a burst of spangles as it hit the water, then came together once more in a bright swirl.

'Nehalennia accepts your offering . . .' the priestess said softly. 'May your journey be blessed.'

The transport Constantius had found for us was a barge laden with salt fish and hides that laboured upriver by the efforts of the twenty slaves who toiled at the oars. It stopped often to take on more cargo, but the delays allowed me gradually to gain a sense of this new land into which I was travelling. At Ulpia Traiana, set at the edge of the river as it meandered through the gently-rolling countryside, we were given dinner by the commander of the fortress. In theory he served Tetricus, but information from the eastern empire also flowed down the river, and Constantius was eager for news.

Thus we heard of the bitter victory at Mons Gessax in Thracia, where the Romans had encircled the last of the fleeing Goths. But the ineptitude of the commander, who had not had the wit to use his heavy cavalry to press his advantage, had cost many lives. Aurelian was now continuing his operations against the Vandals in Dacia. At least it appeared that the barbarian threat had been dealt with, for a time.

By the time we boarded our boat once more a new passenger had joined us. He was called Father Clemens, a round little priest of the Christian cult who had been sent by the Bishop of Rome to visit the congregations in the western lands. I observed him with some curiosity, for apart from the monks of Inis Witrin, he was the first priest of his faith whom I had seen.

'Oh yes, there are Christians in Eburacum,' he assured us when Constantius mentioned our point of departure. 'A small congregation, to be sure, meeting in a house-church belonging to a virtuous widow, but they are strong in the faith.' Father Clemens eyed us hopefully, reminding me painfully of Eldri when she thought I might throw her a scrap.

Constantius shook his head, smiling. 'Nay, I serve the Soldiers' God, and the eternal light of the sun, but there is much good to be found in your belief. Your churches care for the unfortunate and the needy, I have heard.'

'God has so commanded us,' he said simply. 'And what of you, lady? Have you heard the good Word?'

'There was a community of Christians near the place where I grew up,' I said carefully. 'But I follow Elen of the Ways.'

Father Clemens shook his head. 'It is the Christos who is the Truth, the Way and the Life,' he said gently. 'All others lead to damnation. I will pray for you.'

I stiffened, but Constantius smiled. 'The prayers of a man of good will are always welcome.' He took my arm and drew me away.

'I am a priestess of the Goddess!' I hissed when we had reached the prow. 'Why should he pray for me?'

'He means well,' answered Constantius. 'Some of his fellow-believers would damn us both, without waiting for their god to take a hand.'

I shook my head. The monk, whoever he had been, who had appeared to me at Inis Witrin, had spoken otherwise. Still, in Eburacum I had met many pagans who dealt only in the forms and ceremonies of their religion. I wondered if among the Christians, there was also a difference between the common folk and those who understood the Mysteries.

Constantius put his arm around me and I leaned against him, watching the long vistas of plain and forest, edged by marsh or mudflat or sandy strand, slide by. One side was Roman, the other, German, but I could not see much difference between them. I had looked at the maps the Romans made in an attempt to define their territory, but the land knew no such divisions. For a moment I hovered on the edge of some crucial understanding. Then Constantius turned his head and kissed me, and in the flood of sensation that followed, the moment was lost.

Our journey halted again at Colonia Agrippinensis, a flourishing city built on an eminence above the Rhenus. There was more news here – the Emperor had pursued the Goths all the way across the Danuvius and destroyed them in another great battle, killing their king, Cannabaudes, and five thousand of their warriors. The Senate had voted him the title of Gothicus Maximus and a Triumph. But despite his victory, Aurelian had apparently decided that Dacia north of the river was indefensible, and was pulling the limits of the Empire back to the Danuvius.

'And I can't say but that he has good reason,' said the centurion we were talking to, 'just as when he abandoned the *agri decumates* south of here and withdrew all the troops back to the Rhenus. Rivers make nice clear borders. Maybe Aurelian thinks the barbarians will be too busy fighting each other to trouble us. But it galls, just the same, when I think of all the blood we shed to hold that land.'

Constantius had grown very silent. 'I was born in Dacia Ripensis. Strange to think that it will become the frontier. I suppose the Goths will be fighting what's left of the Carpi, the Bastarnae and the Vandals for it now.'

'Not the Vandals,' corrected the centurion. 'Aurelian has brought them in as federates and enlisted them as auxiliaries.'

Constantius frowned thoughtfully. 'It may work; the gods know the Germans breed good fighting men.'

The barge took us as far as Borbetomagus. There, we joined a party of traders who were taking their pack mules along the Nicer and through the hills to the Danuvius. The farther we travelled the stronger my awareness of the density of the land around us became. In all my life I had never lived more than a day's journey from the ocean, but now solid earth surrounded me, and even the mighty rivers were no more than the blood flowing through her veins.

These lands might have been abandoned by the legions, but they had not yet reverted to barbarian rule. The villas and farmsteads the Romans had carved out of the forest still prospered, and we were glad of their hospitality. And for me, this leisurely journey through Germania brought the unexpected benefit of my husband's

141

undivided attention. When he first joined the army Constantius had been posted to the German *limes* and knew them well. To hear his stories of garrison and battlefield gave me a picture of who he truly was that was to stand me in good stead thereafter.

But with each league we travelled my own past fell farther behind me. I became Julia Helena only and entirely, and memories of that Eilan who had been a priestess of Avalon dwindled until they had no more substance than a dream.

A moon of travel brought us to the upper reaches of the Danuvius, where we found another boat that would take us downstream. Here the great river flowed east between the Suevi hills and the lowlands of Rhaetia. When the autumn haze cleared, we could see the snow-clad Alpes glittering on the southern horizon, drawing gradually closer and lower until the river passed through a gap in the hills and presently made a sharp turn southward through the broad Pannonian plain.

This river was in fact far longer than the Rhenus, but going with the current, we moved faster. Presently we turned eastward once more, heading, so Constantius told me, towards the Euxine Sea. To the south lay the lands of Graecia of which Corinthius had told me so many stories, to the north, Scythia and the unknown. The land itself told me that we had journeyed far indeed. As the season advanced towards winter, cold winds blew down from the mountains, but the days were not appreciably shortened, and the trees and plants were different from the ones I knew.

I had thought that we would stay with the boat all the way to the Euxine, but when we stopped at Singidunum, Constantius reported to the fort's commander and found there orders that had been waiting in case he should come that way. The Emperor, having settled the barbarians, was preparing to march on Palmyra, where Zenobia had attempted to wrest her desert kingdom free from Roman rule.

Aurelian wanted Constantius, and he wanted him now. Authorization for posthorses was therefore included, and chits for lodging in the government mansios along the way. Leaving Philip and Drusilla to follow with our goods, Constantius and I set out by horseback along the good military road that led through Moesia and Thracia to Byzantium. From there, a ferry took us across the Straits of Marmara to the province of Bithynia, and the city of Nicomedia, where the Emperor and his court were now in residence.

'Wait until summer – this can be a beautiful land,' said Constantius. His tone was bracing, as if I were a homesick recruit. It was not so far from the truth, I thought, tucking my heavy shawl more firmly around me. We had been here for over four months, much of which Constantius had spent riding back and forth between Drepanum and Nicomedia, where the Emperor was preparing for the Palmyran campaign. Zenobia, who called herself Queen of the East, had laid claim not only to her native Syria, but to Egypt and parts of the province of Asia as well. In another moon, the army being sent to punish her would be gone.

'This is February,' I reminded him. Though we were too near to the straits for snow, the chill had settled in my bones. The villa he had rented for me was damp and draughty – a house built by people who refused to believe it would ever get cold. Not surprising, I thought glumly, since the town of Drepanum, just down the coast from Nicomedia and across the strait from Byzantium, was a popular resort to which the court escaped during the summer heat. In winter, it had only the spa with its hot springs to recommend it.

'Britannia is colder—' he began, the plates of his cuirass creaking as he turned. I had not yet become accustomed to how he looked in uniform, but it was clear to me that the merchant he had played in Eburacum was only half the man Constantius was meant to be.

'In Britannia,' I retorted, 'they build their houses to keep *out* the cold!'

'It's true that it was summer when I was here before,' he capitulated, looking through the opened shutters at the rain that was dimpling the waters of the lily pool in the atrium. For most of the past two months it had rained. He turned to me again, suddenly serious.

'Helena, did I do wrong to take you from your homeland and drag you all the way here? I was so accustomed to the army, you see, and all the officers' wives who have travelled with them from post to post all over the Empire, I never thought that you were not bred up to this kind of life, and might . . . not . . .' He shrugged helplessly, his eyes fixed on my face.

I swallowed, searching for words. 'My love, you must not mind my complaining. Don't you understand? *You* are my home now.'

His bleak gaze brightened, like the sun breaking through clouds. I had a moment to admire him, then he took me in his arms, carefully, for we had already learned that his armour could leave bruises, and for the moment, I was not cold any more.

'I must go,' he said at last, murmuring the words into my hair.

'I know . . .' Reluctantly I stepped away from his warmth, trying not to remember how soon he would be gone indeed, on the Palmyran campaign. The overlapping plates of the cuirass scraped slightly as he bent to pick up his heavy coat. I noted with sour satisfaction that it was a *byrrus*, the hairy, hooded kind we made in Britannia.

'By the time you reach the city, you will be wet through,' I told him, not entirely sympathetically.

'I'm used to it,' he grinned back at me, and I realized that not only was this true, but that he actually *liked* confronting the weather.

I accompanied him to the entry and opened the door. Our house was halfway up the hill above the main part of the town. Tile roofs and the marble columns of the forum gleamed through drifting veils of rain. Philip was holding Constantius's horse, an old woollen mantle drawn over his head against the rain.

'I am sorry, lad – I did not mean to keep you waiting!' Constantius reached for the reins. As he started to mount, there was a squeak, and the horse, a skittish chestnut gelding, tossed its head and swung away. Constantius wrestled it down, and Philip made a

144

step with his laced hands so that his master could swing a leg over the beast and settle himself between the horns of the military saddle.

But I was no longer watching. That odd squeaking noise had come again, or perhaps it was a whimper. My searching gaze fixed on a pile of debris swept against the corner of the wall by the overflow from the gutter. Had it moved, or was it only the wind? I picked up a twig blown down by the storm and bent to poke at the pile. It quivered, and suddenly I was staring down at a pair of bright black eyes.

'Helena, take care! It might be dangerous!' Constantius nudged the horse closer. From the rubbish came a faint but unmistakable growl. Bending closer, the debris proved to be a sodden huddle of hair, as if someone had lost a fur cap in the rain.

'It's a puppy!' I exclaimed, as a black button of a nose appeared beneath the eyes. 'The poor thing!'

'Looks like a drowned rat to me,' muttered Philip, but he was already pulling off his wool mantle and thrusting it at me to keep me from using my own shawl.

Gently, I scraped away the leaves and mud in which the puppy was tangled and lifted it out. There was no hint of warmth beneath my hand: I would have thought it dead had it not been for the desperate regard of those bright eyes. Murmuring softly, I cradled it against my breast, and imperceptibly, an emptiness that had been there since I lost Eldri began to fill.

'Be careful,' said Constantius. 'It may be sick, and it will certainly have fleas.'

'Oh yes,' I answered, though in truth, I wondered if even a flea would be interested in the skin and bone beneath my hands. But I could feel the flutter of a heartbeat. 'I will give this poor mite every care.'

'I will be going, then,' said Constantius as the horse sidled nervously.

'Yes, of course.' I looked up at him, and something that had been strained in his face eased. His returning smile was like a caress.

145

Then he pulled up the hood of his *byrrus*, reined the horse around, and put it into a splashing trot down the road.

When he had gone, I settled the puppy securely against my breast and carried him inside. A bath and a good meal improved his looks, though his breeding was as mixed as the population of the Empire. His ears were floppy, his coat a mixture of black and white, and there was a hint of a plume to his tail. The size of his paws suggested that if early starvation had not stunted him, he might grow to be a big dog indeed.

The eagerness with which he lapped up the bowl of broth Drusilla prepared for him demonstrated a commendable will to live.

'What will you call him?' asked Philip, less dubious now that the dog was clean.

'I was thinking of "Hylas", after the lover of Heracles whom the nymphs drowned in the pool. In these parts that is a popular tale.' Indeed, it was in Chios, a few days' journey to the east along the coast, that Hylas was supposed to have been lost when the Argonauts stopped there on their way to capture the Golden Fleece.

'He certainly looks as if *someone* tried to drown him,' the boy agreed, and so the dog was named.

That night Hylas slept in my chamber, and although my bed was still empty, it comforted my heart a little then and during the lonely months after Constantius had followed the Emperor southward to Syria to once more hear the patter of paws at my heels.

Constantius had been right about the weather. With summer, the sun shone triumphant from a cloudless sky and baked the grass on the hills to gold. The windows that had admitted so many draughts in February were thrown open to let in the sea breeze in the morning, and the wind off the lake in the afternoon. The local people said it was quite reasonable for the season, but after the mists of Britannia, I found the heat oppressive indeed.

By day, I dressed in the sheerest of gauzes and lay beneath a linen shade by the fountain in the atrium, Hylas panting by my side. At night I sometimes walked by the lake, the dog scampering ahead of me and Philip, clutching a cudgel and glaring suspiciously around him, a step behind. From time to time I would receive a letter from Constantius, who was marching, in armour, through country that made Drepanum sound as cool as Britannia by comparison. When we heard of the victory at Ancyra, the magistrates had ordered a great bonfire lit in the forum, and again after the good news from Antiochia.

With summer, a number of noble families from Nicomedia had transferred their households to Drepanum. Several of the women also had husbands who were with the Emperor, but we had little in common. Drusilla, who picked up all sorts of gossip at the market, told me that the word was going about that I was not Constantius's wife, but a girl he had found at an inn and made his concubine, and I understood why the ladies had been so distant. She was full of indignation, but I could hardly resent an opinion that from the legal point of view was true. There had been no marriage contract, no exchange of gifts or alliance of relatives to solemnize our union, only the blessing of the gods.

And in truth, I was glad to be relieved of social obligations, for with the nobles had come some of the Emperor's philosophers, and one of them had a skinny young apprentice called Sopater, who in exchange for what I could spare from the housekeeping money and a taste of Drusilla's cooking, was willing to tutor me.

The Greek I had learned as a child was rusty, and in this country I needed the common tongue to speak with tradesmen, and the more rarefied language of the philosophers to read the works of Porphyry and others who were making such a stir.

Sopater was both young and earnest, but once he relaxed sufficiently to look me in the face at our lessons, we got on well, and if during those long summer days it was too hot to move my body, at least my mind was active. I needed the distraction; for after the great battle at Emesa, I had received no word from Constantius, or of him, at all.

But just at dusk one evening shortly after midsummer, when I had finished my bath and was considering a walk by the lakeside, I heard a commotion outside, and above Hylas's furious barking, a voice that made the breath catch in my throat. I dragged the nearest garment over my head, and with tousled hair and the sheer tunica unbelted, ran out into the entry.

In the light of the hanging lamp I saw Constantius, fined down by the campaign to bone and muscle, his hair bleached to pale gold and his skin brick-red from the sun. He was alive! Only in that moment did I admit to myself how deeply I had feared his death in those desert sands. From the look on his face I realized that with the light behind me I might as well have been naked. But what I saw in his gaze was something more than desire, it was awe.

'*Domina et dea* . . .' he whispered, which was a title even the Empress did not claim, and yet I understood, for in that moment I saw him, as I had seen him at that Beltane on Avalon, as the god.

I motioned to the servants to leave us, and then, holding out my hand, drew him after me into our bedchamber. Hylas, after the first flurry of barking, had fallen silent; perhaps he had recognized Constantius's scent as belonging to this room. As we moved towards the bed, I heard him flop down before the door.

After that I ceased to think about the dog or anything else beyond my own need for the man in my arms.

We came together in that first frantic encounter like wanderers in the desert who finding an oasis, were desperate to assuage our thirst. Struggling with each other's garments, we fell upon the bed. Later, I was to find my tunica in a corner, torn in two. When we had shuddered to completion, I held Constantius in my arms, waiting until his galloping heartbeat slowed.

'Was the fighting very bad?' I asked as I helped him to remove the remainder of his clothing.

Constantius sighed. 'The Arabs plagued us all the way through Syria, picking off men with arrows, trying to raid the baggage train. When we reached Palmyra, Zenobia was ready for us. We couldn't take the place by assault – the Emperor himself was wounded – so we had to sit down to a siege. Aurelian offered terms, but she thought the Persians would save her. Only their king, Sapor, died, and they were too busy fighting each other to worry about Rome. Then Probus finished dealing with Egypt and came to reinforce us. It was all over, and Zenobia knew it. She tried to flee, but we caught her and brought her back in chains.'

'So you won – you should be triumphant,' I commented, reminded of Boudicca, and repressing my instinctive sympathy.

He shook his head, stretching out and settling me with my head pillowed on his arm. 'Zenobia had sworn to kill herself if captured, but she panicked, put all the blame on Longinus and the other men who served her. And Aurelian executed them. So she will walk in his Triumph after all . . . I understand why they had to die,' he added after a moment had passed, 'but it left a bad taste all the same. At least the Emperor . . . did not appear to enjoy it.'

Oh my poor love, I thought, turning to cradle his head against my breast, *you are tempered too finely to be used for this butchery.*

'When we had won the city . . . the other officers took women,' he whispered then. 'I could not do it, not with all that death around.'

I tightened my grip, unreasonably pleased, whatever the reason, that he had been faithful. It was not something I had a right to ask, but it certainly, I thought with secret amusement, explained the intensity of his need.

'You are life . . .' murmured Constantius.

His lips brushed one nipple. I could feel both of them harden at his touch, and the rekindling of the fire between my thighs.

'I have seen so much killing . . . let me make life in you . . .'

His hands moved upon my body with a deliberation and a need more compelling than his first compulsion, and I found myself opening to his touch more deeply than ever before. At the ultimate moment he rose above me and I saw his features by firelight, focused in ecstasy.

'The sun!' he gasped. 'The sun shines at midnight!'

At that moment my own completion came upon me, and I could not tell him that it was only the light of the bonfire they had kindled to celebrate the Emperor's victory.

In the silent hour before dawn, the only time, at this season, that it was truly cool, I rose to relieve myself. When I returned from the privy, I stood for a time, gazing out of the window and enjoying the touch of the chill air on my bare skin. The fire in the forum had burned out, and sleep, that next to death was the greatest of conquerors, had overwhelmed the revellers. Even Hylas, who had roused when I did, had lain down again.

A sound from the bed made me turn. Constantius was clutching at the bedclothes, groaning. As I watched, tears squeezed from beneath his tight-shut eyelids and began to roll down his cheeks. I hurried back and lay down beside him, winding him in my arms. Once, I thought, I had been the one who had the nightmares, but since I left Avalon I did not dream any more.

'It's all right,' I murmured, knowing it was the tone that would reach him, not the words. 'You are all right now – I am here . . .'

'The sun shines at midnight—' he groaned. 'The temple burns! Apollo! Apollo is weeping!'

I soothed him, wondering if this was something he had seen on the campaign. The Emperor's personal deity was the sun-god – I could not believe he would willingly destroy a sanctuary, but I had heard that in warfare the destruction sometimes got out of hand.

'Hush, my love, and open your eyes – it is morning, do you see? Apollo is driving his chariot above the rim of the world—'

With lips and hands I set out to awaken him, and was rewarded presently when he quickened to my touch once more. This time our loving was slow and sweet. By the time we had finished, Constantius was awake once more, and smiling.

'Ah, my queen, I have brought gifts for you—' Naked, he padded over to the bag that someone had brought while we slept and set just inside the door. 'I meant to array you in this for our first night back together, but you are more beautiful clad only in your night-dark hair . . .'

He rummaged in the bag, and pulled out something wrapped in unbleached linen. As the rough cloth fell away, a blaze of colour

150

smote the eye. Constantius shook out a silk chiton dyed the true, imperial purple, and held it out to me.

'My love, it is too splendid!' I exclaimed, but I took the garment, wondering at the fine weave of the fabric, and slipped it over my head. I shivered as the silk caressed my skin and swayed, feeling the soft folds mould themselves to my body.

'By the gods, purple becomes you!' he exclaimed, his glance kindling.

'But I can never wear it,' I reminded him.

'Not outside,' he agreed, 'but in our bedchamber you are my Empress and my Queen!'

And in bed or out, you, my beloved, are my Emperor! I thought, admiring the powerful balance of his naked body, but even here I dared not speak those words aloud.

Constantius put his arm around me and drew me to the east-facing window. I sighed, replete with loving, feeling in my body a sense of fulfilment I had not known before. Surely, I thought then, I must come away from such a night as this had been with child.

Together we stood watching as the sun, like a victorious emperor, lifted above the horizon and banished night's mysteries from the world.

CHAPTER NINE

AD 272

In Britannia, September had been a month of misty sunshine, but the forum at Naissus blazed with light beneath a brilliant blue sky. From the shade of the awning that had been raised to shelter the families of the imperial officers I could feel the waves of heat rising from the cobbles of the square. I had hoped, when Constantius told me of his new posting, that the plains that bordered the Danuvius in Dacia, being farther north, would be cooler than Bithynia, but in the summer, this inland city seemed even hotter than Drepanum, which had at least sometimes got a breeze from the sea. I could feel perspiration gathering beneath the fillet I wore to hide the crescent moon tattooed upon my brow. I took a deep breath, hoping I would not faint. Three months into pregnancy, I was still sick in the mornings and at intervals throughout the day.

Perhaps it was hunger that was making me feel so light-headed, I thought then, for I had not dared to eat before the ceremony, or perhaps it was the heavy scent of the incense. Two priests swung censers beside the altar; with each swing, more smoke swirled into the air. The haze drifted like a gauzy curtain before the columns that formed the western side of the square where the ground fell away towards the River Navissus. Beyond the tiled rooftops, a gleam of water, fields gold with stubble and low blue hills wavered in the heated air, insubstantial as a dream.

'Are you unwell?' Someone spoke nearby.

I blinked, and focused on the bony, dark face of the woman beside me. With an effort I remembered that she was called Vitellia, the wife of one of Constantius's fellow *Protectores*.

'I will be,' I answered, flushing. 'I'm not ill, it's just—' I felt myself colouring agin.

'Ah, of course. I have borne four children, and I was sick as a hound-bitch with three of them – not that dogs generally have morning sickness—' she added, large teeth showing as she smiled. 'The first one I bore when we were stationed in Argentorate, the second and the third in Alexandria, and my last boy was born in Londinium.'

I gazed at her in respect. She had followed the Eagles all over the Empire. 'I come from Britannia . . .' I said then.

'I liked it,' Vitellia gave a decisive nod, setting her earrings swinging. A little golden fish winked from her breast, suspended from a fine chain. 'We still have a house there, and perhaps we'll return when my husband retires.'

The procession was almost at an end. The flute players had spread out to one side of the altar, and the six maidens, having scattered their flowers, took up their position on the other. The priestess who walked behind them halted before the altar and cast a handful of barley into the fire that burned there, calling on Vesta, who lived in the flame.

'I had heard you were from the Isle,' said Vitellia. 'Your man came back from exile there and did so well in the Syrian campaign he's been made a tribune.'

I nodded, appreciating her matter-of-fact acceptance of my some-what ambiguous marital status. Since Constantius's promotion, some of the women who had pointedly ignored me before had become gushingly respectful, but Vitellia struck me as the sort of woman who would behave the same to a fish-wife as to an empress. The thought turned my gaze back to the forum.

The Emperor presided from a shaded dais behind the altar, with his senior officers around him. Seated on his throne, Aurelian looked like the statue of a god, but when Constantius presented me I had been surprised to find him a small man, with thinning hair and tired eyes.

Automatically, my gaze moved to the end of the line where Constantius himself was standing, just at the edge of the shade. When he moved his breastplate caught the sunlight. I blinked – for a moment he had seemed to stand in an aureole of light. But of course, I thought, smiling, he always looked like a god to me. The armour flashed again as he straightened, and I saw that the priests were coming through the archway with the sacrificial bull. The animal was white, its horns and neck garlanded with flowers. It moved slowly; no doubt it had been drugged to prevent any inauspicious struggle from marring the ceremony. The procession came to a halt before the altar and the priest began to intone the prayers. The bull stilled, its head drooping as if the droning incantation had been a sleep spell.

A second priest moved forward, hard muscle bunching in his arms as he lifted the pole-axe. There was a moment of stillness, then it blurred downward. The resounding 'thunk' as it struck the animal's skull reverberated from the columns. But the ox was already sinking to its knees. As it fell, one priest caught its horns, holding them long enough for the other to plunge the knife into the beast's throat and jerk crossways.

Blood rolled across the stones in a red tide. Several of the men who were watching averted their eyes, crossing themselves in the Christian sign against evil. *It is only evil for the bull*, I thought ruefully, *or perhaps not even for him, if he consented to be the offering.* Surely the Christians, who worshipped a sacrificed god, knew that death could be holy. It seemed rather small-minded of them to deny that sanctity to all religions but their own.

Holy it might be, but as the sickly-sweet scent of blood overwhelmed the incense on the air I felt my gorge rise. I drew my veil across my face, and sat very still, breathing carefully. It would be impolitic as well as unlucky to disgrace myself at the ceremony. A pungent whiff of herbs cleared my head and I opened my eyes.

Vitellia was holding out a spray of lavender and rosemary. I took another deep breath and thanked her.

'Is it your first child?'

'The first that I have carried this long,' I answered.

'May God's Holy Mother bless you then, and bring you safe to term,' said Vitellia, looking back towards the forum with a frown.

It was not a scene to enjoy, I thought, but I did not quite understand her disapproval. I tried to remember if her husband had been one of the men who crossed himself when the bull was killed.

The beast had mostly bled out by this time, and the lesser priests were sluicing the blood towards the gutters. The others had the body cavity open and had set the liver in a silver bowl so that the haruspex could examine it. Even the Emperor was leaning forward to listen to his muttering.

For me, trained in the oracular tradition of Avalon, augury by entrails had always seemed a clumsy method of divination. When the mind had been properly prepared, the flight of a bird or the fall of a leaf could be an omen, triggering the insights of prophecy. At least the bull had been killed cleanly and with reverence. When we feasted on its flesh that night, we would accept our own place in the cycle of life and death, even as we shared in its blessing. I placed my hand on my belly, just beginning to harden as the child within me grew.

The haruspex wiped his fingers on a linen towel and turned towards the dais.

'All honour to the Emperor, favoured of the gods—' he declaimed. 'The Shining Ones have spoken. The winter that is coming will be a mild one. If you take the field, you will have victory over your enemies.'

I only realized how tense the crowd had been when I heard the murmur of comment. Several strong men were dragging the bull away to be cooked for the feast. The maidens came forwards, lifting their arms to the heavens and began to sing.

'*Hail, Thou resplendent and sovereign sun,*
Adore we Thy glory, oh Thou holy one!
So help us and heal us, until as above,
Below, all is beauty and all know Thy love . . .'

I felt the tears start in my eyes as the pure sweet voices intertwined, remembering how I used to sing with the other maidens on Avalon. It had been a long time since I had called upon the Goddess, but the singing awakened in me a longing I had almost forgotten. The chant was for Apollo, or whatever name they used for the sun-god in the Danuvian lands. It was the custom for each emperor to exalt the deity who was his patron, but it was said that Aurelian wished to go further, and proclaim the sun to be the visible emblem of a single, all-powerful being who was the highest god of all.

At Avalon also I had encountered such an idea, though it was the Great Goddess whom we saw as Mother of everything. But I had been taught also that any honest impulse of worship will find the Source behind all images, no matter what name is called, and so I set my hands upon my belly and closed my eyes and sent forth a plea that I might carry this child the full term and bear it healthy and alive.

'Come, Lady Helena,' said Vitellia. 'The ceremony is over, and you won't want to keep your lord waiting. They say that Constantius is a man with a future. You must make a good impression at the celebration.'

I had hoped that Vitellia and I might be seated near each other at the banquet, but Constantius escorted me to a couch just below the dais, while she and her husband remained near the back of the room. She had been correct, I thought as I stretched out and spread my skirts modestly over my ankles and watched him speaking with the Emperor. The fact that my husband had won Aurelian's favour was becoming clear. I tried to ignore the murmur of speculation from the women nearby. Constantius would not have brought me here without the blessing of Aurelian, and what the Emperor approved, no gossiping woman, however exalted her status, might deny.

On the next couch lay one of the largest men I had ever seen. Obviously he was a German, from his flaxen hair to his cross-gartered breeches, with muscular arms showing beneath the short-sleeved tunic. But around his neck was a golden torque, and the bands on his upper arms and wrists were also gold.

'You are Lady Helena, yes?' he asked. I flushed, realizing he had caught me watching him, but he did not seem to mind. With such a physique, I thought then, he must be accustomed to attracting attention. 'Constantius says much about you.' His accent was guttural, but he spoke good enough Latin, by which I concluded that he had served with the legions for some time.

'You were on the campaign?'

'In the desert—' he grimaced, holding out one brawny arm, where the fair skin had been baked nearly to the colour of brick by the sun.

I nodded in understanding. I had learned quickly that it was not modesty but necessity that impelled women to go veiled when they walked outside in this land.

'I am a leader of auxiliaries – of Alamanni spears. You Romans cannot pronounce my name.' He grinned. 'So Crocus I am called. Your man saved my life at Ancyra, more than his duty. I give him my oath, I and my kin.'

I nodded, understanding him as, perhaps, a Roman woman could not, and understanding as well that this loyalty extended to Constantius's family.

'Thank you. My father was a prince among the British tribes, and I know what this means to you. I accept your service—' I set my hand upon my belly, 'for myself and my child.'

Crocus bent his head with even greater reverence than before. 'I see that it is true, what he says about you.' He paused as I lifted an eyebrow, and then continued. 'Among my people we know that women are holy, so when he says you are like a goddess, I know it is true.'

That Constantius should think so did not surprise me, but such talk was for the privacy of the bedchamber. I could not help but wonder in what extremity of danger he and this man had found themselves, for him to have revealed his inner mind so far. But I had realized already that there were things that a soldier did not speak of at home, things that Constantius strove to forget when he lay in my arms, and I would probably never know.

'To you and your child,' he repeated my words, 'I pledge my troth, to protect and defend against all foes.'

The babble of conversation had receded, leaving the two of us in a great silence. I bowed my head, my eyes blurring with tears. It seemed a long time since I had used the senses by which the spirit sees truly, but even though there was no altar here, and neither priest nor sacrifice, I knew that the oath that Crocus had just sworn had been witnessed by the gods.

'I see that the two of you have met.' Constantius spoke beside me and I looked up, blinking the tears away.

'Crocus tells me that you saved his life,' I said quickly, lest he misunderstand my emotion, and moving over so that he could recline on the couch at my side.

'Did he tell you that he saved mine as well?' His smile to Crocus was a warning not to frighten the womenfolk with soldiers' tales.

'She does not need to be told.'

Constantius's eyebrows twitched, but he thought better of enquiring further. He leaned on one elbow and waved towards the dais.

'Aurelian is honouring all the heroes of the campaign – he has Maximian up there with him, I see.'

I followed his gesture and saw a thick-set man with a shock of greying brown hair, as formidable as a bull. He looked like a farmer, as indeed, his parents had been, but he had a gift for war.

'And there is Docles beside him,' Constantius went on. Next to Maximian sat a big man with thinning reddish hair above a broad brow. Lines of rigid control marked his features despite, or perhaps because of, the colour of his hair.

'Now there's a man to watch. His father was only a herdsman in Dalmatia, unless some god begot him. He seems to have been born with a genius for fighting, anyhow, and he is a good administrator as well, which is even more valuable in a general.'

'And more rare?' I asked. But just then the slaves began to serve us the first course of the banquet, and he forbore to reply.

Constantius had been posted to the Cohors Prima Aurelia Dardanorum, who were garrisoned near the junction of the Navissus and the Margus. I had hoped that this meant he would be commuting between the fort and the house he had rented for me in Naissus, but at the beginning of November, the Dardanians were ordered to assist in the pursuit of the retreating Goths, and Constantius, his baggage packed with woollens against the suddenly chilly weather, marched north and left me alone.

Only a thin line of hills protected Naissus from the winds that swept across the open Danuvian plain, winds born in the steppes of Scythia that had warmed only enough to pick up some moisture in their passage across the Euxine Sea. Soon, I thought as I wrapped a shawl around my shoulders, there would be snow. Still, in this country they knew how to build for cold weather, and not only did the house have a hypocaust that kept warmth rising from the tiled floors, but in the large room Constantius had chosen for our bedchamber, there was an actual hearth. It was for that reason that Constantius had rented it, he had told me, so that the warmth of an open fire would remind me of home.

As my pregnancy progressed I spent much of my time in that chamber. It seemed unfair that Constantius, who had comforted me through the first three months, should have had to leave me just as the sickness was passing and my belly began to round out as the child grew. I had passed through the phase when women most often miscarried their children, and I now felt certain that I would carry this babe to term. Indeed, I had never felt better. When the weather permitted, I would walk with Drusilla to the market-place in the centre of town; Philip, who had become very protective, a half-step behind us and Hylas scampering ahead.

Good food and affection had transformed the little dog, who now

159

stood nearly as high as my knee, with a silky black and white coat and a wildly-waving plume of tail. To Hylas, the market was a place of infinite possibility, full of fascinating smells and even more interesting and odoriferous objects. It was poor Philip's task to keep the dog from trying to drag them home. For the human members of the household the market was a source of gossip that kept us informed about the progress of the campaign.

The Goths they were fighting were the last survivors of the great incursion that had shaken the Empire two years before. But even in the days when Rome still claimed Dacia, its northern mountains had resisted the penetration of the legions. The Goths had melted into the wilderness like snow in summer. But it was winter now, and a dwindling food supply would put them at a disadvantage before the well-fed legions.

Or at least we could hope so. To think of Constantius on the march, wet and hungry while I sat warm before my fire, chilled my soul. But there was nothing I could do to help him. Only my yearning spirit reached out across the leagues that separated us, as if by doing so I could bring him some comfort.

And more and more, as winter drew in, it seemed that I was indeed touching his spirit. I had tried to do this when Constantius was in Syria, without success. Was it because I now carried his child that the link had strengthened, or perhaps because my successful pregnancy had restored a confidence lost when I was exiled from Avalon?

I dared not question too closely. It was enough, in the long winter evenings, to sit before the hearthfire, humming softly as I combed out my hair, and allow a vision of Constantius to take shape among the glowing coals.

On one such evening, just before the solstice when soldiers celebrate the birth of Mithras, I found the visions I saw in the coals taking on an unusual clarity. A chunk of charring firewood was transformed into a mountainside, and below it, on an outcrop, glowing sticks became the square palisade of a Roman marching camp with neat rows of tents laid out inside. Smiling, I indulged the fancy. Constantius might be settling down for the night in just such a camp even now. I leaned forwards, willing myself to see the tent in which he lay—

—and suddenly I was there in the camp, staring at falling tents and running men lit by the flames of the burning palisade as the Goths burst in. Spearpoints flickered like exploding sparks as the Romans rallied, swords darting in and out in tongues of flame. Frantic, I searched for Constantius, and found him standing back-to-back with Crocus. He was defending himself with a legionary's *pilum*, while the big German fought with a longer German spear, and their valour had swept a circle of safety around them.

But even together they could not defeat the entire Gothic army, and the rest of the Romans were getting the worst of it. There were so many! Now another contingent drove towards Constantius. Instinctively I leapt forwards with an inarticulate cry. I do not know what the Goths saw, but they recoiled.

Suddenly I remembered a fragment of teaching from Avalon, offered as a historical curiosity, since surely we would never have any use for it now. In the ancient days, the Druid priestesses had been taught battle-magic, spells to protect their warriors, and the shriek of the Raven Goddess that had the power to unman a foe.

It was that shriek that I felt building in my breast now, a cry of rage, of despair, of utter negation. I extended my arms and they became black wings, bearing me upward as that fury filled me, body and soul.

The Goths looked up, mouths opening, fingers flexing in the sign against evil as I swooped towards them. They were no Romans, to make divinities of abstractions and abstract principles of their deities. They knew the spirit world was real . . .

'*Waelcyrige! Haliruna!*' they cried as I bore down upon them. And then I opened my throat, and the scream that left my lips separated them from their senses, and me from consciousness as well.

When I opened my eyes once more, Drusilla and Philip were bending over me, faces blanched with fear.

'My lady, my lady! What was it? We heard a cry—'

I looked at them, thinking that I did not want the love with which they served me to change to fear.

'A nightmare, I think,' I muttered. 'I must have fallen asleep before the fire.'

'Are you all right? Is the child—'

In sudden alarm I set my hand to my belly, but all was well. 'He is a soldier's son,' I managed to grin at them. 'It will take more than a little noise to frighten him.'

It was the Goths who had been frightened, I thought in satisfaction, if what I remembered had been true vision, and not a dream.

After that I sent Philip to the market-place each morning, seeking news, until a letter came from Constantius, telling me that he was well, and not to worry if I heard there had been a battle. He had not been hurt, and in the fighting the Gothic king Cannabaudes had been killed. And by the way, and here I could almost hear the uneasy laughter with which Romans responded when they thought the powers they worshipped might actually be real – Crocus said that the enemy had been routed by a goddess with my face . . .

When we had first come together in the Great Rite, Constantius had seen me as the Goddess; and he had done so on the night I conceived my child. Why then, I wondered, should he be surprised?

The Romans, I reflected as I wrapped my shawl around me, were prone to fall into one error or its opposite – either to hold that the visible world was only an imperfect reflection of the Ideal, which the philosopher sought to transcend, or to live in a world of unpredictable forces which must be constantly propitiated. The one despised the world while the other feared it, and the Christians, I had heard, did both, calling on their god to save them from his own judgment.

But everyone believed in omens. If Constantius had not provided for me I could have made a good living as a seeress, using the skills I had learned on Avalon. And what omen, I wondered then, should I find in my vision of the battle? I set my hand on my belly, smiling as I felt the flutter of movement within.

Was it your valiant spirit that inspired me, my little one? Surely you will be a great general, if you are helping to win battles even before you are born!

And what, I asked myself then, did I believe? I did not fear the world, but neither did I reject it. We had learned a third way, on Avalon. My training there had taught me to sense the spirit in everything, and to recognize that for the most part the world went its way with little interest in humankind. The raven that croaked from the rooftop did not know that the man who listened would hear a message – it was the man whose mind must be altered in order to find meaning in it, not the bird. Spirit moved through all things; to learn to live in harmony with that movement was the Way of the Wise.

The babe stirred once more in my belly, and I laughed, understanding anew why we saw a Goddess when we sought to give a face to the Highest Power. Now that the first months of adjustment to pregnancy were over, I had never felt so well. Filled and fulfilled, I was simultaneously acutely aware of my body and one with the life force that flowed through everything.

As the winter progressed and my belly grew ever larger, my euphoria was tempered with an understanding of why the Goddess might sometimes want to let her creation fend for itself. I gloried in my role as human cornucopia, but it would have been a relief at times if I could have set my fertile belly down. By the time Constantius and the Dardanians returned from their campaign, early in the second month of the year, it seemed to me that I could have posed for a statue of Taueret, the Egyptian hippopotamus goddess who presided over pregnancy.

Upon learning of my condition, the wives of Constantius's fellow-officers had been quick to share every story of childbed trauma to be found in what was obviously a rich folklore, while cheerfully offering me the services of Egyptian physicians and Greek midwives. When I was still at Avalon birthing had never been one of my specialties, but fortunately it was covered as part of our training in healing. When I woke in the still hours, still trembling

163

from some nightmare of a botched delivery, I knew enough to quiet my worst fears.

But the midwife I chose was a woman Drusilla had found for me called Marcia, who had a good reputation among the wives of the town. A sturdy, matter-of-fact soul with a frizz of auburn hair and an ample bosom, she insisted on consultations with the mother-to-be well before the delivery, and consented to work only for those who would follow her directions regarding diet, exercise and rest.

When she had measured my girth and calculated my due date Marcia recommended activity. The child was large already, she told me, and the birth would go easier if I could deliver him early. I understood what she did not say. When an infant was too big, it came down to a choice between cutting into the mother, as they said the great Caesar had been born, or dismembering the child to extract it from the womb. It was then that I began to make offerings to Eilythia for a safe delivery. I was willing to die for the sake of the Child of Prophecy, but if it came to a choice between us, I knew that Constantius would wish to save me.

And so as February drew on I walked to the market with Drusilla in the mornings, and down to the river and back up the hill every afternoon, ignoring Constantius's worried frown. I walked on the occasional day of watery sunshine, ignoring the twinges as my womb prepared for its task, and through the rain, even when it turned to sleet and snow.

'You do not train your soldiers for battle by keeping them idle in camp,' I told Constantius. 'This is my battle, and I intend to go into it as fit as I can.'

And on the twenty-seventh day of that month, coming back up the hill to our house I slipped on a wet cobblestone and sat down hard. As Drusilla helped me back to my feet I felt the gush of warm water from my womb mingling with the cold water that soaked my gown, and the first hard pang as labour began.

The household clucked and bustled in panic around me, but I had hoped for just such an accident. As one of the maids rushed off to find Marcia and Philip took horse to go out to the fortress for

Constantius, I lay back upon the bed with a grin of triumph, until the next contraction came.

My time had come upon me early, but my womb, once started in its labour, seemed in no hurry to expel its contents. Through the rest of that day and the night that followed the contractions continued. The merciful amnesia that allows a woman who has given birth to face the prospect again has dimmed my memories of most of that time. Indeed, sometimes it is the fathers who remember so vividly that they fear to let their wives suffer so again.

If I had not been in such good condition I doubt I would have survived, and even so, as the second day drew on and my pangs, instead of becoming closer together, began to slow, the women who attended me looked grave, and I remember telling Marcia that if it came to a choice, she must cut me and save the child. The rain had stopped and the light of the westering sun, coming through the window, flamed in her hair.

'Nay,' she said then. 'It is true that once the waters have broken the birth must not be too long delayed, but fear not to let your body rest for a little while. I have a trick or two left in my bag that can get things going once more.'

In my exhaustion I found it hard to believe her. I closed my eyes, wincing as the child within me kicked. This must be hard for him as well, trapped in a constricting bag that was squeezing him into a passageway too narrow for his frame. But he had no choice about it now, and neither did I.

'*Goddess, was it so terrible for You, when You gave birth to the world?*' came my silent cry. '*I have seen the passion that drives Your creatures to reproduce their kind. Help me to deliver this child! I will give you whatever you ask!*'

And it seemed to me then that from the depths of my pain there came an answer.

'*Whatever I ask? Even if it means that you must lose him?*'

'*So long as he stays alive!*' I replied.

'*You will keep him, and you will lose him. He will trample your heart as he pursues his destiny. The changes that he brings you can neither predict nor control. But you must not despair. Even when they bring pain, growth and change and alteration are all part of My plan, and all that is lost will one day return once more . . .'*

I was in pain already, and could not understand. I knew only the need to bring forth my child. I made some motion of assent, and abruptly I was back in my body once more. Marcia set a cup of tea to my lips whose bitterness was perceptible even through the honey they had mixed in. I tried to identify the herbs, but caught only the astringent taste of yarrow and red cedar.

Whatever it was, when it hit my empty stomach it began to work immediately. The contractions returned with a wrenching agony that overwhelmed my intention not to scream. Again and again I was wracked by the pain, but presently I was able to discern a kind of rhythm in it. Marcia got me up onto the birthing stool and gave me a wad of cloth to bite down on. Drusilla braced herself behind me and one of the maids took either arm. I learned later that I had gripped their wrists so tightly I left bruises, but I was not aware of doing so at the time.

I felt the warm seep of blood and the hot oil with which Marcia was massaging me. 'You're doing well,' she told me. 'When the urge comes, bear down with all your might!'

Then the giant hand squeezed once more, and I pushed, past caring whether anyone heard my cry. Again and again it came, until I thought I must split in two.

'I have the head,' said Marcia, and then a last convulsion seized me and the rest of the child slid free. A purplish, struggling form swung across my vision as she lifted it, ummistakably male, and then the room resounded to a roar of protest that must surely have been as loud as any of my own.

Dimly I was aware of being lifted to the bed once more. Women bustled around me, packing me with cloths to stop the bleeding, washing me, changing the bedding. I paid no attention to their chatter. What matter if I was too badly torn to bear another

– this child lived! I could hear his lusty cries even from the next room.

A face appeared above me. It was Sopater, with a man in the robes of a Chaldean priest whom I remembered being told was an astrologer.

'Your son was born at the fifth hour past noon,' said Sopater. 'We have a preliminary horoscope already. Mars is in Taurus and Saturn lies in Leo. This child will be a warrior, stubborn in defeat and unyielding in victory. But Jupiter reigns in the sign of Cancer and there also sits his moon – your son will care strongly for his family. But above all, Aquarius will rule, rising with his Venus and his sun.'

I nodded and he turned away, still excited. I heard the clink of glassware and realized that they were drinking to the baby's health in the next room. How unfair, I thought then. All the work was done by me! But that was the custom, when a man claimed his son, and I should be glad for it.

I was, by Roman reckoning, an illegitimate child, and though my father had acknowledged me in the British fashion, he had never bothered to draw up papers of formal adoption, having always intended me for Avalon. In Roman law, I was Constantius's *concubina*, a relationship which was legally recognized, but lower in status than a formal wedding. But even had we been married *confarreatio*, in the most ancient and formal of patrician styles, it would still have fallen to my husband to claim the infant as his own and to decide whether he should live.

As I lay in the bed, too exhausted to open my eyes, yet still tense with excitement, it seemed wrong to me that the man should have that power. It was not he who had formed the child out of his own flesh, nor he who would nurse it. A memory came to me of Avalon, when I sat listening with the other maidens while Cigfolla taught us the midwife's skills.

The woman of ancient times had possessed a strength we no longer claimed. If she had too many children, or not enough strength to rear another child, or if feeding it would deprive the tribe at the wrong time of year, she could look into the face of the child and put forth her hand and send that child back into nowhere and nothingness as if it had never been born.

Lying in my bed, listening to the murmur of talk from the men in the next room, I understood her meaning as I had not when I was a girl. I realized then that a woman is never free to bear a child unless she is also free to abort it. A man must know that he is breathing because his mother looked on his face and saw that it was good and chose freely to nourish him. This child, who lived because I had given up so much in order to conceive and bear him, must never be allowed to forget that he owed his life to me.

And then the men came back into the bedchamber, and my little son was laid in my arms. Constantius looked down at us. His face bore the marks of an anguish which I suppose must have been the echo of my own pain, but his eyes were shining with joy.

'I have given you a son,' I whispered.

'He is a fine boy,' Constantius answered, 'but I would have considered him a poor trade for you! We will call him Constantine.'

I looked down at the fuzz of golden down on the baby's head, whose curve repeated the round of the breast against which he nuzzled, already hungry. In law he might be his father's, but it was I, who by my care or my neglect, would determine whether he survived.

And he would survive! For the sake of this child I had suffered through this birthing, and abandoned Avalon and everyone there that I loved. He must be worth saving, to justify my pain! Nonetheless, as I put him to the breast I took a secret satisfaction in remembering that every woman has within herself this tremendous power to give life . . . or to deny it.

CHAPTER TEN

AD 282

In the year that Constantine was ten years old, we took up residence in the old palace in Sirmium. Since his birth, we had moved regularly as Constantius was shifted from one posting to another, contriving not only to survive but to rise in rank through the turmoil that had followed the assassination of the Emperor Aurelian when Constantine was two. That first imperial death had shocked me, for I had come to respect the little man whose order had wrenched us from Britannia into this new life. But by the time Aurelian had been followed by Tacitus, and Tacitus by Florianus, and Florianus by Probus, we had all learned to give the current wearer of the purple no more than a wary courtesy.

Probus was proving to be an effective emperor, suppressing barbarian invasions in Gallia and recruiting the defeated Burgunds and Vandals as federati forces which he then sent to Britannia to put down a revolt led by its current governor. With my mind, I understood the military necessity, but my heart wept at the thought that a Roman had loosed a barbarian horde against my native land. When Probus chose Constantius as one of his tribunes and ordered us to Sirmium I found it hard to rejoice.

Constantine had been quite excited to hear we were going to live in a palace. But by this time I had some experience of administrative housing, and would have been much happier with a snug little villa on the outskirts of town. A newly-built villa. The palace which Probus had chosen as his headquarters had been constructed originally by Marcus Aurelius a century before. There was no telling when it had last been repaired. The frescoes on the walls were disfigured by ominous stains where the damp had got in, and the hangings had holes where mice had done the same.

But here, the Emperor had decreed, was where he and his staff would live, and since Constantius was the most senior officer whose wife was with him, it had fallen to me to make the place habitable for us all. I wiped perspiration from my forehead, for it was one of the hottest days in an exceptionally warm summer, and directed the maidservants to change the water with which they were scrubbing the wall.

'When I am a man, I am going to build *new* palaces,' Constantine had told me when we moved in. I believed him. When he was little he had constructed fortresses out of the furniture. These days he bullied the children of the other officers into helping him erect buildings in the gardens – pavilions and play-houses, guarded by fortifications laid out with military precision.

I could hear the sound of young voices raised in laughter, and my son's bellow of command overriding them all. Atticus, the Greek whom we had bought to be Constantine's tutor, had given them an afternoon's holiday, saying it was too hot to do lessons indoors. Play was apparently another matter. The boys seemed to be working more willingly than the soldiers whom the Emperor had set to digging ditches through the marshes below the town.

'Perhaps he will be an engineer for the legions,' Constantius had commented when he came home the evening before, evaluating the design with an experienced eye.

But I did not think our child would be satisfied with building walls to military specifications, or draining marshland, either. Whatever Constantine created would reflect his own vision of the world.

The doors of the dining chamber had been thrown open to the gardens in the hope of letting in a little air. At least here, on the higher ground at the southern edge of the city, we could expect a breeze. Beyond the garden wall the ground fell away to the

River Savus. Down there, where several hundred legionaries were sweating in the sun, it must be stifling. At least Constantius did not have to labour with a shovel, but I knew that he would be hot and thirsty by the time he returned.

Even the boys might be grateful to stop their play long enough for a drink of something cool. I told the maidservants they could rest for a little and sent one of them to bring the earthenware jug of barley-water from the kitchen.

Constantine stood near the back wall of the garden, directing two other boys as they lifted a framework of wickerwork to roof the structure they had made. As always, the sudden sight of my son could make my breath catch, and now, with the strong sunlight blazing on his fair hair, he was like a young god. He was going to be tall, like my father, but he had Constantius's sturdy bones – he was already bigger than most boys his age.

He would be a magnificent man. Drusilla had tried to console me when it became clear that I would never bear another child. But in time, seeing women of my own age made old by constant pregnancies, I had realized I should be grateful. And why should I wish for other children, with such a son?

'No, it is not quite right—' Constantine stood with hands braced on his hips, head cocked to one side. 'We must take it down.'

'But Con—' protested the younger of his helpers, a son of one of the centurions who was called Pollio, 'we just got it up there!'

I smiled to hear the nickname. It was an obvious shortening of the Latin name, but in my own tongue 'con' was the word for a hound.

'And it's hot,' added the other boy, Marinus, who came from a merchant family in the town. 'We can rest in the shade until sunset and finish it then.'

'But it's not *right* . . .' Constantine gazed at them in incomprehension. 'The slope has to be at an angle or it will be unbalanced—'

My heart went out to him. He could see the desired result so clearly in his mind, and reality kept falling short of his dreams. Well, life would teach him soon enough that one cannot always

171

order the world to one's liking, I thought, remembering my own girlhood. Let him enjoy his illusions while he could.

But it *was* hot. Even Hylas, who usually frisked at my feet like a puppy when we went outdoors, had flopped down in the shade of the disputed wickerwork and lay panting.

'I have brought some barley-water to cool you,' I interrupted, taking pity on the two younger boys. 'When you have drunk it perhaps the task will seem easier.'

I poured cups from the sweating terra cotta jug for the boys and took my own to the garden wall, pausing to pour out a few drops before the image of the nymph of the garden in her shrine. It had taken me some time to become accustomed to the Roman preoccupation with images, as if they needed markers to tell if something was holy. But the shrine did serve as a reminder, and sometimes, in the evening, I would come into the garden to spend half an hour in her company.

Beyond the wall, the ground fell away in a tangle of greenery. Between the slope and the gleaming curve of the river the marsh-land shimmered in heat-haze, distorting the shapes of the men who laboured at the ditches and the tall column of the siege tower the Emperor had ordered brought in so that he could observe their progress. In this weather even the iron-clad tower could not offer much comfort.

I could imagine Probus standing there, thin and intense and as obsessed with his project in the marshes as my son was with his work in the garden. Another idealist – everyone had heard of the Emperor's plan to hire foreign auxiliaries to guard the frontiers. If Probus had his way, there would be no need for the Empire to tax its citizens to maintain a standing army. If so, perhaps I could persuade Constantius to retire to Britannia, where my friend Vitellia and her husband had gone.

In the shade of the linden tree the tiles that topped the wall were cool enough to lean on, though the sunlight that filtered through the leaves was making me perspire beneath my thin gown. Even slaves should not be made to work in such heat, I thought, shading my eyes with my hand. I wondered how Probus had persuaded his men to do so.

But the men in the marshes were moving with surprising vigour – it was hard to see clearly, but there seemed to be some commotion around the tower. My heart began to race, though I could see nothing wrong. As I watched, the wavering of the tower became more pronounced, for a moment it leaned, then dust billowed in a dun cloud as it fell.

'What is it?' asked Constantine at my elbow, as that sense that had connected us since before his birth had communicated my unease.

'Listen—' The clangour of the iron plates that had covered the tower still reverberated in the heavy air. But now another sound was growing, a many-throated roar that I had heard the one time I had gone with Constantius to see the gladiatorial games at the amphitheatre in Naissus, the sound a crowd makes when a man goes down.

It seemed to me that the mob of moving men was swirling towards the road. Suddenly I turned.

'Pollio, Marinus, there is trouble down at the marshes. I want you to return to your homes *now*!' Unthinking, I had used the voice of command in which I had been trained at Avalon. My son stared at me as the boys, eyes widening, set down their cups and hurried away.

'We can't stay here,' I told Constantine, thinking aloud. 'They will know where the Emperor keeps the pay-chest. Go – pack a change of clothes and whatever books you can carry in one bundle.' I was already calling to Drusilla and the maids.

'But why are we running away?' protested Con as I shepherded my household down the road. The maids were weeping, clutching their bundles in their arms, but Drusilla looked grim. 'Surely the Emperor will stop the riot before it can get this far.'

'My guess is that the Emperor is dead, and that is why the soldiers are rioting,' I answered. Philip crossed himself, and I remembered that he had been attending the Christian church in town.

Constantine stopped short, staring, and I reached out to drag him

173

along. He knew in theory that most emperors did not reign long, but Probus was the only emperor he could really remember, a man who in his rare moments of leisure had played board games with the child.

'But what about Father?' he said. Now it was he who was pushing me forwards. My son was as close to me as my own heartbeat, but it was Constantius whom he idolized.

I managed a smile, even though that was the question that had been knotting my belly ever since I realized what was going on.

'He is not the one who ordered them to work in this heat. I am sure they will do him no harm,' I said stoutly. 'Come along now. The basilica has stout walls, and not much that's worth looting. We'll be safe there.'

We were almost in time. The riot exploded with volcanic swiftness, and by the time we reached the Forum, the first bands of maddened soldiers were already rampaging through the town. Some of them might have been from my husband's command – men whom I had nursed when the flux swept the camp the winter before. But they had already broken into at least one taverna, and the unwatered wine in the flasks they were carrying was speedily drowning what reason bloodlust had left them.

As my little group emerged from the colonnaded cloister that surrounded the square, a band of perhaps twenty men came pounding down the main street, their hobnailed sandals ringing on the cobblestones. In another moment we were surrounded. Hylas began to bark furiously, struggling in Drusilla's arms.

We should have stayed at the palace! I thought desperately. *We could have hidden in the stables*— Then I saw Con fumbling for the Parthian dagger his father had given him on his last birthday and pushed myself in front of him.

'Make no move!' I hissed as one of the soldiers made a grab for me, tearing my tunica from the fibula that held it at the shoulder so that it fell, leaving one breast bare.

Abruptly the men grew still, lust transfixing them like lightning as they stared. In another moment they would kill the boy and throw me spread-eagled to the ground. Rape I could endure, but not the loss of the child for whom I had given up Avalon!

'Goddess!' I cried in the British tongue, 'save your Chosen One!' And as my arms lifted in invocation, it seemed as if a great wind swept down and whirled my awareness away.

As if from a great distance I heard a voice too resonant to be human calling down curses, coming from a figure that seemed head and shoulders taller than the diminutive beings that surrounded her, a figure that radiated light. A great hound stood beside her, growling like thunder. She swept down her hands, and her puny assailants recoiled, falling over each other in their haste to get away. The goddess beckoned to the ones she was defending, and led them towards the basilica. When she reached its door she turned, drawing a circle in the air as if to claim the place as her own.

In the next moment I felt myself falling, all power leaving my limbs as I returned to my body and crumpled to the ground.

Exclaiming, my servants half-dragged, half-carried me inside. It took some time for me to catch my breath and calm them enough so that I could speak with Constantine.

'They would have killed *my* mother!' he said hoarsely, clinging to me as he had not done since he was a little child.

This did not seem the time to point out that killing was the least of what the rioters had had in mind. 'It is all right,' I soothed him. 'We are safe now . . .'

'No one is safe if the Emperor loses control,' he muttered. 'It should not have happened. I am young, and they were too strong for me, but I swear to you, mother, such things will not be allowed when I am a man!'

I shook my head, thinking how much he had to learn, then put an arm around him and held him close. 'When you are a man, you will set all things right!' I murmured to comfort him, and only when I had said it did it occur to me that even this might be possible for the Child of Prophecy.

*   *   *

Night came, and with it came the rest of the legion, seeking to drown the knowledge of what they had done in wine and violence. If the officers had survived, like us, they had found some bolthole in which to hide. I believed that Constantius was among them. Surely I would have known if death had broken the bond between us. To the south, where the wealthy had built their homes around the palace, we could see flames, and I thought that I had been right to bring my people here after all. Some of the shopkeepers and the clerks who worked in the basilica were here when we arrived, so we were about thirty in number, in all.

When for a time there was a pause in the sounds of destruction and revelry I could hear chanting from the Christian church.

'*Kyrie eleison, Christe eleison . . .*'

'Lord, have mercy,' whispered Philip, behind me.

They had no more defence than the sheep of which they sang so often, but even drunken soldiers knew there would be nothing worth looting there. I pitied any poor souls who had no refuge at all, for the Roman legionary, who could fight like a hero under discipline, without it was closer to the beast than any barbarian.

Through that night we huddled in the basilica, sitting with our backs against the wall, and though it was the season when the hours of darkness are at their least, to us it seemed very long. But at last I must have dozed, Constantine's solid torso lying across my lap, as if in this extremity he had become once more a little child. I opened my eyes to see a pale light filtering through the high windows. The city outside was, at long last, still.

Con stirred in my arms and sat up, rubbing his eyes. 'I'm thirsty,' he said, blinking at the others, who were beginning to wake as well.

'I'll go,' said Philip, and when I opened my lips to stop him, shook his head. 'The troops will all have passed out and be sleeping it off, or wishing they were. Why should anyone bother me?'

I sighed and nodded acceptance. Philip had filled out as he grew older, but early underfeeding had stunted him and with his crooked nose and shock of wiry reddish hair he was not likely to invite attack of any kind.

'Are you still afraid of the soldiers, Mother?' asked Con. 'I have been thinking, and I am certain now that we will be safe. A goddess protects you, as I have seen, and I know that I am not destined to die here, for have you not told me many times that I am the Child of Prophecy?'

I stared at my son, wondering now if that had been wise. When the rioters surrounded us the day before, I had suddenly remembered that visions showed only what things *might* come to pass. It was my own desperation that had summoned the Lady's power, not destiny. I still believed that Constantine had been born with the potential for greatness, but his own deeds must determine whether, and how, that potential was to be fulfilled.

By the time Philip returned, most of the others were awake. He had picked up an empty amphora and filled it at the fountain, and had found a cup to go with it. The water tasted faintly of wine.

'I am surprised that you found anything unbroken,' I said as I passed the cup to Drusilla. 'How is it, out there?'

'Like the morning after a battle, except that most of the gore is not blood but wine. A tribune on his first campaign could command them, ashamed as they are right now. I heard one man sobbing about how good Probus had been as a general, and they ought to build him a monument.' He shook his head disgustedly.

By mid-morning, the shop-keepers felt brave enough to begin sweeping up the wreckage, and the owners of food-stalls, whose wares were not so breakable, were in business once more. Many of the legionaries had ended their riot in the forum and were now awakening, and as the morning drew on, more joined them, to gather in arguing groups. I was not quite ready to try returning home, however, always supposing the palace was still there to return to, and so we were sitting on the steps of the basilica eating sausages wrapped in flat-bread, when the rhythmic tramp and jingle of soldiers marching in formation brought everyone – mutineers and townsfolk alike – to attention.

177

It was not a junior officer who had rallied them, but the Praetorian Prefect, Carus. As he rode into the forum my heart beat faster, for behind him, with a face that seemed chipped from stone, came Constantius. I rose to my feet with our son beside me, and his gaze, moving across the crowd, came to the porch of the basilica and found me. *You are all right*, for a moment his features contorted. *I can live once more.* I should not have been surprised – he had two of us to worry about. At least I had known that our son was safe. Then Constantius got his face under control, but it no longer seemed made of stone.

No doubt my own face would have displayed a similar transformation if anyone had been watching me, but all eyes were fixed on Carus, who rode as calmly as if he were on his way to the Senate, where he had served before resuming his military career. He had apparently been picking up stragglers as he came through the city, for more soldiers followed, crowding into the square. In the centre of the forum was a fountain raised on three steps. Carus slid off the horse and as it was led away, stepped up onto the broad stone rim of the fountain, from which he could see and be seen. He must be near sixty, but he was still strong and fit, with a bald head which he protected with a shapeless cap, and a preference for the simple dress of the old Republic.

'Soldiers of Rome—' Carus began, 'what god has maddened you? You have done to death the Emperor who was your kind father, made yourselves orphans, dishonoured the spirits of your fallen brothers and the emblems you carry.'

For some time he continued in this vein, speaking with a measured elegance that indicated an excellent education. Soon the men, who had begun by listening in sullen silence, were weeping. But Con had left the shelter of my arm and moved forwards to watch with shining eyes.

'Centurions! Step forwards, and the rest of you, rally to your commanders!' he cried then, and the chaotic scene slowly resolved itself into something resembling military formation. 'You will return to your tents, cleanse yourselves and your gear and present yourselves in formation on the parade ground at the second hour after noon.'

I supposed that even standing in full kit under the blazing sun would be better than digging mud, but fortunately a breeze from the north was bringing the temperature down.

But perhaps, in their current condition, even that much discipline was too much for the men, for a murmur was growing among the ranks. I saw Constantius rein in a suddenly-restive horse, and Carus frowned.

One of the centurions stepped forwards. 'Sir!' He brought his arm to his chest in salute. 'As you say, we are orphans, who need a father's strong hand. Who will be our commander now?'

'The Senate, in Rome—' Carus began, for Probus had not named an heir, but he sounded less certain now.

'Bugger the Senate,' said someone in the ranks, and there was an echo of laughter.

Con shook his head, and I bent my own to hear his whisper. 'The Senate has no power, only the army. Why cannot he see?'

I thought that perhaps Carus did, for there was a tension in his posture as he waited for their silence that had not been there before. Was it hope or resignation? I could not be sure.

'My lord, we need an emperor!' The centurion raised his arm in salutation. 'Hail, Caesar!'

'Hail Caesar!' the men responded with a full-throated roar. 'Carus shall be Emperor!' Suddenly they surged forwards, chanting his name until the columns of the basilica's porch trembled to the sound. I was certain that the rioters had looted the palace when I saw a flash of purple and they draped one of the dead Emperor's togas across his shoulders. At least one of the men had his shield, and the mob that had surrounded Carus got him onto it and raised him high.

'Will you truly have me for your Imperator?' Carus might be a republican by preference, but he must know that if he refused them now they could pull him down as swiftly as they had killed Probus.

'*Ave! Ave!*' they cried.

'I will not treat you gently – I will punish those who killed Probus, and then I will take up the old war in Parthia, that has waited so long—'

The cheering redoubled in volume.

Why are they so happy? I wondered. *He has just promised to lead them to battle in a land where it is as much hotter than Dalmatia as this land is than Britannia.* But the lands of the East held riches, and if the heat killed them, they would die not like slaves but as soldiers.

The noise, as they carried Carus in procession around the forum, deafened the mind as well as the ears. The other officers had drawn back to the shelter of the colonnade. Carus belonged to the legionaries now.

'*Ave Carus!*' came a new cry from beside me. Constantine had extended his own arm in a stiff salute, and he gazed at the figure of the new Emperor with visions in his eyes.

The new Emperor, with no more than a curt announcement of his accession to the Senate in Rome, set about establishing his authority. The Romans rioted in protest, but so long as the army supported him, Carus did not appear to care. Probus had valued his abilities so much that he had requested the Senate to award him a marble palace and an equestrian statue. Now, with the exception of the palace in Sirmium, which was a charred ruin, he had palaces in plenty, and no doubt the statues were already being created, along with the panegyrics that came in from every corner of the Empire.

Carus had no time to read them. He had promised the army glory in Parthia, but before the expedition could set out, there was much to be done. If he was grateful to the legionaries of Sirmium for raising him to the purple it did not prevent him from executing the men who had been the first to attack Probus, an act which apparently did him no harm in the eyes of the survivors, for that autumn they followed him willingly into battle against a horde of Sarmatians who had come down upon Illyria, and gained a resounding victory.

The succession was also provided for. Carus had two sons, both now grown, whom he raised to the rank of Caesar. Carinus, who was the elder, was directed to deal with the latest barbarian raids into Gallia and then take charge in Rome, while his brother Numerianus became the Emperor's second-in-command on the Parthian campaign.

I dared not speak my fear that the Emperor would drag Constantius along with him, but the Goddess must have heard my prayers, for shortly before the army was to depart, my husband returned to Sirmium with the news that Carus had appointed him Governor of Dalmatia.

In my dream, I was moving along the Processional Way at Avalon. I knew it for a dream because I seemed to see everything from a vantage point of several feet off the ground, and because when I spoke, no one noticed me. But in every other regard, I was fully present. I could feel the moist chill of the night air and smell the resins in the torches. I trembled to the reverberations of the great gong that was used to summon initiates to the greater ceremonies.

It had summoned me, I realized, all the way from Sirmium. This was no dream but a spirit journey. But what was the ceremony?

Cloaked and hooded, the priestesses in black and the priests in white, they passed between the last of the pillars and began the spiral ascent of the Tor. Drawn along with them, I could neither lag nor hurry. Soon I recognized Cigfolla and some of the others, and realized that I was in the place in the line in which I would have marched had my body been there. I knew then that in the depths of my spirit I had never ceased to be a priestess of Avalon, and that was why I had answered this call.

Presently we reached the top, and in the midst of the circle of stones I saw the intricately-stacked logs of a funeral pyre. The body was shrouded, but it seemed small to be the centre of so much ceremony. Yet only a High Priestess or Arch-Druid received such a funeral.

Holding a torch beside the pyre I saw Ceridachos, wearing the

181

Arch-Druid's torc of gold. He had taught the boys music when I was at Avalon. It was not the Arch-Druid, then, who lay upon the pyre, but the Lady of Avalon.

For a moment amazement held me, that in the end Ganeda should be so little, whose spirit had been such a towering presence, dominating us all. And now she was gone. I wondered whom they had chosen to follow her.

I was justified! See, I bore my son and my man still loves me! I wanted to cry, as if we were still in contention, but I would never have the chance to tell her so, unless her spirit could hear.

The gong had ceased to resound. Ceridachos stood away from the pyre, turning to face it, and I saw another torch on the other side. A priestess held it: no, it was the new Lady of Avalon, for beneath the open front of the cloak gleamed the ornaments of moonstone and river pearl. Then her hood fell back and I recognized Dierna's blazing red hair.

But she was just a child! Then I looked again and thinking hard, realized that Dierna must be twenty-five years old. When I last saw her, she had been a child, but we would be women together, were we to meet now. She lifted her arms in invocation.

'Hail to Thee, Dark Mother who art the Mistress of Souls! This night we remember before Thee Ganeda, who is passing through Thy kingdom. Her blood flows in the waters, her breath is one with the wind. The holy Tor will receive her ashes and the spark of her life return to the fire that enlivens all.'

The warriors and kings who were Avalon's guardians were buried on the Watch Hill, but the great priests and priestesses, whose ascending spirits might have been constrained by too much adulation, were sent to the gods by fire.

Ceridachos lifted the torch. 'Let the holy fire transform that which was mortal, and the spirit fly free!' A glittering ribbon of sparks trailed behind it as he moved around the pyre, touching it at intervals to the oil-soaked logs. The wood caught quickly, and in moments the shrouded form was hidden behind a veil of flame.

'No part of her will be wasted, nothing lost,' said Dierna as she followed him around the pyre. Her voice was calm, as if she had put herself into an altered state for the ceremony, where no grief could trouble her serenity. 'Even her spirit, taught by life's pains, still evolves towards her true identity.' From the pouch at her waist she took a handful of incense and cast it onto the stacked logs.

Ceridachos turned to face the others. 'But we, remembering that particular coupling of body and spirit in which she walked the world, pray to Thee to guide and guard her on the path she now pursues.' His voice was hoarse as if he had been weeping, and I realized how closely he, as Arch-Druid, must have worked with the Lady over the years. He cleared his throat and continued.

'We have not forgotten – bear Thou our love to her, and ask her to pray for us with the wisdom she has now. And when in time we also come to Thee, receive us gently, oh Thou Dark Mother, as a child is lulled to sleep, and wake us to the Light.'

All around the circle, heads bent. I bowed my head as well, though no one could see. For so many years I had feared my aunt, and fought her, and in the end, tried to forget her. And yet she had done the work of Avalon and done it well. Having managed my own household for a dozen years, I could in some wise appreciate her achievement now. Were there things that Ganeda could teach me?

Dierna handed the pouch of incense to Ceridachos, and he cast a handful onto the pyre, which was now well alight.

'The dead has her release, and the answer to all questioning,' she said gravely. 'It is those who remain who suffer now, from loss, from memory, from regret for things left unsaid or undone. Let us pray now for the living left behind . . .' Her hand swept out in a wide circle to include us all.

Pray for me! I thought grimly, amazed to discover that even my astral body could shed tears.

'Oh Thou Lady of Darkness, lift Thou the darkness that lies upon our souls. As Thou hast cut the thread of life, break Thou the bonds that constrain our spirits, lest our feelings should bind the one we would set free.'

It came to me in that moment that I was not the only one who might have had mixed feelings about the Lady of Avalon, and the spirit of any adept could make a dangerous ghost. The community had the best of reasons for making sure nothing held her here.

Now the incense was being passed around the circle. As each one threw a pinch on the flames I heard the words, 'Thus I release you,' followed sometimes by a murmured message of more personal farewell. Smoke and sparks billowed upward to join the stars. And though my fingers could not grasp the incense, I too moved close to the pyre, and with all the truth of my being, offered the woman who had in so many ways shaped my life both forgiveness and farewell.

'The Lady bounds life with death, and out of death creates life anew,' said Dierna when all had finished. 'We are the children of earth and starry heaven. By our response to this loss let us transcend it.' She took a deep breath. 'I bear now the ornaments of the High Priestess. I pray to the Goddess to give me the strength and the wisdom to lead Avalon!'

As the night drew on the others made their vows, then drew aside to keep watch as the pyre became a framework of glowing lines, and the central core, which had been built with faster-burning fuel, fell to ash. And just as the eastern sky was beginning to pale with the approach of the sun, I willed myself to approach the heap of coals and ashes that remained.

'*Lady, it was you who exiled me, but the Goddess who showed me my way. By example and by opposition you taught me much. Though I walk now in the world beyond the mists, I will do so as a priestess of Avalon!*'

I drew back, for suddenly the world was filled with light as the newborn sun rose above the eastern hills. And in that moment, the dawn wind, rising, lifted the ashes like a swirl of smoke and swept them outwards to fall like a blessing upon the green turf of the Tor.

It had made me shiver sometimes, when I first learned of that custom, to think that I might be treading on what was left of Caillean or Sianna or one of the legendary priestesses who had

184

followed them. But in truth, the earth of the Tor was just as holy as they. Their dust hallowed it as it blessed them. They were one and the same.

The priests and priestesses stirred from the stillness of their vigil as if released from a spell. As Dierna looked up, her eyes widened and I knew that she, alone among that company, could see me standing there.

'This should be *your* place,' she whispered, touching the ornaments she wore. 'Will you return to us now?'

But I shook my head, smiling, and using the full imperial obeisance with which I had always honoured the Lady of Avalon, I bowed.

At breakfast I was silent, still thinking about the night's visions. The palace burnt in the rioting had been rebuilt and most mornings we took our first meal in a pleasant chamber that opened out onto the shaded walkway that surrounded the gardens. Constantius, finishing his gruel, asked me if I was well.

I shook my head. 'It is nothing – I had strange dreams.'

'Well, then, there is something I need to discuss with you. I should have spoken of it before.'

I forced my attention away from my own concerns, wondering what on earth this could be. Since Carus's accession, over a year had passed. The reports from the East had been glorious – the cities of Seleucia and Ctesiphon had surrendered almost without resistance, and the enemy, distracted by warfare on their own eastern borders, seemed unable to resist the Roman advance. It seemed possible that the Parthians, who had been a looming menace since the days of the first Augustus, might be finally overcome. But what did all that have to do with Constantius or me?

'Does the Emperor think you can somehow curb Carinus?'

In the preceding months it had become clear that the gift of imperial power in the city of the Caesars had gone to the young man's head. He had executed the advisors his father had given him and replaced them with his drinking companions. In a few months he had married and divorced nine wives, leaving most of them pregnant, in addition to his other amusements. If Constantius tried to advise him, he was likely to go the way of the others. Surely no amount of devotion to duty would require that useless sacrifice.

'No . . . the Emperor has always been a man of justice rather than mercy, and I fear he has ceased to hope that his elder son will prove worthy. So he is looking for a substitute . . .' he slowed, stirring his spoon around and around in the empty bowl. 'He wants to adopt me.'

I stared at him. This was my own Constantius, his hairline somewhat higher and his frame stockier than that of the young man who had stolen my heart thirteen years ago, but the honest grey eyes were still the same. I gazed at the features of the man who had been my mate for a dozen years overlaid by the splendour he had worn when he first came to me in the light of the Beltane fire. If he became Caesar, everything would change.

'It is not an honour that one can easily refuse.'

I nodded, thinking that I had known from the beginning that Constantius had the potential for greatness. Was this the meaning of my vow to Ganeda's spirit? I would never be Lady of Avalon, but I might indeed become Empress one day.

'But why you?' I blurted suddenly. 'No one could be more worthy, but when did he have a chance to know you so well?'

'The night of the mutiny, after Probus died. Carus and I hid in a fisherman's hut at the edge of the marsh while the men were rioting, and as men will when the situation is desperate, we bared our souls. Carus wanted to bring back the old virtues of the Republic without losing the strength of Empire. And I . . . talked to him about what I thought was wrong with us now, and what, with honest government, Rome could be.'

I reached out to take his hand, that warm flesh that I had come to know as well as my own.

'Oh my dearest, I understand!' With the powers of a Caesar he could do so much – such an opportunity must outweigh any consideration either for his comfort or my own.

'Until the Emperor returns from Parthia I will not be required to decide,' said Constantius, managing a smile. But we both knew that there would only be one possible decision when that time came.

I heard a clatter of sandals on the flagstones of the walkway and then the door crashed open. For a moment Con clung there, panting.

'Father, have you heard the news?' he cried when he had got his breath once more. 'They are saying that the Emperor is dead in Parthia – struck by lightning in a storm, and Numerian is bringing the army home!'

CHAPTER ELEVEN

AD 284–85

As the Empire mourned Carus so did I, though my sorrow was more for Constantius's lost chance for greatness than for the Emperor, whom I had known only for a little while. If I had understood the inevitable consequences of my husband's elevation, I should have rejoiced. Because Carus died when he did, I had Constantius for almost ten more years.

The Emperor had died as a consequence of the flux which was a constant hazard on campaign. But the death had occurred during a thunderstorm, and when the Emperor's tent caught fire, the troops believed he had been killed by lightning, the most evil of omens. Our forces had been well on the way to conquering Parthia at last, but there were prophecies, it was said, that the River Tigris would forever mark the limits of Rome's eastern expansion. Indeed, there were any number of signs, omens and portents for folk to gabble at in those first, horrified weeks after the news arrived.

The troops acclaimed Numerian as co-emperor with his brother Carinus, but refused to continue the war. And so the Army of the East was making its slow way back home while Carinus ran riot in Rome. Did he know that Carus had intended Constantius to supplant him? Suddenly Dalmatia seemed entirely too close to Italia, and when Maximian, who now held the command in Gallia, requested Constantius to join his staff, we agreed that he would be prudent to resign his post as governor of Dalmatia and accept the invitation.

Our new home was a villa in the hills above Treveri. It was not Britannia, but the country folk here spoke a language not unlike the British tongue, and even two hundred years after Julius Caesar had suppressed them, the Druids were remembered. Someone among the servants whom we had engaged to assist our household slaves must have recognized the fading blue crescent upon my brow, for I soon found they were treating me with a respect that went beyond duty. When I went about in the countryside people would bow before me, and from time to time offerings of fruit or flowers appeared by the door.

Constantius thought it was amusing, but it made Constantine uncomfortable, and from time to time I would catch him watching me with troubled eyes from beneath the shock of fair hair. It was his age, I told myself, and pretended unconcern. He was twelve now, leggy as a young hunting dog, the big bones out of proportion, and the superb co-ordination that had carried him through childhood likely at odd moments to let him down. If he could have laughed at himself it would have been easier, but Constantine had never had much of a sense of humour. With the approach of adolescence he was becoming reclusive, fearing to expose himself to ridicule.

But there was nothing wrong with his mind, and Atticus found that he suddenly had a willing pupil, eager to sink his teeth into the meat of Greek philosophy and literature. At present they were studying the works of Lucian. As I directed the girls who were cleaning the mosaic of Dionysos with the dolphins on the floor of the dining room, I could hear the murmur of voices from the study, Constantine's uncertain tenor rising and falling as he translated the passage his tutor had assigned.

Tomorrow would see the beginning of the month the Romans had named after Mercurius's mother, Maia. In Britannia, I thought, smiling, they would be preparing for the festival of Beltane. If I read the signs rightly they celebrated here as well. The weather, which had been chill and rainy, had suddenly turned warm, and wildflowers starred the green hills.

I took a deep breath of the sweet air, then paused to listen, as the maids opened a door and Con's voice grew suddenly louder.

'They saw that . . . the thing that both the ones who fear and the hopeful ones needed and, uh . . . wanted the most was to know about the future. This was the reason Delphi and Delos and Clarus and Didyma had ages ago become rich and famous . . .'

I paused to listen, curious to learn what they were reading and what my son would make of it.

'I don't understand,' said Constantine. 'Lucian says this man Alexander was a fraud, a deceiver, but it sounds as if he thinks that Delphi and the rest of the oracles are just as bad.'

'You must take the statement in context,' Atticus said soothingly. 'It is true that Lucian was one of the leading Sophists of the last century, and naturally prefers to base his conclusions on reason rather than superstition, but what has aroused his ire in this essay is the fact that Alexander intentionally set out to trick people, pretending to discover the snake in the egg, and substituting another, big one, with its head hidden by a mask in the ritual. Then he told everyone it was Aesclepius reborn and said it gave him the oracles that he had written himself. But it is true that he sent clients to the great shrines to keep the priests from denouncing him.'

I remembered now hearing something of the story. Alexander had been quite famous at one time, and Lucian had not only written about him, but actively tried to unmask him as well.

'Do you mean to tell me that none of the oracles are true?' Constantine said suspiciously.

'No, no – my point is that you must learn critical thinking, so that you will be able to judge for yourself whether something is reasonable, rather than accepting blindly what you are told,' Atticus responded.

I nodded: that was more or less what we had been taught at Avalon. It was as foolish to deny that oracles could be faked as to blindly believe in them.

'That doesn't make sense,' protested Constantine. 'Those who are wise should decide what is true and be done with it.'

'Ought not every man be allowed to decide for himself?' Atticus said reasonably. 'Learning how to think should be a part of everyone's education, just as everyone must learn to care for a horse or use numbers.'

'For simple things, yes,' answered Constantine. 'But when the horse falls sick you call in a healer and you employ a mathematicus for higher computations. Surely in the realm of the holy, which is so much more important, it should be the same.'

'Very good, Constantine, but consider this – the flesh is tangible, and its ills can be perceived by the senses. Numbers are symbolic of items that can be physically counted, and they are always and everywhere the same. But each man experiences the world differently. His nativity is ruled by different stars, and he has a unique history . . . Is it so unreasonable to allow him his own perception of the gods? This world is so rich and varied – surely we need myriad ways to understand it. Thus, there are the Sophists, who doubt everything, and the followers of Plato, who believe that only archetypes are real, the mystical Pythagoreans and the Aristotelian logicians. Each philosophy gives us a different tool with which to understand the world.'

'But the world stays the same,' objected Constantine, 'and so do the gods!'

'Do they?' Atticus sounded amused. He had been sold into slavery by his uncle, and I suspected he found it more comfortable to believe in no gods at all. 'How then, do we reconcile all the stories about them, or the claims of all the different cults, each of which declares that its deity is supreme?'

'We find out which is the most powerful, and teach everyone how to worship Him,' Constantine said forthrightly.

I shook my head. How simple it all seemed to a child. When I was his age, there had been no truth but that of Avalon.

'Come now,' Atticus was replying, 'even the Jews, whose god permits them to worship no other, do not pretend the other gods do not exist.'

'My father is beloved of the greatest of gods whose face is

191

the sun, and if I prove worthy, He will extend that blessing to me.'

I lifted an eyebrow. I knew that Constantine had been impressed by the solar cult of Dalmatia, to which most of the officers Constantius had served with belonged, but I did not realize how far his attempt to model himself on his father had gone. I must find some way to teach him about the Goddess as well.

Constantine continued, 'There is one Emperor on earth and one sun in the sky. It seems to me that the Empire would be much more peaceful if everyone worshipped alike.'

'Well, you are certainly entitled to your opinion, but remember, Alexander the Prophet gave his oracles in the name of Apollo. Just because a man speaks in the name of a god does not mean he is speaking true.'

'Then the authorities should stop him,' Constantius responded doggedly.

'My dear boy,' said Atticus. 'The Governor Rutilianus was one of Alexander's most devoted supporters. He married the prophet's daughter for no better reason than because Alexander said her mother had been the goddess Selene!'

'I still think people should be protected from false oracles.'

'Perhaps, but how can you do that without taking away their right to decide for themselves what they believe? Let us continue the translation, Constantine, and perhaps matters will become clearer . . .'

For the first time, I wondered if we had been wise to let Constantine study philosophy. He did tend to take things rather literally. But the flexibility of mind that characterized Greek culture would be good for him, I told myself, secretly relieved that it was Atticus who had the task of getting the point across, not I. Still, I told myself as I opened the door to let in the soft spring air, the time was coming when I must talk to my son about Avalon.

I had sung him to sleep with the teaching songs I had learned as a little girl, and amused him with wonder tales. He knew how the swans returned to the Lake at spring's beginning, and how the wild geese sang in the autumn skies. But of the meaning behind the tales, and the great pattern to which swans and geese both belonged, I had said nothing. Such matters were taught to initiates of the Mysteries. If Constantine had been born on Avalon as Ganeda planned, he would have learned these things as part of his training. But I had willed otherwise, therefore it must be my responsibility to teach him.

Constantine was a child, I thought as I listened to the two voices. It was natural that he should focus on the surface of things. But it was the external face of the world that was the most varied and full of contradictions. On the surface, there was truth in all the different cults and philosophies. It was only at a deeper level that one could find a single truth behind them.

'All the gods are one God, and all the goddesses are one Goddess, and there is one Initiator.' I had heard that watchword more times than I could count when I was at Avalon. Somehow I must get its meaning across to Constantine.

The breeze that wafted through the open doors came laden with all the scents of spring, and suddenly I could no longer bear to remain inside. I slipped through the open door and stepped out along the path that led between two rows of beech trees to the high road. I should tell Atticus to give his pupil a holiday – it was too lovely a day to spend locked in one's head debating philosophy. That was the mistake that some of the Pythagoreans, despite their understanding of the Mysteries, had made, to fix their minds so firmly on eternity that they missed the Truth proclaimed by this green and lovely world.

From our hill I could see fields and vineyards, and the gleam of the Mosella. The town nestled along the river, protected by its walls. Treveri was a place of some importance, a centre for the production of woollen cloth and pottery, with good communications to both Germania and Gallia. Postumus had made it the capital of his Gallic empire, and now Maximian had made it his base of operations as well. They were repairing the bridge again; the local reddish stone glowed pink in the bright sun, but the temple of Diana, higher up on the hillside, was a glimmer of white amid its sheltering trees.

A good road ran up the hill and past our villa. A rider was moving swiftly along it, passing a farmer's cart and continuing up the hill. My interest sharpened as he drew close enough for me to recognize the uniform and realize that he was coming here.

Had there been some disaster? I could see no unusual bustle of activity in the city. I waited, frowning, until the man drew up, retying the neckcloth with which he had been wiping his brow. I recognized him as a youngster on Constantius's staff, and acknowledged his salutation.

'And what has my husband sent you up here in such haste to say? Is there some emergency?'

'Not at all. The Lord Docles has arrived, my lady, and your husband bids me tell you that they will be dining with him here this evening.'

'What, all of them?' I shook my head. 'It is an emergency for me! We were planning to spend the day spring cleaning, not preparing a banquet.'

The young man grinned. 'That's right – Maximian will be coming as well! But I have heard about your dinners, lady, and I feel sure you will gain the victory.'

It had not occurred to me to view a dinner as a military engagement, but I laughed as I waved him on his way. Then I hurried inside to consult with Drusilla.

Despite my words, a meal for three men accustomed to the food of army camps would not place any unusual demands upon my kitchen. They might not be so devoted to austerity as Carus had been, but I knew from experience that all three would pay more attention to what they were saying than to what they were eating. It was Drusilla who felt that both the cooking and the service must be, if not elaborate, at least accomplished with restrained perfection.

Fortunately it was a season when fresh food was plentiful. By the time Constantius and our guests came riding up the hill, we were prepared for them with a salad of spring greens dressed in olive oil, hard-boiled eggs and new bread, and a roasted lamb, garnished with herbs and served on a bed of barley.

The evening was mild, and we opened the long doors in the dining chamber so that our guests could enjoy the flowerbeds and the fountain in the atrium. As I moved back and forth between the diners and the kitchen, supervising the service, I could hear the deep rumble of masculine voices growing more mellow as more of the tangy white wine of the countryside was served.

It was clear that this was to be a business dinner, not a social occasion, and I had not sat down with them. Indeed, even though it had been years since I had celebrated the Eve of Beltane, old habit kept me fasting. The men were talking of troop strengths and city loyalties, but as the evening drew on, I felt the energies that flowed through the land increasing in intensity. Drusilla was complaining because some of the kitchen servants had disappeared as soon as the first course was served. I thought I knew where they had gone to, for when I walked in the quiet of the garden, I could feel the throbbing in the earth and hear the drums that echoed it, and a hilltop above the town blazed with Beltane fire.

My blood was warming in answer to the drumming. I smiled, thinking that if our guests did not stay too late, Constantius and I might have time to honour the holiday in the traditional manner ourselves. The laughter in the dining room had deepened. Perhaps the men did not recognize the energy in the evening, but it seemed to me that they were responding to it all the same. As for me, the scent of the night air had made me half-drunk already. When I heard Constantius calling, I draped a palla across my shoulders and went in to them.

My husband moved over on his couch so that I could sit and offered me some of his wine.

'So, gentlemen, have you decided the future of the Empire?'

Maximian grinned, but Docles's heavy brows, always startling below that high bald brow, drew down.

195

'For that, Lady, we should need a seeress like Veleda to foretell our destinies.'

I lifted a eyebrow. 'Was she an oracle?'

'She was the holy woman of the tribes near the mouth of the Rhenus in the reign of Claudius,' Constantius replied. 'A Batavian prince called Civilis, who had been an officer in the auxiliaries, began a rebellion. They say the tribes would make no move without her counsel.'

'What became of her?'

'In the end, I think we feared Veleda more than we did Civilis.' Constantius shook his head ruefully. 'He was the kind of enemy we could understand, but she had the ear of the eternal powers. Eventually she was captured, and ended her days in the Temple of Vesta, as I have heard.'

In the pause that followed the chirring of the crickets seemed suddenly very loud. Beneath that audible rhythm I sensed rather than heard the heartbeat of the drums.

'I have heard,' Docles said into the silence, 'that you yourself have some training in the seeress's craft.'

I glanced at Constantius, who shrugged, as if to say it was not he who had spread that word. It should not have suprised me to learn that Docles had his own sources of information. His parents were freed slaves who had become the clients of Senator Anulinus, their old master. For Docles to have risen from such humble origins to command the young Emperor's bodyguard indicated that he was a man of uncommon abilities.

'It is true that I was trained as a priestess in Britannia,' I answered, wondering whether this was only idle conversation or if some deeper meaning was implied.

Maximian raised himself on one elbow. He was country-bred himself, and I had noticed his fingers twitching to the drumbeat, though I did not think he realized he was doing it.

'Mistress, I know what powers fare abroad this eve,' he said solemnly. ''Tis a night when the doors do open 'tween the worlds. Don't waste the moment, lads—' he gestured a little tipsily with his goblet, and I realized that they had stopped watering the wine. 'Let the strega use her powers for us, an' show us th' way out o' the tangle we're in!'

I drew back, startled at his language – in my own country folk did not speak so of a priestess of Avalon – and Constantius laid a protecting hand on my arm.

'Take care, Maximian – my wife is no hedge-witch to brew you up a pot of spells.'

'Nor did I ever say she was.' He gave me an apologetic nod. 'Shall I call her a Druid priestess, then?'

They all twitched at that, remembering how Caesar had dealt with the Druids of Gallia. But I had recovered myself: it was no more than the truth, after all, and better they should think my craft a survival of lost Celtic wisdom than suspect the existence of Avalon. Constantius's grip tightened, but my sudden fear had left me. Perhaps it was the power of Beltane Eve, like a fire in the blood. I felt my head swimming as if I already scented the smoke of the sacred herbs. It had been so long, so very long, since I had done trance-work. Like a woman meeting an old lover after many years, I trembled with re-awakened desire.

'Lady,' added Docles with his usual dignity, 'it would be an honour and a privilege if you would consent to divine for us now.'

Constantius still looked uncertain, and I realized that he too had grown accustomed to seeing me as his mate, the mother of his child, and forgotten that I had once been something more. But the other two out-ranked him. After a moment he sighed. 'It is for my lady to decide . . .'

I straightened, looking from one to the other. 'I promise nothing – it has been many years since I practised this craft. Nor will I instruct you how to interpret what you may hear, or even whether what you are hearing is my own ravings or the voice of some god. I can promise only that I will try.'

Now all three men were staring, as if, having got what they asked for, they were wondering whether they wanted it after all. But with every breath the ties that bound my spirit to the waking world were loosening. I rang the little bell that would summon Philip and asked that he take the silver bowl that was kept in Constantius's study, fill it with water, and bring it to us here. Hylas, who had somehow escaped from my bedchamber, settled himself across my feet, as if understanding that I would need an anchor when I fared between the worlds.

When the basin had been brought, and the lamps positioned so that their light swirled in a liquid glitter on the surface of the water, I instructed Philip to make sure we would not be disturbed. He looked disapproving, and I remembered that the Christians were forbidden to seek pagan oracles, though in their own meetings it was said that sometimes young men and women would see visions and utter forth prophecies.

When he had gone, I unbound the fillet that hid the crescent upon my brow, and loosened my hair from its knot so that it tumbled down about my shoulders. Maximian swallowed, his eyes widening. *This one is still close to the earth*, I thought, lowering my gaze. *His soul remembers the old ways.*

Docles's eyes were hooded, his features unreadable. I admired his control. But Constantius was gazing at me as he had when first I came to him by the Beltane fire. *Look well*, I said silently. *For nigh on fifteen years I have ruled your household and shared your bed. Have you forgotten who and what I am?* Abashed, he looked away, and I smiled.

'Very well, gentlemen, I am ready. When I have blessed the water, I will gaze into its depths, and when I begin to sway, you may ask your questions.'

I cast a little salt into the water, consecrating it in the old tongue of the wizards who had come to Avalon from the drowned land across the sea. Then I leaned forwards so that my hair hung down about the bowl like a dusky curtain, and let my eyes unfocus, gazing within.

Light rippled across the dark surface as my breath stirred it. With an effort of will I controlled my breathing, in and out, ever more slowly, sinking into the rhythm of trance. Now the light on the

198

water flickered in time to my breathing. Awareness narrowed to this circle of light in darkness, water and fire. I suppose that by that time my body had begun to move as well, for from what seemed an immense distance away I heard someone calling me.

'Say then, seeress, what shall come to the Empire in times to come. Will Numerian and Carinus rule well?'

The light on the water flared. 'I see flames . . .' I said slowly. 'I see armies that harry the land. Brother against brother, an emperor's funeral pyre . . . Death and destruction will come of their reign.'

'And what comes after?' came a new voice that some part of my mind recognized as that of Docles.

But already the scene before me was changing. Where I had seen bloodshed now lay peaceful fields. Words came to me.

'All hail to the Emperor who is blessed by Fortune. One becomes four, and yet the first is the greatest still. For twenty years he will reign in glory, Jupiter with Herculos at his side, and Mars and Apollo serving him.

'The son of Jupiter is here, but you will bear another name. Your strong right arm bears witness, and another, who blazes like the sun. Only Mars is missing, but when you have need of him he will appear. Fear not to seize the moment when it comes. You will rule in splendour, Augustus, and die full of years, having at length released the sceptre to younger hands . . .'

'And what comes after?' This voice was golden, blazing in my mind with its own light.

'The son of the sun rules in splendour, but sets too soon. And yet a brighter dawn shall follow, and a new sun shall rise whose light will blaze across the world.'

Light blossomed within my vision, shaping itself to a face I knew. Constantius, I thought, for a fair beard fringed the strong line of the jaw. But the face was altogether more massive in structure, with a long nose and eyes deeply set under the curve of the brow, a face of such stubborn strength it made me a little afraid.

Then this vision also, faded. I sagged forwards and my hair touched the water. Then Constantius had his arms around me, holding me as I shuddered with reaction. I opened my eyes, and as I tried to focus, the after-image of my vision superimposed itself upon a shape that was emerging from the darkness of the doorway.

I blinked, and realized it was Constantine. How long had he been standing there? And how much had he heard? I sat up, suddenly aware of how I must look to him, with my hair unbound, my eyes dazed with trance. I stretched out one hand towards him in an unvoiced plea. For a moment longer he stood there, on his face an expression half-avid and half-appalled. Did he think I was like Alexander the Prophet? My eyes filled with tears as he turned and disappeared.

'Lady,' said Docles in his deep voice, 'is it well with you? You have given us a great blessing.' His face had its usual calm, but his eyes shone. In Maximian's face I saw something almost like fear. I looked from one to the other, knowing that all three would wear the purple one day.

'Only if you make it so,' I whispered, remembering how the last two emperors had died.

'You have told me what I needed to know,' answered Docles. 'Constantius, take your lady to her chamber. She has done us good service this night and should rest.'

'And what will you do?' asked Maximian.

'I shall return to Numerian and wait. Jupiter smiles upon me, and will make my way clear.'

In the months that followed, all seemed confusion. In November of that year, Numerian died. Docles seized the opportunity, accusing the Praetorian Prefect, a man called Arrius Aper, of having poisoned him, and executing him on the spot. The next thing we heard was that the army had acclaimed him Emperor. But he had changed his name, and now he was calling himself Diocletian.

Carinus, who was a good commander when he put his mind to it, roused himself from his debaucheries to defend his throne, and Roman warred against Roman once more. Maximian and

Constantius declared for Diocletian and prepared to hold the West against Carinus. But when the compaigning season opened the following spring, the gods, or perhaps it was Nemesis, decreed against another lengthy civil war. In the confusion of a battle a tribune whose wife Carinus had seduced seized the opportunity to slay his commander and take his own revenge.

Diocletian was now supreme. His first act was to name Maximian as his junior colleague. And that summer, when the new Caesar, who had appointed Constantius to be his praetorian prefect, was busy dealing with the latest incursion of Germans, Diocletian sent a letter requesting that my son Constantine join his household in Nicomedia.

Constantine's bedchamber was strewn with gear and clothing. I paused in the doorway, arms full of linen undertunics fresh from the clothesline. In such confusion, it seemed impossible that all this gear would be packed and ready by tomorrow's dawn. A brief fantasy of a midnight raid to steal the baggage played through my imagination. But no attempt to delay my son's departure could achieve more than a momentary confusion, and Constantine was of an age to be embarrassed by his parents even when they were acting sensibly. Even Constantius, had he been at home, could not have resisted an imperial command.

'Has your bodyservant packed your woollen leggings?' I asked, handing the tunics to the maidservant to add to the pile.

'Oh, Mother, I won't need those old things. Only peasants wear them: I'd look like a peasant parading through Diocletian's marble halls.'

'I remember very vividly just how cold it got in Bithynia, the year we lived in Drepanum, and imperial halls are likely to be draughty. If it is cold enough for you to wear the leggings, I assure you that you will also be wearing enough outer gear to hide them from view.'

The young Gaul we had bought to be Constantine's body-servant when he turned thirteen looked from one of us to the other, comparing frowns, then turned towards the chest that held the things his master had intended to leave behind.

'Come with me, Constantine, and let us leave the slaves to their work. Here, we will only get in the way.' In truth, I would have preferred to pack his gear myself, with a blessing on each garment as I put it in, but that was something that others *could* do. No one else could tell my son what was in my heart.

Gravel crunched softly beneath our feet as I led him to the garden and sat down on a bench carved from the local reddish stone. The summer had been a good one, as if the gods were blessing Diocletian's reign, and the garden was bright with flowers.

But soon enough, they would fade. And in the morning my son would be gone. I had thought to have five years more before I lost Constantine to the army, time enough for Atticus to train his mind, and for me to awaken his soul. Con was tall for his age, his muscles developed by exercise. He would be able to meet whatever physical demands might come.

But he still viewed the world with a child's rigid convictions regarding right and wrong. Diocletian might well be the most virtuous emperor since Marcus Aurelius, but his court would be a hotbed of intrigue. How could I armour my son against it without myself compromising his innocence?

'Don't be sad, my mother—'

I had not realized how my face betrayed me. I managed a smile. 'How can I not be? You know how much I love you. You are a man, and I knew that you must leave me one day, but this seems very soon.' I was choosing my words carefully, for it would not do to frighten the child, since this separation must be.

'When the letter first came, I was frightened too, but now I want to go,' said Constantine. 'But I will not forget you, Mother. I will write to you every week, as surely as the sun shines above!' He lifted a hand as if calling on Apollo to bear witness.

I gazed at him in surprise, for that oath had been spoken with adult sincerity.

'It will not be easy,' I told him. 'There will be new things and new people, exciting things to do . . .'

'I know—' He paused, searching for words. 'But kindred are important, and since you have no other children, I must be your whole family.'

My eyes filled with tears. 'Would you have liked brothers and sisters?'

Constantine nodded. 'When I am a man I want a big family.'

'I am sorry I was not able to provide them,' I said with difficulty. 'But I always thought that the purpose for which the gods had put me in this world was to give birth to you.'

His eyes rounded, for I had never spoken of this so explicitly before. 'Do you believe that my stars have ordained some great destiny?'

I nodded. 'I do. That is why I have been so concerned about your education.'

'Perhaps living at the court of Diocletian will be part of it,' Constantine said soberly.

'Oh, I am sure that it will.' I tried to keep the bitterness from my tone. 'But will it be what you need? I had hoped to teach you something of the Mysteries in which I myself was trained when I was young.'

Constantine shook his head. 'I do not think I am meant for a priesthood. When I am grown I will enter the army and command troops, or perhaps even a province, in time. I think I would do well at that, don't you?'

I suppressed a smile. Certainly he did not lack for confidence. I wondered if he, too, saw himself wearing the purple one day. Carinus had been an appalling example of the dangers of gifting a man unprepared for it with imperial power. My son might well be right to think that he could learn much from the Emperor if that was his destiny.

'If you rise high, Constantine, you must never forget that the gods are still above you, and the *Theos Hypsistos*, the Power that is beyond the gods. You must seek to fulfil their will for the people you rule.'

'I understand that,' he said confidently. 'The Emperor watches over his people as a father rules his family.'

I lifted one eyebrow. Apparently the boy had thought about it, and perhaps he had reason. His father had almost become heir to the Empire, after all. Constantine might well dream of an imperial diadem.

'The sun watches over me, just as He does my father.' Constantine patted my shoulder. 'Do not be afraid for me.'

I took his hand and held it against my cheek. My son certainly had the confidence to make his way in the world. Only later did it occur to me to wish that he had possessed a little more humility.

CHAPTER TWELVE

AD 293–296

'*The court has become ever more splendid,*' Constantine's large script straggled across the page. In the eight years since he had gone to join the Emperor's household he had no doubt learned many things, but elegant handwriting was not one of them. I shifted the page so that the wavering lamplight fell full upon it. The house which Constantius had rented for me in Colonia Agrippinensis was elegant, but not quite proof against the winds of a German spring.

'*A simple salutation is no longer enough, when one approaches the Emperor. Our* deus et dominus, *Diocletian, now requires a full prostration, as if he were the Great King of Parthia instead of the Augustus of Rome. But I must admit it is all very impressive, and the foreign ambassadors appear to be appropriately awed.*'

Maximian, thank the gods, remained the same bluff, hearty soldier he had always been, even though he was now co-Augustus with Diocletian. But no one could doubt which of the two was the senior partner. Diocletian's coins bore the image of Jupiter, while those of Maximian were adorned with the muscular form of Hercules.

But even if Maximian had been inclined to indulge in ceremony he would have been too busy to do so. The year he became Augustus, Carausius, the Menapian admiral they had appointed to defend Britannia from Saxon raiders, had been charged with misappropriating the spoils. Rather than stand trial in Rome he had rebelled and proclaimed himself Emperor of Britannia. The man was a brilliant seaman, who had roundly defeated not only the Saxon pirates, but the fleet Maximian sent against him. After that, our forces had been fully engaged with incursions of Franks and Alamanni in the east, and slave rebellions in the west of Gallia, with no time to worry about Britannia.

I missed my garden in Treveri, but Colonia, on the banks of the Rhenus in Germania Inferior, was close enough to the fighting for Constantius to visit me between campaigns. Our house was near the eastern wall, between the Praetorium and the temple of Mercurius Augustus, and had been occupied by the families of many commanders before us.

At least at the moment I did not have to worry about my husband's safety, for he had been summoned to Mediolanum, which Maximian had made his capital, to confer with him and Diocletian. I wondered sometimes if during those months spent away from me Constantius remained faithful, but in truth, if I had a rival it was not another woman but the Empire. When first we met I had loved him for his dreams. I could hardly complain because he now had an opportunity to make some of them reality. Still, with my husband off fighting and my son away with the Emperor there was little for me to do, and I found myself missing the responsibilities that would have been mine on Avalon.

For the moment, Diocletian and Maximian had accepted Carausius as a brother emperor. I wondered how long that would last. When I heard a rumour that Carausius was married to a British princess who had been trained on Avalon I was astonished. Ganeda had always feared and discouraged contact between Avalon and the outside world. That policy of isolation had been one of the reasons I left. But now I could not help thinking that if I had become High Priestess, it would have been I, not Dierna, who would now be deciding what role Avalon should play in this rapidly changing world. Sometimes I wished I could return to Britannia and find out what was happening there, but such a voyage was unlikely so long as Carausius ruled the British Sea.

*   *   *

On a bright day in the middle of March, when the wind, brisk as a hunting wolf, chased the little clouds across the sky, Constantius returned from Italia. At first, seeing his face as stony as it had been once after a lost battle, I thought the Emperor must have given him some reprimand, though I could not understand why Diocletian should be displeased. Surely it was Maximian, if anyone, who would be blamed for not having disposed of Carausius. If Diocletian was unhappy, I thought angrily as I directed the unpacking, he could come to Gallia and try his own hand at dealing with the situation here.

But the Germans led by Crocus, who had become Constantius's permanent bodyguard, were in fine fettle, filling the courtyard with their deep laughter, and surely they would have been gloomier if something were wrong. Most of them were quartered in the barracks at the Praetorium, of course, but there were always a round dozen or so about the house when Constantius was here.

I had grown accustomed to their size and their sometimes grim humour. I was a little surprised, to be sure, that Crocus himself had not come to greet me, as he had treated me with the deference due one of his own seeresses ever since our first meeting. Had something happened to him? That might explain my husband's mood.

I was in our bedchamber, sorting through the tunics from Constantius's baggage to see which ones might require mending, when my husband appeared in the doorway. I looked up, smiling, and saw him flinch. His face grew more forbidding as he glanced around the room.

'Constantius,' I said softly, 'what is wrong?'

'Come for a walk with me,' he said harshly. 'We need to talk, and I cannot do it . . . here.'

I could have assured him that none of our servants would eavesdrop, but it seemed better to change my slippers for sturdier sandals and take up a warm wrap without argument, and in truth, I would not be sorry to get out of the house on such a brilliant, restless day.

Ever since the rebellion of Civilis, in the time of the first Agrippina

207

after whom the city had been named, Colonia had been a frontier town. Other cities might neglect their defences, but Colonia's walls had been rebuilt at regular intervals until they rose high and strong, punctuated at regular intervals by guard towers. In times of peace, citizens could climb up by the stairs at the north gate and walk around to the east all the way to the gate by the Praetorium. Here, the banks of the river were already high, and the walls gave one a spectacular view of the bridge across the Rhenus and Germania Libera beyond.

I followed Constantius up the stone stairs, reassuring myself that it was not his health that was the problem, for he climbed without a pause for breath, the hard muscles of his calves flexing with each step. I, on the other hand, began to wish I had taken more regular exercise, for by the time we reached the walkway I was panting, and had to stop to catch my breath. Constantius put out a hand to steady me, then retreated to the wall, where he stood, arms resting on the crenellations and gazing northward where the barges moved smoothly down the river, until I joined him.

By this time my belly was knotting with apprehension. After so many years, I knew Constantius's moods as well as my own, and an angry confusion of emotion emanated from him so that he seemed wrapped in shadow, even while he stood in the sun. As I began to speak he started off and I followed him, recognizing that I would have to let him get to it in his own time and way.

The walls of the fortress at the other end of the bridge glowed, and sunlight glanced and sparkled from the blue waters of the river, very wide at this point and flowing strongly towards the sea. On the eves of festivals I would pour a little wine into the river, asking the gods of the waters to carry it to Britannia. As we passed the corner tower and turned towards the Praetorium, we moved into the wind off the river and I clutched at my shawl.

Constantius's steps slowed, and I realized that here, halfway between the tower and the gate where the cobbled road between the wall and the cloisters of the Praetorium was widest, must be the best place in Colonia to speak without being overheard.

'Surely,' I said aloud, 'You have not brought me here to speak of treason to the Emperor!' I stopped short, surprised how much anxiety had sharpened my tone.

'Do not be so sure!' Constantius answered harshly. 'He has put me in a position from which I must betray someone. The only choice I have is whom—'

'What do you mean?' I touched his arm and his other hand covered mine, gripping so tightly I winced with pain. 'What did he say to you?'

'Diocletian has had an idea . . . a way to extend the imperial power equally across the Empire and secure a peaceful succession. He vows that when he and Maximian have reigned for twenty years, they will retire in favour of their Caesars, who will then take the title of Augustus, and appoint two more.'

I stared at him, amazed at the idea that a man would voluntarily give up the supreme power. But it might just work, if all four of the emperors remained loyal to each other. The idea of an empire that was not torn apart by civil wars of succession seemed like some fantasy.

'So he means to appoint two Caesars . . .' I prompted, when the silence had gone on too long.

Constantius nodded. 'For the East, it will be Galerius. He's another man from Dalmatia, a hard fighter. They call him "the Herdsman" because his father kept cows—' He realized that he was babbling, and paused. 'For the West . . . he wants me.'

It seemed to me that I had known this even before he said it. It was the dream of a lifetime, this gift from the Emperor. Or perhaps it was not a gift, for why was Constantius so unhappy? I looked up into his dear face, permanently reddened by exposure to weather, the flaxen hair fading now to silver and receding from his broad brow. But to me he was still the fair lad I had met in Britannia.

'But there is a price,' he answered the question I could not ask. 'He requires that both Galerius and I marry into the imperial families.'

I could feel the colour draining from my face, and reached out to the stone to keep from falling. Constantius had his eyes fixed

209

on the horizon, as if he were afraid to see. I had heard that when a man is severely wounded, he feels first the shock, and only later, the pain. In that pause between the blow and my own agony, I found a moment to pity Constantius, who had had to bear this knowledge all the way from Mediolanum. And I understood now why Crocus had not come to see me. He was a man whose thoughts showed clearly in his face, and I would have read the truth of this disaster in his eyes.

'Galerius will marry Diocletian's daughter Valeria,' he said tonelessly. 'They want me to take Maximian's step-daughter Theodora.'

'I didn't even know he had a step-daughter,' I whispered, and then: 'They *want* you to take her? You mean you have not yet agreed?'

He gave a violent shake of the head. 'Not without speaking with you! Even the Emperor could not require that of me. And Maximian remembers you with kindness – he gave me this much reprieve, that I should be allowed to tell you myself, before everything was arranged—' He caught his breath on a sob. 'I vowed my heart's blood to the service of Rome, but not my heart! Not you!' He turned to me at last and gripped my shoulders so hard that the next day I would find bruises there.

I leaned my head against his chest and for a long moment we simply stood, locked together. For more than twenty years my life had revolved around this man; I had wondered sometimes if it was because I had given up so much for him, that I dared not feel any other way. And surely he, with so much more to occupy his mind, must be less dependent on me. But now I realized it was not so. Perhaps because his career had required him to be a creature of mind and will, all his heart was given to me.

'At the end of that river lies the sea,' he murmured against my hair, 'and across the sea is Britannia. I could take you there, offer my services to Carausius, and to Hades with the rest of the Empire! I have thought about it as I tried to sleep in the posting-houses on the way home . . .'

'Constantius,' I whispered. 'This is the opportunity you have dreamed of. All your life you have been preparing to be an emperor . . .'

'With you by my side, Helena, but not alone!'

My arms tightened around him, and then, like a spear to the heart, the realization came.

'You will have to do it, my beloved. You cannot defy Diocletian—' My voice cracked. 'He has Constantine.' And with that, the ice that had armoured me cracked suddenly and I wept in his arms.

Night was falling by the time we made our way back home, our eyes swollen with weeping, but for the moment emptied of tears. I drew my palla down and turned my face away when I told my maidservant to have a meal brought to our bedchamber. Drusilla would have known immediately that something was wrong, but Hrodlind was new, a German girl who was still learning Latin.

Constantius and I lay down together on our bed, while the food sat untouched. I had not even removed my palla, for I was chilled to the soul. If I killed myself, I thought numbly, it would be no better for Constantius, but at least I would be spared the pain. I said nothing, but Constantius had been the other half of my soul for too long not to sense what I was feeling, or perhaps it was his own experience that told him.

'Helena, you must live,' he said in a low voice. 'In every campaign, when danger threatened, it has been the knowledge that you were safe at home that gave me the courage to carry on. I can only do the duty that is being forced upon me now if I know you are still living, somewhere.'

'You are unjust. You will be surrounded by people, distracted constantly by responsibilities. Who will there be to need me, when you are gone?'

'Constantine . . .' The name hung in the darkness between us, my hope and my doom. For his sake I had left my home to follow Constantius, and for his sake we now must part.

We lay together in silence for a long time, while Constantius stroked my hair. I would not have thought that with our spirits so exhausted, the body could make any demands, but after a while, despite my despair, his familiar warmth began to relax me. I turned in his arms, and he brushed my hair back from my face and almost hesitantly, kissed me.

My lips were still stiff with grief, but beneath that gentle touch I felt them softening, and soon my whole body warmed and opened, yearning, one final time, to welcome him in.

In the morning, when I woke, Constantius was gone. On the table he had left a letter.

'*Beloved*—

'*Call me coward if you will, but only thus, when your beautiful eyes are closed in sleep, can I leave you. I will inform the household of the coming change in our situation, so as to spare you the need to explain to them what seems, even to me, to be an evil dream.*

'*I will be at the Praetorium for a short while, but I think it best, for my peace and yours, if we do not meet again. I am transferring this house to your ownership, with all of the slaves. In addition, my bankers have been instructed that you may continue to draw upon my account for whatever you may need, and if you should desire to move elsewhere, to transfer funds in your name.*

'*I will communicate with our son, of course, but I hope that you will be able to write to him as well. It will be you for whom his heart grieves, even as, I suppose, loyalty will compel him to congratulate me. But indeed, he ought to grieve for me as well.*

'*I hope, if the bounty of your heart allows it, that you will find a way to let me know where you go, and whether you are well. Whatever may befall, believe that while my heart beats, it is yours*—'

His usually careful signature trailed off, as if, at the end, his resolve had failed. I let the piece of papyrus fall, staring at the empty bed, the empty room, and an endless, empty succession of days through which I must somehow learn to live, alone.

For the better part of a week I scarcely left my bed, as devastated as I had been after I lost my first child. There was no further word from Constantius, though a badly-spelled note did arrive from Crocus, pledging his continued loyalty. I ate when Drusilla forced food upon me, but I would not let Hrodlind dress my hair, or change the bedding that seemed to me still to bear the impress of Constantius's body and the scent of his skin.

Hylas's silent devotion was the only sympathy I could bear, and I think now that it was the dog's warm body curled against my own and the poke of a cold nose when he wanted to be petted that kept me from losing contact with the outside world entirely. He was white-muzzled now, and moved stiffly when the weather chilled, but his heart was still warm. It would have been so easy, in the first shock of my loss, to retreat into madness. But as long as one creature needed me, as long as Hylas still offered me his unquestioning love, I was not completely alone.

I was not aware of any logic to my mourning, but when Philip came to me one afternoon to tell me that Constantius had departed Colonia for Mediolanum and his wedding, I realized that this was the news for which I had been waiting. Now I was truly alone. It was easy enough, in the end, to dissolve our union. No negotiations over the return of a dowry were required, for all I had brought to him were my skills as a priestess and my love, which could not be priced; or the custody of children, since our only son was in the keeping of the Emperor. In Rome, we had never truly been married, only in Avalon.

My mind seemed to move very slowly, but eventually I allowed Hrodlind to bathe and dress me, and the servants to come in to clean the room. But I did not leave the house. How could I bear to go abroad, where any passer-by might point to the cast-off concubine of the new Caesar, and laugh?

'Lady,' said Drusilla, setting down a platter with spring greens dressed with a little olive oil, hot barley cakes, and some new cheese. 'You cannot live like this. Let us go back to Britannia. You will be better at home!'

Home is Avalon . . . I thought, *and I cannot go there, where I would have to admit before them all that Constantius has aban-doned me.* But though relations with Carausius's island empire were tense, Britannia and Rome were not yet at war. Ships still sailed across the British Sea to Londinium. Surely there, a wealthy woman could live alone in respectable anonymity.

Philip made arrangements for us to embark from the port at Ganuenta just after the first day of summer. My first act, when I finally emerged from my chamber, had been to free him and the other slaves Constantius had left to me. Most of those we had purchased to staff the house in Colonia accepted their manumission gratefully, but I was surprised by how many of the older members of my household chose to remain. So it was that Philip and Drusilla and Hrodlind, whose own father had sold her into slavery, along with Decius, the boy who had tended my garden, and two of the kitchen maids, were to take ship with us for Londinium.

On the day before we were to depart, I walked out along the road to the old temple of Nehalennia. Hrodlind followed, carrying Hylas in a basket, for he could no longer walk so far, yet he whined pitifully whenever he was parted from me.

Perhaps the lichens covered more of the stones, and the tiles of the roof had a more mellow glow, but otherwise the place seemed unchanged. And the Goddess, when I confronted Her inside the temple, gazed past me with the same serenity. It was only I who was different.

Where was the young woman who had made her offerings at this altar, the British tongue still adding its music to her Latin, her gaze apprehensive as she faced this new land? After twenty-two years my speech had flattened, though it was much more eloquent, and it was Britannia which I would view with a stranger's eyes.

As for this temple, how could it be expected to impress me, now that I had seen the great shrines of the Empire? And how could the Goddess speak to me, now that I had lost my soul?

But I had brought a garland of spring flowers to lay before her, and when I had done so I stood with head bowed, and despite my depression, the peace of the place began to seep into my soul.

The temple was quiet, but not entirely silent. Somewhere in the eaves sparrows were nesting, their cheeps and twittering the grace-notes to a deeper murmuring which I eventually identified as the sound of the spring. And suddenly I had no need to descend to those waters, for the sound of them was all around me, an overwhelming sense of Presence that told me the Goddess had entered into her temple and I stood on holy ground.

'Where have you been?' I whispered, tears smarting beneath my closed eyelids. 'Why did you abandon me?'

And after a while, as I waited, I sensed an answer. The Goddess was here, as She had always been here, and in the running water, and upon the roads of the world, for those who were willing to be still and listen with their souls. Hylas had poked his head above the rim of the basket and was staring at a spot near the statue with the look usually reserved for me when I came home after a journey. I thought the place was just above the hidden spring.

I turned, lifting my hands in salutation. 'Elen of the Ways, hear my vow. I am a wife no longer, and I have been cast out of Avalon, but I will be Your priestess if you will show me what you wish me to do . . .'

I closed my eyes, and perhaps the sun, descending, chose that moment to shine through the high windows, or perhaps one of the temple servants had brought a lamp into the room, but suddenly I sensed a blaze of light. And though my eyes were still shut, that glow shone into the darkness that had engulfed my spirit when Constantius left me, and I knew that I would survive.

Londinium was the largest of Britannia's cities, larger than Sirmium or Treveri, if not so great as Rome. I was able to purchase a comfortable house in the northeastern part of the city, near the main road that led out towards Camulodunum. It had belonged to a silk merchant before his trade was disrupted by Carausius's wars, and in this part of the city, there was still enough open land for vegetable gardens and pasture, so that it was almost like being in the countryside.

I settled into the quiet life suited to the widow most of my neighbours believed me to be. I did not trouble to correct them, but made a regular circuit to the baths, the theatre, and the markets. And little my little, my inner turmoil eased. Like a legionary who has lost a limb in battle, I learned to compensate, and even at times to enjoy the things I had without immediately remembering those I would never have again.

From time to time, news would reach us from Rome. Constantius had taken Flavia Maximiana Theodora in marriage at the ides of Maia, a month which was said to be unlucky for marriages. I could not help hoping that in this case the tradition would prove to be true. But if Constantius still mourned for me, it did not prevent him from doing his husbandly duty, for at the end of the year we heard that Theodora had borne him a son, whom they called Dalmatius.

Theodora was not only younger than I, but she appeared to be the kind of woman who gets pregnant as soon as her husband hangs his belt on the bedpost, for after Dalmatius, another son, Julius Constantius, and two daughters, Constantia and Anastasia, were born in quick succession. I never saw Theodora, so I do not know whether she was, as the panegyrists were bound to say, beautiful.

I was now cut off from army gossip, but I could not help hearing talk in the market-place, and the political situation was degenerating. After getting Theodora pregnant, Constantius had returned to the army, and used his new authority as Caesar to mount an attack on Gesoriacum, the port from which Carausius had maintained his foothold in northern Gallia. The naval fortress was impregnable, but by building a mole across the entrance to the harbour, Constantius was able to cut the place off from support by sea, and shortly after mid-summer the garrison surrendered.

His next move was an attack on the Franks who were Carausius's allies at the mouth of the Rhenus. Trade was already suffering, and now, for the first time, people began to murmur against their upstart Emperor. It was said that his wife Teleri, the one who had been trained on Avalon, had gone back to her father, the prince of Durnovaria. Had she loved her Roman husband, I wondered, or was the marriage a political arrangement from which she was happy to be freed? And if so, had the alliance been made by the Prince of Durnovaria, or the High Priestess of Avalon? Teleri might be the only woman in Britannia who could understand me. I would have liked to talk with her.

And then, just before the feast that begins the harvest, men came crying through the streets with the news that Carausius was dead, and his minister of finance, Allectus, had claimed his throne, rewarding his old master's Frankish auxiliaries richly to support his claim. When it was announced that he would marry Teleri I shook my head. Allectus might call himself an emperor, but clearly he meant to be High King in the old way, by wedding the queen, and with her, the land.

I stood among the crowds who watched them on their way to their wedding feast. Allectus waved with a feverish gaiety, though there was tension in the way he gripped his reins. When the carriage in which Teleri was riding with her father passed by, I caught a glimpse of a white face beneath a cloud of dark hair, and thought she looked like a woman going to her execution, not her marriage bed.

Surely, I thought, Constantius would put an end to the pretensions of Allectus soon. But one year passed, and then another, with no challenge from Rome. Allectus pressed out an issue of hastily-minted coins and then lowered taxes. I could have told him that short-term popularity might prove a poor trade for repairs to fortifications when the Picts attacked or Rome decided to reclaim its errant province.

But I had taken care that no one should learn my identity. Constantine wrote regularly, letters filled with robust good cheer but few personal opinions, as if he suspected someone in the Emperor's household was reading his correspondence. I doubted that anyone was reading mine. It was not unusual to have a son in service abroad, after all. It was not my connection with Constantine that was the danger.

I had not heard from Constantius since he left me, but sometimes I saw him in my dreams and I did not think he had forgotten me. I would have made a valuable hostage, if Allectus had known who was living in his capital.

In the third year since I had come to Britannia, at the beginning of autumn, I had a series of dreams. In the first of them, I saw a dragon that emerged from the waves and coiled itself along the white cliffs of Dubris, guarding the shore. A fox came, and fawned upon it until the dragon ceased to pay attention to it, and then the fox leapt and bit the dragon's throat, and so the great beast died. And now the fox grew great, and decked himself in a purple mantle and a wreath of gold, and rode in a golden chariot about the land.

That dream was not hard to interpret, though I wondered why the gods had sent me a vision of something that had already come to pass. Still, I thought that perhaps some change was coming, and sent Philip more often to the forum to hear the news.

The next dream came with more urgency. Across the sea I saw coming two flights of eagles. The first group was driven back by the wind, but the second used mist and cloud to hide its approach and soared to the land. A flock of ravens rose up to combat it, and I saw they were protecting the fox, but the eagles overcame them and killed the fox, and the ravens retreated, shrieking, towards Londinium. Then the first group of eagles reappeared, descending just in time to defeat the ravens once and for all. And when they had done so, a lion appeared among them, and the people came out of the city to greet it, rejoicing.

When I awoke, a storm was lashing the rooftops. Bad weather for sailors, I thought sleepily, and then sat bolt upright with the sudden conviction that Constantius was out in that storm. But he would be safe, if my dream was a true one. It was Londinium which was likely to be in danger if the Frankish troops, whom I had seen as ravens, were defeated and in retaliation attacked the town.

I told Drusilla to lay in enough food to last us for several days. By sunset, we knew that the Roman army was on its way at last. Some said the legions would attack Portus Adurni, where

Allectus's fleet was waiting for them, while others thought they would come to Rutupiae and march on Londinium. But if I had dreamed true, Constantius was splitting his forces and would attack both places. That night I slept badly, waiting for what the morning would bring.

Throughout the next day, reports and rumours flew through the city. The storm had driven the Romans back, said some, while others told of an advance north from Clausentum and fighting near Calleva. Darkness had already fallen when Philip came back from the forum to tell us that a rider had come with the word that Allectus was dead, and his Frankish barbarians, who had taken most of the casualties, were falling back towards Londinium, vowing to make the city pay for their losses.

Philip was all for fleeing, having lived through the sack of a city when he was a child, but so far, all I had dreamed was coming to pass, and I had faith that Constantius would arrive in time. I had not yet determined what I would do when he did. Could I resist the temptation to see him once more, and if I did so what would become of my hard-won serenity? I went to bed that night as usual, partly to reassure my household, and somewhat to my surprise, I dreamed once more.

The fox lay dead on the battlefield. From its side rose a black swan that winged desperately through the stormy air, pursued both by the eagles and the ravens. When it settled to earth at last beside the governor's palace, it was the lion that menaced it. But from one of the side-streets appeared a greyhound, that held off the lion until the swan had the strength to make her escape.

When I woke, the first light of morning was filtering through the bed-curtains. From outside I could hear shouting, but someone would have roused me if there had been immediate danger. I lay still, going over the details of my dream until I was sure I could remember it.

When I did rise, I found the household gathered in the kitchen.

'Oh, Mistress,' exclaimed Drusilla, 'there's been a battle outside the city! Asclepiodotus, the Praetorian Prefect, beat Allectus at

219

Calleva, and here's the Master's fleet come up from Tanatus to save us from the Frankish barbarians!'

He is here — I thought, *or he soon will be.* I felt my heart beat more quickly, and the wall which had protected me from my memories was beginning to crumble away. If we met, would he still find me fair? I was past forty now, my body grown more solid with time, and there was silver in my hair.

'They are saying that by afternoon his legion will enter the city,' said Philip. 'The garrison Allectus left here has already fled, and his ministers and clerks and the rest of his household are scurrying about, gathering up their belongings and preparing to be gone before Constantius arrives.' He laughed.

But in my dream, I thought then, the swan had been unable to flee. I finished my porridge and set down the bowl.

'Philip, I will want the carriage in an hour, with you and Decius to walk beside it. Bring your sticks to discourage any trouble from the crowds.'

His face showed his amazement, but he had learned that commands given in that tone were not open to discussion. A little before noon we were turning out of our gate into the road. The cart was more suitable for country transport, but the top had leather curtains which could be drawn. Through the space between them I could see that the streets were full of people in a holiday mood. Some were already building an arch of greenery across the main road that led to the forum and adorning it with flowers.

I fingered the fabric of my gown nervously. I had bought it many years ago, because it was almost the blue of Avalon, and for the same reason rarely worn it. My thin woollen palla, of a darker blue, shadowed my face like a veil. Philip had not dared to question me. If we came home empty-handed he would think me mad, though he might doubt my sanity more were we to succeed.

There was no one guarding the gates to the palace. I directed my driver to a side door that I remembered from the one time I had accompanied Constantius on a visit to Britannia, descended, and slipped inside. The corridors showed the signs of a hasty departure.

I made my way swiftly to the suite of rooms that were normally occupied by the Governor, which I suspected Allectus had made his own.

And there, sitting alone in the great bed, half-dressed and staring, I found my black swan.

As I had expected, she was very lovely, with white skin and curling black hair that fell about her shoulders. And not as young as she had looked at first glance, for there were lines of bitterness at the corners of the full lips and shadows beneath the dark eyes.

'Teleri—'

It took a long moment, as if her spirit had been wandering, before she stirred. But her vague gaze focused as she saw the blue gown.

'Who are you?'

'A friend – you must come with me, Teleri. Gather up whatever you would take with you.'

'The servants took my jewels,' she whispered, 'but they were not mine, but *his*. I have nothing . . . I *am* nothing, on my own.'

'Then come as you are, but quickly. The Caesar would do you no harm, but I do not think you would wish to be a trophy of his victory.'

'Why should I trust you? Everyone else has betrayed me, even Avalon.'

I was glad to see she retained some sense of self-preservation, but this was no time to waver. In the distance I could hear a sound like the surf on the shore and knew that the people of Londinium were cheering. I pulled back my palla so that she could see the faded crescent between my brows.

'Because I too was once a priestess. In the name of the Great Mother of us all, I beg you to come away.'

For a long moment we stayed with locked gaze. I do not know what she read in my eyes, but when I held out my hand and turned to go, Teleri gathered up one of the bedcovers for a mantle and followed me.

We were just in time. As my carriage creaked through the gate and turned down the side-road, from the direction of the forum I heard the blare of military clarions and the rhythmic slap of hobnailed sandals. My grip on the wooden seat of the waggon tightened until the knuckles showed white. The people were shouting – the words came clearer as we moved on:

'*Redditor Lucis, Redditor Lucis!*'

Restorer of the Light . . .

My closed eyes could not shut out the brightness that was blossoming in my awareness. Constantius was coming, his presence a radiance in my soul. Did he feel that I was near, or were the responsibilities of his office and the tumult around him a sufficient distraction?

As the people of Londinium cried out in welcome to their saviour, my cheeks grew wet with silent tears.

CHAPTER THIRTEEN

AD 296–305

During the weeks that Constantius spent in Britannia I remained
true to my vow and made no attempt to see him, but my self-
discipline took its own toll. My woman's courses, never regular,
had almost ceased, and now a variety of other symptoms, from a
pounding heart to waves of heat that left me drenched as if even
my body were weeping, added to my misery.

Meanwhile the city was rejoicing at the word that Theodora had
borne Constantius another child. I knew he had been devastated by
our parting, but by now he must be appreciating the advantages of
a wife who was royal, young and fertile. Prudence, which had kept
me out of his sight before, gave way to despair.

The counsels of wisdom I had meant to give Teleri went unspoken.
For her sake I had missed even the glimpse of him I might otherwise
have had, though at the time I had thought even that much unwise.
Constantine wrote to tell me that he was going to Egypt with
Diocletian to fight someone called Domitius who had started a
rebellion there, and so to my other troubles I could add anxiety
for his safety.

And then Constantius left Britannia, and I learned the true
meaning of despair. Lying with curtains drawn in my bedchamber I
refused to rise and dress myself, and neither Drusilla's most delicate
recipes nor Hrodlind's pleading could persuade me to eat. For most
of a week I lay, accepting no company but that of Hylas, who was
now grown so old that he spent his days dozing by the brazier,

223

though when I was in the house he still insisted on following me from room to room. I rejoiced in my growing weakness, for though I had promised Constantius I would not take my life, this gentle slide into oblivion seemed a welcome surcease to my suffering.

And as weakness loosed the fetters of my mind, a vision came.

It seemed to me that I was wandering in a misty landscape like the borders of Avalon. I had come to confront the Goddess, to learn the next step in my own passage, to go beyond the Mother and meet the Crone. Before, I could never see beyond the Mother, who must be the central face of the Goddess, and the two on either side, Nymph and Crone, only Her handmaidens.

But what I was enduring now was the ultimate childbirth, the ultimate test of strength and courage. Now, confronting my own transition from the status of motherhood, I was forced to see the world-tragedy of mothers. Even Jesus, according to the Christians, had a mother, and again and again and again I saw him leaning on her arm, and when life deserted and defeated him he cried out to her too. I said, 'Just like a man; he went on and died bravely and left the women to put his work together again afterwards.' Fear for my own son overwhelmed me and I cried bitterly, 'Does the Mother have to let her children go just to be crucified?'

I asked what was beyond. Again and again I received only the sense of being a ship's figurehead cleaving water towards the unknown.

Then I seemed to perceive woman's central tragedy. I had lost my own mother before I could even know her, and was left alone, lost, desperate, crying out for comfort. It was a situation in which we women continue to find ourselves lifelong. We are forced to lend strength to men, to bear and feed our own children. Outsiders saw me as strong, but I was a child crying in the dark for comfort and my mother had gone away and would never be there for me again.

And then the twist of the knife. Before I was barely old enough to stand alone, before I had had time or strength to know who I was, a smaller hand had been tucked into mine and the Voice had said, 'Here. This is your little cousin. Look after her.'

224

And this is the confrontation with Life, the first awareness that perhaps we should cry out, 'No,' and strike down that little form and batter it until it lies dead and cold and no longer demanding, and run on free, untrammelled, shouting, 'Mother, wait, there's only me.'

Or else we must make the other choice, being deprived of the Mother, to *become* the mother, and pick up the little one when she falls down, and wipe away her tears, and rock her to sleep, clinging together against the dark because she is as much in need of comfort as you, and you are the stronger so it is yours to give . . .

And that, I realized as the bright images misted away, was what I had done, first for Becca and Dierna, and later for a succession of maidservants and soldiers' wives and junior officers in my husband's command. And for Teleri, though I had failed her, at the last.

And then I realized that someone was with me in the room. I had left strict orders that I was not to be disturbed, but I was too weak now even for anger. I opened my eyes.

Teleri was sitting beside my bed, slumped a little in the chair, as if she had been there for some time. In her lap she held a bowl of porridge. It still steamed, and the scent brought back memories of the Hall of the Priestesses on a frosty morning, when we had all gathered to eat our daymeal around the central fire. It was this scent, I realized, that had brought me back from my vision, the fragrance of porridge with honey and dried apples as they made it in Avalon.

'Your servants dared not trouble you,' she said softly, 'but I will not add to the sins I already bear that of letting you die when there is something I can do.'

I reached out for the bleak security of despair, but my stomach was growling. Apparently my body had decided to live, and it was no use arguing. With a sigh, I held out my hand for the bowl.

'When you are well,' said Teleri, 'I will leave you. I am going back to Avalon. I should never have left it, and if Dierna casts me out, I will wander until death takes me in the Mist between the worlds.'

That was what I had been doing, I thought grimly, and without the trouble of travelling to the Summer Country, but it seemed to me that I had lost the right to criticize.

'Come with me, Helena. I do not know your story, but it is clear that you are a priestess of Avalon.'

I swallowed a bite of porridge, considering. Had I been forgotten already? Ganeda might well have been bitter enough to erase my name from the rolls of priestesses. But perhaps the explanation was simpler.

'When I dwelt on the Holy Isle I was called Eilan,' I said slowly, and saw her eyes widen.

'You are the one who ran away with a Roman officer! Not since the days of the first Eilan who was High Priestess at Vernemeton has there been such a scandal. But Dierna said that you were kind to her when she was a little child, and always spoke well of you. Is your Roman dead, then? Your servants do not speak about him.'

'Not dead, except to me,' I said through stiff lips. 'He is Constantius Chlorus, the father of my son Constantine.'

Teleri's eyes filled with tears. 'I was married to Carausius, who was a good man though I could never love him, and to Allectus, whom I did love, though he was good neither for Britannia nor for me.'

'This was Dierna's will?' In the end, it would seem that Ganeda had trained her grand-daughter well.

'She wanted to bind the Defender of Britannia to Avalon.'

I nodded, understanding that this was the same hope that had originally sent me out to seek Constantius.

'Dierna is a great priestess, however badly things turned out for me,' Teleri said earnestly. 'I am sure that she would welcome you—'

And then attempt to use me, all for the good of Avalon, I thought bitterly. Once, I might have had as good a claim to be Lady of the Holy Isle as she, but I had been away too long, and though Constantius had abandoned me, his son, whose last letter lay even now on the table beside my bed, had more need of my counsel than the priestesses of Avalon.

'To Dierna, and to her only, you may say that I still live, and that I send my love to her. But I think that the Goddess may still have work for me in the world.'

A week later, when I came down to breakfast, they told me that Teleri had gone. She had what was left from the money I had given her to buy clothing, and all I could do for her now was to ask the blessing of the Lady upon her journeying.

Spring had come to Londinium. The Tamesis ran high with rainfall and new leaves were springing from every branch, welcoming the returning birds. Life returned to my limbs, and suddenly I needed to be outside, walking through the pastures and along the stream that divided the city. At other times I would go past the forum and over to the baths, or farther still, to the Temple of Isis that had been built near the western gates to the town. With each day I grew stronger, and less content to sulk at home, brooding on my misery. I missed the patter of paws at my heels, but as soon as I began to recover, Hylas had died, as if he felt his duty was now done. He had lived a long time for a dog, but I could not bring myself to get another.

A stone-carver had his workshop between the Isaeum and the Temple of Diana, and I conceived the idea of commissioning from him a relief of the *matronae*, the trio of ancestral mothers who were honoured all over the Empire. But it had come to me that my carving should be different, and so in addition to the usual three figures, two of them holding baskets of fruit and the third a child, I asked the sculptor to carve a fourth Mother, this one holding in her lap a dog.

Perhaps the Mothers were grateful, for within a moon, I met three people who were to make a profound difference in my life during the remaining years I spent in Londinium.

I encountered the first immediately after finishing negotiations over the carving. I had set out in search of a cookshop where I could have a bit of bread and sausage before starting home. But as I turned the corner, I nearly tripped over something furry, and looking down, found myself surrounded by cats. If this was an omen, I did not understand it. There must have been two dozen, of all shapes and colours, waiting impatiently in front of a rather ramshackle building that had been added on to the back of the Temple of Isis.

I heard a ripple of words in some foreign tongue, turned and saw a small, round woman draped in several tunicas and a palla of brightly clashing colours, and leaning on a cane. Dark hair was partly covered by windings of purple, and she was carrying a basket that smelled strongly of fish even from here.

She looked up and saw me. 'Oh I am sorry,' she said in Latin. 'They get very insistent, the greedy pusses, but I am the only one who will feed them, you see.'

As she opened the bag and began to dole out fish heads I could see that her dark eyes had been elongated with kohl, and her skin had a warm glow that had never come from a British sun. Around her neck hung a pendant of a cat in the Egyptian style.

'Are you a priestess?' I asked.

'I am Katiya, and I serve the Lady Bast—' She started to touch one hand to her forehead in homage, realized that she was holding a piece of fish, laughed, and cast it to a big orange tomcat who waited to one side.

'Eastward we gaze upon Bast, the Queen-Cat,' she chanted softly. 'In the east we seek for the soul of Isis, Light-bearer, Moon-mother, gentle protectress. To the shrine of Per-Bast we direct our prayers . . . But I am the only one in Londinium who does so,' she added, shaking her head. 'In Egypt all people know that the cat is sacred to the Goddess, but merchants bring cats to Britannia and leave them, and no one seems to care. Only the priests of Isis let me stay here because they know that Bast and Isis are sisters. I do what I can.'

'My goddess favours dogs,' I told her, 'but I suppose that Bast is *her* sister as well. Will you accept an offering?'

'In my Lady's name,' she answered, and from amongst her draperies fetched out a net bag, somewhat less redolent of fish than the basket, into which I could drop a few coins. 'I feed my little ones, and I make songs. Come to me when you are sad, noble lady, and I will cheer you.'

'I think it very likely you will!' I answered, laughing in spite of myself. And thereafter, for as long as I lived in Londinium, I would visit Katiya every week or so and make my offering. Just to keep the scales balanced, however, I made a donation to the Temple of Diana, who loves hounds, for the care of the city's stray dogs. From time to time I would take one of these foundlings home with me, but though I enjoyed the patter of paws about the house, with none of them did I find the bond I had had with Hylas and Eldri.

The second meeting occurred one day when I noticed the name 'Corinthius' on a sign above a door and paused, remembering the old Greek who had been my tutor when I was a child. From inside I could hear the sound of young voices declining Greek verbs. Corinthius had told me he intended to set up a school. I asked Philip, who was with me, to knock and enquire, and soon I was taking wine with a young man who told me he was the son of my old tutor, who had married when he got to Londinium, and begotten this son to eventually inherit his school.

'Oh yes, my lady, my father often spoke of you,' said Corinthius the Younger. Crooked teeth showed as he grinned. 'He used to say that you were brighter than any boy he ever taught, especially when I had not done well at my lessons.'

I could not help smiling in answer. 'He was a good teacher. I wish I could have studied with him longer, but I was lucky my father believed a girl-child should be educated at all.' I did not tell him that my studies with the old Greek had been followed by a much more extensive education at Avalon.

'Oh indeed,' Corinthius nodded. 'I am so sorry sometimes, when I see my lads with their sisters, that I am not able to teach the girls as well. I think that some of their parents would be willing, but they do not like to send their girls to a male teacher, and of course there are not so many educated women here as in Rome or Alexandria . . .' He poured more wine.

'Do you know,' I said eventually. 'I have always wished that I had a daughter, to whom I could pass on some of the things I know. You might suggest to the mothers of some of these boys who have sisters that they pay a call on me. My husband left me with enough to live on, but I find myself a little lonely, and would welcome a . . . circle . . . of friends.'

'You will be like Sappho in the meadows of Lesbos,' exclaimed Corinthius, 'beloved of the gods!'

'Perhaps not quite like Sappho,' I replied, smiling, for when we lived in Drepanum I had read some of her poems that my tutor had never shown me. 'But tell the women, and we shall see.'

Corinthius kept his word, and by the time the carving of the *matronae* was finished and installed in a shrine, a group of mothers and daughters were coming to my home at the new moon and the full, and if what I taught them owed more to Avalon than it did to Athens, it was no one's business but our own. But not even to these, the first sisters in spirit I had had since I left the Holy Isle, did I confide whose wife I had been.

The third meeting took place at the baths, where one was assured of eventually meeting everyone in the city, during the hours reserved for women. Seen through clouds of billowing steam, everyone looks mysterious, but it seemed to me that the voice that was so loudly complaining about the price of wheat was familiar, and the long-boned, dark face as well.

'Vitellia, is it you?' I asked when she drew breath at last. Through the steam I could see that the golden fish still hung from its chain about her neck.

'By Heaven's blessings, it is Helena! When I heard about – the marriage – I wondered—'

'Hush!' I held up one hand, 'I do not speak of that here. I was well provided for, and people think me a rich widow with a son serving abroad.'

'Well then, let us be widows together! Come, let us eat a bite, and you shall tell me all that has happened since your son was born!'

We dried and dressed ourselves and went out through the marble portico. As we passed the statue of Venus I saw Vitellia glance at it nervously, but there was nothing there to account for the disgust with which she hurried past, only a garland of flowers that someone had draped across the pedestal.

'I am sure that people would not do that if they knew how difficult it is for us,' she muttered as we passed out into the road. 'I know that you are not of the true faith, but in the days when our husbands were serving together, all the officers paid honour to the Highest God, so perhaps you can understand. We are commanded to avoid idolatry, you see, and yet we are surrounded by graven images and sacrifices.'

She gestured down the street, and I saw, as I had seen a hundred times without thinking anything of it, that we were surrounded by gods. An image of Neptune rose from a fountain, nymphs and fauns grinned from the corbels of houses, and the crossroads was marked by a shrine to some local spirit who had recently received a plateful of food and a bunch of flowers as an offering. I remembered being struck by the lavish display when first I came from Avalon, where we knew that all the earth was holy, but saw no reason to emphasize the point with all these decorations, but I had become accustomed to it, after more than twenty years.

'But no one asks you to honour them,' I said slowly – for it had been years since any emperor had tried to enforce that requirement.

'Even to touch them, to *see* them, is a pollution,' Vitellia sighed. 'Only in the church we have built in the woods outside the walls can we feel truly free.'

I lifted one eyebrow. I had walked out along the north road at Beltane, when even the fields inside Londinium were too confined for me. I thought now that I remembered the building, a modest daub-and-wattle structure with a simple cross over the door. But the woodland that surrounded it had hummed with the power of the spirits that were abroad that day, and patches of flattened grass showed where young couples had honoured the Lord and the Lady in their own way the preceding eve. How could the

231

Christians imagine they would avoid the old gods by moving outside the town?

Still, it was not for me to open their eyes to what they so manifestly did not desire to see. Vitellia was still talking:

'And one of our older members donated a building near the wharves that we have made into a refuge for the poor. Our Lord commanded us to care for the widow and the orphan, and so we do, nor do we ask what faith they hold, so long as they speak no demon's names within our walls.'

'That seems a worthy work,' I told her. Certainly it was more than any of the magistrates were likely to do.

'We can always use helpers, to treat their ills, and serve out the food,' said Vitellia. 'I remember hearing that you knew something of herb-lore, when we were in Dalmatia.'

I suppressed a smile. Teaching had blessed, but did not quite fill, my days. It might prove interesting, I thought, to work with these Christians for a while.

And so it proved, and for the next seven years, my life was both rich and full, and more useful, I suppose, than it had been when my only responsibilities were to keep Constantius's house and share his bed.

It was at the end of February in the third year of the new century that the news that was to change everything arrived. I was on my way home from my weekly visit to the priestess of Bast, when I heard a tumult from the market-place. When I turned in that direction, Philip, who had been my escort that day, stopped me.

'If there is a riot, Mistress, I may not be able to protect you. Stay here—' He grimaced as he realized we were in front of the Mithraeum. 'Here you will be safe, and I will go and see what the excitement is all about!'

I smiled a little as I watched him stride down the road, remembering the scrawny boy he had been when he first joined our household. He was still lightly built, but he had a very solid presence now. I tried to remember whether that change had come when he became a Christian, or when Constantius freed him. I rather thought it was the former, that had liberated his spirit even before his legal status was altered. Perhaps that was why, given his freedom, he had chosen to stay with me.

It seemed a long time before he returned. I seated myself on a bench in front of the Mithraeum, contemplating the relief of the god slaying the bull. I wondered if Constantius had visited this place when he was in Britannia. I knew that he had continued to rise in rank in the cult, for I remembered times when he had been absent for additional initiations, but of course the worship of Mithras had no place for women and he was forbidden to tell me what went on. Still, to sit here was almost like being under his protection. I was glad to find that the thought made my heart ache only a little, now.

Then I heard quick footsteps and saw Philip coming, his face white with shock and anger.

'What has happened?' I rose to meet him.

'A new edict! Diocletian, may God curse him, has begun the persecutions again!'

I frowned, hurrying to catch up as he started down the street again, for the murmur of the crowd was beginning to sound ugly. I remembered hearing rumours of trouble a few years before when the presence of Christians was said to have spoiled the Emperor's ritual. A few officers in the army had been executed for refusing to join in the sacrifices, and some others expelled, but nothing more had come of it. In most places, the Christians, though considered peculiar, got along well enough with their neighbours.

How could Diocletian be so stupid? I had been around Christians long enough by now to know that far from fearing martyrdom, they welcomed it as an easy way to cancel out all sins and win the favour of their gloomy god. The blood of the martyrs, they said, was the nourishment of the Church. Killing them only reinforced their belief in their own importance and made the cult stronger.

'What does the edict *say*?' I repeated as I caught up with Philip.

'Christianity is outlawed. All copies of the scriptures are to be turned in and burnt, all churches to be seized and destroyed.' He spat out the words.

'But what about the people?'

'So far, only the priests and bishops are mentioned. They are required to offer sacrifice in the presence of a magistrate or be jailed. I must get you home, Lady – the garrison is coming out, and the streets will not be safe.'

'And what about you?' I asked, between breaths.

'With your leave, I will go out to the church and offer my help. Perhaps something can be saved if we are in time.'

'You are a free man, Philip,' I said, 'and I do not presume to command your conscience. But I beg you in the name of your god, take care!'

'If you will also do so!' He managed a smile as we neared my door. 'Keep the rest of the household indoors. Though you are still a worshipper of demons, the High God loves you well!'

'Thank you! I think!' I watched him hurry off down the road. Still, blessings should be welcomed, from whatever quarter. Shaking my head, I went in.

For a day and a night, the detachment from the fortress tramped through the streets, searching out Christian leaders and property. By the time it was over, the bishop of Vitellia's church was in custody, and the little church in the woods by the north road had burned to the ground. The holy books, however, had been hidden safely, and a pile of church accounts given to the authorities to destroy.

The smoke of the burning was carried away by the wind, but the stench, both physical and metaphoric, lingered longer. Diocletian had ruled wisely for almost twenty years, but in his attempts to preserve our society, the Emperor was effectively dividing it. As I had predicted, persecution only made the Christians more stubborn, and there were more of them than most of us had realized.

These days the Christians met in secret in their houses. Philip reported to me that letters from the eastern part of the Empire told of arrests and executions. But to my relief, Constantius did no more than enforce the letter of the new law in those portions of the Empire under his control. And once the first excitement was over, the general population showed little enthusiasm for persecuting their neighbours. How those Christian neighbours might view the rest of us was not a question which at that moment applied.

Still, it seemed to me that in times such as these, I ought to offer the maidens I was teaching something more relevant than Homer and Virgil, and so, from time to time, I would turn our discussions to the issues that divided men today.

'It is necessary,' I said one morning, 'that the educated person understand not only what she believes, but why she believes it. And so I ask you, who is the Supreme God?'

For a long moment the girls looked at each other, as if not quite certain I really meant what I was asking, much less that it applied to them. Finally, Lucretia, whose family exported wool, raised her hand.

'Jupiter is the king of the gods, that's why the Emperor puts his image on his coins.'

'But the Christians say that all deities except the god of the Jews are demons,' offered Tertia, the sandal-maker's daughter.

'That is very true, and so I ask you, how many gods are there?'

This elicited a babble of discussion, until I held up a hand for silence once more. 'You are all correct, according to our way of thinking. Every land and district has its own deities, and in the Empire, our practice has been to honour them all. But consider this, the greatest of our own philosophers and poets speak of a supreme divinity. Some call this Power "Nature", and others "Aether", and still others, "the High God". The poet Maro tells us,

> 'Know first, the heaven, the earth, the main,
> The moon's pale orb, the starry train,
>   Are nourished by a Soul,
> A Spirit, whose celestial flame
> Glows in each member of the frame,
>   And stirs the mighty whole."'

'But what about the Goddess?' asked little Portia, pointing towards the altar in the corner of the sunny chamber we used as a classroom, where a lamp was always kept burning before the relief of the Mothers. Sometimes, when no one else was present, I would pat the head of the dog in the fourth Mother's lap, and feel it warm and smooth beneath my hand as if Hylas had come back to me.

I smiled, having hoped that someone would raise this point.

'Certainly, it makes more sense to see the Highest Power as female, if one must assign a gender to Deity, for it is the female who gives birth. Even Jesus, whom the Christians say was the son of God, or even God himself, had to be born from Maria before he could take human form.'

'Well of course!' answered Portia. 'That's where the heroes and demi-gods come from – Hercules, and Aeneas, and the rest of them.'

'But the Christians say their Jesus was the only one,' observed Lucretia. The rest of the girls contemplated this lack of logic and shook their heads.

'Let us return to the original question,' I said when the discussion came to an end. 'Pythagoras tells us that the supreme Power is "a soul passing to and fro, and diffused through all parts of the universe, and through all nature, from which all living creatures which are produced derive their life." This is very much the same teaching as I received among the Druids, except, as I said, that we tend to think of this Power as being female when we give it a gender.

'This being so,' I gestured towards the *matronae* once more, 'why do we feel impelled to make images of that which cannot, in truth, be pictured, and divide it up into gods and goddesses and give them histories and names? Even the Christians do it – they say their Jesus is the Supreme God, and yet the stories they tell about him are just like our own hero tales!'

There was a long silence. In a way, I thought, it was unfair to ask these girls to answer a question whose solution had eluded the theologians and philosophers. But perhaps, just because they were female, they might find it easier to understand.

'You have dolls at home, don't you?' I added. 'But you know they are not real babies. Why do you love them?'

'Because . . .' Lucretia said hesitantly after another pause, 'I can hold onto them. I pretend they are the babies I will have when I grow up. It is hard to love something that has no face or name.'

'I think that is a very good answer, don't you?' I asked, looking around the circle. 'In our minds we can understand the Highest God, but so long as we are in human bodies, living in this rich and varied world, we need images that we can see and touch and love. And each one of them shows us a part of that supreme Power, and all the parts together give us a glimpse of the whole. So the people who insist there is only One God are right, and so are those who honour the many, but in different ways.'

They were nodding, but I could see a glaze of incomprehension in some of their eyes, and others were looking out into the garden, as if they found more truth in the play of light on the leaves. Still, I could hope that something of what I had said would stay with them. Laughing, I dismissed them to go out and play.

For two more years, Diocletian's edict remained in force in Britannia. The year after the edict, when everyone was ordered to sacrifice, a soldier named Albanus had been put to death in Verulamium for refusing to do so, and one day I found Vitellia weeping because she had heard that her fourteen-year-old nephew, Pancratus, had been killed in Rome, but in Londinium there were no executions, though the bishop had been imprisoned and stayed under guard.

The Christians continued to meet in their houses, and when even that became too dangerous, I allowed them to hold services in mine. Or rather, in my atrium, since even with veils thrown over my images and altars, the interior was considered too polluted for them to expose the holy things of their god. They were happy, however, to welcome me to those parts of their service open to the uninitiated.

Nathaniel the rope-maker, who, since he was only a deacon in the church, had escaped arrest with the others, was holding forth to his congregation, the men on one side of the garden and the women on the other, heads covered and eyes cast down in piety.

'*Oh God, the heathen have come into thy inheritance;*' he intoned, moving his finger along the line of writing.

Vitellia sat in the first row, eyes closed and lips moving. Why did they not allow her to speak, I wondered, since obviously she knew the holy writings as well as he?

'*They have defiled thy holy temple; they have laid Jerusalem in ruins. They have given the bodies of thy servants to the birds of the air for food . . .*'

As he continued I reflected on the appropriateness of the words, which had been written, so I was told, by one of the ancient Jewish kings.

'*We have become a taunt to our neighbours, mocked and derided by those round about us . . .*'

Apparently those who served the god of the Jews had always had difficulty in getting along with their neighbours. Was it because they were wrong, or because, as they believed, they were ahead of their time? I had suggested that since the Christians did not believe in our gods, it could do no harm for them to go through the motions of making an offering, but Vitellia reacted with horror. I realized then that the Christians *did* believe in the gods, and considered them evil. I did not understand her reasoning, but I had to admire her integrity.

'*. . . let thy compassion come speedily to meet us, for we are brought very low. Help us, O God of our salvation, for the glory of thy name . . .*'

For the past few minutes I had been aware of a distant murmur. As Nathaniel paused, it grew louder – the sound of many feet and many voices. The Christians heard it too.

Softly, one of the women began to sing—

'The eternal gifts of Christ the King,
The martyrs' glorious deeds we sing;
And all, with hearts of gladness, raise
Due hymns of thankful love and praise . . .'

I caught Philip's eye and nodded, and he got up and went through the house towards the door.

Then we heard a heavy banging, and even Nathaniel's voice failed. Some of the women were weeping, but others sat straight with burning eyes, as if hoping for martyrdom. And they continued to sing.

'They braved the terrors of the time,
No torment shook their faith sublime;
Soon, holy death brought peace and rest
And light eternal with the blest.'

I rose to my feet. 'Do not be afraid. I will go out to them.'

When I got to the door, Philip had it open, confronting the crowd. I stepped past them, and as the first man opened his lips to speak, stared him down.

'I am Julia Coelia Helena. For twenty years I was the wife of Constantius who is now your Caesar, the mother of his first born son. And I promise you, it is his wrath that you will feel if you dare to invade my home!'

Behind me, the Christians were still singing—

'Redeemer, hear us of thy love,
That, with thy martyr host above,
Thy servants, too may find a place,
And reign forever through thy grace.'

'Oh Lady!' the leader shook his head, and I saw that he was laughing. Now I could see that many of those in the crowd had

239

garlands on their heads, or carried wineskins, and I began to realize that the fervent souls who were singing behind me were going to be frustrated in their desire for martyrdom.

'That was never our intention! In the name of Jupiter and Apollo, we are not bent on slaughter, but celebration! Have you not heard the news? Diocletian and Maximian have abdicated, and your Constantius is now Augustus!'

CHAPTER FOURTEEN

AD 305–306

In my dream I was walking with Constantius along the banks of a river. I could not tell if it was the Rhenus or the Tamesis, for the sky was a dim, featureless grey. It hardly mattered, since my beloved was with me. His features were shadowed, but my body knew the strong grip of his hand. It was unexpectedly sweet, after so many years in which I had denied even my memories, to have his companionship.

'Where are you taking me?' I asked.

'To see me off on my journey—'

'Not again!' I stopped, trying to hold him, but his steady progress drew me on. 'Please, do not leave me again!'

'This time,' he told me, 'it is only by leaving you that I can be with you once more.'

'Is night falling?' I asked through my tears.

'No, my beloved, look – it is the morning!'

I blinked, for his face was growing more radiant as the sun rose above the horizon. And then he was all light, slipping through my fingers as I reached out to embrace the dawn . . .

Light blazed through my eyelids, and someone was banging on the door. I struggled free of the bedclothes, rubbing my eyes as the ordinary reality of my bedchamber, frescoed with scenes of the nymphs of wood and fountain, replaced the misty radiance of my dream. It could not be danger – though Vitellia was still living with me, in a new wing we had built onto the house where no one had ever honoured the gods. Since Constantius became Augustus, even the pretence of Christian persecution had ceased. But spring sunlight was flooding through the windows. Clearly I was going to get no more sleep, and it was time to start the day.

As I pulled off my sleeping shift and began to wash from the basin I could hear voices below. My hair showed a few threads of silver at the temples, but I still walked everywhere instead of taking the carriage or a chair, and my body was firm. Hrodlind appeared in the doorway, and seeing that I was up, hurried to set out a fresh shift and one of my finer tunicas, the saffron silk with embroideries of wheat sheaves around the hem.

When she saw the surprise on my face she grinned. 'You have a visitor, Mistress. You will want to look your best today!'

I considered forcing the truth out of her, but apparently it was not some disaster. I held out my arms for her to pin the gown without a word, suppressing a smile at her expression. She had not expected me to give in so easily.

By the time I approached the dining room, settling a palla of light-weight, creamy wool across my shoulders against the early morning chill, I could smell the tantalizing aroma of nut custard, which Drusilla used to make as a holiday meal when Constantine was a boy. And with that, I stopped short, understanding who, beyond all hope or expectation, my visitor must be.

My heart pounded in my breast and I took a deep breath, grateful for the sense of smell which is the key to memory, and which had given me this warning. Constantine could not be bringing bad news, I thought, or the servants would not have been so cheerful. I waited a little longer, summoning up the courage to face this son whom I had not seen since he had been home for a visit when he was eighteen years old. He had written, of course, but guardedly, as if he suspected his letters were being intercepted. I no longer knew where his heart lay, and I wondered if the intervening thirteen years had changed him more than they had me.

242

Then I rearranged my palla and made my entrance into the dining room.

A strange officer was sitting by the window, positioned where his moulded bronze cuirass would catch the morning sun. At least he had had the courtesy to remove his helmet. I noted the fair hair, worn rather long with a hint of curl, and my view of him doubled suddenly into the image of a stranger and the recognition that this was Constantine. He had opened the window, and was looking out at the birds splashing in the bath I had set up for them in the atrium, and had not heard me come in.

For a moment longer I indulged myself with the sight of him. A long-sleeved tunic of white wool edged with crimson showed beneath the armour, and well-worn breeches of tan suede. In fact the entire outfit, though it was of the best quality, showed the effects of long use. Perhaps Constantine had not intended to show off, but had come to me in his armour because he had nothing else decent to wear. But I must, I thought then, allow him his pride.

'Uniform becomes you, my son,' I said softly.

He turned swiftly and jumped to his feet, surprise changing swiftly to joy that lit his face as if the sun had risen in the room. In the next moment I was being crushed in a hard embrace, held away so that he could look into my face, and hugged again.

'I trust that cuirass is more comfortable from the inside.' I smiled ruefully when he let me go, rubbing my flesh where the edges of the armour had dug in.

'One becomes accustomed,' he said absently, still holding my hand. After a moment I felt myself flushing beneath that intense gaze. 'Oh, my mother, do you know how often I have dreamed of this day? And you have not changed at all!'

That was not so, I thought, smiling back at him. Was the image he had of me so strong that he could not see what I looked like, or was it that most of my changes were inside?

'Sit down, and let Drusilla bring in the breakfast she has been cooking for you,' I said at last. 'What are you doing here, and how long can you stay?'

'One day only,' he said, answering the last question as he sat down. The chair creaked beneath his weight, for he had grown as tall and big-boned as my own father, everything about him just a little larger and more solid than other men. *Surely*, I thought with satisfaction, watching him, *he is worthy to be the Child of Prophecy*!

'Father gave me special permission to land here instead of at Eburacum, and tomorrow I must be on my way north to rejoin my legion. The Picts will not wait on my pleasure.'

I felt my heart pound suddenly in my breast. Constantius was in Britannia! I suppose I should have expected it. After several years of peace, the wild tribes of the north were trying once more to break the border, and in several places they had overwhelmed the troops stationed on the Wall. It was the responsibility of the ruler of the West to defend Britannia.

I shook my head, trying to deny the sudden, traitorous wish that Constantius had come with his son to Londinium.

'But how do you come to be here at all? I thought you were serving in the East with Galerius—'

Constantine's face grew dark, but clearly, he had learned to control his temper. If he had not, I told myself, no doubt he would not have lived long enough to be sitting in my dining room now.

'Oh, I was,' he said grimly. 'I was on that dreadful march across the plain east of Carrhae, the one that killed Crassus and ten legions two hundred years ago. Scarcely a tithe of our men made it home again from that campaign. I was surprised Galerius himself survived Diocletian's wrath when we reached Antiochia – did you know he had to walk for a mile behind Diocletian's chariot?'

I shook my head. I was glad now that I had not even known my son was involved in that disaster.

'You did not write to me about this.'

Constantine lifted an eyebrow, a habit I recognized as my own.

'My dear mother, my father is an honourable man, and there has always been trust between him and Maximian. Things are quite otherwise in the eastern part of the Empire. Even when I served in Diocletian's household, one of his freedmen read our mail, and Galerius had even less reason to trust me.'

I sighed, realizing that my own letters, perhaps in response to the restraint in his, had over the years become increasingly perfunctory, with the result that neither of us really knew the other at all.

Drusilla brought in the porridge and Constantine rose to embrace her. There were tears in her eye when he let her go again.

'Did you go with him on the second campaign as well?' I asked when he had eaten a little.

'By that time I was serving in his bodyguard. I have to say that Galerius learns from his mistakes. The Emperor gave him an army of Illyrian veterans and Gothic auxiliaries, and we took the northern route, through the mountains of Armenia where the people were our friends. I will also admit that the man has courage – he scouted the enemy camp by night with only two men to guard him, and led the charge when we overran them. That day, there was enough glory for everyone. Narses was put to flight, and the treaty we finally made bids fair to secure our eastern borders for at least a generation.'

'Galerius must have appreciated you, to keep you in his guard.' I set down my own spoon.

Constantine grinned. 'Oh, I can fight. I will not tell you about my narrow escapes – they would only frighten you – but I know the gods protect me, for I came through both campaigns with scarcely a scratch. Still, I think Galerius wanted me close so he could keep an eye on me. He thinks he will outlive Father, and be supreme, and I am a threat to his plans.' Abruptly his gaze grew grim. 'How much news about the abdication did they release to the provinces, Mother?'

I looked at him in surprise. 'Only that it had taken place, and two men I've never heard of were appointed as Caesars.'

'Galerius made those choices,' Constantine said through stiff lips. 'I don't know what pressure he put on Diocletian to do it – perhaps he threatened civil war. Do you know, the mint at Alexandria had actually minted a coin with my name on it? I was ready to ask Maximian if he would set a date for my wedding to his daughter Fausta, who was betrothed to me when Father was made Caesar, and is finally of age. Everyone was sure the choice was going to fall on Maximian's son Maxentius and on me.

'We stood waiting on that damned hill, beneath the column of Jupiter, and Diocletian tottered to his feet and complained about how frail he was becoming and that he was seeking rest after his labours, and so my father and Galerius would become the Augustii, and to assist them he was appointing Maximus Daia and Severus as Caesars! People were whispering, wondering if I had changed my name, until Galerius shoved me aside and pulled out Daia, the son of his sister!'

'Some have said it is just because you and Maxentius are the sons of emperors that you were passed over, to avoid establishing a hereditary monarchy,' I said mildly.

Constantine swallowed an oath. 'I could name you a dozen men who would have been more worthy of the honour! Men I would have been proud to serve. Severus is Galerius's best friend and neither he nor Daia has ever commanded anything bigger than a detachment. Galerius does not want colleagues, but servants, and all Diocletian wants is peace and quiet so that he can continue to believe he saved the Empire!' he said furiously. 'Galerius was a good servant, but by the gods, he will make a poor master. He is continuing to harass the Christians in his dominions, when clearly the persecution has failed.'

I took a deep breath. 'I am surprised he let you go.'

Constantine began to laugh. 'So was he! Father had written to him, pleading ill-health and requesting my presence. Galerius took his time about replying, and it is amazing how accident-prone I became thereafter. My patrols were ambushed, the beaters who were supposed to hold a boar we were hunting somehow failed, footpads attacked me outside a taverna. Things got so bad I bought a slave to taste my food.'

I bit my lip. No use to ask why he had not written to tell me of his danger – the letter would never have arrived. But every morning since he had left me I had prayed for his safety when I made my daily offering.

'Finally, Galerius gave me his permission,' Constantine continued. 'This was at the end of the day, and he obviously expected me to leave the next morning. But by that time I was wondering if I would live that long. I got a friend in the clerk's office to frank the pass for the post-horses and did my best not only to out-run pursuit but warning, especially once I was travelling through country Severus holds.' He grinned wolfishly, then applied himself to his food.

I sat back with a long sigh, reviewing his story as I waited for my heartbeat to slow.

'And so you came to your father,' I said presently. 'Was it a ruse, when he said he wanted you because he was ill?'

Constantine sat back with a frown. 'Well, I don't know. He says so, but he grows short of breath easily, and he doesn't look well. That is the other reason I insisted on coming to you now. He will not allow the physicians to examine him, and I thought that perhaps you—'

I shook my head. 'My darling, that right belongs to another woman. It would only bring pain to both of us if I went to your father now.'

My son's frown grew deeper, and I realized that despite, or perhaps even because, he had for so long had to act the part of a loyal subordinate, he disliked not getting his own way. But a mother has certain advantages. I met his grey stare, and in the end it was he who looked away.

After that, things grew easier, and when he had finished eating, I showed him my house and introduced him to Vitellia, and then arm in arm, we made a circuit of the town. Constantine did most of the talking, and I delighted to rediscover this glorious young man whom the gods had made my son. By the time we returned to Drusilla's most lavish dinner, night was falling. And this time, Constantine waited until morning before he set out once more.

That summer I followed the military news with more interest

than I had since the days when I was an army wife in Dalmatia, and the garrison in Londinium, who had been mightily impressed by Constantine, kept me supplied with news. Asclepiodotus, the prefect who had served Constantius so well in the campaign against Allectus, was once again second-in-command of his army. I remembered him as an earnest young officer when we had been stationed in Sirmium.

The man who had been my husband had always been able to inspire devotion. I, after all, had followed him from Avalon. And Constantine still idolized his father. If Galerius had made Constantine Caesar, my son would have supported him as he did his father. As it was, the Eastern Augustus had made two important enemies.

The troops Constantius brought from Germania had landed at Eburacum and joined with selected detachments from the garrisons on the Wall. As the spring turned to summer, they pressed north through the territory of the Votadini, following an ever-retreating enemy all the way past the Bodotria to the vicinity of Mons Graupius, where Tacitus had defeated their ancestors a little over two centuries before. And there, the reports told us, the Emperor had won a great victory.

This news was proclaimed from the forum and posted on the gates of the Governor's palace. The priestess of Bast, who was one of those to whom I had introduced Constantine, offered her congratulations. I thanked her, but despite the general rejoicing I found myself uneasy, and continued to the Temple of Isis to make an offering.

The goddess in the shrine was portrayed in the Roman fashion, with a crown of wheat and flowers surmounted by a crescent moon, and flowing draperies. The sounds of commerce outside seemed to fade as I cast frankincense upon the glowing coals in the brazier before the altar.

'Goddess,' I whispered, 'for the sake of your son Horus, the mighty warrior who is the Hawk of the Sun, watch over my child and bring him safely home.' I waited for a moment, contemplating the play of lamplight on the marble features, and then cast a second handful on the coals. 'And watch over the Emperor also, as you watched over Pharaoh.'

Any citizen might make offerings on behalf of the Emperor, but I no longer had the right to pray for him as my husband, and even if I had, the fidelity of Isis is remembered because Osiris died. I went home, but found myself still uneasy. Still, the reports continued to be positive. *I am becoming an old woman,* I told myself. *There is no reason to worry so . . .*

At the end of June, I received a letter from Constantine.

'My father collapsed on the way back from Alba. He is up again now and we have reached Eburacum, but he seems often to be in pain. The physicians will say little, and I am afraid for him. Please come. He is asking for you . . .'

Constantine had sent an order for post-horses. Travelling by carriage and changing horses at each government mansio, it took a little over week for me to travel north to Eburacum. A fifty-five-year-old body was not meant for this kind of travel. By the time I reached the fortress, I was bruised and exhausted by the constant sway and jolt of the carriage, but though the word of the Emperor's illness had spread through the countryside and I saw many worried faces, at each stop I was told that Constantius still lived, and so hope sustained me through my journey.

I was realizing now that the sorrow of our separation had been eased a little by the knowledge that Constantius still walked the world. And yet, as I travelled, I could not keep from remembering the image of Isis sorrowing for her husband. Even the gods lost those they loved, so why should I think myself immune?

Word of my coming had run ahead of me. Constantine came out of the presidium as we rumbled through the gate, and when the carriage halted, lifted me out. For a few moments I clung to him, drawing strength.

'How is he?' I asked, when I could stand alone.

'Each day he insists on getting dressed and attempting to do a little work. But he tires very easily. I told him that you were coming, and each hour, it seems, he has asked where I think you are now.' He managed a smile. 'But we persuaded him to lie down a little while ago and he is sleeping.'

He escorted me into the building and showed me the chamber they had set aside for me and the slave girl who would attend me. When I had washed and changed my gown I found Constantine waiting in the adjoining room where a table with wine and honey-cakes was laid.

'And how are you?' I asked, noting the dark smudges beneath his eyes. Physically, I might be the more exhausted, but he was suffering too.

'It is strange. When I go into battle I feel no fear. But this is an enemy I cannot confront, and I am afraid.'

It is true, I thought sadly, *even the strength of a young man who does not believe he can die is helpless against some enemies.*

'I remember,' he said slowly, not meeting my eyes, 'from when I was a child . . . you can do strange things sometimes. You must help him, mother, or we are lost.'

'Did you call me here as your mother, or as a priestess?'

He looked up, and for a moment I thought he was going to crouch against me with his head upon my breast as he had when he was a little child.

'I need my mother, but my father needs the priestess.'

'Then it is as a priestess that I answer you. I will do what I can, Con, but you must understand that there is a natural rhythm to our lives that not even the gods can deny.'

'Then they are evil gods!' muttered Constantine.

'My heart cries out against this as loudly as yours, but it may be that all I will be able to do is to help him let go.'

The chair scraped loudly as he stood up and gripped my hand. 'Come—' He pulled me to my feet, and scarcely waiting for me to wrap my palla around me, drew me from the room.

'He stirred a moment ago,' said the physician on watch as we appeared in the doorway. 'I think he will wake soon.'

The Emperor lay on his bed, his upper body raised on pillows. I paused, making an effort to pull myself together. Constantine was right. The wife and mother would dissolve in tears, seeing her beloved lie so still. It was the priestess that was needed now.

I came to the bedside and stretched out my hands above Constantius's body, extending my awareness to sense the energy flow. Above the head and brow the life-force still flowed strongly, but the aura above his chest flickered weakly, and lower down, though it was steady, it was not strong. I bent close to listen to his breathing, and could hear the rasp of congestion inside.

'Does he have fever?' I did not think so, for his skin was not flushed, but abnormally pale; however, I had hoped it might be, for the lung-fever, though serious, was something I knew how to fight. The physician shook his head, and I sighed. 'The heart, then?'

'I have made up an infusion of foxglove, for when it pains him,' said the physician.

'That is well, but perhaps there is something we can do to strengthen him. Do you have a trustworthy man you can send for the following herbs?' As he nodded, I began to dictate my list: motherwort and hawthorn, nettle and garlic, and Constantine's grim look eased.

Then the man on the bed stirred and sighed, and I knelt beside him, chafing his cool hands between my own.

Eyes still closed, Constantius smiled. 'Ah, the goddess returns . . .'

'The Goddess was always with you, but now I am here as well.' With an effort I kept my voice firm. 'What have you been doing to yourself, to get in such a state? Is it not the place of the Augustus to sit in his palace and leave the fighting to younger men?'

'I have not even opened my eyes, and she is scolding me!' he said, but in truth I think he was not yet certain I was real.

'Perhaps this will take the sting away,' I leaned over to kiss his lips, and as I released him, he looked up at me.

'I have missed you,' he said simply, and read my answer in my eyes.

*　　*　　*

251

Throughout the week that followed, I dosed Constantius with my potions, but though Constantine talked loudly of his improvement, I began to suspect that he had used up the strength that remained to him in holding on until I arrived. Constantine and I took it in turns to sit with him, holding his hand as he rested, or speaking of the years we had spent apart.

One day, as I bathed him, I noticed a livid scar up the side of one thigh and asked when he had risked himself so foolishly.

'Ah, that was in Gallia, three summers ago, and I assure you I did not intend to run into such danger!'

Three years, I thought, and the scar was still red and angry. It had not healed quickly or well, a sign that his circulation was failing even then. I could have given him medicines to strengthen his heart, if I had known. But perhaps it would not have mattered. It was not Theodora who was my rival. Constantius had given his heart to the Empire before he ever offered it to me.

July was drawing on, and even in Eburacum the days were warm. We opened the windows to let in fresh air and covered the sick man with a light woollen cloth, and the chirring of the crickets blended with the rasp of his breathing.

One afternoon when I was alone with him in the room Constantius woke from a brief sleep and called my name.

'I am here, my dearest,' I took his hand.

'Helena . . . I feel that this is one battle I am not going to win. The sun shines brightly, but he is declining, and so am I. I have done most of what I set out to do in this world, but I fear for the Empire, at the mercy of Galerius and his puppet Caesars.'

'No doubt Augustus thought the same, but Rome still stands,' I told him. 'Her safety, in the end, depends on the gods, not you.'

'I suppose you are right – when an Emperor receives divine honours, it becomes hard to tell the difference, sometimes. But the gods do not die. Tell me, my Lady, can this body heal?'

For a moment I stared at him, blinking back tears. His gaze was clear and direct, and there had always been truth between us. I could not deny it to him now.

'It has been long since I studied the arts of healing,' I said finally. 'But each day you spend more time in sleep. The life-force in your body sinks lower. If it continues to do so, I think you may stay with us a week, but no more.'

Astonishingly, his face brightened. 'That is more than I have been able to make my physicians say. A good general needs as much accurate information to plan an orderly retreat as he does when he seeks victory.'

I would not have thought of it that way, and despite my tears I returned his smile.

'Constantine asked you to heal me, but now I ask you a harder thing, my beloved priestess. I have spent too much of my life in trying to stay alive on battlefields, and it is hard to let go. Now you must teach me how to die.'

'I can only do this if I become wholly the priestess, and when I do so, the woman who loves you will not be here.'

He nodded. 'I understand. When I led Constantine in battle, it was the Emperor, not the father, who ordered him into danger. But we have a little time, my darling. Be my beloved Helena today, and we will feast on our memories.'

I squeezed his hand. 'I remember the first time I saw you, in a vision that came to me when I was only thirteen years old. You shone like the sun, and you do so still.'

'Even now, when my hair has faded and my strength is gone?' he teased.

'A winter sun, perhaps, but you light the world for me all the same,' I assured him.

'The first time I saw *you*, you looked like a wet kitten,' he said then, and I laughed.

We spent the rest of that day in talk, replaying our every meeting in the gentle light of memory. For a time Constantine sat with us, but it was clear that this was something in which he had only a peripheral part, and he went away to rest before his watch. When

253

I went to my bedchamber that night I wept for a long time, knowing that this had been our farewell.

In the morning, I came to Constantius robed in blue and wrapped in the invisible majesty of a priestess. When he opened his eyes he recognized the difference immediately. Others responded to the change without understanding, except for Constantine, who gazed at me with a child's panic at the loss of the familiar mother he thought he knew.

You are an adult now, I tried to tell him with my steady gaze. *You must learn to see your parents as fellow travellers upon Life's road.* But I suppose it was not surprising that he still saw us with a child's eye, having been separated from us when he was only thirteen years old.

'Lady, I salute you,' said Constantius in a low voice. 'What have you to teach me about the Mysteries?'

'All men who are born of woman must one day come to life's ending,' I murmured, 'and the time is coming now for you. Soul to soul, you must listen, and not allow yourself to be distracted. Your body has served you well, and become worn out in that service. You must make ready now to release it, to depart from it, to rise from the realm of the tangible, which is subject to change and decay, to that place where all is Light, and the true and eternal natures of all things are revealed . . .'

It had been many years since I had learned these words, and I had spoken them only once, when the other novices and I took turns to read them to an old priestess who was dying; but now need called them forth, complete and perfect.

Throughout that day I repeated the instructions, explaining how the body would become a weight too heavy to be moved, and all sensation would disappear. When that happens, the soul must be ready to will itself upward and out through the crown of the head, seeking its union with the Source of All. The cares of the world and affection for those one has loved conspire to drag the spirit back again, but it is necessary to be steadfast in determination to leave them behind.

'You will pass through a long, dark tunnel, as once you were forced from the darkness of the womb. This is the journey of your birth in the spirit, and at the end of it you will emerge, not into the light of day, but into that radiance that is the true source of the sun . . .'

Constantius had fallen asleep, but I continued to speak, knowing that some part of his spirit was still listening. It seemed to me that the gods meant to give him a gentle death, and from one of these sleeps there would be no waking, and the soul would depart from the body, and at last the flesh, without a spirit to direct it, would give up as well.

By this time it was apparent to everyone that the Emperor was dying. In the city, I was told, the clamour of the market-place was hushed, and incense smoked on every altar. The people of Eburacum had always considered Constantius to be one of their own: he had saved them from the Picts, and they were grateful. In the fortress the soldiers stood guard around the Praesidium, and Crocus and his senior warriors had crowded into the corridor outside the Emperor's chamber, waiting with the uncomprehending patience of good hounds.

That night Constantius woke long enough to speak for a while with Constantine. Exhausted, I had gone to bed, but in the grey hour before the dawn a soldier came to summon me. I dashed water on my face, struggling to focus, but in truth, I was not surprised. I had given Constantius permission to depart and instruction in how to do so. There was no reason for him to linger on.

'He is drifting in and out of consciousness,' whispered the physician as I came to the door. 'And he labours to breathe.'

'Here is Mother, come to see you,' said Constantine a little desperately as I eased myself down on the low stool beside the bed. Constantius struggled for breath, choked for a moment, and then exhaled.

'Put more pillows behind him,' I said, uncapping the vial of attar of rose that hung from a chain around my neck. I saw his nostrils flare, and the next breath came more easily, and then he opened his eyes, and his lips twitched in an attempt at a smile.

For a moment it was enough simply for him to breathe. Then he gathered his forces and turned his gaze towards Constantine. 'Remember. . .' he whispered. 'Take care . . . of your mother. . . and your brothers . . . and sisters . . .' Gaze focused in concentration, he drew breath again. 'Pray to the Highest God . . . to preserve the Empire . . .'

His eyes closed, but he was clearly still conscious, still struggling. The windows were shuttered, but I could feel a change in the air. I gestured to one of the physicians—

'Open the windows!'

As the shutters were folded back, a pale light filled the room. With each moment it grew stronger. The sun was rising; on strong men's cheeks I could see the glistening track of tears. Moment by moment, the face of Constantius was growing brighter. I leaned forwards, and clasped his hands together upon his breast.

'The world fades around you . . .' I whispered, 'it is time to move into the Light . . .'

His gaze turned towards me, but I was not certain what he was looking at, for in that moment his features were transfigured by an expression of astonished joy. 'Goddess . . .' The word hovered at the edge of sound. Then his eyes widened, unseeing, the body fought for a last breath and failed, and he lay still.

For the eight days between the death of Constantius and his cremation, Constantine had kept to his chamber, eating little and speaking to no one. For me those days passed like a nightmare, in which the memories that came to me waking were worse than my dreams. But when the eighth day came to a close I put on the white garments of mourning and went out to follow my husband's body to the pyre. Constantine was waiting, washed and shaved and wrapped in a snowy toga, and although his eyes were deep-shadowed, he had clearly recovered his self-command.

I remember that night now as a series of images – torches

whipping in the wind, pale in the gathering dusk, and the white marble of the new-made tomb glowing faintly in their light. Not for Constantius a burial along the road outside the town – the magistrates of Eburacum had claimed him, and if he could no longer protect them in life, the honours paid to a tomb in the forum might persuade his hovering spirit to confer a blessing.

I have another image – Constantius's body, wrapped in purple and crowned with the wreath of gold, lying upon a pyre, stacked high with good British oak and studded with spices. I remember torchlight on the grim faces of Asclepiodotus and Crocus, who had escorted us, and the glitter of their armour. And Constantine's silence, as if he had been carved of the same marble as the tomb.

There is a sound, a wail that goes up from the populace when Constantine thrusts his torch between the logs. The soldiers who had filled an entire side of the square are murmuring, but their discipline holds, and as the smoke swirls skywards, hiding the still form of the Emperor, except for the weeping of women it becomes quiet once more. I have seen this before, in the vision at my passage into womanhood, but I saw myself wearing the purple, and that never happened, so how can this be true?

I remember the pyre beginning to fall into coals as the first stars pricked through the velvet pall of the sky, and the deep voice of Asclepiodotus, telling Constantine he must speak to the people now. Like a sleepwalker, Constantine turns, and now his eyes burn. He lifts his arms, and it becomes utterly still.

'My brothers and sisters, brothers-in-arms, and fellow-children of the Empire. My father and yours is dead, and his soul ascends to heaven. We are orphaned of our protector, and who will watch over us?'

And a wail rises from among the women, as swiftly overwhelmed by a deep cry from the throats of many men.

'Constantine! Constantine will protect us! Constantinus, Imperator!'

Constantine lifts his hands once more as if to quiet them, but the shouting only grows louder, and now the soldiers surge forwards,

Crocus in the forefront, one of them bearing a purple robe, and Asclepiodotus has my arm and is pulling me away.

I do not remember how we got back to the praesidium. But throughout that night it seemed to me that the heavens echoed back the cry—

'*Constantine for Imperator!*'

Part III

THE WAY TO WISDOM

CHAPTER FIFTEEN

AD 307–12

In all the years I had travelled about the Empire as Constantius's wife, I had never been to Italia. I had yet to see Rome, but Maximian's new city of Mediolanum, on the north Italian plain, was said to be nearly as magnificent. Today, with the streets newly washed by the spring rains and every archway garlanded with flowers, I could well believe it, as the masters of the Empire attempted to forge yet another alliance by the marriage of Maximian's young daughter Fausta to my son Constantine.

They had been betrothed in the year Constantius became Caesar. At the time, Fausta was only an infant, and in the long years when Constantine was hostage first to Diocletian and then to Galerius, it would have surprised no one if the potential relationship had been forgotten by everyone, including Constantine, except that I was beginning to realize that Constantine never forgot anything he had claimed as his own. I hoped that self-interest would dispose him to affection, and the fact that Fausta had grown up as his intended wife would incline her to respect, though it was asking a great deal to expect much companionship in the mating of a girl of fourteen with a man of thirty-five.

Certainly the past nine months had been bewildering. Although the troops, led by Crocus, had hailed Constantine as Augustus, he had deemed it more politic to claim no more than the rank of Caesar when he informed Galerius that he had a new colleague in rule. Meanwhile, Maximian's son Maxentius had decided to follow his

261

example, and Maximian himself had come out of retirement to help him. They were *all* calling themselves Augustus now.

I would have been quite content to wait at the palace, but Constantine insisted that all his family, including the half-sisters and brothers, Theodora's children whom we had brought with us from Treveri, should ride in the procession. And so I was seeing Mediolanum from the vantage of a triumphal cart, garlanded and gilded and shaded with pink silk which clashed with the purple palla I wore, though I trusted that it flattered my complexion.

From the sound of the cheers, Maximian and Constantine, riding together, had passed through the triumphal arch leading to the main square. More cheering behind me proclaimed the advent of the bride, riding in a chariot drawn by four milk-white ponies which had been fitted with wings, so that each resembled a miniature Pegasus, her face hidden by the flame-coloured silk of her veil.

I still did not know whether Crocus's acclamation had taken Constantine by surprise, or if he himself had planned it. In retrospect, it was inevitable that Constantius's oldest son should claim the imperium. If he had not done so, I suppose Galerius would have made some pre-emptive strike against him, and why should I blame my son for doing what he had been conceived and born to do?

In fact, Constantine had acted with wisdom and decision, establishing himself in his father's capital, Treveri. So far as anyone knew, to rule his father's territories was the extent of his ambition, and now everyone was courting him.

There were days when it all seemed like some dream. With Constantius I could have enjoyed all this, but I had trouble believing I belonged here, with a son I loved but hardly knew. Still, I had rented out my house in Londinium and brought all the household to Treveri, where Drusilla took charge of my kitchens and Vitellia the management of everything else as if they had been born to live in palaces. I missed my students and Katiya and my other friends in Londinium, but Constantine's enthusiasm was infectious. Constantius had done his duty, but Constantine *enjoyed* the exercise of power.

262

My head was beginning to ache from the clamour by the time we reached the palace, and I was more than ready to sit down on something that did not move. I could see Constantine eyeing the marble facings in the hall as if he were considering copying them for his new basilica. They were magnificent – pink and grey polished slabs laid in patterns on the lower walls and the floor. But though the building itself was impressive, a close examination made it clear that it had been put back into use rather hastily. The long tables so beautifully swathed in brocade were plain wood, and the fittings where tapestries should have curtained the windows were still bare.

The richly-dressed guests who sat at those tables did not seem to notice. Crocus was there, with two of his senior officers, and a rotund little man called Ossius who was the Bishop of Corduba. Though the wedding had been a traditional Roman affair, Constantine had asked the bishop to give it his blessing, which had no doubt pleased the Christians here.

Nonetheless, once the sacrifices had been made, the omens read, and the marriage contract signed, the feast to which we sat down was memorable, even if the little bride had not yet lost her puppy fat and was unbecomingly flushed – with excitement, I hoped, not with wine. Fausta had fine reddish hair, to which her maids had given rather too much curl, and grey eyes. When she grew into her looks, she might be handsome, but for now, her cheeks full of sweetmeats, she brought to mind a bright-eyed squirrel.

During one of the breaks in the entertainment when the guests were milling about, Constantine made his way to my couch.

'My darling,' I gazed up at him, 'you outshine your bride!' Surely no woman had ever been blessed with such a splendid son. On this day, all my sufferings seemed justified.

Constantine grinned. His cream-coloured tunic of Eastern silk was bordered and banded with gold that set off his burnished hair. 'She is pretty enough when she is not laden with ornaments like a heifer at a festival. But it is true that she is still very young. Will you rule my household, Mother, until Fausta is old enough for the job?'

I pretended to think about it, but he knew I could not refuse, and he seized my hand and kissed it when I smiled.

'And there is another request I would make of you, even dearer to my heart,' he paused, as if searching for words. 'When I was in the East, I formed a . . . connection . . . with a woman named Minervina, and two years ago she bore me a son.'

I lifted one eyebrow, understanding why he might feel unwilling to bring up the subject, when from his point of view this Minervina's story sounded so much like my own.

'And what have you done with her, now that you have a legitimate bride?' I asked tartly, and saw the betraying flush stain his skin.

'She died of a fever a year ago,' he replied with some dignity. 'I had no choice but to leave the boy with his uncle when I escaped Galerius, but now I have sent for him. His name is Crispus, mother. Will you take charge of him for me?'

'Pater familias,' I teased him gently. 'You are taking all of your relatives under your wing. Did you dislike it so much that I was not able to give you sisters and brothers of your own?'

For a moment he looked confused, then he gave me the sweet smile that I remembered from the days when he was a boy. A grandchild! I was surprised at how that thought excited me.

'Never mind,' I said then, 'bring your little lad to me. If he smiles at me like that I am sure I will love him well.'

'*Avia*! *Avia*! See – Boreas will jump for me!'

I turned, smiling, as the golden-haired boy held up the branch. The male greyhound puppy, one of a pair that Constantine had recently sent to me, leapt over it, and the female, Favonia, gambolled around them, barking.

'They are still young, my love – do not make them too excited,' I warned, although in truth it was as much the nature of a puppy to live in a state of excitement as it was for a little boy.

Crispus was curious about everything, and charmed everyone. Constantine never spoke of the boy's mother, but it was clear that she had had the raising of the child long enough to give him a certainty that he was loved. Even Fausta, though she was more of an age to be his sister, played with him like a doll and swore that she would adopt him as her own.

In the three years since Crispus had come to Treveri I had become accustomed to the cry of 'Avia!', 'Grandmother!' It seemed to me sometimes during these first years of Constantine's reign that I had lived three lives, and the third was the happiest of all.

In my first, I had been a maiden of Avalon, struggling to survive Ganeda's hostility and come into my own power. The second had given me the joy of a woman's fulfilment and the pain of a woman's passions, but even during the years when we were apart, like a flower forever turning to the sun, my identity had been determined by my relationship to Constantius. But now my body had found a new equilibrium, no longer at the mercy of the moon, and I had a new existence as Empress-mother, the most unexpected identity of all.

Tiring of his play, Crispus came running up to climb into my lap, and the dogs, panting, flopped down beside us. I popped a candied fig from the painted plate on the bench beside me into the boy's mouth, and cuddled him against my breast.

For the first time in my life I had no need to practise economy, and I had servants in plenty to do the actual work of the imperial household. I was free to spend most of my time with Crispus, who had all his father's brilliance, and, as it seemed to me, even more sweetness, though that may have been the partiality of a grandmother, who can afford to love her grandchildren more openly because their success or failure does not so directly reflect upon her own.

'Tell me a story about when Pater was a little boy!' mumbled Crispus through the fig.

'Well—' I thought a moment, 'when he was your age, he loved figs, just like you. At that time we lived in Naissus, and we had a neighbour who was very proud of the fig tree in his garden. Now we also had a dog called Hylas who loved fruit, and would even climb trees to get at it. So Constantine made a muzzle for Hylas, and very early one morning he dropped him over the wall into the neighbour's garden and encouraged him to climb the fig tree and knock the ripe figs down. Then he nipped into the garden with a basket and gathered them up and took them into the playhouse he had built in our garden to eat.'

'Did he eat them all?' asked Crispus. 'Didn't he give the doggie even one?'

'Oh yes, and smeared fig around Hylas's muzzle as well, and when the neighbour discovered his loss and came over, shaking his fist and demanding that we punish our son, Constantine pointed to the dog and swore by Apollo that Hylas had done the deed, which was, of course, true. When the man didn't believe him, he insisted on going to the fig tree and letting Hylas climb it again, and this time of course he was not muzzled, and managed to grab one of the figs he had missed before.'

'What did the neighbour say?'

'Well, first he wanted us to destroy the dog, but he settled for a promise that the animal would be prevented from ever getting into his garden again. So we swore by Apollo as well, and paid the man the worth of the figs in silver, and he went home.'

'I'm glad the dog was safe,' said Crispus. 'But didn't Pater get in trouble?'

'Oh yes, because, you see, Hylas had been trained not to climb that wall. Constantine thought he had been very clever, until we explained the difference between being truthful and being honest, and made him help our gardener dig the flowerbeds until he had worked off the price we paid.'

I saw the child's eyes grow round as he contemplated the idea that his father had once been less than perfect. In recent years, Constantine had developed a distinct taste for splendour, and I thought it would do Crispus no harm to realize that his father was human too.

If I had a worry, it was the continued political turmoil as Constantine struggled with his competitors for supremacy. I had no real doubts that he would eventually triumph, for was he not the Child of Prophecy? Still, I waited eagerly for my son's letters, and finding in his mother his safest confidante, Constantine wrote to me often.

When Crispus jumped down to go and play with the dogs some more, I took out the latest letter, sent from somewhere near Massilia. After the wedding, Maximian had quarrelled with his son and for a time taken refuge with us. Galerius, having failed to rectify the situation by force, had made another treaty and installed a man called Licinius to replace Severus, whom Maxentius had executed.

And now Maximian, who in my opinion was showing signs of senility, had seized the treasury and dug himself in at Massilia, after first having written a letter to Fausta proclaiming that soon he would be the sole ruler of the West once more.

Constantine was at that point reviewing troops on the Rhenus, and Fausta, who idolized him, had promptly written to inform him of what was going on. By now, Constantine might be fighting his father-in-law. We had received no word since this letter, written from the temple of Apollo at Grannum, where Constantine had stayed three nights before.

'Grannum was on our way, and so I took the opportunity to sleep overnight in the shrine there. And the god gave me a dream. Apollo himself came to me, attended by Victory, and offered me four laurel wreaths. Perhaps you will know how to interpret this portent better than I, but I believe that each one represents a span of years during which I will reign. The Almighty Sun has always favoured our family, and so I claim His protection. If Apollo gives me victory in the coming conflict, I will inscribe "soli invicto comiti" on my next issue of coinage in His name. Pray for me, mother, that I have dreamed true, and will indeed gain the victory . . .'

A sound, like the distant murmur of trees in a storm, caught my attention, but there was no wind – the sound was coming from the city. The gardens attached to the palace were extensive. If I could hear noise from the street beyond our gates, where the new basilica rose above the trees, it had to be loud. I felt my gut tensing as I rose to my feet, but I folded Constantine's letter carefully and slid it into the bosom of my gown where it bloused over the waist cord.

Crispus and the dogs were still chasing each other around the garden. If it was good news, I told myself, I could wait to hear it, and I had no need to hurry sorrow if it was bad.

Yet it was not some dust-coated military messenger, but Fausta who came running out of the palace as if the furies were at her heels. The cramping in my belly tightened as I saw her face contorted and her cheeks smeared with tears.

'Mater! Mater! He killed himself, and it is my fault!'

Abruptly my own terror eased. My son believed in his destiny too strongly to take his own life whatever disaster might befall. I took the girl in my arms and held her until her sobbing eased.

'Who, Fausta? What has happened?'

'My father—' she wailed. 'They caught him at Massilia and now he is dead, and it is all because I told Constantine what he wrote to me!'

'Your duty was to your husband, you know that,' I murmured, patting her, 'and Constantine would have found out soon in any case, and the end would have been the same.' It was a very convenient suicide, I observed silently, wondering if Maximian had been given assistance in expiating his crime. Gradually, Fausta's sniffles ceased.

'Mourn for your father, Fausta, for in his day he was a great man, and he would have hated to live until he was feeble and old. Wear white for him, but do not let your eyes be red and puffy with weeping when Constantine comes home.'

She nodded. Constantine liked to have everyone happy around him. I wondered sometimes if the uncertainties of his childhood had given him this desire for a perfect family, or whether he simply believed it necessary if he was properly to fulfil his role as Emperor.

When Constantine was at home, it was his custom to sit with me for an hour at the end of the evening. We would speak sometimes of the family, and sometimes of the Empire. I suppose that I was the only advisor whom he could trust absolutely, but even to me he rarely opened his mind completely. I regretted sometimes the loss of the open-hearted boy he had been before he went to Diocletian's court, but I knew that innocence would never have survived the dangers and intrigues that surrounded an emperor.

I had a small sitting room between my bedchamber and the gardens, with doors that could be opened in the heat of summer, and a hearth in the British fashion for the days of winter and autumnal chill. Now, at the end of summer, I sat by the fire with my spinning. The work was no longer the necessity it had been at Avalon, but I found it focused and calmed the mind.

'How do you make the thread so fine and even, Mother? No matter how long I watch you, when I try the wool always breaks in my clumsy hands!' Constantine sat with his long legs stretched out to the fire, his deep-set eyes half-closed as he watched the spindle turn.

'It is a good thing, then, that you were not born a girl,' I answered, catching the spindle with my foot as I paid out more wool from the distaff and adjusted the tension. Then a deft twist set it spinning again.

'Oh yes,' he laughed. 'But the fates, who have laid out my course from the cradle, would not have erred in so fundamental a matter. I was born to be Emperor.'

I raised one eyebrow. There was something a little disturbing about such certainty, but I could not dispute what I also believed to be true.

'And to father a dynasty? Crispus is growing to be a fine lad, but one son is not much of a family. Fausta is nineteen now, and ripe to be bedded. She will get into mischief if you do not give her children.'

'Has she been complaining?' He laughed. 'You are right, of course, but I will sire no more offspring until I can be sure of being at home often enough to supervise their upbringing. The death of Galerius has upset the balance of power. I have reason to believe that Maximin Daia has made an alliance with Maxentius. I myself have been in communication with Licinius, who also claims the East, and offered him the hand of my sister Constantia.'

He gave me a quick glance, as if wondering how I would take this mention of his half-sister, but I had long ago accepted the fact that Constantius had asked Constantine to watch over the children of Theodora. Her birth might have been better than mine, but it was my son who was Emperor.

'So, the lines have been drawn . . .'

'Maxentius has defaced my statues. He says it is in response to my treatment of the images of his father Maximian, but Maximian died a rebel, whereas I am supposed to be Maxentius's brother-emperor. I will have to go against him, and soon, before snow closes the Alpine passes. It is as good an excuse as any.'

'If the rumours that *I* have heard are true, the Senate will applaud you. He has made free with too many patrician wives and daughters, and imposed too many taxes. But do you have the forces to match the men he has added to the Praetorian Guard, and the troops brought over from Africa?'

'In quality—' he grinned whitely. 'In quantity? No, but I am the better general. Superior numbers will not matter if they are not led well.'

'May the blessing of all the gods be with you,' I said, frowning.

The last of the laughter left his face. 'If I knew which god could guarantee me victory I would promise him a temple – I would make his cult first in the Empire. I must fight Maxentius, and it must be done now, but you are right in thinking that the result will hang upon the favour of heaven. Pray for me, Mother – you have the ear of the gods!'

'You are always in my thoughts and in my prayers,' I answered when the silence threatened to go on for too long. I loved Constantine. He was the centre of my life. But there were times when he seemed to need more than I understood how to give to him.

The next day he was gone, to gather his faithful troops from the Rhenus,

I assumed, though no announcement had been made that might warn his enemy. Later I was to learn that Maxentius, anticipating some move from Constantine, had entrusted the defence of the north to Ruricius Pompeianus, staying in Rome himself in case Licinius should finish dealing with the Persians in time to attack him. But at the time I was unable to appreciate even what news we had, for Crispus had taken some illness from the gardener's children, and though he recovered quickly, I, who had been nursing him, contracted it myself.

First came the red rash, and then the fever, that seemed to burn in my very bones. If this was a disease we had in Britannia, my upbringing on Avalon had sheltered me from it. And as often happens when an adult catches a childhood disease, I became far more ill than Crispus had been.

I lay in alternating stupor and delirium as the month of October drew to its end. In my moments of clarity I heard the names of cities: Segusio, Taurinorum, Mediolanum, and later, Verona, Brixla, Aquilela, Mutina. Afterward, I was to learn that they were the towns Constantine had taken. By refusing to allow his soldiers to plunder the first of them, he had won the swift surrender of those that followed. But I was fighting my own battle, and as the days passed, I sensed that I was losing.

Events around me passed like a troubled dream, but in that in-between state in which I hovered, neither the world of humankind or the spirit world, I sensed the tides of the seasons swinging onwards towards Samhain, when the Britons hold that the old year ends and the gestation of the new begins. There comes a moment, then, when a doorway opens between the worlds and the dead return.

A good time, I thought dimly, for my own passing. I regretted only that I had no chance to say farewell to Constantine. Yet it was not my life, but an era, that was ending, though it was to be many years before I clearly understood the signficance of that Samhain-tide.

A day came when the fever rose once more, and my spirit, freed from a weakening body, fared forth between the worlds. I seemed to see the land laid out below me, and love carried me eastwards where my son was about to come to grips with his enemy. I saw a great city beside a river which I knew must be Rome. But Maxentius's forces had crossed the Tiber upstream from the city, and were drawn up in formation, facing the smaller number of troops led by Constantine. Winter was coming early, and in the crisp air the sun seemed to shatter, sending a refraction across the horizon that rayed out in a cross of light.

Constantine's forces charged the enemy, his Gallic cavalry evading the more heavily armed Italian horse and overwhelming the lightly-armed Numidians. I could see Constantine in his golden armour, and his bodyguard, all with a Greek Chi Rho painted for luck upon their shields.

Maxentius's Praetorians died where they stood, and the remainder broke and ran. The bridge cracked beneath the sudden weight, spilling men and horses into the swift grey waters. The attackers swarmed after them, repairing the damage, and by sunset they were entering Rome.

As shadow swept across the land I also fell into darkness. The disease had run its course, but I was dreadfully weakened. I would eat and drink when they roused me, but most of the time I slept. Sometimes, half-conscious, I would hear conversation around me.

'She grows no better,' came the voice of the Greek physician. 'The Emperor must be told.'

'We dare not distract him. If Constantine is defeated, none of our lives will be worth a denarius. Maxentius will treat us as Maximian did the wife and daughter of Galerius.' That was Vitellia. She sounded as if she had been weeping. I wanted to tell her that Constantine had triumphed, but I could not make my body do my will.

'Even if we sent a message now, my lord could not come in time,' said Fausta. She was Maxentius's sister, and might expect to be spared if he triumphed, unless he blamed her for the death of their father. The early emperors had not hesitated to kill their own kin. Why should I fight my way back to life in a world where such things could be?

But by the next morning a messenger had come to confirm my vision, and in the general rejoicing, little Crispus slipped into my chamber, and as he hugged me, laughing for joy at the news and weeping to see me so thin and pale, I felt a pulse of strength leap from his strong young body to mine, and knew that the gods were not going to take me this Samhain after all.

It was past the feast of Saturnalia when Constantine returned to Treveri. By that time I was recovering my strength, with only an occasional shortness of breath to remind me of my fight to breathe, but my hair, which until now had shown only a few strands of grey, had gone white in the course of my illness. I trusted that it would distract him from noting any other changes, for I had not allowed them to tell him how close to death I had come.

I chose to receive him in my sitting room, where the reflected light from my red-painted walls would give me a healthier colour. Even so, I was glad to be sitting when he came to me, for the aura of power that blazed out around him was like the blast of heat from a roaring fire.

'Hail *Sol Invictus*! You are surely the sun in his splendour now!'

I lifted a hand, in welcome, or perhaps to ward him away, for in that moment he was a giant, dwarfing all else in the room. Later, when I saw the statue that he had commissioned in Rome, whose head alone was the height of a tall man, I realized that the sculptor had sensed the same quality of something beyond the scale of humanity as I.

Constantine grinned, bent to kiss me, and then began to pace around the room, as if the power that filled him would not let him sit still. He did not comment on my appearance; perhaps he was still too transfixed by his visions to really focus on the outer world.

'Oh Mother, I wish you had been there, for surely the God of Light was with me on that day!' He took another turn around the room and came to my side once more.

'I have heard there were many signs and wonders. What happened, Constantine? What did you see?'

'Oh yes, now they are all saying how my victory was foretold, but at the time the prophets on both sides were predicting their sides would win. The Sibylline Books prophesied that an enemy of Rome would perish on the day of the battle, and of course Maxentius said it must be me, and the astrologers were muttering darkly about a conjunction of Mars, Saturn, Jupiter and Venus in Capricorn. But I am the Child of Prophecy, and I knew how to make even my enemies serve me!'

I gazed at him in wonder. Constantine had always been confident, but now he spoke with the fervour of a priest in trance.

'Maxentius had become a tyrant, and Rome was bound to see me as a liberator. He was on the bridge when it collapsed, and the weight of his armour drew him down into the mud and he drowned. As for the stars, the night before the battle I dreamed that a shining figure showed me a scroll with the Greek letters that the scribes use to signify a passage that is good, and told me that was the Sign by which I should conquer. When I woke, I told the fabricators to affix the Chi and Rho to a military standard, and my guard, to draw the Sign on their shields, and then the sun rose and divided in a cross of light, and I knew I would have the victory. Sopater believes that I saw Apollo, but Bishop Ossius assures me that my vision was given by the Christos.'

'And what do you believe?' I asked him then.

'The Jewish Jesus, whom we crucified, is a god for slaves,' said Constantine. 'But the great Father whom the Christians worship, the King and Creator of all the world, is the same as the god of the philosophers, and worthy to be patron to an emperor. I do not think it matters what name folk use for Him, so long as they recognize that One God is supreme in the heavens and on the earth, one Emperor.'

'The Senate may have acclaimed you as senior Augustus,' I observed gently, 'but in the East, Licinius still rules, and is about to become your brother-in-law . . .'

'That is true,' Constantine frowned. 'I do not know how the god will arrange matters, but in my heart, I know that what I have said is true. It is my destiny.'

'I believe you,' I said softly, for in that moment, with the last of the winter sunlight bathing him in a golden glow, he did indeed seem touched by a god. And surely, after the civil disorders of the past years, a single strong hand on the reins of Empire would be welcome.

The prophecies of Avalon had foretold a child who would change the world, and with every year it became clearer that Constantine was the one foretold. My rebellion had been vindicated. I wondered why I still felt that flicker of unease even as I rejoiced in my son's victory.

The spring that followed was one of the most beautiful I could remember, as if the entire world were celebrating Constantine's victory. A goodly mixture of sun and rainfall brought out the flowers and the winter wheat produced an abundant harvest.

I was in the garden, talking with the man who took care of the roses, when Vitellia came running out of the palace, clutching a scroll, her cheeks streaked with tears.

'What is it?' I cried, but as she drew closer I could see that her eyes were shining with joy.

'He has made us safe!' she exclaimed. 'Your son, blessed by God, has preserved us!'

'What are you talking about?' I took the piece of papyrus from her hand.

'This comes from Mediolanum – the Emperors have made a policy regarding religion—'

I pulled open the scroll, scanning the words that referred to the earlier edict of toleration of Galerius and adding to it:

'. . . *to no one whomsoever should we deny liberty to follow either the religion of the Christians or any other cult which of his own free choice he has thought to be best adapted for himself, in order that the supreme Divinity, to whose service we render our free obedience, may bestow upon us in all things his wonted favour and benevolence.'*

The paragraphs that followed restored to Christians the property and freedoms that had been taken in the persecutions, stipulating that all cults should have an equally free and unhindered liberty of religion. No wonder Vitellia was weeping, I thought then. The shadow that had hung over her and her church was lifted, and the Christians might now emerge to stand beside the followers of the traditional religions in the blessed light of a new day.

I had not seen such recognition of a Truth that lay beyond cult or creed in all my years among the Romans, whose gods seemed to vie for the favour of their worshippers like magistrates at the elections, or the philosophers, who denounced other schools as errors, or among the Christians, who simply stated that all other religions were wrong.

This recognition of a Power in whose light all faiths might stand as equals reminded me of the teachings I had learned as a child on Avalon, and at the thought, I found my own eyes filling with grateful tears.

CHAPTER SIXTEEN

AD 316

To sit on the shore at Baiae was like being in the heart of the sun. Light reflected with blinding intensity from the white sand that bordered a bay whose waters glittered a clear azure only a shade darker than the blue of the sky. To a child of the north, this light was overwhelming, banishing every darkness not only of the body but of the soul. As I lay upon the couch on the terrace, set between the sea and the freshwater bathing pool, I could feel the heat baking out the agues that a winter in Rome had set in my bones.

It seemed to me that the anxieties of the past few years were dissipating as well. There were still those who challenged my son's authority, but he had proven himself a brilliant general, and I no longer doubted that one day he would rule supreme in the Empire.

For several years the imperial household had been settled in Rome. But the great city, which was plagued by a raw chill in the wintertime, was just as bad in the summer, when a damp, sticky heat blanketed the seven hills. Fausta, who was now in the last moon of her first pregnancy, had complained that the heat was stifling her, and so I had brought the imperial household here, to the palace the Emperor Severus had built beside the Bay of Puteoli in the gulf of Neapolis fifty years before.

Fausta lay on a couch beside me, with two slaves to fan her and a sunshade to protect her fair skin. But I had only a hat to shade my eyes. To me, the heat everywhere in Italia was equally intense, but on the coast the air had a purity that invigorated even as it overpowered, and so I spent most of my time in the sun, listening to the sigh of the glittering wavelets on the shore.

An occasional shout of laughter came to me from the bathing pool, where Crispus was playing with the sons of noble Roman families who had come along to bear him company. If I turned I could see the flash of their smooth young bodies, gilded by the sun. Crispus was fourteen now, big-boned as his father, with a voice that was, most of the time, that of a man. By the time my son turned fifteen he had already been at the court of Diocletian for two years. Every year that Crispus remained with me was a blessing, as if the years during which Constantine had been lost to me were being restored.

Of Constantine himself I saw little. The defeat of Maxentius had made him undisputed master of the West. Licinius was now his brother-in-law, but the pact the two emperors had made did not last long. Within two years they began a series of conflicts that was to continue for a decade. Still, my son now felt secure enough to take Fausta to his bed, and at the age of twenty-three she had become pregnant at last. She swore it would make no difference to her affection for Crispus, and indeed, she had adopted him as her own child as well as Constantine's. Still, I could not help but wonder if her attitude might change when she had a child of her own.

The noise from the pool crescendoed as the children began to climb out, glistening in the strong sun. Boreas and Favonia, who lay sleeping in the shade of my couch, lifted their heads to watch, feathered tails beating gently against the flagstones. Slaves hurried forwards with towels to dry the boys, while others brought out trays of fruit and little pastries and pitchers of mint-water chilled with ice brought all the way from the Alpes and stored in a deep cellar, wrapped in straw. Drusilla would have snorted at such extravagance, but she had died the year after Constantine's great victory. I missed her plain cooking, surrounded as I was by all this luxury.

Still laughing, Crispus led the others to the terrace and I sat up, smiling as the dogs fawned at his feet. As he grew, he was coming to resemble his grandfather Constantius more and more, save that where my beloved had been so fair of skin he burned at the slightest touch of the sun, Crispus had inherited his mother's complexion, and the sunshine that bleached his hair only turned his skin a deeper gold. Save for the towel slung over one shoulder, he was as naked as a Greek statue, trained muscles rippling, as beautiful as a young god. *But he is only a boy* – I told myself, surreptitiously flexing my fingers in a sign against ill-luck, irrationally afraid that one of those deities might hear my thought and resent it.

I have been among the Romans too long, I told myself then, for the gods of my own people were not so prone either to lust for mortals or to jealousy. Nonetheless, Crispus was approaching that age which in these southern lands was held to be the apogee of splendour. Fausta was watching him with an appreciation as great as my own, and I found myself suppressing a shiver.

'*Avia, Avia*! Gaius says that the lake on the other side of the hill is the place where Aeneas descended into the Underworld. Let's get up a party to go look for it. We can take a lunch, and picnic on the shore, and read passages from the *Aeneid*. It will be educational.'

'Who will read them?' Fausta laughed. 'Not Lactantius!' She tried to sit up, but the great round of her belly prevented her, and she held out a hand so that her maid could help her.

I smiled. The eminent rhetorician had in later life become an ardent Christian and had recently been sent by Constantine to become his son's tutor. The Emperor had made it clear that the Christos was now his patron deity, and those who wished to rise at his court had found it in their interest to become Christian too. So far he had not insisted on a formal commitment from his family, though we were expected to attend those parts of the services open to the uninitiated. I missed Vitellia, who had gone back to Londinium to rebuild the church there in honour of her nephew.

'Do not be so sure!' retorted Crispus. 'Lactantius is a great admirer of Virgil, and says that he is one of the virtuous pagans who predicted the coming of our Lord.'

'Then I suppose he will not forbid the expedition,' I put in. 'Very well. Let us plan to set out early tomorrow, so as to arrive before the heat of the day.'

Somewhat to my surprise, Lactantius not only made no objection, but decided to come along, a scroll of the *Aeneid* firmly in his hand. Fausta remained at the palace, resting, but the old man and I travelled in litters, while the boys rode little surefooted donkeys from the nearby village up the winding path. A waggon full of picnic gear brought up the rear.

Even in the north of Italia I could find scenes that reminded me of home, but here I knew I was in another land, where the heated air was fragrant with the scent of artemisia and the perfume of the flowers that grew in such profusion in the rich volcanic soil. As we reached the top of the hill above Baiae I called for a halt to rest the bearers and the donkeys and turned to gaze out over the brilliant blue waters of the bay to Neapolis and the perfect cone of Vesuvius beyond. Today no smoke curled from its summit, though the slopes of Vulcan's forum, a half-day's journey away, steamed with a variety of foul smells. They called this place the 'Fields of Fire', and I could sense the earth-fires below the surface, a constant reminder that nothing was eternal, even the solid ground beneath our feet.

Then we were jolting our way down towards the round blue mirror below. The white columns of the healing baths built on the shore by the first emperors gleamed in the summer sunlight, but we halted in a shady grove in the lee of a hill, and the slaves began to lay out our meal. The boys were already running about, dashing down to test the water, daring each other to dive in.

'Are you sure this is really Lake Avernus?' asked Crispus as Lactantius and I settled ourselves in wicker chairs. 'Look, birds are flying across it without harm, and though the water smells a little stagnant, it did us no harm.'

'Virgil must have known it was all right,' said one of the other boys. 'They say that Julius Ceasar himself visited those baths.'

'Well, perhaps things were different when Rome was founded,' I said, smiling. 'After all, it was over eight hundred years ago. And this is bright summer, remember. In the winter, with a storm coming on, this place might look much more menacing.'

'But where is the "wide-mouthed cavern" of which Virgil tells us?' asked Crispus.

'Perhaps there was once a chasm which has now closed,' answered Lactantius, 'for they say that this is a land of changes.' He stretched out one arm in the pose of an orator. Even in this heat he wore a long robe, and with his white beard flowing over his chest, looked the part of an ancient sage as he unrolled the scroll and began to intone:

'There was a wide-mouthed cavern, deep and vast and rugged, sheltered by a shadowed lake and darkened groves; such vapour poured from these black jaws to heaven's vault; no bird could fly above unharmed . . .'

'And when the ground begins to shake, it was an earthquake and not Hecate coming at all?' asked Crispus.

Lactantius nodded, smiling. 'Such evil spirits are no more than dreams and delusions, made demonic by men's fears. When the earth shakes, it is by the will of the Lord God who made it, but it was necessary that Aeneas, who lived long before the light of the Christos came into the world, should be led to found Rome.'

'Yet Virgil himself was a pagan,' I observed.

'He was,' answered Lactantius, 'but so noble in soul that the light of God was able to reach him, as it did so many of our greatest poets, men of the highest genius. Seneca and Maro and Cicero, of our own Roman writers, and Plato and Aristotle and Thales and many another among the Greeks, all touch upon the truth at times, and only the custom of their times, which insisted that God was not One, but many, caused them to continue to honour false gods.'

'If there was a chasm here, perhaps it closed when Christ was born,' said young Gaius, whose father was one of the few senators who had converted wholeheartedly to the new religion.

'Indeed, it might be so,' said Lactantius approvingly.

By this time, the food was ready and the boys, who were at that age when a meal was always welcome, were attacking it with their usual gusto. In addition to the hard breads and olives and cheeses, the cooks had included a crock of the seafood stew that was a specialty of Baiae, featuring various shellfish cooked with sea nettles and spices. I eyed it dubiously, but the cooks had packed it with snow from the cellars, and it seemed to be good.

'What is the temple whose dome I see shining above those trees?' I pointed towards the top of the hill behind us.

'It is the Temple of Apollo that crowns the hill of Cumae,' answered one of the slaves.

'Cumae!' exclaimed Lactantius, gazing upward with interest. 'But of course, it would be, for the Sibyl gave her oracle to Aeneas from her cave and then led him down to the lake to enter the Underworld.'

'Is there still a seeress there?' I asked, remembering how Heron had prophesied the coming of Constantius and wondering, with a remnant of professional curiosity, how the oracle was conducted here.

'Oh no,' replied Lactantius. 'Have you never heard the tale? In the time of Tarquin, the last king of Rome, the seventh seeress of Cumae brought to him nine books of prophecy. When he, considering her mad, refused to pay her price she burned three of them, and then another three, and then at last the king bought the remaining three for the price she had originally asked for all of them. And after that the words of other sibyls were collected from all the cities of Italia and Graecia, expecially those of Erythraea, and the leaders of Rome have been guided by them from that day to this.'

'So there is no sibyl resident at the shrine of Cumae?'

'No, Noble One,' replied the slave. 'Only the priestess who tends the temple of Apollo. But the cave in which the sibyl gave her oracles is there still.'

'I should like to see it,' I said then, 'if the bearers have finished their meal.' Cunoarda, the little Alban girl who had become my maid after I freed Hrodlind, went off to the water's edge where the slaves were eating, and returned with the eight strong Germans whom Constantine had given to me. Her red hair reminded me of Dierna, the little cousin I had loved so long ago.

'It should be safe enough,' Lactantius said seriously. 'There is no wind, and the demon Apollo will be still. And perhaps the spirit of the Sibyl who proclaimed the unity of God will speak to you. I will stay to watch over the boys.'

I refrained from raising an eyebrow. After so many years, the crescent of Avalon had nearly faded from my brow, and I had no wish to explain to the old man why I did not fear the voice of the daimon of Cumae, whether it were that of a spirit or a god. Lactantius had never questioned me about my faith, but he knew that I was not a communicant of his church, and Crispus had confided to me that his tutor worried about the state of my soul.

I have never resented the prayers of anyone who wished me well, no matter what god he prayed to, and Lactantius was a kindly soul, as well as a learned one. If my grandson must be tutored by a Christian, he was fortunate to have the old man.

An hour of travel brought us to a bare cliff of golden sandstone, pierced by a shadowed tunnel that was the entrance to Cumae.

'Do not tell them who I am,' I cautioned Cunoarda as she helped me to descend from the litter. 'Say to the doorkeeper that I am a widow from Gallia called Julia, and will make an offering if they will show me the Sibyl's cave.'

I sat down on a bench beneath an oak tree, glad that we were now high enough to catch the sea breeze, and watched the sunlight glisten on the girl's russet braid as she made her way to the gate. When she returned she was smiling.

'They have sent for the priestess of Apollo herself to guide you. I think they no longer get many visitors to the shrine.'

A few moments later a middle-aged woman in a white tunica

emerged from the tunnel. As she drew closer I could see that her gown was growing threadbare, but it was scrupulously clean.

'Holy One, I will offer this golden bracelet to the god in the name of my husband, who honoured Him, but my deepest interest is in the cave of the Sibyl. Can you take me there?' I had not brought a purse with me, but the heavy cuff bracelet I was wearing had enough gold in it to feed this woman for some time.

'Of course, domina. Come this way.' The priestess turned towards the cool shadows of the tunnel and I followed her, Cunoarda at my heels. As we emerged into the light, she pulled the gauze veil up over her head and I did the same.

Before me was a court paved with worn sandstones, and a plinth bearing a statue of the Sibyl, arms uplifted, with wildly waving hair.

'When Aeneas came here, he called upon the oracle. The Sibyl was standing there, before the doors, when the power of the god came upon her suddenly,' said the priestess. She pointed to an oddly-shaped door in the side of the hill, like an elongated triangle from which someone had cropped the point.

'She seemed taller,' the priestess went on, 'and her voice boomed. It is the nature of a human to resist when such power tries to take possession – they say the Sibyl rushed to and fro like a frightened mare, until the god overwhelmed her. And then, they say, His power rushed through the cave like a great wind, and all its doors were flung open, carrying her words to the waiting men.'

'A hundred gates, was it not, in Virgil?' I asked.

'There are not so many as that, but there are openings all the way,' said the woman, smiling. 'Come, and you will see.'

She lifted the bar, touched a sliver of wood to the lamp that was kept burning by the entrance, used it to light a torch, and pulled back the door. Now I could see that this was no natural cave, but a passage carved into the solid stone. To the right a series of bays had been cut through to the sloping surface of the hill. A little light filtered through their shuttered openings.

To the left a long trough ran along the side of the passage, through which water flowed. As we moved forwards the flickering torchlight glittered on the water and sent strange shadows dancing along the dusty floor. After the bright heat outside, the air here seemed damp and cool and very still.

Apollo might not be present, I thought as I followed, but I sensed power of another kind waiting within the silent stone. Was it indeed Apollo who had once spoken through the oracle here, I wondered then, or had Virgil, writing five hundred years after the last of the sibyls of Cumae had departed, simply assumed she served the god who had taken over most of the other oracles in the Mediterranean world? I reached out with senses long unused, wondering if the force that had once dwelt here retained enough coherence to respond.

Between one breath and another, I felt the familiar dip and shift of consciousness that signalled the approach of trance. Cunoarda took my elbow as I stumbled, but I shook my head and pointed towards the dark bay at the tunnel's end.

'Yes, that is where the Sibyl is said to have sat when she gave her answers,' the priestess said then. 'We do not know what sort of a seat she had, but we have always kept a tripod there, as they have at Delphi.'

I was moving forwards on feet that scarcely felt the ground, but the three-legged stool at the end of the passage seemed to glow with its own light. *The belief of centuries has made it sacred,* I thought then.

'I will sit there,' I said in a voice that did not sound like my own. I pulled off the bracelet from my other wrist and held it out to the priestess. For a moment she was taken aback, glancing at the tripod nervously, but this was not the temple of her god, which she would have been bound to defend from any possible sacrilege. It was clear that she could not feel the power that was beginning to make my head spin.

Shivering, I sank down upon the three-legged stool, and the veil slipped away, leaving my head bare. The position awakened memories buried in my bones; my trembling became a convulsive twitch as my body tried to adjust to the influx of power.

'Lady, are you unwell?' cried Cunoarda, reaching out to me, but the priestess prevented her, and that part of my mind that was still my own noted with relief that though the woman was no seer, she had enough training to recognize what was happening to me.

'Do not touch her,' she cautioned, and then: 'This is all highly irregular. She should have told me she had the Gift, so I might take precautions, but there is no help for it now.'

But indeed, came a thought that was swiftly being pushed into the background, I myself had not known that the trance skills in which I had been trained long ago would awaken so swiftly here.

'*So, daughter, will you let Me in*?' came an inner voice, and with a long sigh, I relaxed into that bright darkness as into a mother's gentle arms.

I was distantly aware that my body had straightened, my hair coming loose from its pins. My arms extended, fingers flexing as if Someone were rediscovering the sensations of wearing flesh once more. I was only sorry that this body, which had endured for sixty-seven years, was all I had to offer her.

'Who are you?' whispered the priestess.

'I am the Sibyl . . .' my lips moved in answer. 'I am always the Sibyl. In Erythraea I have spoken, and in Phrygia, in Samos and Libya and many other holy places in the lands of men. But it has been long, so long, since there was anyone to give Me a voice in this shrine.'

'Do you speak with the voice of Apollo?' the priestess asked suspiciously.

'Go to your temple that stands upon the heights and open your doors to the wind and the sunlight and He will speak to you. But my power comes from the depths and the darkness of earth, and the perpetually upwelling waters of the sacred spring. I am the Voice of Fate. Would you seek an oracle?'

There was an uncomfortable silence, and then the Sibyl's laughter.

'Woman, you have served the gods your whole life long. Why are you so surprised that a Power should speak to you? Ah well – I read in the mind of this old woman who carries me that many things have changed. Rome still endures, but among her people there are some who have abandoned their ancient gods.'

'It is the fault of the Christians!' exclaimed the priestess. 'They say that there is only one god—'

I felt my consciousness shift once more, deepening and expanding as the persona that had overshadowed me was itself overwhelmed by a blaze of illumination that swept all mortal awareness away.

'Indeed, the Divine Source is a single deity of pre-eminent power, who made the heavens and sun and stars and moon, the fruitful earth and the waves of the waters of the sea. This is the One, who alone was and is from age to age.'

'Are you telling me that the Christians are right?' the voice of the priestess sharpened in horror. 'And their god is the only one?'

'No mortal, save in the utmost transports of ecstasy, can touch the ultimate deity. You who live in flesh see with the eyes of the world, one thing at a time, and so you see God in many guises, just as different images are reflected in the many facets of a jewel. To each facet you have given a form and a name – Apollo or Ammon, Cybele or Hera, who once gave oracles at this shrine. Jahweh of the Jews watches over only one people, and this Jesus blesses those who call on his name. They desire to touch the One, but their human limitations allow them to see only a single face, which they identify as the whole. Do you understand?'

In that moment I did comprehend what she was saying, and prayed that I would be allowed to remember these words.

'Then they are wrong!' the priestess exclaimed.

'They do well to serve the Christos, if they will truly follow his teachings, as you do well to serve the radiant Apollo. They are in error only in supposing that there is no truth but the one they see. But I will tell you this – their vision is a powerful one, and I foresee a time when the temple of your Apollo will be a tumbled ruin, his

287

worship as forgotten as that of the goddess who was honoured here before he came.

'Lament, oh ye high gods, and mourn you dwellers on Olympus, for a time is coming when your altars will be cast down and your temples will lie beneath the Cross.' Vision extended in a mosaic of scenes as I saw the Cross lifted above buildings of dignity and splendour, or blazoned upon the coats of men who nursed the sick or fell upon each other with bloody swords. Onwards rolled the vision, as the Sibyl spoke words I could no longer hear and the priestess crouched at her feet, weeping.

Eventually the images ceased, and I realized that the Sibyl had turned her gaze towards Cunoarda.

'And you, child – is there nothing that you would ask?'

Cunoarda's gaze fell, then lifted with a blaze of hope that transformed her. 'How long will I stay a slave?'

'When your mistress goes free, then you will be free as well, and a distant land shall grant you both a refuge. But before that comes to pass she must endure many sorrows and make a great journey.'

'Thank you,' whispered the girl. Her head was bowed, but I could see that her cheeks shone with tears.

'There is more that I could say, but this body tires. It is a sorrow to me, for I tell you that it will be many centuries before another comes who will allow me to speak through her.'

My head drooped, and for a moment then I was two beings in one body: the immortal Oracle, and an old woman who ached in every bone. I tired to cling to the consciousness of the Sibyl, but it was like attempting to hold back the ebbing tide. And then that vital presence that had upheld me was gone, and I collapsed into Cunoarda's arms.

By the time we returned to the palace at Baiae I was in full possession of my faculties once more, though my body, strained beyond its normal capacity by the power that had filled it, felt as limp as an emptied wineskin. As soon as I could speak I had cautioned Cunoarda to say nothing of what had happened, but to remember what had been said and write it down, for already the details were fading from my memory as a dream fades with the day. As regards the free folk of the palace she obeyed me, but I think now that she must have said something to my German litter-bearers, for from that time on they treated me with a reverence that went beyond duty, and I would hear the whisper, '*Haliruna*' when I went by.

Crispus and the others were concerned for me, but they thought my collapse no more than the weakness of an old woman who had overtaxed her strength, and apologized for having dragged me on this journey on such a hot day. But I assured them that I had taken the risk willingly, though they did not know just how great that risk had been. And indeed it was so, for though my body ached, my spirit was soaring with the knowledge that the ability to touch the Otherworld that had been the delight of my youth was not lost to me after all.

We passed through the palace gates as dusk was falling, but the place was full of lights.

'What is it?' I asked, holding open the curtain of the litter. 'Has the Emperor arrived? Are we having a feast that I had forgotten?'

'Oh my lady!' exclaimed the eunuch who was our steward. 'Not the Emperor, but perhaps a Caesar – the Lady Fausta began her labour this afternoon! She has been calling for you, domina. I beg you – go to her.'

I lay back with a sigh, wishing this had not happened now, when I was already so tired.

'I will be no use to her until I have washed and eaten. This is her first child. There will be time.'

When I came to the birthing chamber I found Fausta alone, whimpering with each pain.

'Why have you sent your servants away, my child? They only want to help you.'

'They fussed and fussed until I could not bear it! Oh *Avia*, it hurts so much! Am I going to die?'

'You are young and healthy, Fausta,' I said bracingly, taking her hand. 'I know this is not comfortable, but it will take a while for your womb to open enough to release the child.' I had borne only the one child myself, but in later years I had often assisted at the labours of the wives of officers in Constantius's command, and added that experience to what I had learned of the birthing woman's craft at Avalon.

I glanced towards the door where the midwife was hovering and motioned her to come in.

'She is doing very well,' said the woman cautiously. I wondered what Fausta had said to her before.

Fausta's fingers tightened painfully on mine as another pang came on. Her auburn hair was dark with perspiration and her face blotched with weeping above the distorted belly. It was just as well, I thought then, that her husband was not here to see her now.

'Talk to me, *Avia*,' she said when she could speak again. 'A poem or a joke or a story about Constantine when he was a little boy, anything to distract me from the pain.'

'Very well—' I patted her hand. 'Has he never told you the story of how he won his first laurels? It was when Probus was Emperor, and we were living in Naissus.'

She shook her head. 'He talks to me sometimes about what he will do in the future, but he has never spoken of his boyhood.'

'Then I suppose it is for me to do, so that you may tell the tales to your children in turn.' I waited as a new pang rolled through her, but I think my presence had eased her tension, and her contractions were now not so hard to bear.

'Constantine had just passed his seventh year, though he was always large for his age and looked older, and the Emperor Probus had offered a prize for the foot-races at the feast of Apollo.' As I continued, I let my voice deepen, making my words rise and fall with the contractions that were squeezing Fausta's womb.

'Constantine began to practise, running each morning with Hylas, who was the dog we had then. I would have breakfast waiting when they returned, panting, from the run.'

Gradually, Fausta was relaxing, riding my rhythms to find her own, even panting a little at the word.

'He won that first race easily, for among the boys of his age he was tall and strong. But the next year he moved to a higher division, and though he was as tall as many, they were stronger and more experienced. He finished respectably, but he was not the winner, and you know my son does not like to lose.'

'What did he do?'

'I remember that he grew very silent, with that stubborn frown that we all have come to know. And he practised – morning and night throughout the spring. My son has always been a dreamer, but a practical one, who will make whatever effort is required to make his dreams come true. When summer came once more he was the winner again.'

Fausta gave a great sigh, then grimaced, remembering that her race was still going on. 'And the next year?'

'The next year we were transferred to Sirmium, and that summer the Emperor was assassinated before the races could be held.'

'Tell me something else about Constantine,' Fausta said quickly. 'What games did he like to play?'

I frowned a little, remembering. They say that the child is father to the man. It occurred to me now that I should not blame Diocletian for what he had made of my son – the signs of his future character were there in his childhood, if one had the eyes to see.

'He liked to gather the children of the other officers and parade down the street, pretending they were holding a Triumph. I remember once he tried to train two of the stable cats to pull a cart. That was one time he failed, and had to use the dog instead. I don't think he ever quite accepted the fact that sometimes you simply cannot gain agreement.'

And that, certainly, was a trait he had still. And now he was Emperor, with the power to enforce his will, unable to understand why the quarrelling Christian factions to whom he had granted his favour still clung to their enmities. The Donatists in Africa and the followers of the Egyptian Arius elsewhere, were being slandered by the orthodox with more energy than they spent on the pagans, and giving as good as they got.

'My husband is brave, and persevering and confident,' said Fausta, 'and his son will be just like him.'

'Are you so certain it will be a boy?' I smiled, but in truth I had no right to tease her, having been so certain I was going to bear the Child of Prophecy. I heard the sound of shutters being opened, and turning, saw through the window, the first light of dawn.

As the new day strengthened, Fausta's pains began to come more swiftly, and her whimpers became screams. The midwife tried to encourage her by saying that it would not be long now, but Fausta had reached that point where labouring women call for their mothers and curse their husbands.

'Tell that woman not to lie to me!' gasped Fausta. 'I am dying, I know it. Soon I will join my father and my brother among the shades, and I will tell them that Constantine sent me there!' She groaned as her belly clenched again. 'But you will stay with me, won't you, *Avia*?'

'I will stay with you, my dear,' I leaned to smooth the lank hair from her brow. 'And rejoice with you when your child comes into the world. Remember, the pangs you suffer are part of the work of the Great Mother – not pain, but power.'

Fausta's eyes closed in exhaustion, but I continued to smooth her hair, and never had I come so close to truly loving her as I did in that hour. I could feel the mighty forces that were working through her, and reached out to the Goddess, seeking Her harmony.

In another moment Fausta's womb was contracting once more, but this time her eyes opened in surprise.

'*Avia*, I want to push – is something wrong?'

The midwife began to smile, and I patted Fausta's hand. 'It means that it is all right,' I said. 'The baby is almost ready to come. We will set you on the birthing chair, and when you feel the urge to push again, bear down—'

In the next moment the power of the Mother surged through her once more. When it passed, we levered Fausta onto the narrow-seated chair, and the midwife knelt between her knees while I braced her, all my earlier exhaustion disappearing in the exhilaration of the miracle we awaited now.

'Get warm water,' I snapped to the hovering maids, 'and make sure the swaddling clothes are ready. It will not be long.'

Grunting, Fausta writhed against my hands. Now that we were come to the test, she had given up whining and was showing the courage of the soldier stock from which she came. Once, twice, a third time she pushed, and then fell back with a sigh as the wriggling infant, red with blood and already squalling in protest, slid into the midwife's waiting hands.

I continued to hold Fausta as the other women bustled around her, cutting the cord and helping her to deliver the afterbirth while the maids washed and swaddled the child. Then the new mother was lifted into a clean bed, and I could stand, trembling with reaction, at last.

'Where is it?' called Fausta. 'I want to see my child!'

'Here he is,' answered the midwife. 'As fine a boy as I have seen.' She handed me the swaddled infant, who was still crying.

My grandson . . . I thought, gazing down into the contorted face. All newborns resembled their grandfathers, but I could see no trace of Constantius here. Flushed with frustration beneath a cap of dark hair, the child I held resembled his other grandfather, Maximian.

Carefully I transferred the bundled baby into his mother's arms.

'A son?' she asked, 'and unblemished?'

The midwife nodded. 'He is perfect in every way.'

Fausta relaxed with a sigh and the baby quieted, though his features were still creased in a frown.

'My Constantinus . . .' she kissed the top of the baby's head and held him closer, 'the Emperor's first legitimate son.'

'There are some who question the validity of my relationship with the Emperor's father,' I said drily. 'I would advise you against speaking in those terms to Constantine, lest you appear to doubt his own legitimacy. And in any case, the Roman tradition has been that the man best qualified shall wear the purple, not necessarily even a relative, much less the most legitimate son.' *And surely it is Crispus, with the advantage of maturity and his native brilliance, who will be chosen when the time comes*, I thought then.

Lost in contemplation of the wonder she had produced, I do not think that Fausta even heard. It was I, remembering tales I had heard of kin-fights among the Persians when a new Great King came to the throne, who felt the first chill of fear.

CHAPTER SEVENTEEN

AD 321–24

'Domina – there is a letter from Crispus—' Cunoarda paused in the doorway to my sitting room.

'Close the door, please, and let's see it.'

The brazier was doing its best to counter the dank chill of a Roman February, and I rested my feet upon the flank of Boreas, son of the first hound to whom I had given that name. But even after the renovations I had ordered when Constantine bestowed the Domus Sessorianum upon me, the place was subject to draughts. I had done my best to keep it home-like, hoping for a restoration of the relative simplicity of the suburban villa this palace had once been, but the architects were infected with the new notions of Constantinian grandeur, and only in this room, whose walls were hung with British weavings, and where striped British rugs covered the cold mosaic floor, did I feel truly warm enough to keep at bay the periodic attacks of shortened breath that plagued me in the winter.

'Mistress, what are you doing?' asked Cunoarda as she held out the cased scroll.

'Spinning . . .' I flushed a little as I twisted the loose wool around the distaff and set it and the spindle down, well aware that this was peculiar behaviour for an emperor's mother. 'When I was a girl the spindle was scarcely ever out of my hand. I wanted to see if I still knew how.'

'I used to spin too, when I was a child in Alba,' said Cunoarda, her voice softening.

'Then we shall get you your own spindle, and you may sit with me by the fire,' I replied. 'But first, let us see what my grandson has to say.'

The scroll was in Crispus's own careful writing. He was now nineteen, with the title of Caesar, and for the past two years had been residing in Treveri as Constantine's deputy, between campaigns on the German frontier. Only last summer his troops had gained a major victory against the Alamanni. I missed him, for Fausta and her children lived with their mother in Mediolanum, and I rarely saw them. After a late beginning, she had proved exceptionally fertile. A second son, Constantius, had been born the year after Constantinus, and a third, called Constans, just this year.

'Avia Nobilissima,' he began. '*I have tidings of great happiness. I am to be married to a most charming girl, the daughter of the senior magistrate of Treveri. Her name is Helena too! Is that not a fortunate coincidence? I call her Lena. I learned to love her this past winter, but I did not know if we would be allowed to marry. Now my father has given permission, and we will hold our feast next month, before I leave to rejoin my legion on the Rhenus. I hope that you can be with us for the celebration, but if it is not possible, I ask for your blessing.*

'*May the most high God keep you in health, dearest* Avia. *I remain, your loving Crispus.*'

'Bless the child indeed, and blast him for marrying in such haste. He must know that the roads and the seas alike will be too rough at this season for me to be there!' I exclaimed.

'Well, one can understand his hurry, if he is going off to war. No doubt he will settle his bride in Colonia or Argentoratum while he is with the troops,' said Cunoarda, picking up the spindle, which in my excitement I had knocked off the stool.

'How can my little Crispus be getting married?' I shook my head. 'It seems only yesterday that he was sitting on my knee.'

'Perhaps he will make you a great-grandmother soon,' Cunoarda smiled.

I sighed. I found it hard to imagine Crispus a father, but at this season, when all the agues of the marshlands around the city seemed to settle in my bones, I could well believe myself old enough for great-grandchildren. It had been a hard winter, and I had heard that there was a new plague in the poorer quarters of Rome.

'I will gift them with my palace in Treveri,' I said then, 'and order my bedchamber redecorated for the new bride. And I will send her my long pearl necklace. It will look better against her young skin than it does on me.'

'Oh my lady, you must not say so. Don't you know that gossip holds that you have been granted an extension of youth by the gods?'

I raised one eyebrow. 'Cunoarda, I would not have believed you to be a flatterer! Bring me my mirror – perhaps there has been some miracle since last I looked upon my image there!'

Flushing a little, she brought me the round of polished silver whose handle was formed in the shape of the Three Graces, their arms entwined. I turned my face into the light and held it up. The face that looked back at me was framed by silver hair, drawn back to a knot in two smooth wings held in place by a woven band. The flesh that once had clung to my strong bones so smoothly was sagging now, my eyes deep set and shadowed beneath my brows.

'What I see, my dear, is the face of a healthy woman of seventy-two. If it is not quite the image of a hag, it is because I am careful of my diet and force myself to take exercise. But just because I live in a palace is no excuse for me to ignore life's realities,' I said tartly. 'Now take this thing away. The hour in which I am scheduled to give audience is almost upon us. How many people are waiting in the reception room?'

'Not as many as usual, but one of them is Sylvester, the Patriarch-Bishop of The See of Rome.'

'Very well, I suppose it is time to put away my spinning and become a *Nobilissima Femina*, even if I am an old one, once more. I will wear the tunica of forest-green silk, and over it the sea-green pallium.'

'Yes, my lady, and the earrings and necklet of emerald and pearl?'

I nodded, reached for my stick, and levered myself upright, sighing as if I were already weighed down by the brocade and jewels.

Since taking possession of the Sessoriana it had been my custom to hear petitioners just before the noon meal. I was always astonished by how many people would make their way across the city to my domus, tucked into the south-eastern angle of the walls the Emperor Aurelian had built to protect the sprawling suburbs of Rome.

Today, despite the foul weather, the hall was full. Above the aromatic scent of the herbs laid on the coals in the brazier I could smell wet wool, and smiled, for it brought back memories of Britannia. Escorted by Cunoarda, my greyhounds padding by my side, I took my place in the carven chair on the dais, and surveyed the crowd.

I recognized Iulius Maximilianus, who was supervising the reconstruction of the baths on the domus grounds. It was my intention to open them to the public once they were completed, as an establishment of such size was hardly required to keep one old woman clean.

Maximilianus was no doubt here to report on the progress of the baths, which had been delayed by the winter rains and sickness among the labourers. Some of the others were my clients, and had come simply out of courtesy. But what was the Christian Patriarch of the city doing here?

Sylvester waited with surprising patience, a wiry little man with a fringe of fading reddish hair around his tonsure, clad in a plain white tunic and cloak. The only mark of rank he bore was the large cross that lay upon his breast, which was fashioned of gold. It was the young priest who had escorted him who fidgeted and muttered at the delay.

If some of the others were unhappy with the speed with which I dealt with their petitions, they did not dare to say so, and

298

by the time an hour had passed, only Sylvester remained to be heard.

'My Lord Bishop, I am certain that only a matter of great moment could have brought you to me on such a day. Yet I am an old woman, and not accustomed to fasting. So that you may have leisure in which to set forth your business will you share my midday meal?'

I could see amusement flickering in his eyes, but he assented with a gravity equal to my own. Bishop Ossius had become one of Constantine's most trusted advisors, but I had never warmed to him. Sylvester seemed different. I found myself curious to know more of this priest who was the heir of the Apostle Petrus and Patriarch of the See of Rome.

After Cunoarda had sent the younger priest off to eat in the kitchens, Sylvester and I were escorted to the triclinium. I saw him gazing around at the marble facings of the lower walls and the paintings above and felt a certain embarassment, even though the scenes portrayed were of nymphs and shepherds from the romance of Daphnis and Chloe, and innocent enough.

'I apologize for the grandeur, and the chill,' I said as I motioned him to take the couch on the other side of the brazier. In the large room the two of us seemed like a pair of peas in a large bowl. 'I never eat in here when I am alone, but my household would be mortified if I told them to serve us in my little sitting room.'

'We are all at the mercy of our servants,' answered Sylvester. 'My housekeeper bullies me mercilessly.'

'If there is anything you may not eat, you must let me know,' I said a little nervously, and saw him smile.

'It is not a fast day, and in any case the holy Petrus himself once said that it is not what goes into a man's mouth, but what comes out of it that defiles him.'

'Very true,' I agreed, but nonetheless I whispered to Cunoarda to instruct the cook to prepare something simple.

I do not know whether it was my order or respect for the Patriarch that compelled him, but in a while we were served with barley broth and a dish of lentils and cow-parsnips along with our eggs and bread and cheese. The Bishop's appetite was good, and I wondered suddenly if this was his first meal of the day.

'So,' I said, when we had taken the edge off our hunger and were sipping hot spiced wine, 'what is it that you want of me?'

'Are you so certain that I have come as a petitioner?'

'You are too busy a man to make this journey yourself if a mere message or a delegate would do.'

'It is true,' Sylvester said with a sigh. 'The need is great, or I would not have come to you. You may have heard that there is sickness in the city, but perhaps you do not realize how bad it has become. This is not one of the fevers that strikes us every summer, but something new, in which the victim coughts up blood or chokes to death on his own phlegm. Some are saying it is a precursor of the Final Days, and have lain down upon their beds to wait for Our Lord to come, but I think that it is only another trial to test us.'

'It sounds horrible,' I said. 'What can I do?'

'For the sick, not much. I have opened the Lateran Church as a hospital, and we are caring for them as we can. But so many are ill or dead that there is hardship in parts of the city. I have already emptied my own treasury. We need authorization to distribute corn from the city granaries, and to requisition other items from the merchants for the poor.'

'And the consuls will not give it?'

He nodded. 'I thought that perhaps the mother of the Emperor could persuade more eloquently than I.'

'I can try,' I said thoughtfully. 'I will drape myself in cloth of gold and visit them tomorrow. And perhaps some other ideas for help will come to me after I have seen your hospital.'

This was a man, I thought, who was rarely astonished by the vagaries of human nature, whether for good or for ill. But I was pleased to see that my response had surprised him.

My way to the Temple of Saturn, where I was to meet with the consuls, led through the centre of Rome, and it seemed to me that indeed the heart of the city was less crowded than I remembered. As we passed through the streets I saw doors hung with garlic and amulets or worse things in a desperate attempt to ward the spirit of sickness away. Just beyond the Flavian amphitheatre, I parted the curtains and ordered the bearers to pause at the arch Constantine had erected there, on the ancient triumphal route between the Caelian and Palatine hills. I had not been surprised to learn that it was the largest such arch in Rome.

But though its size might excite admiration, its decoration had caused considerable amusement, for only the topmost frieze actually referred to Constantine, celebrating his victory over Maxentius. The rest of the panels, reliefs and medallions had been cannibalized from monuments to earlier emperors such as Hadrian, Trajan and Marcus Aurelius. The architect had justified this thievery by proclaiming Constantine the summation and fulfilment of the imperial genius, but as I inspected the monument I could not deny that the workmanship on Constantine's panels was visibly inferior to the rest.

You were in too great a hurry, my son, I observed silently. *You have no need to steal other men's glory.*

As Sylvester had expected, the word of the Empress-Mother was a command no magistrate of Rome dared ignore. On the way back to my palace I put on a veil to shield myself from the contagion, and ordered my bearers to make a detour so that I might view the hospital.

Constantine did not spend much time in Rome, but he had been generous in the giving of churches. Rather than seize property from the aristocracy, who were mostly pagan still, he had built most of them on imperial lands outside the old city walls. But in the year of his marriage to Fausta he had presented the imperial palace of the Lateran, where she was born, to the Patriarch of Rome. After razing the barracks of Maxentius's cavalry, he had built his first cathedral beside the palace.

I remembered the little boy who had so enjoyed making fortresses in our garden and realized that for him, one of the attractions of Christianity was the opportunity to build something new—

Something new, and grand in scale. As I entered, I could see the huge row of columns that supported the nave, and the green marble pillars that bore the lower arcades of the aisles. Light streamed in from high windows over the apse, glittering on the silver filigree roodscreen and the statues of the Resurrected Christ and Jesus as Teacher, flanked by angels, watched over the scene within.

But as my eyes adjusted I forgot the splendour. The nave itself and the aisles behind the columns on either side held row upon row of rude pallets, and on each pallet lay a human being, most of them either hawking and choking horribly or ominously still. Some had family to care for them, but for the most part it was the priests and the old women of the Christian community who moved among them, giving water to those who would drink and comforting the dying. The reek of old blood and human wastes assaulted the nostrils.

Sylvester had looked dubious when I spoke of trying to help, and I saw now that until this thing had run its course there was no help to be had, and no miracle but the fact that anyone was willing to nurse these people at all. Surely not all of them were Christians. All Sylvester needed to know was that they were human and in need. I understood then how, despite the gaps and incongruities in its theology, this new faith had become so strong.

I did not stay long. The Patriarch, who had greeted me when I arrived, did not expect it, and was already turning back to his work as I left the basilica. During the short journey back along the walls to the domus I said nothing, and I retired early, but sleep was slow to come.

Like most of the educated classes of Rome I had scorned the simple fervour of Christianity. But these folk had more compassion and more courage than I, who had been trained on Avalon. I realized then that I was ashamed. But even now I do not know whether it was shame or pride that drove me the next morning, when I borrowed a headwrap and tunic from one of the kitchen slaves, and instructing

Cunoarda to tell everyone I was resting, set out to make the short walk to the basilica. I had barely rounded the corner, however, when I heard footsteps behind me and saw Cunoarda.

Her features set in a stubborn frown as I started to order her home again.

'Mistress, I must obey, but if you send me back I promise I will tell everyone where you have gone! Please – I saw your face when you returned from visiting the cathedral. I cannot let you go into that horror alone!'

I frowned at her, but I had long ago learned to accept the peculiar tyranny that servants can exercise over those who ostensibly own them, and common sense told me that it might be wise to have someone young and strong at my side.

I thought that if we could avoid Sylvester, I need not fear being recognized, for I had worn a veil when I visited before. And in the event, no one even asked who we were – they were too hard-pressed, and grateful for every pair of hands. And so I, who for ten years had been the most powerful woman in the Empire, worked as I had not since I was a girl on Avalon, carrying water and attempting to keep the patients clean. And Cunoarda laboured at my side.

It surprised me, how swiftly one could become accustomed not only to the smell but to the horror. Blood and feces were something to be cleaned, that was all. But exhaustion sharpens tempers even among the best of men, and it quickly became clear that although they might be selfless, risking their lives by nursing the sick since the authorities would no longer oblige them with martyrdom, not all the Christians were saints.

I was gently washing the chest of an old man who had just tried to cough out his lungs when I heard an exclamation from behind me. The man with the pail had apparently just been bumped by a woman whose arms were piled high with clean rags, and some of the water had slopped onto the floor.

'Will you look where you are going? For someone to slip on this and twist their ankle would be all we need!' His voice was thin with weariness, but the woman looked little better.

303

'Who are you to reprove me? Everyone knows that during the persecutions you burned incense to the demons the pagans call gods.'

'And have I not done penance for that sin?' He gestured at the suffering around us. 'Have I not risked my life every day here? If the Lord God wishes to punish me, it will be easy enough to strike me down. But you were so unimportant they never even bothered to persecute you. Beware lest you yourself be damned for the sin of pride!'

'You should be ashamed to squabble in the presence of the dying!' I said in the voice that had ruled a household for fifty years. 'You, woman, give me a clean rag, and you, sir, some water to wet it in, that this poor fellow may at least spend his last moments clean!' But by then the sick man's body was arching in a final convulsive fight for breath, before he lay still. Wincing as stiffened muscles complained, I rose to my feet and gestured for the men who carried out the bodies to take him away.

The first few days had been a horror, and in self-defence I erected a psychic shield against the suffering. By day I laboured mindlessly, and each evening I would slip away and make my way home to soak the contagion away in my baths and sleep without dreams until morning. Perhaps because my thoughts were so focused on the needs of others, I had little attention to spare for my own pains.

Gradually we came to realize that not quite all of our patients were dying. Some few, if they could drink enough water, were able to keep their secretions moist enough to cough them up instead of choking. Eventually they recovered, though they were so weak that any other contagion was likely to carry them away. Grimly, we redoubled our efforts, but the priests who were working beside us were still kept busy giving last rites when we failed. Sometimes I saw Sylvester labouring with the others, wearing a stained robe and a cross of simple wood instead of gold, but I managed to stay out of his way. In truth, I doubt he would have recognized me if I had stood before him. Most people's vision is limited to what they expect to see.

It was not until the end of the second week, when the epidemic seemed at last to be faltering, that something occurred to shake my composure. A young girl had been brought in – a Syrian slave called Martha who had nursed her master and mistress until they died and then taken the illness herself, with no one left to help her. She was a Christian, and though she knew what was in store for her, I had not yet encountered anyone who faced it with such serenity.

'Our Lord suffered greater pains to redeem us,' she whispered when she was able. 'I offer Him this martyrdom.'

I had thought myself past all emotion, but when I saw the hope that glowed in her eyes, I found awakening within me a stubborn determination.

'The water of baptism may have saved your soul,' I muttered grimly, 'but what's in this cup will save your body. Drink it down like a good girl – I am not going to let you die!'

I forced water into Martha until her urine ran clear once more, but I could feel her heart fluttering beneath my hand, and I knew that the battle was going against me. In order to evaluate her condition I had to let down my defences, and through the bond between nurse and patient I touched the pure fervour of her soul.

The life-force within was flickering like a guttering candle flame. They say that for the old, the past is more vivid than the present day, and in that moment it was not a Syrian slave girl I was holding in my arms, but my beloved Aelia, who had died when I was far away. I closed my eyes, and powers so long unused I had thought them forgotten roused within me.

I took a deep breath, and as I exhaled, drew up life-force from my own depths and projected it into hers. *Lady*! I prayed, *grant life to your child*! Again and again I did this, as if I were blowing the breath of life into her lungs, but it was something less tangible and more powerful that flowed from my astral body into hers.

And presently the laboured breathing began to ease. For a moment I stilled in the fear that she was leaving me. Then I opened my eyes and stared in wonder, for Martha was sleeping, each breath deep and clear.

My own heart bounding in reaction, I straightened. It was only then that I realized that we were not alone.

Cunoarda was by my side, her eyes wide, but kneeling across from me I saw Sylvester, with the young priest who had apparently summoned him when he saw he would not be required to give the last rites after all.

'Who *are* you?' he breathed, gripping his wooden cross. Our eyes met, and I saw the simple awe in his gaze give way to astonishment as he recognized me. 'Lady, what are you doing here?'

I thought for a moment, searching for a reason he would understand. 'I am doing the work of the Most High,' I answered, deciding he did not need to know whether I called that Power Goddess or God.

'Christ be praised, you do indeed!' he said warmly.

'Say nothing of this!' I exclaimed. The ceremony that surrounded me as Empress-Mother was constricting enough, without adding superstitious hopes or fears.

The ardour in his gaze chilled as he, too, began to think of the political implications. 'I understand, but my lady, you must not stay here! Will you promise to return home and stay there? I could not face . . . your son . . . if anything should happen to you.'

'Do you not believe that God will preserve me?' I said a little bitterly, for I realized that I would miss this time of being fully used, and useful, now that it had come to an end. 'Never mind. I will do as you say. But when this little one is recovered, bring her to me. If her master had heirs, I will give them her price and take her into my household.'

I staggered as I got up, for I had spent more strength than I knew, and Sylvester took my arm. The lamps had been lit, and I knew that it was time to go.

'Thank you. If you will assist me to the door, Cunoarda can help me the rest of the way. You know my home is only just down the road.'

'I will praise God tonight in my prayers,' said Sylvester softly as we went out the door, 'for He has shown me a miracle.'

306

I sighed, suspecting that he did not mean Martha's recovery. But the old tattoo upon my brow was throbbing, and I felt that I had experienced a miracle as well, to know that after all these years I was still a priestess.

'I hear great praise of you from the Patriarch,' said Constantine. It was now high summer, and the last cases of plague had died or recovered some months before, but Sylvester and I had continued to work together on behalf of the city's poor, and I trusted that this was what my son was referring to.

'But you should not have risked yourself,' he went on. 'If I had known, I would have forbidden it. You do not realize how important you are.'

An old woman, important? I wondered. Then I realized that it was the Emperor's Mother who mattered, not the real Helena. He was not seeing me, but an icon with my name. It was natural enough for a child to think of his mother only in relation to himself, I thought then, but it was a mark of adulthood to be able to see one's parents as people, with lives of their own. These days I was even beginning to understand Ganeda, though I had still not forgiven her. I bit back a retort that might have angered him, thinking I ought to be grateful that Sylvester had said no more.

Constantine had been campaigning on the Dacian border, and in the strong morning light, he looked all of his nearly fifty years. My son had grown more massive with middle age, as if he were striving to equal the heroic dimensions of the statue that was being carved for his basilica. But his fair hair, though fading now to a shade between flax and silver, still grew thick and strong.

'The need was great,' I answered him. 'I had no choice but to give what help I could.'

'You had a choice,' he corrected. 'How many of the noblewomen of this city were labouring among the sick beside you?'

I thought for a moment, and offered some names.

'They are Christians already, and only needed an example,' he

307

replied. 'You do not find such self-sacrifice among the pagans. Do you see now why I favour the Christian God?'

I nodded, for among the Romans that was true, but we had tried to give what help we could to all who came to us on Avalon.

'It has been long since we have had a chance to talk together, my mother, and I have much to say to you,' Constantine went on. 'With each year it becomes more clear that the old ways are without virtue. It is the One True God whose will we must obey if we are to preserve the Empire, and the family of the Emperor is the model for all. That is why I permitted Crispus such an early marriage.'

'You must be very proud of him,' I answered, thinking of last year's victories against the Germans. In Crispus, I saw Constantine reborn, and even more glorious, without the suspicions that my son had learned from Diocletian.

'Yes. I am naming him and little Constantinus as this year's consuls.'

'Licinius will not like that,' I observed. 'Last year you named yourself and Constantius, with no mention of Licinius or his son. And if you continue to spend most of your time in Serdica, so close to his border, Licinius will think you are planning to attack him.'

Constantine shrugged. 'Did you really believe that we could share the Empire forever? If the Armenian Christians appeal to me, I will help them, and if the Visigoths attack Thrace, I will repel them. Licinius will no doubt object, and there will be another war.'

'I hope you can delay it for a year or two longer, until Crispus has enough experience to be a truly effective commander.' I replied.

'Yes, the boy is developing well . . .'

It seemed to me that his answer came a trifle reluctantly, and in that moment, random memory reminded me of the ritual of the running of the stag that the little people of the marshes near Avalon performed sometimes when there was need. And it seemed to me that I could hear the whispered echo of their cry, *'What of the King Stag when the Young Stag is grown?'*

But this was Rome, I told myself, and Constantine was a civilized man. With a shiver, I thrust the memory back into the darkness from which it had come.

'. . . but he is still young,' Constantine was continuing, 'and subject to the lusts of the flesh, which lead men into sinful entanglements.'

I suppressed a smile. 'Not all so-called entanglements are unlawful, or he would never have been born. For that matter, your father and I would have been living in sin.'

'No!' Constantine exclaimed. 'You were my father's true wife! He told me so!'

I sighed, realizing there was no point in trying to explain that our marriage had been valid in the world of the spirit rather than in Roman law. I remembered now that Constantine had always been stubbornly attached to his own version of reality.

'The days of pagan immorality are ending! Soon Christianity will be the only faith, and the imperial family must set an example. I am building a basilica in honour of the martyrs Marcellinus and Petrus on the road adjoining your palace grounds. You will become its patroness.'

'Constantine! Not even the Emperor can command another's conscience, as Diocletian and Galerius learned to their cost. Will you deny your own edict, that granted toleration to all?'

'Oh, I will not persecute the pagans—' He gestured dismissively. 'When they see the glory of the Church they will beg to come in! But if God is to bless my reign, my family must serve only Him!'

'Indeed . . .' my voice grew softer. 'And when were you baptized? I would like to have been there . . .'

He stilled suddenly, and I wondered if the shiver I had just felt was a flicker of fear. This was an emperor, and emperors had been known to execute close relations, even their mothers, in times past. In the next moment he smiled, and I told myself I had been insane to entertain such a notion. This was Constantine, the child whom I had borne to change the world. And indeed he was doing so, even if the manner of it was very far from anything we might have imagined on Avalon.

'Baptism is a very sacred rite,' he said in a voice as soft as mine. 'So sacred it can be performed but once, to wash away all sin and leave the soul cleansed and ready for Paradise. But I am Emperor, and must rule in a very imperfect and sinful world—'

And you suspect you may have some sinning yet to do . . . I thought wryly, but I did not voice the thought aloud.

'I live in the same world,' I said instead. 'Until you make that commitment yourself, you cannot require it from me. But I will take your new church under my protection, and receive instruction in the faith as a catechumen.'

Inspired by Martha's fervour, Cunoarda was already doing so. I had freed both women when I took Martha into my household, for I could not treat the Alban girl as a slave when we had laboured together like fellow priestesses in the hospital.

'Then you are a Christian!' Constantine exclaimed.

'Call me what you like,' I said tiredly. 'The Truth does not change.' I did not tell him that it was not his example that had inspired me, but the simple faith of a Syrian slave.

'Praise be to Christ, by whose Name we shall be saved!'

Constantine's deep-set eyes blazed with conviction and I found myself recoiling, trying to remember where I had seen such a look before. It was not until evening, as I was preparing for bed, that it came to me. In that mood, Constantine had been the image of Ganeda, laying down the law with self-righteous certainty.

CHAPTER EIGHTEEN

AD 325–6

'In Christ's holy name, why can they not agree?' exclaimed Constantine. 'I called this council so that the bishops might *resolve* their differences.'

'Yes, Augustus,' said Bishop Ossius, his face reddening, 'but these matters are both subtle and important. A single syllable may make the difference between salvation and damnation. We must proceed carefully.'

Bishop Eusebius of Caesarea, who had come with him to report on the deliberations, was frowning. The pagans in the room looked confused, and my old tutor Sopater, who had become a noted teacher of rhetoric and a member of Constantine's court, was suppressing a smile. The two thousand bishops who had come to the Council at Nicaea at the beginning of May were already arguing about the nature and relationship of God and His Son.

My hip-bones had begun to ache, and I tried to shift position unobtrusively on my ivory chair. The first time I had seen the Emperor's audience chamber in the palace at Nicomedia I had felt overwhelmed by its splendour. But that had been over fifty years ago. Now that I was accustomed to Constantine's ideas of the state befitting an emperor, Aurelian's throne room seemed classic and restrained. Only its human ornaments showed the taste of the Constantinian age.

Where Aurelian had allowed the vivid purple of his toga to proclaim him Emperor, and contented himself with a simple curule

311

chair, Constantine's gilded throne was raised on a dais, and his robes, which were of cloth of gold over purple and adorned with precious stones, outshone it. And where Aurelian had presided alone, Constantine was flanked by his two empresses, for he had given both me and Fausta the title of Augusta the preceding year, when he finally defeated Licinius.

I had been placed at the Emperor's right hand, resplendent in amethysts and cloth of silver, and at his left was Fausta, glittering in emeralds and bronze. Imprisoned in the heavy robes, we sat like the images of Jupiter flanked by Juno and Minerva in the temple at Rome, though I knew better than to say so to Constantine.

'Do they not understand that the unity of the Church is essential to the unity of the Empire?' he exclaimed.

It did no good to point out that the Empire had flourished for more than two centuries while tolerating a wide variety of cults and creeds. The bishops who had come to the council were representing the people who had let themselves be slain rather than throw a pinch of incense on an altar fire. I wondered sometimes if they had become so accustomed to persecution that now that they were the Emperor's favourites they were compelled to attack each other.

Even after several years of Christian instruction, I, like Constantine, found it hard to understand the fine distinctions over which the bishops were arguing. What ought to matter was what Jesus had said, not whether he was God or Man.

'Indeed,' objected Ossius, sweating, 'but if the Empire is not founded upon truth, it will fall. If the Son and the Father are not one and the same, equally God, then we are no better than the polytheists.'

'We are no better than fools if we deny logic!' exclaimed Eusebius, a flush animating the intellectual serenity of his features. A high forehead merged into his tonsure and he wore his beard long, like a philosopher. 'If the Father begot the Son, then there must have been a time when the Son did not exist.'

'But they were of the same substance!' Ossius replied, '*Homoousios*,' he added the Greek term, 'Light from Light, True God from True God!'

'Could we not say *Homoiousios*? Of *like* substance?' offered Eusebius rather desperately. I had heard that he was noted for his writings on Church history, a scholar who would care about every shade of meaning.

Constantine shook his head. '*Consubstantialis* – "of the same substance", has been good enough for us in Rome. Let men interpret it as they will. Then we can address ourselves to objects more within our power. All these fine words are distracting us from reality, and we become no better than the philosophers who reason about a thing without looking at it at all.

'If the bishops, who are the pastors of the people, attack each other, the people will fight as well,' he went on. 'You should never have raised such questions, and if they were raised, they should not have been answered! This is philosophical frivolity! With the Persians on our eastern borders and the Germans to the north, I have enough to worry about without these squabbles. I beg you – give me back peaceful nights so that I can live in the pure light of the Spirit and use my energy for the protection of the Empire!'

During this speech both bishops had gone a little pale.

'*Consubstantialis*?' said Eusebius weakly. 'Well, perhaps we can get them to agree on that. My lord, I will bear your word to my brethren.'

'No – I will come myself,' answered the Emperor. 'Perhaps if I plead with them in person they will understand!'

The two bishops abased themselves, foreheads touching the marble floor, and backed away from the imperial presence. Constantine smiled as if he had persuaded them, and I suppose he had, for though he might not be their master in logic, he was surely their superior in power.

At least my son did not require *me* to bow down before him. I shifted my weight to the other hip and addressed a prayer to the Son, whatever His relationship to the Father might be, that the imperial audience would not last too long.

No part of the palace at Nicomedia could be called home-like, but the red dining salon was small enough that our voices did not echo when a dozen people were gathered there. Fausta was reclining on a couch upholstered in crimson brocade which clashed with the purple tunica she wore. Neither colour suited her complexion, but perhaps the flush was due to wine. After giving Constantine three sons, she had borne him two daughters, Constantina, and a new baby whom they had named after me. Her figure had suffered, and palace gossip said that she no longer shared a bed with the Emperor. On the other hand, Constantine was not sleeping with anyone else, but whether this was the result of morality or because he was incapable no one dared surmise.

It occurred to me that in my old age I was becoming cynical, and I gestured to the servant to bring me some wine as well. These days I found getting up and down from a dining couch more trouble than it was worth, and had claimed a comfortably padded chair, but all of us rose as the Emperor came in.

His couch groaned a little as he stretched himself upon it, but his bulk was more muscle than fat, even now. Swiftly the servants set tables before us and began to bring in the food.

'Do you think that the bishops will be able to agree on the wording of the creed?' I asked. These days I had little appetite, and a few bites of the cuttle-fish croquettes in liquamen had been enough for me.

'It is necessary that they do so. I must make that clear,' answered Constantine.

'If they know what's good for them, they'll comply!' Fausta giggled. There was an uncomfortable silence, as everyone immediately thought of Licinius and his young son, who despite Constantine's pledge to his half-sister (who was married to Licinius) to spare them, had been executed only a few weeks before.

'I meant, of course, for the sake of their souls,' Fausta added, and someone suppressed a snort of laughter, for the Empress, unlike the

314

rest of the imperial family, was still avowedly pagan. Constantine was frowning, but he continued to chew steadily on the stuffed shoulder of wild boar they had just brought in.

'Has there been any new word of the Visigoths?' asked Sopater in an attempt to change the subject. It was not terribly successful, since suspected communication with the barbarians had been one of the reasons given for executing Licinius. Constantine had defeated them in Thrace two years before, going into Licinius's territory to do so and provoking the last civil war.

'Well, if they make any trouble, you can send Crispus to deal with them!' Fausta laughed a little too loudly. 'Don't they call him "Invictus", the Unconquered?'

I felt a prickle of unease. During the war against Licinius, Crispus had been put in charge of the Aegean fleet and by defeating the enemy admiral, he had enabled Constantine to take Byzantium. Only last year the Emperor had struck a medallion showing Crispus and young Constantinus together, but since then Crispus had been transferred from Treveri to frontier duty in Dacia. Old Crocus was long dead, but his tribe had continued to send young warriors to serve as Caesar's bodyguard. Perhaps that was what Fausta had been referring to, but there was something I did not quite like in her laugh.

'These bishops are too concerned with words,' said Constantine, pushing his plate away. I wondered if he really had not heard, or only pretended not to. 'They forget the need for faith. Words divide, but the symbols of religion inspire the soul.'

'What do you mean?' asked Ossius.

'The pagans have shrines where they venerate the treasures that they believe were given by their gods. If we are to wean the people away from such delusions, we must offer them something to take their place. How can true believers walk in purity when every grove and crossroad is dedicated to a pagan god?'

'What would you have them worship instead?' asked Fausta.

'The places where our God has shown Himself to men. Why have we no basilica to honour Christ's empty tomb?'

'Does anyone even know for certain where it is?' I asked.

'That is precisely the problem!' exclaimed the Emperor. 'It is in my mind to send an expedition to excavate the site. Do you know what stands on the hill of Golgotha now?' he added indignantly, 'A temple to Aphrodite the Whore!'

'Abomination!' exclaimed Ossius.

But surely, I thought, it was the place of execution that had been the abomination. I wondered what irony of fate had transformed it into a temple of the Lady of Love.

'Oh indeed,' muttered Fausta. 'We all know that *She* has no power any more . . .'

In July the Council of Nicaea concluded with the creation of a creed to which everyone, even Arius, was willing to subscribe, respecting, if not the will of God, the wishes of their Emperor. At the beginning of the next year, Constantine, euphoric in the conviction that his leadership had brought the quarrelling Christians to a state of unity, moved his court to Rome to celebrate the twentieth year of his reign.

Our entry into the city was, if not a Triumph in the traditional sense, certainly triumphal. Every window was hung with white, and each archway garlanded with spring flowers. Slowly we made our way down the ancient route along the Via Triumphalis, between the pine-crowned Palatine and the Circus Maximus to the Caelian Hill, where we turned towards the Flavian Amphitheatre and the arch that Constantine had set up twenty years before. There the procession paused to allow a delegation of youths and maidens to present a panegyric and song.

Following the procession of senators and a group of flute players came several cohorts of crack troops from various parts of the Empire. The first of the imperial family to appear was Fausta, enthroned with her younger children on a low cart which had been fashioned into a representation of the Empire, bound with a banner proclaiming her the health and hope of the republic, the legend that had appeared on the coin that bore her image the year

316

before. Her eldest son Constantinus, now ten years old, followed on a white pony.

Next was a float depicting the battle of the Hellespont in which the fleet led by Crispus had destroyed the much larger force belonging to Licinius. It was quite effective, I thought, with model ships poised on a silver sea. Crispus himself came after, resplendent as Apollo in full armour, mounted on a flighty Iberian mare who danced and tossed her head at each new wave of cheering.

My own cart looked rather like a shrine, with columns and a gilded pediment, for I had insisted on some kind of shade before I would consent to participate in the procession. Its legend bore the words 'Securitas Republicae'.

I felt less and less like the Security of the State as the morning wore on, for the jolting of the cart set every bone to aching despite the deep pillows that cushioned my throne. At least, this early in the year, the weather was still cool enough that I did not suffocate in my stiff robes, but it seemed to me that a painted statue would have done as well.

In a traditional Triumph, the floats would have been followed by the animals garlanded for sacrifice, but Constantine had replaced the pagan custom with two ranks of white-clad youths and maidens, singing hymns and waving palm branches, and the senior Christian clergy of the city, led by the Patriarch Sylvester, in their festive robes. The imperial bodyguards who escorted them carried the *labarum*, the gilded spear with a transverse bar which was at once a religious banner and a military standard. At its top was a jewelled wreath surrounding the Greek letters 'Chi' and 'Rho', which in the years since Constantine's victory at the Milvian Bridge had come to signify the beginning of Christ's name.

By now, the first part of the procession had made its careful way down the Sacred Way past the basilica Maxentius had begun and Constantine had completed and the old shrines that nestled against the base of the Palatine Hill, and was moving up and around the hill crowned by the temple to the Capitoline Jove. In order to endure the incessant jolt and sway, I found myself retreating into a tranced state in which it seemed to me that it was not I that was moving, but all the fading glories of old Rome that were passing before my eyes.

But even as we curved back to the palace on the Palatine where the feast was being prepared, I could hear a rising tide of sound behind me as the Emperor was borne onward in a chariot drawn by two snowy horses, blazing like the sun-god in cloth of gold.

'Constantinus!' they shouted, '*Io Constantine!*'

Twenty years . . . I thought dimly, *it has been twenty years since Constantius died. Oh my beloved, look down from among the blessed spirits and rejoice in the triumph of our son*!

Summer came early that year, bringing with it a crop of rumours as bountiful as the growing grain. I had declined to accompany Constantine's triumphal progress through the rest of the Empire, and he had left me as his deputy in Rome, with authority to draw upon the Treasury. But even in my palace I heard that people were predicting that the Emperor, having reigned for twenty years, would follow Diocletian's example and abdicate in favour of his glorious eldest son.

But others denied it, and pointed out that Crispus was being kept tethered at his father's side while the government of Gallia went to young Constantinus. A young patrician called Ceionius Rufius Albinus had been arrested for seducing a girl, and Crispus, who was his friend, was held guilty by association.

I found that hard to believe, for I knew my grandson was still in love with his wife, who had given him a son who died and then a little girl. But there were other whispers that were more disturbing. The crime of Crispus was to be too successful, too good. And I could not help remembering that on the day of the procession, the crowd had cheered as loudly for him as it did for Constantine.

And so, it was not so much with surprise as with the shock with which a man who has been ailing hears the physician's sentence that I heard that Crispus had been arrested and taken to the town of Pola, which is in Illyria at the head of the Adriatic sea.

The order for the boy's arrest had been sent from Sirmium, but

Constantine could move swiftly when the mood was on him, and no one was quite sure where he was now. My immediate response was to write an impassioned letter pleading with the Emperor to reconsider and send it off with a trusted messenger.

Surely, I thought, *Constantine will do no more than keep Crispus under guard for a while*. But why should the boy have been arrested at all? Crispus was his own child, but I could not help remembering that his sister Constantina had begged the Emperor to spare the lives of her husband and son. He had promised their safety – and executed them all the same. My stomach knotted when I considered the possibility that my letter would not reach the Emperor, or worse still, might fail to move him.

But if I did not know where to find Constantine, I did know where they were holding Crispus, and I had the imperial Tablet of Authority which the Emperor had given me when he left Rome. My bones ached at the very thought of travel, but by the time the sun rose the next morning I was in a swift carriage with an escort of German guards clattering behind me and Cunoarda at my side, heading north from Rome.

In the heat of summer it was a terrible journey, for our shortest route was the Flaminian Way over the spine of Italia. Changing horses at each post-house, it took us a week of travel, and I was half-dead by the time we reached Ancona on the Adriatic Sea. The sight of the imperial Tablet and the few pieces of gold bought me the services of a swift liburnian galley, and after a day and a night and another day upon the ocean, the rugged coast of the Istrian peninsula came into view.

I will demand to see my grandson, and get to the bottom of this, I told myself as the litter we had hired in the port swayed up the road. *If Crispus has done something that the Emperor misconstrued . . .* I stopped the thought. I had spent a week imagining things that might have made Constantine believe his son was betraying him. Further speculation was pointless now.

Pola was a typical provincial town, with a grid of streets built around the crossroads, an amphitheatre and baths on the outskirts and temples, shops and dwellings farther in. We passed through the gate to the forum and pushed through the crowd to the basilica. As I waited for the officer who commanded my guard to find me someone in authority I realized that the people I could see through the curtains of the litter were not ordinary folk gathered for market day.

Men, most of them in the togas of provincial land-owners, stood in frowning groups as if they had been arguing. A tension that could not be attributed to the sudden appearance of a troop of legionaries hung in the air.

I will not allow fear to overcome me, I told myself, *or jump to conclusions. I have come so far, I can wait a little longer now.*

In a little while my commander emerged with a sweating magistrate in tow. *It is the heat*, I thought, but beneath the perspiration the man's face was white with fear. I had put on the pearl diadem with which I was always portrayed on the coinage. I pulled open the curtains to let him see.

'I am Flavia Helena Augusta, and I bear the authority of the Emperor. I wish to see my grandson – I understand you have him here.'

'Yes, Augusta, but—' he squeaked.

'Take me to him.' I swung my legs over the edge of the litter and prepared to descend.

His face worked. 'Yes, Augusta—'

Escorted by the commander and Cunoarda, I followed the magistrate into the shadows of the basilica. I remember how loudly my stick tapped on the tiles as we crossed the large central hall to the row of offices behind it. At such times, the mind fastens upon little things.

A man stood on guard before one of the rooms, but the door was open. The magistrate stood aside to let me go in.

It had been someone's office, converted into a prison by replacing the desk with a military folding bed. Crispus was lying there. Some power beyond volition moved me forwards, noting with an odd

320

detachment how his golden complexion had already gone sallow, the cheeks beginning to hollow as the flesh changed. Seen thus, the fine bone structure of his face was even more beautiful.

He had been dead, I judged, for some hours.

Was that wind I felt in the dawning the passing of your spirit, my beloved? I wondered numbly. *Could you not stay long enough to bid me farewell*?

Gradually I became aware that the magistrate was speaking.

'The order came from the Emperor, from Sirmium. The young Caesar was to be tried by the magistrates, for treason. Evidence was provided. The Emperor . . . did not specify how we must impose the penalty, but we were afraid to let him have a weapon, for we knew his deeds in battle. He asked then for the death that was given Socrates. A Christian priest gave him the rites of the Church before he died . . .'

I do not know what the man saw in my face, but he stepped back, swallowing hard. I wanted to rage like a maenad, to order the men who had condemned my Crispus slain. But they were not to blame.

'What are we to do now, Augusta? There were no orders . . .'

'Do you have a sculptor in this town? Tell him to bring his wax to make a death-mask. Meanwhile, prepare a funeral pyre.'

I would have taken the body to throw at Constantine's feet, but at this season it was not possible. Shock still numbed most of my emotions, but a few thoughts were beginning to stir. I would take the image of Crispus to confront his father, and I would have vengeance, against Constantine himself or against those who had driven him to destroy his child.

When the magistrate had gone off to do my bidding, I made them leave me alone with my dead, and allowed the burning spark of grief to flare into a raging flame at last.

Silently I raged against my own denial of power. I had cried out to God, but now I understood the great secret, which was that beyond my own strength there was nothing. How could I believe in a god who would allow Constantine to do this thing? It seemed to me then that men had invented their male God to comfort them in the dark when Mother wasn't there to hold their hands.

I had been brought up to see the divine with a different face, in Avalon. I thought of the proverb, 'God could not be everywhere at once so he invented Mothers,' and it seemed to me that it should be the other way around, 'Mother did not have enough breasts for everyone, so man invented deities enough so that every man would have a Mother who would never leave him for another . . .'

Yet the Christians held that their terrible deity was the only one. Sylvester had preached the love of Christ, but I was a woman, and I knew that the only strength and the only god is that strength which is there when we are small and helpless, and it was for that support that I cried out now.

I remembered Hecuba, wailing over the death of Troy, old and stricken with age and powerless, seeing her daughters raped, imprisoned, scattered one by one to the far corners of the earth, destroyed, maddened, their children taken from them . . . But even Hecuba had not had to endure the sorrow of seeing a beloved grandchild slaughtered by his father, who was her own dear son. This was my punishment, I thought, for denying my gods.

By the time I caught up with Constantine in Treveri, almost two months had passed, and autumn was beginning to tint the leaves with shades of bronze and gold. The town had grown since I had last seen it. Constantine's great basilica had been completed, and so had the baths. As we passed beneath the great arch of the gate and turned down the main thoroughfare towards the palace I noticed the changes with a weary curiosity.

By now our caravan had grown to include a cart for the baggage in which Cunoarda was riding, and a second set of bearers for the litter, for I could no longer endure any other form of transportation. It was only large enough for one person, but I was not alone, for the death-mask of Crispus and the urn that held his ashes were my companions.

During the long journey we had held many conversations, Crispus

322

and I. I knew that the bearers had told the others how they heard me murmuring behind the curtains. I could see how Cunoarda sought for signs of madness when she looked into my eyes. But they could not hear that other voice that answered, as Crispus told me of his love for his Helena and the little daughter who was left to them, of his pride in his victories, and the hopes he had cherished for a future which now would never be.

It was as well, I thought as the gates to the palace swung open, that my journey had been long enough to cool my rage. Now, my purpose was hard as quenched steel. No one was safe, if Constantine could kill his own son, and while the life of an old woman was of little value, I wanted to live long enough to see justice done.

I pretended not to hear the whispers as the servants settled me in my old apartments, or the curious glances at the bundle I cradled in my arms. All of the staff here were new. Drusilla had died long ago, and Vitellia had retired to Londinium, and most of the people who had served Crispus and his Helena had been sold off as well. Constantine and Fausta were still at the summer palace in the hills north of the town. I wondered how long it would take him to get up the nerve to come to me.

The next morning I ordered my bearers to take me to the home of young Helena's parents, where she had been living while Crispus was with the Emperor. Lena was, as my grandson had told me, beautiful, with pale skin and smooth dark hair. But that white skin was almost translucent, and when I embraced her I could feel the fine bones, as if her own grief were gnawing at her from within.

In all her life she has never known tribulation, I thought, releasing her. *She does not know how to survive.* Then the nursemaid brought in little Crispa, almost a year and a half old and bright as a sunbeam, and I sat down so that I could take my great-grand-daughter into my arms. What future awaited this child? I wondered as I breathed in the sweet scent of her hair.

'My Crispus was no traitor,' murmured Lena as the child slid from my arms and ran to her. 'He could never have done what they say of him. He loved the Emperor.'

323

'I know it, and I swear to you that I will vindicate his memory,' I answered her. Inscriptions and statues to Crispus were being defaced already as men sought to rewrite the past by *damnatio memoriae*. 'In the meantime, you must write to me and tell me how you are getting on. Be brave and take care of yourself for the sake of your child.'

Her eyes filled with tears. 'I will try . . .'

That evening, the court arrived. I waited for some word from Constantine, but in the morning it was Bishop Ossius who came to me.

'He is waiting for you.' The bishop's gaze flicked to my face and then away. 'I know what you have come to say. I have tried, myself, to remonstrate with the Emperor for this . . . atrocity. But he does not seem to hear me. I think it preys upon his mind, but he will not face it. Come, perhaps a mother's words will reach him where mine cannot.'

'If they do not,' I said softly as I picked up the silk-wrapped bundle I had brought so far, 'I have something here that may.'

We moved along a corridor which terrified rumour had emptied. They were wise, I thought as I limped after Bishop Ossius, my black robes hissing like the whisper of Nemesis along the tiles. When the gods quarrel, mortals must take cover lest a stray thunderbolt destroy them as well.

Constantine was sitting in the little dining room, whose ochre-painted walls were frescoed with scenes from the *Æneid*. Light from the door to the garden lay like a barrier across the mosaic floor, but the Emperor was sitting in shadow. A flagon was on the little inlaid table, and a wine cup in his hand. I paused by the door.

'Augustus . . .' the Bishop said softly.

'Have you come to nag me again, Ossius?' Constantine answered tiredly without looking up. 'You speak of the laws of heaven, but I am responsible for the Empire. You have no right to reproach me—'

Ossius started to object that he was responsible for the Emperor's soul, but my gesture silenced him.

'Perhaps not, but here is one who does!' Pulling the cloth away, I stepped forwards and thrust Crispus's death-mask into the light.

'My son!' Constantine recoiled, hands splayed in self-protection, and the table lurched and sent cup and flagon flying. Spilled wine spread like a tide of blood across the tiles.

Constantine's gaze moved from the mask to the wine and then, finally, to me. His face was pasty and there were dark circles under his eyes as if he had been unwell.

'I had to do it! I had no choice!' he cried. 'God called me to sacrifice the son I loved, just like Abraham, but He provided no substitute, no lamb. So Crispus must have been guilty! God would not be so cruel!'

His head swung back and forth, eyes bulging, as if he could not see me at all. I wondered suddenly if he ever had seen me, or only an icon that he called 'mother', with no more resemblance to the person I really was than a holy image painted on a wall.

'Did God send you a vision, or was it some mortal who persuaded you, Constantine? What did you think Crispus had *done*?' Did he even know who was talking to him, or was my voice echoing the accusations of his own soul?

'He wanted me to abdicate, and when I would not he was going to rebel against me – he had consulted an oracle! He meant to make Fausta his wife to legitimize his rule. Another civil war would have destroyed the Empire. Crispus consorted with sinners. He was an adulterer, and God would have cursed us all. One God, one Emperor – we must have unity, can't you understand?'

Fausta! Perhaps Constantine did not understand, but for me, a picture was beginning to come clear.

'Is that what Fausta told you?' I said in a still voice. 'Has she given you hard proof of all this – or any proof at all? Did you allow Crispus to defend himself – did you ask him any questions, or were you afraid to see the judgment of God in his clear eyes?'

Constantine flinched at each question, but he was still shaking his head in denial.

'You are wrong! You hate her because she is the half-sister of

Theodora, who took my father from you! But Fausta's first loyalty has always been to me – she told me when her father was plotting against me, she supported me against her own brother—'

'She betrayed her own blood for the sake of power – do you think she would hesitate to sacrifice yours?' I spat back at him. 'She did this for the sake of her own sons, not for you, intending that one day they would give her the authority you have given me!'

'Your mother speaks reason, my lord,' said Ossius softly. 'My investigations have revealed no evidence of treachery.'

'Are you a traitor too?' A vein bulged at the Emperor's temple as he turned. 'I had to safeguard the succession,' he said then. 'Crispus was only a half-brother. There would have been war between him and Constantinus . . . Fausta kept on and on about it, and I could see how the people loved him . . .'

'Did you think she would poison you in a dish of mushrooms as Agrippina poisoned the Emperor Claudius, for the sake of her son?'

'She said that Crispus had tried to make love to her!' he cried.

'You are not Abraham – you are Theseus, and a fool!' I raged, waving the mask in his face until he cowered away. 'Even if he had tried, which I do not for a moment believe, what kind of sin is a failed seduction compared to the murder of your own child?! Perhaps the Christian god can forgive you – He allowed his own son to die! No pagan deity could forgive such a crime!'

Like a great tree falling, Constantine sank to his knees. 'God has abandoned me . . .' he whispered.

'God will forgive you.' With a reproachful look at me, Bishop Ossius stepped past and set his hand on the Emperor's head. 'But you must repent and make restitution.'

'If it is Fausta who persuaded you to this deed then you must punish her,' I echoed. 'Do it, or Crispus will forever haunt you, and so will I!'

'God, have you forsaken me?' whispered Constantine. 'Father, forgive me for my most grievous sin . . .'

'Leave us,' whispered the Bishop, pointing towards the door. 'I will deal with him now.'

326

I nodded, for I was sick and shaking, and had no desire to watch as the master of the Roman world grovelled before his god.

For the rest of that day I lay in a darkened room, refusing food. Cunoarda thought I was ill, but if so, it was a sickness of the soul. I was waiting, though until I heard the shouting late that afternoon I did not know what I had been waiting for.

I was already sitting up when Cunoarda hurried into my chamber.

'Lady! The Empress Fausta is dead!'

'How did it happen?' I snapped back. 'Was it an execution?' I had demanded Fausta's punishment, but I had not expected Constantine to compound one crime by committing another, scarcely less terrible.

'No one seems to know,' Cunoarda replied. 'She had gone to the new baths, and guards came to take her to the Emperor, but before they could arrest her they heard screaming. Someone had raised a sluice to let in the scalding water, and Fausta was caught in it, boiled to death in her bath! They are bringing the body back now. They say it is horrible to see.' Her voice shook with an awful suppressed glee.

'Crispus, you are avenged!' I sank back upon the bed, wondering why the knowledge only increased my desolation.

My son had become a monster, at the mercy of his fears. But was I any better, who had urged him to an equal crime?

Of course there was an investigation, but no one ever learned how the accident had been arranged. In truth, although the Emperor meant to punish her, I am not certain that the manner of Fausta's death was ordered by Constantine. Crispus had been very popular in this city where he had governed for so long, and it is possible that some servant at the baths, hearing that the Empress was condemned, had taken advantage of the opportunity to give her a foretaste of the hell she so richly deserved.

327

CHAPTER NINETEEN

AD 327–8

'I think you should see him,' said Bishop Sylvester. 'I believe the Emperor to be sincerely repentant, but he is still troubled in mind. They say he has caused a sculptor to make a golden image of his son which he has placed in a kind of oratory. He stands before it, lamenting. Perhaps you can give him ease . . .'

I stared at him in amazement. Surely I was the last person to offer Constantine comfort now.

'I know that you are still grieving, and perhaps you blame the Emperor for what happened, but if Christ could forgive His murderers as He hung on the Cross, can we do less?'

I might have found it easier, I thought grimly, if my son had sinned against *me*. I had spent the eight months since the death of Fausta in Rome, but neither in the new chapel that had been made from one of the rooms of my palace nor in the church of Marcellinus and Petrus, had I attended any service of the Christian faith. Nor had I entered any temple of the old religion. I was bereft of both Goddess and God. Indeed, since returning, I had hardly stirred beyond my own doors.

They say that the old dwell much on the past, as if reliving their lives backwards towards the beginning. Certainly I preferred to remember the days when Constantius and I had been young together, and more and more often, the dreams that filled my nights were of Avalon. I knew that my servants feared I was dying, and with good reason, for I was now in my seventy-seventh year, and life held nothing that I still desired.

I suspected, also, that while I was away the Syrian girl, Martha, had said more about the manner of her healing than I would have liked. When I did go abroad, people bowed even more deeply than my rank required, and offerings of flowers were often left at my gates.

In the same period, Constantine had relieved his feelings by directly attacking pagan religion for the first time. He had the prophets of Apollo at Didyma and Antioch killed, and destroyed the shrine of Aesclepius at Aigai. But the greater part of his wrath was directed towards what he called immorality. Increasingly strict laws against seduction, even when it was a willing elopement, were prescribed, and the temples where priestesses served Aphrodite pulled down.

I heard Sylvester clear his throat and realized that he was still waiting.

'The Emperor is in the audience chamber, Augusta. It is not good for mother and son to live in estrangement. If you do not feel well enough to rise, may he come to you here?'

I have no son, I thought bitterly, but I nodded. Constantine was still the Emperor.

Cunoarda rearranged the folds of my woollen mantle more becomingly. Spring had come to Rome, but I still felt cold. These days I spent most of my time in the small chamber with its British hangings – Constantine had never been here before. The dogs, sensing my tension, got up as he entered, and I motioned them back to their accustomed place at my feet.

'Are you not happy with your palace, Mother?' he asked, looking around him. 'Surely you have somewhere to sit that is more . . . appropriate . . .'

Bishop Sylvester, whose own private chambers were even less luxurious, winced a little, but kept still.

'The room is comfortable and easy to keep warm. You must forgive an old woman her eccentricities, my lord,' I replied.

'But your health is good—' He looked at me in sudden concern. 'You can travel.'

I frowned. 'Where would you send me?' Was I about to be exiled?

Constantine straightened, his expression brightening. 'To the Holy Land, mother, to Palestine!'

I blinked up at him, confused. I knew that Jesus had lived in Palestine, but after all, his own country had rejected him. These days it was one of the poorest of our provinces. Antiochia and Alexandria were the great Christian centres of the Empire.

'Our Lord once walked that sacred earth! Every stone He touched is holy. But except for Caesarea, there are only a few house-churches in the entire province. The sites of His miracles, which should be thronged with pilgrims, have no shrines!' Constantine's face flushed with excitement.

'That is unfortunate, but I do not understand—'

'I will build them! Work at the site of the Holy Sepulchre is progressing. Bishop Macarius has sent me some pieces of the True Cross already – I will give you one for your chapel here. To beautify the places where God manifested Himself will be my penance and my offering. Surely then He will forgive me my great sin!'

An offering, I thought cynically, but hardly a penance, except perhaps for those whose taxes would support this ambitious programme of construction. I nodded, still wondering why my blessing was required.

'I want to do it now, but the Visigoths are restless and the Persians will have to be dealt with soon. I cannot take the time to visit Palestine, but you could go as my representative. You would know how to find the sacred places and how to bless them,' he drew breath and added ingenuously, 'and show the East that the family of the Emperor is still strong!'

'That would be a difficult journey for a woman of my years,' I said, trying to conceal my astonishment.

'Eusebius of Caesarea will take good care of you. Palestine is a land flowing with milk and honey, and the sun is warm . . .' Constantine's voice was cajoling, but his eyes were full of dreams.

'I will have to pray over this . . .' That was something to which he could not object.

'I must go now, but Bishop Sylvester is still here. He will explain.' Constantine started to embrace me, his sanguine smile faltering a little as his eyes met mine, and compromised by kissing my outstretched hand.

'You are still angry,' said Sylvester when the Emperor had left us, 'and you have good cause. But nonetheless I ask you to make this journey.'

'Why?' I rasped. 'What possible interest should I have in visiting the holy places of a religion whose protector is responsible for such deeds as Constantine has done?'

'God Himself grieved as you grieve when He saw what men did to His Son, but He did not destroy humankind. When you consider how far we Christians are from perfection, is it not a proof of our religion that it has survived at all? Go to Palestine, Helena, not for the Emperor, but for yourself. In the desert, God speaks clearly. If there is any purpose to this tragedy, perhaps you will come to understand it there.'

I made him some neutral answer, and presently he left me alone. I was determined to wait until Constantine had left Rome and then send him my refusal, but that night I dreamed that I stood in a sere land of golden sand and white stone, beside a silver sea. It was a place of terrible beauty, a place of power. And I knew, even as I gazed upon that bleached landscape, that I had seen it before.

It was only when I woke, perspiring, that I realized that it was not from this life that I recognized it, but from the vision that had come at my initiation into womanhood on Avalon. I understood then that there might still be something left for me to do, and that this journey to the Holy Land was my destiny.

Constantine, having got his way, spared no expense in transporting me to Caesarea, the port that the infamous Herod had built two centuries before. In the middle of August, I took ship from Ostia with Cunoarda and Martha, for they had sworn not to leave me

331

even though I had freed them both some time before. We made a leisurely progress around the toe of Italia, past the shores of Graecia to Creta, where we took on fresh food, and then straight across to the Asian coast.

We came in with the setting sun behind us, illuminating the flat strip of tilled land, so rich in orchards and vineyards, and the rising ground beyond it with a rich, golden glow. The fortress loomed over one horn of the little harbour, with the walled town behind it, but more whitewashed buildings showed among the trees to the south, and as we drew closer I could see the smooth crescent of the amphitheatre, its tiered seats facing the sea.

Since the second Jewish rebellion had left Hierosolyma in ruins Caesarea had been the capital of Palestine. Here the Procurator had his palace, and it was here that Eusebius, the senior bishop for the province, had his church and see. I could see why the Romans liked it – in climate and atmosphere it reminded me strongly of the area around Baiae.

On the third day after my arrival, when I was sufficiently rested, my bearers carried me from the Procurator's palace to dine with Eusebius at a little house he had among the olive groves above the town. It was now the end of summer, and our couches had been arranged on a terrace where we could watch the sunset and wait for the relief the sudden drop in temperature brought at the end of the day.

'It is a beautiful country,' I said, sipping some of the local wine.

'The coastal strip is fertile, if it is cared for,' anwered Eusebius, 'and some of the valley of the Jordan, and around Lake Tiberias in the Galilee. Inland, the country grows arid, fit for grazing, and farther south it is desert, fit only for scorpions.'

Here in his own home he looked more relaxed, but he was the same thin, sallow-skinned intellectual I had met in Nicomedia. It was said that the library he had amassed here was better, especially in relation to the Church, than anything in Rome, and he was noted as an apologist and historian. I estimated his age at about ten years less than my own.

'My lady is unaccustomed to heat,' said Cunoarda. 'I hope that she will not be required to spend much time in the wilderness.'

Eusebius cleared his throat. 'Augusta, may I speak freely?' I gestured permission, lifting an eyebrow in enquiry, and he went on. 'If the decision were mine, you would not be required to travel at all. To identify the places associated with our Lord can be a useful aid to faith, but to make them places of veneration and pilgrimage, as if they were in themselves holy, is to fall into the error of the pagans and the Jews. The religion of Moses was founded upon the Holy City, but even the name of Hierosolyma has been lost. Without the Temple, their religion must die. No Jews live in Aelia Capitolina now.'

I lifted one eyebrow. There were Jews in every great city in the Empire. The ones I had known in Londinium seemed to be flourishing. Perhaps Hadrian had reinvented Judaea and turned it into Palestine, but the Jews seemed to have reinvented their religion as well. Still, I knew better than to say so.

'But there are Christians—' I probed gently instead. Sylvester had taken care to brief me on the rivalry between Eusebius and Bishop Macarius of Aelia Capitolina.

He shrugged. 'A small community. And the locations of some of the sites associated with the incarnation of the Christos are known. Since the Emperor has ordered it, I will be happy to escort you there.'

'We must all obey the Emperor,' I agreed blandly.

Two days later we began our journey, following the Via Maris southwards in easy stages across the Plain of Sharon. For me there was a litter with two teams of trained bearers, while Cunoarda, Martha and Eusebius rode mules. Through the gauze curtain I could see the flash of sunlight on the helmets of my escort, sent to guard me and the chests of coin with which I, on behalf of the Emperor, would fund the building of churches in those places I deemed worthy. The rhythmic clash and tramp of the rearguard echoed from behind.

The next morning, the bishop himself arrived to escort me to the site of the Holy Sepulchre. It seemed to me that he greeted Eusebius with a hint of pious triumph, as if he already had the primacy of Palestine in his grasp. But Macarius was growing frail, while Eusebius was a veteran of Church politics. No matter what relics were found here, I did not think he would be dethroned so easily.

'It may not look as if we have made much progress,' said Bishop Macarius apologetically, 'but indeed the place looks very different than it did a few months ago. The abomination that was the Temple to Venus is gone, and we are making good progress in removing the rubble with which they covered the sacred ground.'

Rubble indeed, I thought as I gazed around me. Several marble columns, which some thrifty architect had saved for re-use elsewhere, lay stacked at one end of the forum, which was littered with ropes and other gear. Workmen were emerging from the excavation beyond it like so many ants, bent beneath wicker baskets of earth and stone, and dumping their loads onto a steadily increasing pile. Women, their wrappings so impregnated with dust they seemed themselves to be creatures of the soil, were picking over the rubble.

'Each night waggons take the sifted earth to the valley to extend the fields,' said Macarius. 'The larger stones are saved for building, and the little ones will be used to repair the roads when the winter rains come. And sometimes they find other things – vessels of pottery or glass, a piece of jewellery, or coins. It is the coins we seek above all.'

'To help defray the cost of the work?'

Macarius shook his head. 'Not entirely. We allow the workers to keep what they find, or they would try to hide things, and we might miss some relic of our Lord. So long as the coins we find are later than the time of Tiberius, we will know that we must dig deeper.'

I nodded, amused, and a little surprised, to find the old man so practical.

'In the gospels,' he went on, 'we are told that soldiers diced for Christ's clothing at the very foot of the Cross. May we not hope that when the earth shook and the heavens were darkened they might have dropped some of their winnings there?'

At that moment one of the women held up something small, and the Bishop limped over to see.

'This talk of relics is superstition, though his idea about dating the coins shows a sound grasp of history,' said Eusebius beside me. 'It is the empty tomb, the Sign of the Resurrection, that should concern us here.'

Together we moved closer to the excavation. 'In the time of the Incarnation,' he went on, 'this spot was just outside the city walls. But the new wall that was built by Herod Agrippa included it, and when Hadrian refounded the city he placed the forum here, at the crossroads.'

One could count on Eusebius to stick to the facts, I thought as I gazed at the gnawed earth below. A knob of rock seemed to be emerging to one side. Still, there was something rather engaging about Macarius's simple enthusiasm.

'I have heard it said that the Emperor placed the Temple of Aphrodite there on purpose, to scandalize the Christians.'

Eusebius shrugged. 'Perhaps, though he was not one of the great persecutors. It is the Jews who earned his wrath. I suspect that Hadrian put the temple here simply because it was convenient, and the site was covered in an attempt to level it.'

I could see his point. The city was set on a plateau surrounded on three sides by canyons, and even the top had irregularities. The earlier wall had ended where a quarry had bitten deeply into the ground, but beyond it the ground rose in a hill. I could see what looked like the beginnings of a deeper ditch at the edge of the forum as well. I knew that the thought of the events that had taken place on this spot ought to move me, but I could find no meaning in the confused scene before me now.

Eusebius frowned. 'Until the diggers have finished there will not be much to see here. Perhaps you should look at some of the other sites – the Galilee, or perhaps Bethlehem, which is only a half a day's journey to the south.'

'To begin at the beginning?' I nodded. For some, like the Bishop, the proof of his religion was in the elegance of its theology. But I came from a place where power flowed through the earth and gathered in sacred pools. If God had become Man here in Palestine, surely the land itself would bear witness in some way to the miracle.

It was the season of the grape harvest, and in the villages, the people were picking the ripe fruit in the little vineyards that patched the hills. Patient donkeys made their way along the road before us, almost hidden by the great baskets of grapes they bore. On our journey to Aelia, I had been insulated from contact with the people, but even the commander forgot to be suspicious when confronted by laughing girls who offered him frothing cups of freshly-pressed juice along the way.

The village of Bethlehem had not changed much since the time of Jesus. A cluster of flat-roofed mud houses interspersed with stock-pens and clumps of greenery spread over the hilly ground.

'Do you see where some of the structures are built out from the slopes?' asked Eusebius. 'There are caves behind them that the people use for stables and storage, because they are cool. They press out the oil of their olives there as well.'

'Do you mean that Jesus was born in a cave?'

'A cave that was being used as a stable. There it is, ahead of us. This site has been known for a long time. The clay manger is still there.'

He did not sound very excited, but by now I had realized that what mattered to Eusebius was not the place itself but its value as a historical proof of the Incarnation. Any lack of enthusiasm on his part was more than made up for by the villagers who swarmed around us, offering to show the sacred cave.

Somewhat to my surprise, the way was partially blocked by a grove of cedar trees.

338

'It is the grove of Tammuz,' said the little girl who had taken my hand. 'The pagans mourn him at the same time as we weep for Jesus in the spring.'

I blinked at this easy acceptance, but Eusebius had warned me that some of the Christians in the country district were little better than pagan themselves. It did not seem so bad a thing to me, if it allowed them to live in amity.

The cave seemed very dark after the bright afternoon, but an oil lamp was flickering, and as my eyes adjusted I saw the clay feeding trough where the walls sloped sharply inward to the grotto's end. Inside the manger someone had laid a bunch of flowers. It was very still.

Eusebius had knelt to pray, with Martha beside him, but I stood, eyes closed and feet rooted firmly in the ground, and something that had been tensed since I had first been ordered to make this journey began to relax. Beneath the scents of old incense and lamp oil and a hint of goat there was something else, which after a moment I identified as the clean aroma of damp stone. *Stone is eternal*, I thought, and moved to the side so that I could lay my hand against the cool surface. *Stone holds memories.*

I extended my awareness into the rock, searching for impressions of the past. For a time all that came into my mind were the elemental needs of the beasts that had been kept here. Then, for a moment, I sensed a woman's pain, the profound relief of birth, and a flare of ecstasy as the child was put into her arms. *Whatever Jesus was, I can believe that he was born here*, I thought then.

When I opened my eyes, Martha and the little girl were both gazing not at the manger but at me, with wonder in their eyes.

'I am thirsty,' I said briskly. 'Is there water here?'

'A well – among the trees,' whispered the girl.

It was late afternoon by now and the light slanted golden through the grove. Strips of cloth and ribbons had been tied to the branches of one of them, that overlooked the little pool.

'Thus they do also in my own land,' I laid my hand upon the

rough trunk and closed my eyes, allowing awareness to follow the life of the tree down to its roots and upward once more to the leaves that drew in life from the sun.

And then, for a moment it was not a tree but a female body that I was sensing, feet rooted in the soil and arms reaching for the sky. The image transmuted and I saw a tree trunk carved into the image of the goddess. Women whirled around her, garlanded with flowers. 'Asherah . . .' they chanted, 'Asherah . . .'

These were the Asherim that the prophets cut down in the Courts of the Temple! I realized in amazement. *They were trying to destroy the Goddess. And it is She, before Tammuz, who was honoured in this holy grove!*

As the vision released me I realized that the girl was still speaking—

'Trees are for the Mother, the Virgin who gives birth to the Child of Prophecy. In Mamre, which is just down the road, there is an ancient terebinth tree where Abraham dreamed of his descendents. The family of King David is a tree, and Jesus is at the top of it . . . I hope they will not cut these trees down.'

'When I give orders for the building of the church here I will ask the architects to save them.' I replied.

No doubt Eusebius would have disapproved of the child's mixed theology, but it seemed to fit that moment, and I realized that in their own way, the rustling trees were also witnesses to the fact that once more the Mother was being worshipped here.

It was growing dark by the time we got on the road once more. The villagers had begged us to stay the night and join their celebration, but I judged that a journey with my own bed at the end of it would be less taxing than a night on a lumpy mattress with fleas. But as we started to descend the last slope I heard a squeal and one of the soldier's horses reared.

Above the centurion's curses as they got the animal calmed I heard a soft whining. 'Wait,' I called. 'There's something out there.'

340

'A wild beast,' said the commander, loosening his javelin. 'But nothing large enough to hurt us, by the sound of it.' He motioned to a trooper to follow him with the torch.

'It sounds like a dog—' I watched the flickering light move along the side of the road.

'You were right, my lady!' the commander called back. 'It is one of the wild dogs that roam the hills, with a broken leg. I'll put it out of its misery.'

'Don't harm it!' I cried. 'Let one of our men wrap it in a cloak so it can't bite and we'll take it back to the city.'

'Augusta, you can't make a pet of a wild dog!' exclaimed Eusebius.

'Are you presuming to tell the Empress Mother what she cannot do?' Cunoarda asked dangerously.

I ignored them, my attention on the squirming mass of red wool from which emerged a golden, short-furred head with frantic dark eyes. Gently I spoke to the animal until at last it quieted. Only then did I give the order to resume our journey.

That night I dreamed I was once more a girl on Avalon, bending to drink from the sources of the blood spring, where the water trickled out from a cleft in the side of the hill. In the dream, it was somehow the same as the cave in Bethlehem, but now I realized how much the opening looked like the gateway to a woman's womb.

In my dream, I wept for all that I had lost, until there came a voice that whispered, '*You are the child of Earth and starry Heaven. Do not forget the soil from which you have sprung . . .*' and I was comforted.

My foundling proved to be a female dog just past puppyhood. I called her Leviyah, which is 'Lioness' in the Hebrew tongue. She bit two of the troopers before the legion's horse-doctor could splint her leg, but once I had put her into a small dark room she grew calmer. Perhaps she thought it was a den. From then on I allowed no one else to bring her food or water, and gradually the dog's panic became acceptance, and acceptance grew to trust, until she was taking food from my hand.

Leviyah remained shy with others, but from then on she followed at my heels, hiding beneath my skirts when there was too much commotion, and springing forth with bared teeth if she thought me threatened. She made some of my entourage nervous, but what was the use of being an empress if I could not indulge my whims?

A few weeks later, we made another expedition, to the Mount of Olives which rose to the east of the city. With age, I had come to wake early, though I often needed a nap in the afternoon. When Eusebius suggested that I should arise in time to see the sun rise upon the city, I agreed, although when I emerged into the chill gloom of the hour just before dawn, I wondered why.

But inside my litter I was wrapped warmly, and Leviyah radiated heat against my thigh. We passed through the silent streets and down into the valley of Kidron, then started up again through the rubble-strewn slopes and past the garden of Gethsemane, where Jesus had wrestled with his mortality and been betrayed.

When we reached the summit the stars were fading, and before us, the dim inchoate mass of the city was assuming shape and meaning, as if this were the morning of Creation and we were watching the first emergence of the world. Like Rome, Hierosolyma took much of its character from its sacred hills. Now I could make out Mount Moriah, on which the Jews had built their temple, and glimpse Mount Sion, just outside the wall on the southern side. More and more buildings became visible, though they still seemed lifeless against the grey sky.

And then, of a sudden, the air was filled with radiance, and my shadow stretched out before me as if reaching for the luminous city beyond the gulf of shadow that lay below. Buildings which a moment before had been lifeless mud and plaster and stone glowed suddenly in a hundred shades of gold.

'Our Lord stood here,' whispered Eusebius, his voice harsh with unwonted emotion. 'He taught his disciples in the cave beneath our feet, and He prophesied that not one stone of Hierosolyma should be left upon another. And Titus fulfilled His word.'

And yet the city still stands before us, I thought then. I shivered, recognizing the sink and shift of consciousness that was altering my vision. I still saw Hierosolyma, but now I saw it as a series of layers, its outlines continually shifting while its essence remained the same. Words echoed through my awareness.

'*The Romans were not the first to destroy this city, nor will the Jews be the last to lose it. It has fallen many times before, and will go down in blood and fire and be rebuilt in clean stone again and again, as one conqueror replaces another upon this land. The followers of Christ will make it their sacred centre, yet men of a faith yet unborn shall rule it until the children of Abraham return to claim it again.*

'*And again and again the blood shall flow across those stones, until not only the three faiths of Jahweh, but all the cults whose altars have been cast down shall worship here once more. For I tell you that Hierosolyma is indeed a place of power, and it is not men who have made it so, but rather they who have been touched by the force that rises up from the depths of its rock to seek union with the sky . . .*'

Blinking, I came to myself once more. The ghostly outlines of the cities past and yet to come were fading, and the city of the here and now lay revealed with brutal clarity by the hard light of day. And yet I knew that those other Hierosolymas were still present, part of the eternal Holy City that would always be.

'Lady, are you unwell?' whispered Cunoarda. I found that I was leaning against her. Eusebius was still gazing at the view, and I realized with relief that I had not spoken aloud.

'A momentary distraction,' I replied, pulling myself upright.

Eusebius gestured towards the hilltop, where an outcrop of bare stone was encircled by olive trees. 'And from this point Christ ascended into heaven. Christians have worshipped here ever since that day.'

I bowed my head in reverence, but I knew that when I instructed the architects to build the church here, it would not crown the summit, but rise above the cave in the earth where Jesus had revealed to his followers the deepest mysteries.

343

That night I dreamed I was climbing a mountain. At first I thought I was ascending the Mount of Olives with a company of Christian pilgrims, but this was a smaller hill, and as the light grew I saw that it was the Tor. Below I could see the cluster of beehive huts and the round church that had been built by Joseph of Arimathea, and I realized that this was Inis Witrin of the monks, not Avalon. And yet, as I climbed, my vision altered, and I knew that I was seeing both at once. And still my sight sharpened, until I could look beneath the surface of the Tor to the crystalline structure of caves within.

With December, winter came to the Judaean hills, with violent storms and a perpetual damp chill that bit to the bone. Storms on the Mediterranean made a return to Rome inadvisable, work on the Sepulchre had become almost impossible, and when I developed a racking cough that worsened my usual winter breathing problems, Bishop Eusebius suggested that I move down to Jericho, where it was warmer, while he stayed to watch over the excavation.

As we made our way along the Jericho road, I could see that the terrain was changing, the trees that had clothed the hills around Hierosolyma giving way to scrub, which diminished until it seemed to disappear into the stony hills. At the slow pace my aching joints required it took us three days to reach the palm-girt oasis whose mud buildings huddled below the ancient mound. The palace of Herod was in ruins, but once more, a local merchant was happy to give up his house to an empress.

Eventually I began to feel well enough to explore the surrounding countryside and give Leviyah a chance to run. Compared to the great rivers of Europe I found the Jordan a modest stream, even when swollen by the winter rains, but the greenery that edged it made it pleasant. Venturing farther, we followed the river down to the shores of the Dead Sea.

To the west, the clouds which were no doubt still drenching Hierosolyma hung above the hills, but here, the sky was an intense blue. At this season the folds of the hills sheltered some vegetation, but it seemed impossible that men should live here, until our guide pointed out a brushwood shelter or a hole in the cliffs where one of the Perfecti had come to escape the temptations of the world. We made camp below the ruins of a place called Sekakah, where a community of Jewish holy men had lived in earlier days.

In this bare land I found a curious peace. A messenger was sent to bring back the supplies we would need for a more permanent encampment, and we settled in. I bathed in the saline waters, warm as blood and so thick with minerals that I floated upon the surface like a child in its mother's womb. And I took long walks along the sun-baked shore with Leviyah frisking by my side.

It was during one of these walks, in the middle of the day when the rocks – water-worn or sculpted into fantastic mushroom-shapes – blazed white in the sun, that I encountered the old man. Like me, he had come out to greet the noon, standing with uplifted arms at the edge of the sea.

Surprisingly, Leviyah remained still until he had finished his devotions. As she danced up to him, he turned with a smile. But I held back until he gestured a welcome. Life in this arid land had fined him down to bone and whipcord, his skin too leathery for me even to guess his age, beyond the evidence of his grizzled hair and beard. Save for a bit of goatskin tied around his skinny hips he was unclad.

'I thought you might be one of those who is not permitted to speak to a woman,' I said when we had turned to look out over the water again. Its lead-coloured waters shimmered in the sunlight, and I blinked, trying to pin down the sense that I had lived this moment before.

'What is male or female when we stand as spirits before God? In the desert, true opposites are obvious – light opposes darkness, heat battles the cold,' he answered. 'Truth is easier to see. Men come here now to live as anchorites because they can no longer hope for the martyrdom of blood to wash away their sins. But they are not the first to seek enlightenment in this wilderness. The men of Sekakah lived a life of purity in their caves, and our Lord Himself spent forty days and forty nights wrestling with illusions not so far from here.'

'And are you one of those who seek wisdom?' I said, watching Leviyah hunt among the stones and sticks cast up upon the shore.

'Since before His day there has always been a small community here, passing on certain teachings that the established religions have forgotten. In times past, persecution was likely to interrupt traditions. In these days, I fear that certain aspects of the ancient wisdom will become unacceptable to a church that is learning how to live with wealth and power.'

'Why do you say such things to me?' I asked, focusing on his face at last. Suddenly I was certain that I had seen him before. 'I am the mother of the Emperor.'

'Even in this life that is not all you are—' he reached out and touched the spot where once the crescent of Avalon had blessed my brow. How had he known? My forehead was deeply lined and my skin browned by the sun; the old tattoo was no more than a discoloration now.

'By this I recognize you as a sister in a tradition kindred to my own, an initiate of the Mysteries.'

I gazed at him in astonishment. From time to time I had met priests of the Mediterranean gods who recognized that behind all their cults lay a greater truth, but I had never expected to hear a Christian speak this way.

'And there is something more. I have had a vision,' he said then. 'For a time the holy Joseph – he in whose tomb Christ was laid – dwelt among us, before he sailed away across the sea. In my vision, he appeared and told me that you would come. When I saw you, I was to speak these words:

'"*Follow the setting sun to your journey's beginning, and through the mists of morning you shall pass between the worlds . . .*"'

'Does this mean something to you?'

I remembered now – twice, I had dreamed this. I nodded, weeping, though the warm air dried my tears before they could fall.

346

CHAPTER TWENTY

AD 327–328

We travelled up to the Holy City just before the Feast of the Resurrection. On the lower slopes, the vivid green of spring was already ripening to summer gold, but the heights around Hierosolyma were bright with new leaf and meadows jewelled with red buttercups, with little pinkish-purple orchids and hairy flax and a host of other flowers. It seemed that every migrating bird in this part of the world flew over Palestine, and the air rang with their cries.

'Rejoice! Rejoice in the spring!' they sang, 'Kore returns from Hades, and the Son of God arises from the tomb!'

On the slopes around the city dense colonies of rock-rose were covered with snowy white bloom, as were the spiky sprays of desert thorn. Inside the gates, one became suddenly aware of hidden gardens when a trill of birdsong and a whiff of perfume came drifting over a wall.

Bishop Macarius's round face was as bright as the flowers. In the past two months his diggers had made great progress. They had unearthed a hard knob of stone which was clearly the site of the Crucifixion, and laid bare the hillside beyond it, into whose slopes had been dug a number of tombs. But his very success presented a new problem, for none of the openings still held bodies, so how were they to tell from which one the angel had rolled back the stone?

With my stick to steady me on one side and a strong young priest ready to catch me on the other, I crossed the ditch and made my way across the uneven ground. A philosopher would have welcomed the

347

current situation as a way to test the hypothesis that great events can sanctify a location, for this site, though historical, had been inaccessible until now. At Bethlehem and the Mount of Olives, the devotion of two centuries had left an impression, and there, I could not be entirely certain whether the images I was perceiving came from the events that had taken place there or the focused yearnings of the pilgrims who believed in them. To Eusebius, simply identifying the location was a powerful aid to faith, but Macarius, and Constantine, wanted a place of power.

I paused, turning to my left to study the knob of stone.

'We believe this to be the place they called Golgotha, because it looked like a skull. The stone here is more fissured than the rest, and I suppose that is why it was not quarried.' Macarius pointed to the uneven surface.

I laid one hand upon the stone, and after a long moment jerked it away, shuddering at the echoes of agony it retained. 'Surely this was a place of execution – the very stones still cry out in pain,' I whispered, though I could not say with certainty whose it had been.

There was a murmur of awe from behind me and I sighed, realizing the story would be all over the city before night fell.

'Be comforted, my lady,' said the young priest when he saw how I had been shaken. 'Behold the empty tomb!'

There were in fact two chambers in the side of the hill that were still in good condition, and several others that might have been tombs before the stone crumbled away. Clearly neither Eusebius nor Macarius had dared to make a choice for fear the other would object to it. I, representing the Emperor, was expected to decide.

To those with the skill to sense such things, places retain memories of great deeds that have been done there. But this tomb, unlike all others, was important because the body of Jesus had not remained within.

'We must pray to God to guide us . . .' I told them. 'Celebrate the Divine Services for the holy days on this spot, and perhaps He will communicate His will.'

*   *   *

Palm Sunday had already passed, and the town was full of visitors. The air throbbed with tension as the Church, triumphant in the Emperor's favour, launched into the traditional round of ceremonies, and the tide of devotion carried me along. On the eve of Good Friday I went once more to the site, hoping for inspiration.

The tombs gave me no help, but as I returned, I noticed in the ditch a sprig of green. One of the workmen dug it up for me and I took it back to my chamber, where Cunoarda, who was accustomed to my eccentricities, found a pot for me to plant it in. It sat on my windowsill, next to the little clay image of the tree goddess that had been dug up by one of the workmen.

The very air of Hierosolyma seemed to darken with the emotions of Good Friday, and the people gathered at the foot of Golgotha wailed as once they had wept for Tammuz, who also died in the spring. During all the day that followed I lay upon my bed, fasting. And in that half-aware state that can result from deprivation, many thoughts took root in my imagination and flowered there. As I wondered about the tomb chambers, memory brought to mind the other caves that I had seen. It seemed to me then that all three were earthen wombs. From the first cave in Bethlehem, Christ was born into the mortal world, the second, on the Mount of Olives, was a birth of wisdom, and from the third, by Golgotha, he was born into immortality. His followers denied the Goddess, but She was here, in the figure of Mary – Virgin, Mother and sorrowing Crone, and in the female recesses of Earth herself, who receives the dead into her embrace so that new life can arise with the spring.

And I thought then that this was what Eusebius, whose religion was of the mind, did not understand – that if there is only one Divinity to be worshipped, it must be addressed in many ways, as Man and God and Mother, as pure Spirit, and in the physical icons which bear witness to the Divine Presence having made itself manifest in the world. Even superstition could promote faith. In this, Constantine spoke for his people – his heart was still pagan enough to know that outward and visible signs were needed to lead earthly men to inward and invisible grace.

When darkness fell I passed into an uneasy sleep in which I experienced a series of dreams. In the first I thought I was awake, for I was still in my chamber, but the sunlight was shining on my potted plant and I knew it was day. However, the plant had grown, dividing into several twisty branches that sprouted both green leaves and thorns. As I watched, it began to put forth starry white flowers. I recognized it then as the thornbush that the monks of Inis Witrin said had grown from the staff that Joseph of Arimathea had stuck into the ground.

From that recognition I passed, in the way of dreams, to Golgotha, as it was in the days when Tiberius ruled. I stood with a crowd of people before the knob of stone. Three crosses had been set there, but as I watched, the central one began to sprout leaves and branches and starry white flowers. It was not dead wood but a living tree that we honoured, renewal instead of sacrifice.

And again the scene shifted. It was evening, and the city trembled beneath a lowering sky. Two men bore a rude stretcher from Golgotha, while weeping women followed behind. They were carrying the broken body of a man. As they neared the hillside in which the tombs were situated a solider motioned to them to hurry, and they manhandled the corpse into one of the dark openings and laid it upon the clay slab. A great stone was leaning against the hillside beside it, its edges still white where it had been hewn. Grunting, the two men managed to roll it across the entrance.

Then the younger man went back to the women, trying to give comfort. But the older paused for a moment, and seeing that the Roman was watching the others, drew upon the stone with his finger the sigil of an initiate of the highest Mysteries. He was better dressed than the rest of them – a man of middle age with silver in his beard. As he turned, the last light of the sun illuminated his features, and with the certainty of dream I recognized him not only as the anchorite I had met by the Dead Sea, but as the old monk I had spoken with so long ago at Inis Witrin.

In the morning, I was carried out to join in the celebration of the Resurrection in a sedan chair, for I was too exhausted to walk. The day had dawned fine and clear, and above the murmur of the crowd came the triumphant choruses of the birds. The deep singing of the priests made the fine hairs rise on the back of my neck and arms. Gold and jewels flashed in the sunlight from the robes of the priests, and the smoke of incense from the altar they had set up in front of the tombs hung in blue swirls in the still air.

There is power here, I thought as the drama of the Mass came to a conclusion. *It may not be the only truth in the world, but this story they are telling is true.* I could feel the life returning to my limbs, and as the bishop lifted his hands in dismissal I rose from my chair. In the morning sun the openings to the tombs showed clearly beyond the altar. By one of them lay part of a large stone.

It seemed to me now that if events had happened as the gospels described them they would have left an impression of power within the tomb, a power so great I was afraid even to try to touch it. But the mark upon the stone I might seek after, for I was an initiate of the same Mysteries.

And so I did, and did not even know that the people had grown silent, watching me, for I was staring at the dark opening beyond the stone that I had found.

Upon the rocky floor lay a scattering of white petals from the holy thorn.

I stayed in Hierosolyma throughout that spring and into the summer, conferring with the architects whom Constantine had sent to build churches above the sacred sites that I had found. From my window I could see the foundations of the Church of the Holy Sepulchre, with its long nave extending to the east, as was so common in Constantine's churches, so that when the doors were opened, the high altar would blaze in the light of the rising sun. The Rock of Golgotha had been trimmed to fit into the courtyard on the southern side, and the hillside behind the tomb cut away so that it could be covered by a rotunda.

I had been brought up to believe that the eternal powers cannot be contained in temples made by human hands, and sacred space should be honoured, not owned. But if this building, gilded and jewelled with mosaics from ceiling to floor, was more likely to impress pilgrims with the glory of the Church than the wonder of the Resurrection, that was the tradition of the Mediterranean world. I could foresee a time when the pagan shrines that had sanctified the landscape and scandalized the Christians would be replaced by Christian icons. I wondered if by then there would be any pagans left to be upset by the change.

One evening Eusebius arrived for dinner, beaming. The Emperor, he told me, had decided to refound the city of Drepanum as Helenopolis in my honour, and build a church to the martyr Lucian there.

'It is a victory for the Arian way of thinking,' he told me over the lamb and barley. 'For Lucian was not only the best student of the theologian Origen, but he himself taught Arius.'

'I thought he was a priest in the church at Antiochia who published a new edition of the scriptures—'

'That is so, but he was executed in Drepanum by Maximinus. You must visit there on your way home and give it your blessing.'

No doubt that would please Constantine, I thought unhappily. My son had taken to calling himself the thirteenth apostle, a status which in practice seemed to demand the adulation formerly reserved for gods. The Roman Emperors had been deified for centuries, but normally they waited for death to assume full godhead. Constantine seemed to be adopting the Eastern fashion of looking upon rulers as living avatars of a god. Obviously no one dared to remind him that the kingdom of Jesus had not been of this world.

'It is time I made plans for my departure,' I said aloud. The words of the anchorite echoed in my memory, and images of Avalon haunted my dreams. But my present life of privilege was also a prison – how could I escape it? For now it would be enough to return to Rome. Perhaps from there I would be able to see my way.

*   *   *

By the time I left Palestine a full year had passed. I did not detour to visit Drepanum, preferring to remember it as it had been when I lived there with Constantius. Martha, her fervour undiminished, had remained to serve in the household of Bishop Macarius, but my faithful Cunoarda was still with me, and my Canaanite dog, and the little thorn tree. With us came several chests full of souvenirs, both gifts and things I had somehow ended up buying – Palestinian robes and pottery, Tyrian textiles and glass from Askalon. It was Rome that now seemed strange, a vast labyrinth of decaying splendours which included the Domus Sessorianum.

Constantine was still in the East, supervising the demolition of the old town of Byzantium so that he could create a new Rome that would bear his name. The little boy who had built fortresses in our back garden now had an entire city to play with. Even the Emperor Hadrian's building projects had stopped short of such ambition. When Constantine had finished with Constantinople, would he compel God, I wondered, to let him re-create the world?

Shortly after my return I went to the church of the saints Marcellinus and Petrus to attend services and to donate a golden vessel that had been given to me by the Procurator in Palestine. In one of the courtyards stood a sarcophagus of white marble with reliefs of horsemen. Constantine had ordered it, said the priest, but now the Emperor was planning a great mausoleum in Constantinople, and no one had said what was to be done with the thing.

I suppressed my amusement and assured him that they would no doubt find some use for it, and encouraged him to return to his report on the church's charities. I had had some thought of occupying my days by helping out here, but it was clear that Helena Augusta was far too important a figure to be allowed to dirty her hands in that way. At least I assumed that the reverence with which I was treated was due to my position. But since I returned from the Holy Land the offerings of flowers had begun to appear at my door again, and sometimes people would make me an obeisance that even the Emperor did not demand. It was disquieting, and I realized that I would either have to become a recluse, or go about the city in disguise.

Cunoarda was scandalized, but in Palestine I had grown accustomed to a simpler life. I was now nearly eighty years old, and surely, as I told her, I had earned the right to do as I pleased, or at least as much of what I pleased as my ageing body would allow. Too often the old were thrust into a corner, sent off to some country cottage where they would not get in the way of their descendents, or even put into the street, if they had no children who would, however grudgingly, provide for them. To become a gilded icon, set safely in a niche on the wall and brought out on holidays, was only a more comfortable way of being put aside.

But I had been set aside before, when Constantius left me to marry Theodora, and I had no mind to let it happen again. I might be old, but I was not powerless.

Remembering how I had nursed the sick during the plague, I told Cunoarda to go to a shop that sold used clothing and purchase garments suitable for a poor widow. She came back with two long-sleeved gowns, one of dusty brown, the other a faded blue, and both of them neatly mended, sturdy sandals, and several bleached linen veils. The priests at the Church of Marcellinus and Petrus had only seen me jewelled and scented, my features half-hidden by purple gauze. I doubted they would recognize me with white linen bound across my forehead and wearing a shapeless gown.

And so it proved. I was only one of a covey of old women who helped to distribute food to the hungry and clothes and medicines to the poor. The activity eased my frustration, but after a year in Palestine the Roman winter seemed raw and cold, and I fell ill myself in December, and for some months I went nowhere at all.

As I lay in my bedchamber, alternately shaking with cold and burning with fever, it came to me that my life was drawing to an end. This was the ultimate parable of Age, ancient, powerless, useless. I cried out for strength and God's help, and like an initiate plumbing the depths of the Mysteries, I came to rest at last in an empty shrine. And there the secret was confided to me – there is no God, and no

354

Goddess, only the power of the Mother within, giving what little strength one has.

And then I realized that, as in childbirth I had created my own tormentor who would feed on me and destroy me, at the end of life I must endure the painful process of giving birth to the Self, for myself alone. I had to give up power over my child to become detached and uninvolved and let him build his world. Why was this such a surprise? Had I not always known that what I did was by my own will – to leave Avalon with Constantius, to accept responsibility for my child? When I did that, I became the Goddess, with the same ruthless power.

Now I had renounced my child, and the grandchild I loved had been taken from me. It was for younger women to bear and care for children now. I might lend wisdom and counsel, but it was no longer my part to meddle in the affairs of the world, unless it was to teach the young ones what I had learned.

There was nothing left to me but old age and declining strength, and in the end, death. But I was beginning to see that this might also be an opportunity. As a mother, I had had to deny myself in favour of others. Now, it was given to me to be free again, to be uniquely myself, living for myself, procreativeness giving way to creativity.

By the time I had the strength to get up and around, spring had come once more. The little thorn tree, which I had put into the earth just outside the chapel in my palace, had survived its transplanting and was now putting out strong green shoots, starred with white bloom. When I looked at it, I did not see my well-tended gardens, but mist on the water and the smooth green slope of the holy Tor.

I summoned a magistrate, and with his help and Cunoarda's I began work on my will. Every detail must be covered, from freedom for those members of my household who were still slaves to the disposition of the items I had brought back from Palestine. A man's robe, which the merchant had assured me was the very garment worn by Jesus, was to be sent to the bishop at Treveri, and a set of diadems worthy of the Wise Men to the church at

Colonia. To Bishop Sylvester I left the Domus Sessorianum itself, with instructions to use its resources as needed, and to take care of the little thorn tree.

Cunoarda pulled a long face, but I found that even simply planning to give so much away left me feeling lighter. How much freer would I feel if I simply walked away? Though I assured Cunoarda I was feeling better, it was likely enough that death would soon release me. But if it did not, perhaps one day I would abandon all that held me in Rome.

Attached to the Church of Marcellinus and Petrus was a kitchen and a covered area where the poor could come for a meal. There was also a small building, lone survivor of the barracks that had formerly occupied the space, where the sick could be nursed for a while. It was a long time since I had been trained in the use of herbs and simples, but I knew more of such things than the priests did, or most of the other women, and they were happy to have my help when I could come.

I had told them that I served a family that had estates in many places, and must often travel with them, which excused me from becoming too close to the community. Still, it was good to go among ordinary people again. In the spring that followed my return from Palestine, I was spending three afternoons a week at the church, while Cunoarda told any enquirers at the palace that I was resting.

It was on one of those afternoons that the old woman from Gallia collapsed over her soup and was carried into the shelter. She had been coming in for the past several weeks. Her name was Drusa, and she had moved to the city with her son, but now he had died and left her alone. I had noticed her particularly because the other helpers thought she resembled me. Perhaps it was the Celtic bone structure we shared. She did not know her age, but I guessed her to be a few years younger than me.

Drusa died just before the Feast of Pentecost, on the day that a messenger had come to tell me that the Emperor was on his way to Rome. Ever since, my stomach had been acid with anxiety, for I

356

knew that there must be a confrontation, but the old woman's death put my own fears into perspective, and in that moment of clarity, from the depths of my soul emerged a plan.

'Drusa is my sister in Christ,' I told the priest, 'and I will act the part of a kinswoman and see to her burial. A waggon will come for the body this afternoon.'

Constantine made a triumphal entry into the city. I did not attend, though even from my palace I could hear the cheers. He was scheduled to attend services at the Lateran cathedral and on the following day, to address the Senate, and then, no doubt, there would be a banquet. It was not until the third day after his arrival that the messenger came to tell me that the imperial entourage was on its way.

By then the domus was worthy of sheltering the imperial presence, every surface polished and shining. Constantine should have no reason to scorn his mother's surroundings now. I received him in one of the private chambers, more intimate than the audience hall, though no less splendid, since I had added the draperies of Tyrian purple and richly-coloured carpets I had purchased in Palestine.

It suited him well, I thought as I rose to greet him. He had come from some formal reception and was still wearing the purple toga brocaded with flowers. I had decked myself out in the robes of an Empress Mother, my hair confined by the pearl diadem.

Three smaller figures, dressed in similar garments, followed him. For a moment I thought they were dwarfs, intended to make the Emperor look even larger. Then I looked again and realized that they were boys, all three of them dark-haired, with skin that did not get enough sun. They gave a supercilious glance at the room's beauties, then flopped down on two of the large cushions next to the table where I had placed a tray of the fig pastries drenched in honey that Constantine used to love.

'Mother, you look well—'

I look old, I thought as the Emperor took my hands and pressed his cheek to mine. Even if I had desired it, court robes did not permit a more affectionate salutation.

'I have brought my boys to see you – Constantinus, Constantius, Constans, salute your grandmother.'

Their names might proclaim their sire, but in features these were Fausta's sons, whom I had not seen since they were very small. The oldest must now be about eleven, and the others a year and three years younger. As they reluctantly relinquished the sweetmeats and got up to make their bows I wondered what they had been told about their mother's passing.

'Do you have horses?' asked Constantinus. 'I have a white pony that I rode in the procession.'

I repressed the memory of the white stallion that Crispus had ridden in our triumphal entry into Rome. At least this child was trying to be polite. His brothers were already roaming about the room, tugging on the curtains and picking up the alabaster vases and delicate bronze figurines.

'I am too old to ride, but I have dogs. If you wish to go out into my gardens you may play with them.' Leviyah would avoid these children with the caution of a wild thing, but my other dogs were friendly. With another pang I pushed away the memory of how Crispus had used to play with my dogs.

'Yes, why don't you boys run outside? It is a fine day!'

Clearly the boys recognized the difference between fatherly indulgence and an imperial command, and made no protest when the servant I summoned arrived to lead them away, especially when I picked up the silver tray of pastries and set it into Constantinus's hand.

'They are fine lads,' said Constantine fondly, gazing after them.

They are mannerless brats, I thought, but they were his problem, not mine, and he deserved them.

'I like to keep them with me,' he went on. 'There are those who would use them against me, you know, young as they are.'

I nodded, and seated myself on one of the carved ivory chairs, whose rounded back had been carved with scenes of Penelope and

Ulysses. Its mate, which creaked as it took Constantine's weight, portrayed Dido and Aeneas.

How did I come to have a son so old? I wondered then. Since I had last seen him the flesh had begun to sag a little on the big bones, and the skin of his face was deeply scored by lines of anger and suspicion as well as power. He seemed to have bounced back from the tragedy of Crispus and Fausta, but not without scars.

'Your journey to Palestine was a great success—' Constantine poured a goblet of wine from the flagon that had been left with the pastries upon the table. 'Even if they can agree on nothing else, both Eusebius and Macarius are unanimous in praise of your virtues.'

He grimaced as he remembered his battle to force the bishops to consensus. I had heard that the compromises of Nicaea were already fraying. In the old days, men had served the gods as their temperaments inclined and no one would have seen any point in trying to make them all see things the same way.

'As I hoped, the image of the imperial family is beginning to shine brightly once more. Now I would like you to make a journey to the churches founded by Saint Paulus in the cities of the Greek diaspora.'

'No.' Though I found great beauty in the words of Jesus, I was becoming increasingly aware of a difference between the truths he taught and the church that Paulus had established in his name.

Constantine was still talking. I cleared my throat. 'No – I will make no more journeys for you.'

'But why? Are you ill?' The Emperor's eyes opened wide as he realized that I had denied him.

'I am well enough, for now, but I am old. I have served you and the Empire. In the time that is left to me I must care for myself – the true Self that lay so long neglected while I was paying attention to other people's needs.'

'Do you wish to retire from the world? Perhaps to a community of holy women, praying for the Empire—'

I could see the beginnings of calculation in his eyes. I could not really blame him – this ability to extract political benefit from

359

everything was, I suppose, one of the things that made him an effective emperor. But in a world that was full of stories of young people rebelling against their parents, I had never considered how hard it might be for an elder to win freedom from her children.

'I will not head your congregation of Christian Vestals, Constantine,' I said tartly. 'But I *am* going away . . .'

'I cannot allow that—' Constantine shook his head. 'You are too useful to me here.'

'Useful!' I was growing angry at last. 'How useful will I be if I begin to call the death of Crispus a murder, or proclaim myself disillusioned with Christianity and go to make offerings at the Temple of Juno Regina on the Capitol?'

'You will not! I can imprison you here—' Constantine was half out of his chair, his face flushing dangerously.

'Do you think I have taken no precautions?' I snapped back at him. 'I am your mother! I have distributed letters to be sent out in a week's time unless a word from me recalls them.'

'You will say that word—'

'Or you will murder me, as you did Fausta? I am *old*, Constantine, and death holds no terrors. Neither threats nor pain will bend my will!'

'Are you still a Christian?' This was not self-interest, but a deeper and more superstitious fear.

I sighed. How could I make him understand?

'I have always wondered why a man who can see only one colour is considered disabled, and yet is praised when he will accept only one deity. I believe that Christ bore the power of God, and I honour his teachings, but I know that the Goddess in her many guises loves her children as well. Do not try to define me as Christian or Pagan, Constantine.' I took a deep breath, remembering the sigil I had seen Josephus of Arimathea inscribe upon the tomb. 'I am a servant of the Light. Let that be enough for you.'

There was a long silence, and in the end it was Constantine's gaze that fell.

'I do not understand, Mother – what do you want?'

Even now there was a part of me that longed to take him in my arms and comfort him as I had done so many years ago, but I could not allow it to rule me.

I took a deep breath, and answered gently, 'I want my freedom, Constantine . . .'

At last I understood the error I had made so long ago. We give birth to our children, but we do not create them. In my pride I had believed Constantine to be the justification for my existence, and claimed his sins, as well as his achievements, as my own. I could pray for him, but Constantine was an immortal spirit, and though it was through me that he had come into this world, I must neither take upon myself the fate his deeds had earned, nor blame him for my own.

'But how? What will people say?'

'You may tell them I am dead, for indeed I will be dead to you, and to this world.'

'What do you mean? What are you going to do?'

'I will leave the world you know, and make my way to a place where you will never find me. In the chapel of my palace lies the body of a poor woman of this city. You may bury her in that tomb at the Church of Marcellinus and Petrus – one old woman looks much like another, and people will see what they expect to see. Tell whatever tale you like, Constantine, mourn the icon of Helena that you have created to feed your glory. But let me go!'

'You are my mother,' he protested, his heavy head turning blindly. 'You cannot abandon me . . .'

'Your mother is dead,' I rose to my feet. 'You are speaking to a memory.'

He reached out, but I had drawn a veil of shadow about me in the way I had learned long ago on Avalon, and his grasping fingers closed on air.

'Mother!' he cried, and then: 'My mother is dead, and I am alone!'

Despite my resolution, I felt my own eyes filling with tears. I turned away, shadow into shadow, and hurried from the room. But as I hobbled down the corridor I could still hear the master of the Empire, weeping for the mother he had never really known.

That night, Flavia Helena Augusta passed away.

With the help of Cunoarda and one or two other servants who knew the truth about what had happened to Crispus and Fausta and were willing to assist us, the body of Drusa was placed in my bed, and taken from thence immediately to the embalmers, as word of the death of the Emperor's mother spread through Rome.

It was very strange to assist at my own demise, though it was a necessary prerequisite to my resurrection. I was astonished by the tumult of grief that swept the city, even knowing that the people were not mourning *me*, but an icon of Saint Helena that was more than half the creation of Constantine's propagandists. Perhaps I had done some good in the city, but I did not recognize this worker of miracles.

The air around the palace grew heavy with perfume from the flowers that people had heaped before the doors, already hung with cypress as a sign of mourning. Indeed, it was said that there was not a flower to be had in Rome, so many had been offered here and at impromptu shrines all over the city.

In all this, Constantine was the chief mourner, exchanging his purple for funeral white, his features gaunt with anguish. No one could have doubted his sorrow, and indeed, I believe that he convinced himself that the shrouded body in the chapel truly was his mother. Even if I changed my mind there was no turning back from my decision. I had hurt Constantine too badly, and he would see me dead in truth if I tried a public resurrection.

Bishop Sylvester was to be my executor, assisted in the distribution of my goods by Cunoarda. I had provided for her generously, and we had planned that I would wait at Ostia until she could join me. But I was seized with a morbid desire to observe my own obsequies, and disguised in my peasant clothes, I took refuge in the modest rooms near the Church of Marcellinus and Petrus that I had rented as a part of my disguise.

*   *   *

362

On the eighth day after my 'death', Bishop Sylvester celebrated my funeral mass. The great Lateran cathedral was crowded, for all the notables of the city were in attendance, whether or not they were Christian. The poorer folk, myself among them, crowded around the entrance. The tall doors were open, and from within one could hear the echo of singing and catch an occasional whiff of incense. But on the whole, I was relieved not to have to listen to the eulogies.

When it was finally over, the funeral procession emerged to carry the cedarwood coffin the short distance to the sarcophagus waiting at the Church of Marcellinus and Petrus. Constantine walked before the bier, barefoot, with his sons beside him. I could see Cunoarda among the veiled women who followed it. The crowd surged after, weeping, and I was borne along with the rest.

I had never quite understood the Christian attitude towards bones. The pagan Romans had had a horror of pollution, and required that their dead be buried outside the city. The roads that led out of every Roman city were lined with tombs. The tombs of heroes and emperors were separate mausoleums, where the offerings of pilgrims sustained them on their progression towards godhood. Even in Palestine, people honoured the tombs of the patriarchs. The graves of the great rooted their people in the land.

But the Christian dead were buried in the churches, in the midst of the cities. Already, every Christian church with any pretension to grandeur had its *martyrium*, where the body of some saint who by being murdered had achieved instant holiness was enshrined. But the ending of the persecutions had cut off the supply of martyrs. I wondered if they would be forced to take the bodies apart to make them go further – a finger bone in one place and a foot in some other church miles away? Bishop Macarius was right. People hungered for some physical evidence that their faith existed in this world as well as in heaven. But at some point they would have to learn to do without such tangible links. I suppressed a cackle of hysterical laughter at the image of God attempting to gather up all

363

these scattered bits in order to restore the bodies of the saints at Judgment Day.

Of course the most famous tomb of all was empty, and I had my doubts about the graves of some of the apostles, after so many years. So perhaps I should not trouble myself over the fact that the bones in this sarcophagus would not be mine. What would matter was the fact that people believed my body was there. And if their prayers lifted the poor soul whose corpse had become my substitute more swiftly towards heaven, that was surely no more than I owed her, whose death had set me free.

CHAPTER TWENTY-ONE

AD 329

'To be dead is not so terrible. Indeed, I am feeling livelier every day.' I gave Cunoarda a reassuring smile.

We had considered passing me off as her mother, but the Empress's freedwoman was well known, and it seemed wiser to say that I was an old British servant called Eilan. It would have been amusing to watch her trying to avoid giving me an order if I had not known how much it troubled her. She was thirty now, and although she was no longer a girl, her red hair and round figure would have been handsome were it not for the anxious frown. My will had provided her with enough money to buy herself a nice little estate anywhere in the Empire and a husband to go with it if she so desired. Each day that she stayed with me I was humbled by her loyalty.

Almost two months had now passed since we took ship from Ostia in the grey dawn of an early summer day. In Massilia we had purchased a modest carriage and begun the long journey north to Britannia.

'You are truly feeling stronger?' asked Cunoarda.

I nodded. I had not realized how the stiff robes and ceremony of my old identity had weighed upon me. Without them I felt lighter in body and spirit, and the shortness of breath that had plagued me in Rome had almost disappeared. I took a deep breath of the hay-scented air, as if I could drink in the sunlight. *Soon*, I thought, *I will become so light I will float away*.

To be sure, floating would have been a more comfortable mode of transportation. The route we had chosen led up the valley of the Rhodanus from Arelate to Lugdunum, and from there, through the fields and hills of Gallia. Unfortunately, the condition of the road in any given section was dependent on the dedication of the magistrates responsible for it. A year ago I would have refused to stir without a well-upholstered litter and a team of soft-footed Nubians to carry it, but I was enduring the jolting of the carriage surprisingly well.

If I had known how much I would enjoy my freedom, I thought then, I would have made my escape years ago. But years ago, I reminded myself grimly, I had still been hoping to save the Empire through my son.

Now I began to recognize the hills around Treveri. To stop here was a risk, but I doubted that anyone would look twice at an old woman with a sun-browned face beneath her broad hat, wrapped in a mended shawl.

Even as we crossed the old bridge over the Mosella and wound through the town I could see changes. The palace that I had given to Crispus had been partially demolished, and was being rebuilt as a double cathedral. By now, the frescoes of the imperial women which had decorated his nuptial chambers probably lay in fragments under the new floor.

The woman who kept the inn where we took lodgings was a fount of gossip. From her we learned that the baths where Fausta had died were now the property of the bishop. The exercise hall was being converted into another church, and the rest of the buildings knocked down.

Nobody said so, but clearly they thought that Constantine was trying to buy enough prayers to purge the memory of his crimes. But it was Crispus's memory that was being purged. The people of Treveri had loved their young governor, and resented the fact that the statues and inscriptions that once had honored him had not been restored.

And it had been many months since I had heard from his wife, Helena.

*　　*　　*

'Remember, until we know the situation you are to let me do the talking—' Cunoarda glanced nervously back down the street. Save for a slave who was sweeping the horse-droppings from in front of his master's door it was empty. It was always possible that someone in the Emperor's service was having Cunoarda followed, but we had seen no signs of it during the long days on the road.

I pulled my veil down to hide my features. 'I understand.'

The house of Lena's parents was in a quiet street near the outskirts of Treveri, lined by well-kept houses, though the area where we stood had not been swept recently, and there was a chip in the plaster of the wall near the door. It seemed a long time before our knocking was answered, and the door was opened by a girl with her hair tied up in a rag as if she had been cleaning.

Cunoarda and I traded looks. We had been admitted by a doorkeeper when we were here before. But from somewhere deeper in the house I could hear the happy laughter of a child.

'Is your master or your mistress at home?'

'Caecilia Justa is lying down. She has been ill.'

'Or the Lady Helena – is she here?'

The girl looked at us with sudden suspicion, and then, evidently deciding that Cunoarda had an honest face, nodded. 'She is in the atrium, with the child.'

As we passed through the hallway I glimpsed the altar to the ancestral *lares* with an oil lamp burning before it, and realized that like many in the old aristocracy, the family held to the traditional religion. Though they had clearly fallen on hard times, the household was trying to maintain decent standards. The worn flagstones that paved the atrium were clean, the flowers in the earthenware pots had been watered and pruned.

On the other side of the fountain a small girl was playing, her fair hair flashing from gold to ash as she skipped in and out of the sunlight. By now she must be almost four years old. This, I thought, was a true child of Constantius's line. What would her future be when Fausta's black-browed offspring came to power?

I wanted to scoop her into my arms, but I remained hidden behind my veil. *I am dead*, I told myself, *I have no right to her now*.

As we entered, the woman who had been watching her turned on her bench to greet us. Crispus's wife was even thinner than she had been when I saw her before, but she was still beautiful. Her shadowed gaze fixed on Cunoarda.

'I remember you. You came here with the Empress.'

Cunoarda nodded uncomfortably. 'My mistress charged me to fulfil certain commissions she did not wish recorded publically in her will. I have brought you a draft for a banker here in Treveri to provide for the little girl.'

Lena's eyes filled with tears. 'Blessed be her memory! I am sorry now that I did not reply to her last letter, but I was afraid. Crispus is avenged, but that woman won. Everyone knows that we are in disgrace, and we have been ostracized. My father died last autumn, and we have had to learn to scrape by.'

'Then I am glad to bring you the Empress's legacy,' said Cunoarda. We sat down on the other bench, and the maidservant brought a tray of preserved fruit and a pitcher of barley-water, very welcome on so warm a day. Though Lena might be thin, she no longer seemed so fragile, as if adversity had brought out a strength she had never needed before.

'I wish money was my only concern,' said Lena. 'With my father dead, my mother is under the authority of my uncle. He is willing to take her in, but Crispa and I are a liability which even a legacy cannot negate. I fear it will only make me more attractive to one of the farmers to whom he has offered me. . . . I no longer care what happens to me,' she added bitterly, 'but what about my little girl, when her only choices are safety as a farmer's drudge or death if she tries to claim her heritage in Rome?'

I could bear it no longer. Cunoarda gasped as I leaned forwards, throwing back my veil. 'She has another heritage . . .'

Lena's eyes grew huge, and for a moment I thought she would faint.

'But you died in Rome . . .'

'I died *to* Rome,' I corrected. 'By revealing myself now I place my life in your hands. Listen to me, Lena – you and Crispa are all that is left to me of my grandson, who was the beloved of my heart. I am going where even the Emperor will not follow. Do you have the courage to come with me?'

I could feel Cunoarda radiating disapproval at my side. She had never really believed we could escape together, and no doubt counted our chances even smaller burdened with this fragile woman and a child.

A flush of colour suffused Lena's cheeks and then drained away, leaving her even paler than before. 'I always wondered,' she whispered, 'why Crispus wanted to marry me. He was so glorious and brave, and I was always afraid. But I see that the time has come to prove myself worthy. We will go with you, my lady, whether it be to the Hesperides or Hades!'

'It is to the Hesperides that we shall travel, my dear,' I said softly, 'to the apple isle of Avalon . . .'

Crispa, sensing her mother's emotion, came skipping over to stand at Lena's knee, her gaze straying from our faces to the candied figs on the table and back again.

'Crispa,' I said softly. 'Do you remember me?'

She frowned a little, and then for a moment I saw an ancient soul looking out of her blue eyes.

'You are my mother,' she lisped. Lena and Cunoarda exchanged worried glances, but I reached out to take the small warm hand.

'Yes, perhaps I was, but in this life I am your other *avia*, little one,' I said softly. 'Would you like to take a journey with me?'

By the time we arrived at Ganuenta, there were new silver threads in Cunoarda's red hair. But if the Emperor's agents were watching us, they had orders not to interfere. When we reached the Rhenus at Mogontiacum we sold the horse and carriage and took passage on a barge carrying timber. It was a pleasant way to travel, and the drama of the gorge just north of the town moved even Cunoarda to wonder. The greatest danger was that Crispa, who clambered all over the barge with the agility of a monkey, would fall overboard.

The Rhenus carried us swiftly past the outposts Rome had built to guard the border. As we drifted by Colonia I gazed at the wall where Constantius had told me we must part, and realized that the old wound to my heart had finally healed. These days I had only to close my eyes to call up his image, and relive the times of our happiness.

Sometimes, when I sat thus, I would hear Lena whispering to her daughter to be quiet, for old people sleep often and should not be disturbed. But these days it was not sleep that claimed me, but the waking dream called memory. Crispus cuddled, warm and golden, in my arms, as real as the little daughter I saw when I opened my eyes. When I lay in my bunk on the barge, Constantius stretched out beside me, telling me what he had been doing during our years apart. Even Constantine came to me at times in the shape of the boy he had been before he became infected with that disease called Empire. And as our journey continued, I was visited more and more often by the folk of Avalon.

Very quickly I learned not to mention these ghostly encounters. At worst, my companions thought my mind was wandering, and at best it made them uncomfortable. Fortunately Lena had improved in health and strength with every mile away from Treveri, and she and Cunoarda had forged an alliance. Anyone who resisted Cunoarda's blunt competence could usually be impressed by Lena's aristocratic manner, and I found that I could leave the ordering of our journey in their hands.

Why had no one ever told me that old age held gifts as well as pains? As a child, I had wondered why the old priestesses looked so content as they dozed in the sun. They knew, I thought, smiling. And sometimes, as I hovered on the threshold between sleep and lucid dreaming, I seemed to glimpse people and scenes that I recognized from some other lifetime. Little Crispa was the only one I could talk to when these far-memories lay heavy upon me, for the very young have just come in over the threshold which the old are about to cross, and at times she remembered the life we had shared before.

Then the moment would pass, and she would be darting away, Leviyah panting at her heels, to hang over the rail and watch the green waters rush by, and I would be abandoned, though not alone.

In Ganuenta I had hoped to visit Nehalennia's shrine, but they said that a flood some years back had damaged it, and the ground was unsafe now that the river's course had changed. My first thought was to endow a new temple. After contributing to so many Christian churches, surely that was the least I could do for the goddess who had guided me for so long. But such an act might have aroused unwelcome questions, and the funds that remained to me were needed to support the two women whom I now spoke of as my daughters, and the child.

If Nehalennia was being forgotten, I alone could not restore her worship. I reminded myself that the Goddess is ever constant and ever changing. When in the slow cycle of years men realized their need for her once more, surely Nehalennia would return. But that night I wept in the darkness, grieving for something lovely and precious that had gone out of the world.

We came to Britannia in the season of harvest, when the air was scented with curing hay and the songs of the reapers rang across the fields of nodding grain. The crossing had been a rough one, and even I found the jolting of a carriage a relief after being tossed about for three days at sea.

'Britannia seems small,' said Cunoarda, looking out at the gentle alternations of wood and field beyond the rounded shoulders of the downs.

'I suppose it is, considering how far we have come. No doubt Londinium will seem little, compared to Rome. But I know the scent of that hay, and the way the power flows through the land.'

'This is still a very different country from my home,' she said with a sigh. 'I was taken in a raid by a rival clan when I was not much older than little Crispa. I have memories of slopes purple with heather, and the baaing of the sheep as they came down from the hills. But I cannot see my mother's face. I think perhaps she died when I was small.'

'Then I shall be your mother, Cunoarda—'

'Oh, but that was only a part of our disguise, while we are on the road—' She flushed to the roots of her hair. 'You are—'

I laid a finger to her lips. 'I am only Eilan, now, and I have reason to know that the children of one's body are not always the children of one's heart.' Gazing at that familiar strong-boned face, I was amazed that through all those years when I had thought myself destitute of love, I had not noticed the treasure that lay beneath my hand.

'I never imagined . . . I never dared . . .' She shook her head, sniffing and wiping her eyes on her sleeve. 'Oh my lady – my mother! You gave me my freedom, but I was still empty. Now you have given me a soul!'

I opened my arms then and held her until her sobs had ceased.

In my will, I had bequeathed the house in Londinium to Cunoarda, and she had written from Treveri to tell the tenant she was coming there to live. When we arrived, the place was empty – indeed, it was practically without furnishings, and Cunoarda and Lena spent a busy day in the market-place purchasing bedding and kitchen gear.

I had looked forwards to seeing what more than twenty years had done to the city, but that morning I was having trouble with my breathing, and I thought it best to stay indoors with Crispa to bear me company.

'*Avia*, who are the pretty ladies?' Crispa pointed at the relief of the four *matronae* which I had commissioned so long ago. It was one of the few decorations that had survived my absence, perhaps because it was bolted to the wall.

I took a careful breath, then turned. 'They are the Mothers.'

'Look! One of them has a dog!'

Leviyah stood up, tail wagging, at the word.

'Not you, silly!' exclaimed Crispa, reaching up to pat the carven flank of the hound in the lap of the third figure in the frieze. 'And one has a baby, and the other two have fruit and a loaf of bread. Are they goddesses?'

'They are the Goddess – but She has many faces, as many faces as there are mothers in the world, and when they grow old and leave their bodies to pass over to the Otherworld they continue to watch over their children . . .'

I had tried to keep my voice calm, but Crispa was a sensitive child, and she climbed into my lap and put her arms around my neck.

'*Avia*, will you always watch over me?'

As I hugged her, I felt an ache in my throat, and knew it was not caused by shortness of breath, but unshed tears.

That night my illness reached a crisis. Gasping for breath, I saw terror in the faces of Cunoarda and Lena, and could not comfort them.

'Shall I send for a priest?' asked Cunoarda anxiously.

I managed a bark of laughter. 'What use? I have already been buried! You heard the funeral oration Bishop Sylvester gave!' Then I began to cough again.

At the height of my paroxysms I would have welcomed death gladly, and continued to fight only because the two women begged me not to leave them alone.

A little after midnight, the mint-scented steam with which Cunoarda filled the room began to relieve me, and I was able to drink some comfrey tea. At length I fell into a state halfway between sleep and waking, cradled against Lena's breast.

During the crisis, I had raged against my weakness, unready to go into the night. But now, I realized that in our old age, what we lose in infancy is miraculously given back. Instead of crying in the dark for the mother who abandoned us before we were able to stand alone, now, with children and kindred having come and gone, we are free. In our darker moments we feel ourselves wholly alone, weak, aged. But in the end the Mother is given back to us and we are reborn, going back to infancy, lying in trust on the breasts of our daughters . . .

Everything is taken from us, even God; we spend ourself to the death. And then the Goddess comes back to us. From *becoming* the Goddess, the mother, we have *created* the Goddess in our daughters, our sisters, as we turn to Her, knowing that even if we must die still not knowing anything else, we die in Her arms and on Her breast.

But I did not die. Waking to the clear light of morning in Lena's arms, I took a deep breath and rejoiced as the life-giving air filled my lungs. Nonetheless, I was desperately weak, and I could feel my heart bound in my breast. For the first time I faced the possibility that this body might fail me before I reached my goal.

I remembered times during my illnesses when death would have been a welcome release. At other moments I had called on the teachings of Avalon to counter my panicked fear. I had reason to believe that death was only a passage from one kind of existence to another, but I had still dreaded the moment of transition. Now, however, I realized that my fears were not for myself but for those I would leave behind me.

'You are awake!' Lena exclaimed as she felt me stir. 'And you are better, thank the gods!'

'For now, but if I do not recover, I must tell you how to get to Avalon.'

Lena's cheeks grew pink with embarrassment. 'Do you mean it is a real place? I thought you were speaking as the poets do, to describe the safety we would find in Britannia.'

I opened my mouth to correct her, then closed it, realizing how deeply ingrained was the prohibition against telling outsiders of the sacred isle.

'It is real, though . . . difficult . . . to attain. It lies in the land called the Summer Country. There is a vale between two lines of hills, so low that when the rivers are in flood or the winter storms

374

back up the tides the water covers it, and any bit of higher ground becomes an island. And there is one such, crowned by a pointed tor, that is called Inis Witrin.

'When you reach it, do not go to the monks who have their little church at the base of the Tor, but stop at the village of the fisherfolk who live in the marshes, and tell them that you are Eilan's grand-daughter, and you wish to be taken to Avalon.'

She looked dubious, and I sighed, for in truth, I could not even guarantee that *I* would be admitted after so many years. And was I justified in taking Lena there? This vital young woman, whose cheeks were glowing despite the shadows a difficult night had painted beneath her eyes, was a very different creature from the fragile and frightened girl I had helped to escape from Treveri almost two months ago.

'The holy isle is a refuge where no king or emperor can follow. But you are not required to go there. If you and Crispa take new names, I think it likely that you will be able to live in perfect safety here in Londinium.'

The winged brows drew down. 'Don't you want us to come with you?'

'Lena, do you not understand how I have come to love you? That is why the choice must be yours. I only know that *I* have to go there, or try.'

I recovered slowly, and it was October before I was strong enough to attempt the journey. The carriage in which we had travelled from Dubris was fitted with a soft mattress and loaded with provisions. But before departing Londinium there was one last task.

I had seen how swiftly, with Constantine's favour, Christianity was becoming the religion of the Empire. I could foresee a time when its shrines and symbols would displace those of the old religion entirely, reinventing Britannia as a Christian land. In the time that was coming, there would be few to understand that it was possible to honour both the Goddess and the God.

It pained me to think that my carving of the Mothers might one

375

day be mocked by folk who no longer saw it as holy. And so workmen were summoned to remove it from the wall and load it into a barrow, and in the night, when the men had gone home, Lena and Cunoarda pulled it to the stream that ran through the fields behind my dwelling, and tipped the carving in. Hidden in its depths, the Mothers would bless the city through which its waters ran.

'Tell me about when you were a little girl on Avalon . . .' Crispa had elected to ride for a while inside the carriage with Cunoarda and me, though I knew she would want to sit with Lena, who was driving, before long.

'I had a white dog called Eldri—'

'Like Leviyah?' Crispa pulled back the curtain to point to the dog who was trotting beside us, head up to catch all the scents of this new land.

'Smaller, with curly fur. A boy at the Lake village gave her to me, and said she was a faerie dog, and I think it was true, because she guided me once to a land even farther from this world than Avalon, and brought me safely back again.'

Cunoarda's lips quirked, and I could see that she thought I was telling the child a fairy story. I found it strange that she, who had been born in Alba, found it harder to believe in Avalon than Lena, the child of a thoroughly Romanized Gallic aristocracy. But perhaps Cunoarda still needed the walls she had erected to protect her from the pain of her loss, and did not dare. I knew that she had found great comfort in Christianity, and when we were in Londinium, she had attended the rituals at the Church of Saint Pancras which I had long ago endowed.

'Did you have other girls to play with?'

'I lived in the House of Maidens,' I answered, remembering the murmur of girls' voices in the darkness with a sudden overwhelming clarity. 'I had a little cousin called Dierna, with hair as red as Cunoarda's. I believe that Dierna is the Lady of Avalon now.'

I realized with a flutter of anxiety that I did not know. I remembered dreaming Ganeda's funeral – would I not know it if Dierna, whom I had loved, had also died?

If she was gone, there might well be no one left at Avalon who remembered me.

After we left Lindinis we turned north on the Aquae Sulis road. It was now the end of October, the season of Samhain when the spirits of the dead return. A fitting time, I thought, for my own homecoming. The landscape was growing very familiar now. It was I myself who seemed unreal, as if I had died in truth as well as seeming and was being summoned with the other ghosts who walked at this time of year.

For two days it had been raining, and a silver sheen of water lay over the lowlands, but I insisted that we press onward, for I remembered these marshes as a country with little provision for travellers. We were surprised, however, to find a small inn where the track that led towards Inis Witrin turned off from the Sulis road.

'Oh yes, we have been here for nigh on twenty years,' said the round-faced woman who brought us our food. 'Ever since the good Emperor granted protection to the Christians. My father built this place to serve the travellers who come on pilgrimage to the monks at the Tor.'

I blinked at this, for in my day the monks of Inis Witrin had been a tiny community whose safety depended on being overlooked by the authorities. But the Christians *were* the authorities now, and it remained to be seen if they would use the power given them more wisely than those who had held it before.

In the morning we set out once more, bracing ourselves as the carriage lurched across the log causeways. And as the sun sank we saw the pointed cone of the Tor rising against the golden sky, haloed in light.

'It *is* real,' breathed Lena.

I smiled, for in that moment even the isle that lies in the mortal world was touched with glory, and yet our true destination was a place more wonderful still.

I could see the smoke of the monastery's cookfires as we skirted the isle. From here we had to go on foot, for the Lake village could not be reached by a vehicle. It was almost sunset, and Cunoarda and Lena were growing nervous, but now that we were here, anticipation gave new strength to my limbs. The path, at least, looked the same – I doubt it had changed for a thousand years. Leaning on Cunoarda's arm and feigning a certainty I did not entirely feel, I started down it.

'No, honoured ones – you go back to houses of the shaven heads—' the headman of the village touched his forehead to indicate a tonsure. 'No place for you here—'

The little dark people of the village whispered behind him, eyeing us nervously. On this night, the mound on which the round huts huddled was lit by torches whose red flicker seemed kindled from the setting sun. If we had come a little later, they would have thought us spirits and refused to admit us at all.

This was a difficulty I had not anticipated. I stared at the man, frowning. I should have renewed the crescent on my brow with woad, I thought then, as the elder priestesses used to do on festival days. How could I convince him to send word of my coming to Avalon?

'Do your people remember a daughter of the sun people who was brought here long ago to be trained as a priestess? A boy called Otter gave her a faerie dog. Does that boy live still?'

There was a murmur from the crowd, and a woman who looked as old as me pushed forwards. 'Otter my father – he like to tell the story. A princess of the tall folk, he said.' She gazed at me in wonder.

'I was that little girl, and I became a priestess on the holy isle. But that was many years ago. Will you send word to the Lady of Avalon and tell her that Eilan has returned?'

'If you are priestess, you can call mists and go—' The headman still looked dubious.

'I have been long away, and may not return without the Lady's leave,' I answered him, remembering how Ganeda had cut my link to the holy isle when she banished me. 'You will be well rewarded – please . . .'

He gave a snort of laughter. 'Is not for gold we serve Avalon. I call the Lady, but this night they have ceremonies. She cannot come before morn.'

In my dreams, it was Ganeda who came to me, with Cigfolla and Wren and the other priestesses and Aelia whom I had loved. I knew this must be a dream, because Ganeda was smiling, her arm around the waist of another woman with dark hair whom I recognized, without knowing how, as my own mother, Rian. They were robed in priestess blue, garlanded as if for a festival, and they held out their arms in welcome. I knew then that it was my own belief, not Ganeda's word, which had exiled me from Avalon.

Laughing, I started towards them. But as I was about to touch Aelia's hand, someone called my name. Annoyed, I reached for the dream image, but the call was repeated, in a voice I could not deny.

I opened my eyes to light that streamed through the open door of the roundhouse in which we had been sleeping, glowing in Crispa's bright hair and on Leviyah's golden hide, outlining Lena and Cunoarda as they helped me to sit up, and falling full upon the blue robe of the woman who stood before me.

I do not know why I had expected that Dierna would still be a young girl. The body of the woman who had called me had thickened with time, and her flaming hair was now the colour of sunset on snow. But I, who had known so many emperors, had not encountered anyone with such an aura of authority. Next to her, the man and the woman who attended her looked frail. Did Dierna remember how I had loved and protected her, I wondered then, or had she, like my son, been warped by the temptations of power?

'Eilan . . .' Her voice trembled, and suddenly I saw looking out of her eyes the little cousin I used to know.

I motioned to Cunoarda to help me up, wincing as stiffened muscles took the strain.

Dierna embraced me, one priestess to another, then her gaze grew stern. 'I will use that name, but I know who you were, in that other world. You have been used to position and power, and you are heir to the elder line of Avalon. Have you come to claim rule here?'

I looked at her in amazement. Then I remembered that she had been trained by Ganeda. Had the old woman taught her to fear that I would return to challenge her one day?

'It is true that I have had power, and all the glory the world can bestow,' I answered stiffly, 'and for that very reason I need them no more. Now it will be enough if I may find peace, and safety for those I love.'

'Come,' Dierna gestured towards the open door. 'Walk with me—'

We all followed her outside into a misty autumn morning that veiled the marshes as if we were already between the worlds.

'Forgive me, but it was my duty to ask,' Dierna said as we started along the path around the edge of the mound that kept the village above the floods.

I was still not quite steady, and Lena took my arm.

'I have known the fulfilment of prophecy and its deceptions. Through the child I bore, the world has indeed been changed, and if I do not like the results, I have only my own pride to blame.'

'Do not judge yourself too harshly,' Dierna replied. 'I myself tried to shape the fate of Britannia, and I tell you that though our choices may determine the manner of its working, it is the Goddess who decides our ultimate destiny.'

It is not only the Christians who sometimes need absolution, I thought, blinking back tears.

For a little while we walked in silence. The morning sun was burning the fog away. Silver ripples gleamed as a heron stalked among the reeds. Beyond them I saw the green slope of the Tor, and the huts of the monks clustering around Joseph's round church.

A gesture summoned Dierna's companions. 'Do you remember Haggaia?' The silver-haired Druid gave me a smile, and I recognized in his face an echo of the laughing boy who had loved to play ball with Eldri so long ago. 'And this is Teleri, whom I have been training.'

To be your successor, I thought, smiling at the dark-haired woman beside her. "Teleri: I know and give thanks to the Lady for bringing her safely home."

'I bring with me two who have become my daughters, and my own great-grandchild,' I said then.

'And do they also wish to cross over to Avalon?'

Lena's eyes were shining. 'This is like a dream that turns out to be true! If you will have us, I and my daughter will gladly go.'

Dierna's gaze grew wistful as she looked at Crispa. 'My own children died,' she said then. 'It will be good to train another child of our blood for Avalon . . .'

But I had turned to Cunoarda, and my heart sank as I saw on her cheeks the silver track of tears. 'What is it, my dear?'

'I will miss you till my life's end, lady, but I cannot go,' she whispered. 'I need to learn how to use the freedom you have given me. And it is the Christ, not your Goddess, whom my heart follows, and I cannot do that on your isle.'

'Then stay, with my blessing.' I kissed her on the brow. It would be no use to tell her that there was a place beyond all such divisions where Truth was One. She still belonged in this world.

'That is settled, then,' Dierna said briskly. 'The barge is waiting. We will breakfast on the holy isle.'

'Not quite—' I pointed out over the waters. 'For you to accept me means much, but Ganeda cast me out. I must prove – to myself, if not to you – that I am still a priestess. Let me call the mists, and win my own way back to Avalon.'

The barge rocks to the push of the poles as the boatmen move us away from the shore. I can see the silver waters part before the prow. Dierna sits beside me, trying to hide her doubts, and Cunoarda is watching from the village, hoping that I will fail and return with her to Londinium. Perhaps they are right to question, and this vow of mine is no more than a final act of pride.

381

But since I came to this decision I have been silently rehearsing the words of power. If I have got them wrong, everyone will pity the foolish old woman who thought she was still a priestess. But if I succeed . . .

It is the gift of age to remember the events of fifty years ago more clearly than what happened yesterday. Suddenly the timing and distances of this journey are clear. My heart is pounding, and when the shifting flow of energy around us peaks, it is hard to breathe. Crispa steadies me as I get to my feet, shoulder-joints protesting as I raise my arms high.

I fight for air, and then, all at once, power surges through me. Words pour from my lips, and now it is easy, so easy to bring down the mists and slip through the chill dark passage between the worlds. I can hear the others calling out in alarm, but I cannot allow them to distract me now, for the silver veils around us are thinning, wisping away in coruscations of rainbow radiance—

Light is everywhere, light all around me, light that grows beyond all the words I have for vision until I see, glowing as if lit from within, the shores of Avalon . . .